W9-BZT-253

THE ALL YOU CAN
DREAM BUFFET

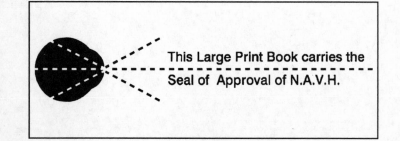

THE ALL YOU CAN DREAM BUFFET

BARBARA O'NEAL

WHEELER PUBLISHING
A part of Gale, Cengage Learning

GALE
CENGAGE Learning·

Farmington Hills, Mich • San Francisco • New York • Waterville, Maine
Meriden, Conn • Mason, Ohio • Chicago

GALE
CENGAGE Learning

LIBRARY OF CONGRESS CATALOGING-IN-PUBLICATION DATA

O'Neal, Barbara, 1959–
    The all you can dream buffet / by Barbara O'Neal. — Large print edition.
        pages ; cm (Wheeler publishing group hardcover)
    ISBN 978-1-4104-6769-0 (hardcover) — ISBN 1-4104-6769-4 (hardcover)
    1. Older women—Fiction. 2. Friendship—Fiction. 3. Organic farming—
Fiction. 4. Large type books. I. Title.
PS3573.I485A78 2014
813'.54—dc23   2014002996

Published in 2014 by arrangement with Bantam Books, a division of Random House LLC, a Penguin Random House Company

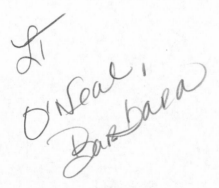

Printed in the United States of America
1 2 3 4 5 6 7 18 17 16 15 14

Dearest Amara:
May you be filled with loving kindness.
May you be well.
May you be peaceful and at ease.
May you be happy.
All the days of your life.

Lavender Honey Farms
yamhill co., oregon

Home Shop Blog Directions Philosophy

Dining partners, regardless of gender, social standing, or the years they've lived, should be chosen for their ability to eat — and drink! — with the right mixture of abandon and restraint. They should enjoy food, and look upon its preparation and its degustation as one of the human arts.

— M.F.K. FISHER, *Serve It Forth*

PROLOGUE

In the stillness just after dawn, Lavender Wills walked the perimeter of the farm, as she did every morning. Rain or shine — and it could be a lot of rain in the Willamette Valley in Oregon — she strode with her dogs along the lavender fields and the greenhouses, following the line of the fields where meat chickens were pastured in movable pens, checking to be sure they hadn't been raided overnight. She eyed the fences around the chicken houses and rounded the beehives, then headed back along the vegetable fields, some of them still tucked under their temporary spring blankets of easily constructed and deconstructed plastic greenhouses.

It was nearly a five-mile walk, counting detours. It kept her alert and healthy, and even now, at eighty-four, she made the distance without much trouble, most days.

Most days.

Every now and again lately, she could feel the shadow of time following along behind her. She glimpsed herself walking this path at four and eighteen before she left to seek adventure, at thirty-two and forty-six, home to visit, at fifty-seven and seventy-three, running the place at last. Always rangy, always walking this same path, forward or backward, always with a dog or two or three. Border collies, mostly, such good working dogs. There had been so many over the years, but she could remember the names of all of them. Jacob and Mike and Andy, Percival and Athena and her beloved Rome, the best of the lot, gone three years now.

Many more. Humans, too. She'd outlived all four of her siblings, despite being the oldest. Her parents were long gone, as were any cousins she knew about and a nephew she mourned deeply. Even most of her friends were gone now.

Sometimes, walking the perimeter, she imagined she spied one or another of them, people or canines. Someone she had loved once upon a time. Her mother, wearing a straw hat as she picked raspberries. Her grade-school friend Reine, who'd died only last spring, looking for mushrooms. Sometimes she saw Rome trotting just ahead, his black coat gleaming, tail high and swishing.

She had no preternatural warning that she might be ready to toddle off this good earth; in fact, she felt as hale and hearty as ever, despite the odd creaks. Her mind was still pretty sharp, sharp enough that she kept up a blog three times a week, a venture that had begun as a marketing gimmick a decade ago and had become much, much more. It was her forum, a place to express her love of the land, of the right and honorable way to bring food to the table, of the way to care for food animals and to grow healthy vegetables in uncontaminated soil. It was the way she had connected with three other bloggers, too, forming a tight-knit group they called the Foodie Four.

Mainly, it gave her an excuse to revel in her passion for lavender — growing it, harvesting it, using it.

No, she felt plenty lively.

And yet . . . this morning she had awakened in the predawn quiet, and knowledge filled her. Life circled. The land taught you that. Soon or late, she'd sleep in the earth she had tended all of her life. What would become of the farm then? This farm, which had been her greatest achievement.

She could not let it pass into the hands of her remaining, indifferent nephews, two of them, businessmen in Portland who rarely

11

came to visit. They had no love of the land, and they would sell it. She didn't blame them. But it was too valuable, too important to the growing organic movement, to let just anyone buy it.

As she walked, she mused. Lavender and honey, fresh eggs and fine wool. An empire for the right heir. An honorable heir.

It was only as she turned the last corner that she saw Ginger near the beehives, her long red hair loose over her shoulders, her face young and remarkably beautiful again. It was the first time Lavender had seen this particular ghost, her friend of nearly sixty years, who had died last year in Carmel. She was kneeling to gather wildflowers from the forest, her knees bending just as they should, her hands — the hands that had betrayed her in the end — free of the gnarled knots that had ruined them. Lavender waited, but Ginger did not turn, did not seem to know Lavender was there.

By the time she returned to her little office, she knew exactly what to do. Firing up the computer, she wrote an email.

FROM:
   Lavender@lavenderhoneyblog.com
TO: FoodieFour@yahoogroups.com
SUBJECT: Birthday bash

Well, gals, it's official. I've decided I'm going to have a little fiesta for my eighty-fifth birthday on June 30. That is, in case you don't know, the night of the blue moon, which is a sign none of us should ignore.

You all know the house is tiny, but there's lots of land around it. Bring those trailers you haven't driven; I'll get you fixed up for water and power, no problem. We're set up for extra help during the harvest and shearing seasons, so there are plenty of hookups.

The lavender will be in full bloom — a sight you do not want to miss — and we can all take turns showing off our fancy cooking skills. Or not, as the case may be (not naming names, but, Valerie, you can serve the wine. As long as it's Oregon wine).

Who's in? Ruby, it's time to stop mooning (snort!) over Liam and have some fun. You're too young to be moping around so long. Valerie, you've been fretting about that daughter of yours, so bring her and we'll put her to work in the sunshine. That'll cure just about anything. And, Ginny, I hear you coming up with all kinds of objections about why your thankless family can't do without you, but I reckon that Bambi you've been showing off in your blog arrived in your life to be taken somewhere, not parked in your driveway just to aggravate your neighbors and husband. COME!

Adventure awaits, chickadees. And I'm not getting any younger.

Lavender

Chapter 1

Dead Gulch, Kansas

Camera in hand, Ginny Smith bent over the still life she had created on the kitchen counter. Her husband, Matthew, had built her a photographer's light box, but she preferred natural light when it was available, and this was one of the prime spots in her house. The pale-green counter and heavy swaths of indirect light pouring through the big kitchen window gave everything a serene look. It was one of the secrets of her blog, this very spot.

This afternoon, she was shooting a slice of pistachio cake. Two generous layers of white cake frosted with the palest shade of green. The beauty was in the depth of field, the fine, pure white crumb of the cake against the cracked satin of the antique plate, the alluring color of the frosting. In the background of the shot was an antique green glass vase overloaded with roses she'd just clipped from the bushes surrounding the house, and in the foreground were six pistachios in various stages of undress, suggesting decadence.

As she clicked and moved and clicked and moved, zooming in and zooming out, changing angles, she hummed along with Bach. The music played on her iPod, a gift from her daughter, Christie, two Christmases ago, and it was loud. Ginny hoped it would drown out the emptiness in her chest.

She thought about the invitation from Lavender. Again.

This morning she had rushed out to the grocery store to pick up a small bag of pistachios for this photo shoot. She had forgotten last night to set some aside when she made the cake. Although they were not strictly necessary, she had time to run out to the Hy-Vee after Matthew left for work — the light this time of year reached its prime glow around ten-thirty — and she took pride in having the best details in her photos.

She came out of the supermarket and decided to make a quick stop at the drugstore for some ribbon — seeing in her mind's eye a curl of thin, shiny dark pink satin to pick up the color of the roses. To get there, she passed the Morning Glory

Café. . . .

And stopped dead.

Standing there, staring through the window, she made up her mind to go to Oregon.

It was a shocking decision. She had never gone anywhere, except once to Minneapolis when her cousin got married. She hadn't even gone to Cincinnati for the funerals of Valerie's family, because — she would admit this only to herself — she was a coward and had been afraid to go alone.

She certainly had not ever driven herself nearly two thousand miles, even without a trailer. Much less driven herself *and* a trailer.

But this bright morning, she happened to catch sight of her three best friends sitting in the Morning Glory, eating pancakes and bacon without her. They were dressed up, probably heading to Wichita after breakfast to do some spring shopping. Karen had her long hair swept up into a comb, with feathery bits carefully falling over the top like a fountain, and she wore her beaded earrings. Marnie wore her gray top from Victoria's Secret, embroidered around the edges, and Jean had red lipstick on, making her, with her cropped hair, look sophisticated.

The three of them plus Ginny had been the best of friends for nearly forty years, ever since they sat together in Mrs. Klosky's fourth-grade class. Ginny knew everything about them, and they knew nearly everything about her. Not the part about her sex life, of course. That would be too humiliating. And nobody had known about the blog until the piece in Martha Stewart's magazine seven months ago had blown Ginny's cover.

What did you expect? Matthew had asked in some disgust. *That nobody would know it was* you?

Maybe that *was* what she had expected. That nobody would connect Ginny the housewife they'd known their whole lives with the "Cake of Dreams" blog, even if they saw a picture of her in it. How many people in Dead Gulch read *Martha Stewart Living,* after all? It wasn't exactly *Family Circle.*

Or *maybe* what she had expected was that people would be proud of her. The blog had sixty thousand readers. *Every day.* She'd had no idea that people would like her pictures so much, or her recipes, or whatever it was, but she was secretly very, very proud of it. She didn't know anybody in real life (not counting her online friends, of course) who had ever done anything like it.

And it was paying her, too, from several

18

directions, a lot more money than she'd made at the supermarket. It came in through ads, first of all. She could pick and choose among the best ones and charge a pretty penny for them. After that, funds came through demands for her photos, which had become so cumbersome to supply that she finally had to pay someone to fill the orders and set up a store on Etsy. Her assistant, a woman who worked with her virtually from Wisconsin, suggested that Ginny offer some framed and matted versions of her stuff, which tripled the income stream from that end. That same assistant also suggested that Ginny should have a subscription service for photographer wannabes, and that had proved to be the most lucrative of all. Every week she sent out tips and lessons. It seemed crazy at first — what did she know? — but some students had begun to have success on their own, so maybe it wasn't so crazy after all.

When the *Martha Stewart Living* people contacted her for a feature story, Ginny had started to realize her secret wouldn't stay secret that much longer anyway. Sooner or later, someone in town would put together the Ginny of "Cake of Dreams" with Ginny Smith, who was a supermarket cake decorator until the blog freed her.

Matthew had known she was making money on photos, of course. But he had not understood what kind of reach the blog had, how famous she had become, until the magazine people showed up.

Standing on the sidewalk this Monday morning, with a pounding hollow in her chest, Ginny blinked back tears.

What had she expected?

What she had *never* expected was this, that her friends would exclude her. That her husband would be embarrassed. That her mother would needle her slyly. Only her daughter, her sister Peggy, and Karen had been genuinely happy for her. But as much as Karen cheered her on, she was never the strongest in the group. Faced with Marnie, who was *furious* with Ginny, Karen didn't stand a chance.

Stinging, Ginny marched toward the door and yanked it open. The bell attached to the top rang violently, banging back toward the glass, and a lot of people looked over, including the traitorous three, who had the grace to look uncomfortable.

"Did you forget to call me?" she asked with a tight smile.

Karen looked abashed. She covered by pulling out the fourth chair at the table. "Hey, girl." She patted the seat. "Join us."

For a minute Ginny wavered, wanting to believe it was a mistake or something.

Jean dabbed her mouth with a napkin. "Sit down, Ginny. You're making a spectacle of yourself. And maybe you like that, but we don't."

Ginny felt her cheeks burning, and tears welled up in her eyes, the same thing that happened anytime she became furiously angry. A part of her wanted to take a seat, to offer the forgiveness they would ask for now that they'd been cornered, to just not rock the boat. That good-girl part of her had been a straight-A student and the president of the PTA and never colored her ordinary dark hair even though she knew she'd look better if she did. *That* girl screamed for Ginny to sit down.

But the day she had opened up a blog and posted her first photograph of a slice of German chocolate cake, crumbs trailing over an antique plate with a cracked glaze and flowers ringing the edge, another Ginny had been born. Now, whether she or they liked it or not, there was no turning back.

"I thought you would be proud of me," she said, "but you're embarrassed. And I don't know if it's because you didn't do it yourself or because now you have to start thinking about what you could do if you didn't spend all your time gossiping and having pancakes and focusing on all the ways life has cheated you, but it doesn't matter."

All three of them stared at her as if she'd grown devil ears. Karen began, "Ginny, you're making too big a deal —"

Marnie, her face bright red, interrupted. "You just think you're so important now," she hissed, glancing over her shoulder. "You ruined everything."

"No," Ginny said. "You did."

Bending now over the still life she had created in her kitchen, she knew she would go to Oregon. She also knew that Matthew would be furious. That her mother would warn her about all the bad things that would happen to her "out there," a woman alone.

But she didn't care. She would bring her dog and drive herself to Oregon, and she would have an adventure for the first time in her life.

THE FLAVOR OF A BLUE MOON

a blog about great food . . .

Recipes   Appetizers
Main dishes   Sides   Sweets
Sort by Name   Sort by Category
About Ruby

O Cherries!

I am in bliss. Purest, deepest cherry bliss. I am going to *become* a cherry in my next life, born to open my soft pink petals to the new spring sun. Honeybees will buzz around my stigma and drink of my juices and bring me the secret nectar to impregnate me. I'll close my petals tightly and rest in the cradle of bright mornings and rainy afternoons until I grow big and fat and red, the very red of lips and lusciousness, and then I will be plucked with gentle fingers and carried, ever so tenderly, into the hot, waiting mouth of a hungry woman. I'll feel her tongue wrapping around my roundness, feel myself explode into her throat and cascade into her belly to nourish her, to bring sunlight into her body.

Cherries are in season. You can cook them if you want to, make them into pies, or put them in pancakes or slice them into a salad. But, really, why? Just eat them.

Cherries are packed with vitamin C and

fiber. They've been used as anti-inflammatories for gout and arthritis. Legend has it that cherries signal fertility.

Eat some.

Love,
Ruby

CHAPTER 2

Ruby Zarlingo was the first to arrive at Lavender's. She drove up from San Francisco to be on hand a week early to help set things up. Lavender was strong, Ruby knew that. But nobody should have to set up a giant party all by herself.

And, honestly, Ruby needed to get away from her father. He'd objected to her driving "all this way," as if she were seventeen, not twenty-six, and experienced in driving much bigger rigs than her tidy little camper and the trailer she'd talked him into helping her refurbish as a kitchen.

She had to admit now that the trip had been harder than she'd expected, with the morning sickness rolling through her constantly, not just in the mornings. For the first time in her life, she was a grouch, a giant, insane grouch, because mainly she spent her time throwing up, then trying to settle her stomach, then throwing up some more.

She'd always imagined that an Oregon farm would be shrouded in forest, with trees marching up to the field lines, all of it huddled beneath a glowering of clouds. She had also imagined that it would be totally Hicksville.

Instead, as she sat waiting to make a left turn into the farm (thus backing up the impatient Portlandians and out-of-state tourists ambling around Yamhill County wineries), she saw that she was wrong on all counts. Lavender Honey Farms sat in greeny-golden glory beneath a sunny sky, surrounded on all sides by mountains in the distance and rolling hills closer in. Lambs frolicked in a neighboring field. A pair of young-looking black-and-white cows with big ears munched grass and watched her idly. (How did she know they were young-looking? she asked herself. It wasn't as if cows got wrinkles.) Vineyards were sketched on the hills in the distance, like a painting of Italy.

She felt the pressure of the cars stacking up behind her, but there was no rushing a left turn when hauling a trailer, and she whistled an old ballad to calm herself. The anxiety made her think of her father, the number one anxiety in her life at the moment, since he had strongly — strongly! — disapproved of her making this trip for all kinds of reasons, some of which might actually have had some basis in reality, and some of which were only leftovers from her childhood, when she had worried him to pieces by nearly dying of leukemia.

A longish break appeared in approaching traffic. Ruby gunned it, making the turn in her camper with exactitude, and hauled the trailer into an open graveled area, where she parked in front of an old, rambling two-story farmhouse that had been converted to a shop. A big wooden sign, carved and beautifully painted, announced LAVENDER HONEY FARMS in purple and green. Beneath the name were the products: HONEY, LAVENDER GOODS, FRESH PRODUCE.

An iridescent bubble of happiness engulfed her, and Ruby laughed aloud. She was here! Putting a hand over her tummy, she said, "What do you think, baby? Let's go see."

Leaping out of the truck, she inhaled the earthy, farmy smell of manure and hints of grass, but no lavender. Clumps of it grew in front of the store, and she reached for a blossom and pinched it, bringing her hand to her face.

"If everybody did that, pretty soon there

wouldn't be any blossoms for anyone to look at," said a rumbling, cranky voice behind her.

"Sorry!" Ruby said, turning. "It's a habit. I'm a chef. I smell things."

The man was in his early thirties, maybe, and she knew exactly who he was from Lavender's emails about the dilemma he'd posed upon arrival for work. She'd hired him, sight unseen, by his résumé — a farm lad, veteran of Iraq, hungry to get back to the land. Lavender was desperate for a manager to help her with the expanding business and liked the sound of his voice on the phone.

But when he arrived, he was taciturn, broody, and much too good-looking. The kind of good-looking, Lavender had complained to the Foodie Four, that caused trouble.

Ruby cocked her head. He was older than she was, but Ruby could see what Lavender meant. Clearly more ethnic than white, but, as with so many people these days, what that background might be was hard to decipher — it all melted together in caramel and golden brown and an aggressive nose. He might be Tillamook — the local Indians — or Mexican, or Iranian, or . . . impossible to know. His hair was very thick and black and curly, and his body was shaped by his work of hauling hay and ice and raking manure and loading produce trucks, but it was a certain untouchable, unhappy aloofness that caught you.

"You must be Noah," she said. "I'm Ruby, one of Lavender's friends."

"I figured." He gave her hand a cursory shake and glanced at her trailer, which Ruby had painted in a Frida Kahlo style in keeping with her fresh-food principles. "The vegan, right?"

She didn't think he meant it as derisively as it sounded, though people took her diet very personally at times. "That's right. I had leukemia as a child, and my father put us both on a vegan diet the day I was diagnosed." She gave him her best, sunniest smile, the one that dared foodies and blood-centered chefs to be grumpy about it all, and gestured to her robust figure. "As you see, it seemed to work."

He grunted. "Lavender's in the meadery. I'll show you."

"The meadery," Ruby repeated, and forced herself not to skip. "That is *so* cool."

He gave her a single glance, not quite rolling his eyes, but Ruby was used to people reacting that way to her. Her old boyfriend Liam — the thought of his name sent a sharp pain through her ribs, right under her left breast — used to actually be embarrassed by her relentless good spirits. He was a native New Yorker and said her cheerfulness made her stick out like a sore thumb.

But there were things you couldn't help. Ruby had been born cheerful. Now, as she trailed behind Noah, joy swelled through her, golden and buoyant, lifting her elbows and knees. Every turn revealed a new delight. Chickens just wandering around! That view of blue mountains hanging like curtains around the valley! A slice of sky visible between barn and roof!

They walked along a well-beaten path, down a slight hill. A pair of chickens, one shiny black with a red thingy on its head (what was it called? she wondered) and the other a mottled brown, waddled along with them. On a hill to her left, near a stand of outbuildings, barns, and open sheds, were a handful of others, pecking along in the dirt. "Hello, Mr. Chicken," Ruby said. "You're looking well."

"It's Ms. Chicken, actually," Noah said. "These are some of the layers, and of course that would make them hens."

"Ah." He probably knew what the thing was called. "What's that thing on her head called?"

"Comb."

"Oh, sure. I've heard that." Under her breath she repeated, *"Comb,"* making sure to capture the word.

In front of them stretched a wide field planted with rows of vegetables, rising and falling like tidy hills across the acreage. The tops of the mounds were covered in straw. A man in a plaid shirt and a brimmed hat bent over one of them, gently plucking carrots and shaking off the soil. Nearby, a woman collected beets and placed them in baskets. Ruby shaded her eyes. "That's a lot of vegetables!"

"Couple acres," he said.

Ruby had often risen with the dawn to find the freshest, most beautiful produce. "Do you sell them at the farmers' market?"

"Some." His posture eased a little. "Some go to our CSA subscribers. A lot more are going to restaurants these days."

She nodded. CSA stood for "community-supported agriculture." "Multiple revenue streams are always good." The restaurant world taught you that.

"Yep." He turned onto a path running between the fields and barns. A band of trees marked the boundary of the vegetable gardens, blocking her view of the rest of the farm.

"Where is the lavender?" Ruby finally asked.

"You'll see."

They passed the barn and a corral, then Noah led the way through a line of shrubs with dark-green heart-shaped leaves — maybe lilac bushes, but she wasn't always that clear on what was what in the plant world. Ruby stepped through behind him, as if she were entering a magic kingdom.

He stepped sideways, out of the way, and gestured. "Here it is."

"Oh!" she breathed. "Oh, my."

The lavender stretched out in long, long lines that followed the contours of the fields, soft purple and dark purple and white and pale pink, in perfect rounded tufts that grew as high as her waist. A breeze swept over them, and the flowers swayed languidly, revealing the pale undersides of their leaves and making the field look like waves, like water. Ruby actually put her hands to her face. "Oh, my gosh."

"Take your time," he said. "The meadery is right there on your left. I've got some work to do."

Ruby did not move. She barely breathed. Maybe, she thought, maybe *at last* she could discover her purpose. Maybe it would be here in these amazing fields, amid the lavender.

Had she ever seen anything so beautiful? *Ever?*

A tall, rangy woman with cropped, no-nonsense white hair emerged from the utilitarian outbuilding. "Told you it was a sight to see," she said, hands on her hips. The voice was not at all old but sturdy and sure.

"Lavender!" Ruby flung open her arms exuberantly, and Lavender met her with a fierce hug.

"Oh, girl, I'm so glad to see you."

Against Ruby's lush frame — not fat, never that — Lavender was as lean as a teenage boy, all shoulders and wiry strength. "Me, too," Ruby said, and, to her surprise, tears welled up in her eyes.

And she was suddenly, overwhelmingly, nauseous. Pulling away urgently, she rushed for the edge of the field and tossed her cookies right in a little ditch. Wiping her mouth with the back of her hand, she turned, unconsciously putting a hand over her lower belly, which was swelling sweetly with the baby. "Sorry," she said. "I thought morning sickness was supposed to be mornings, but I have it all the time."

Lavender cocked her head. Her face was

shaped into angles by high cheekbones and a hard jaw. "Pregnant?"

Ruby nodded. "Five and a half months."

"I thought you couldn't have children."

"Me, too," she said, and the whole impossible business of it struck her again. She opened her eyes wide. "But here I am. Really, it's kind of a miracle, they said."

"So you're happy?"

Ruby put both palms open on her belly and laughed. "Yes. Very. *Very.*"

"Well, then, congratulations, my friend." Lavender flung an arm around Ruby's shoulders and bracingly moved her away from the meadery. "I was going to give you a taste of mead, but first let's get some food in you. Maybe a cup of tea, how about that?"

"Perfect. As long as we can come back to the meadery later."

"Promise. You aren't going to get away that easily!"

Lavender helped Ruby set up her campsite. She parked in a wide spot beneath a sheltering of tall pines, which had been shorn of their lower branches to allow open views of the rolling hills around the farm. The spot gave Ruby a sweet vantage point over the lavender and the shop. She hooked her camper and trailer up to the amenities.

It was mid-afternoon, and Ruby was sleepy the way she had been as a child. That was the other thing about pregnancy. Sleep could overtake her like a spell, so insistent she had no choice but to crawl into whatever hole she could find and succumb. Just now she didn't bother to open up the kitchen trailer but crawled into her camper, propped open the door to the breeze, and fell onto the bed.

Most of the camper was the bed, with a portable toilet tucked in a closet. She'd gutted the camper when she was eighteen and wanted to explore the country, then put in the biggest, softest bed she could find and added bigger windows to let breezes flow over the mattress. Storage was tucked beneath the bed, and shelves with netting held the little things that made life rich: books and a brush, socks for cold nights, maps of her travels. The walls had been covered with fabric to make it more feminine, in a pattern of pastel stripes that made it feel more homey. Over the fabric, she'd découpaged photos of her life — her father and her; one ancient picture of her mother and father and her together, before Ruby got sick; her mother laughing, long blond hair tumbling over her brown shoulders and bikinied back; various pets, friends. And Liam. Lots of Liam. She needed to cover them with something but hadn't yet had the heart to do it.

Sprawled on top of the bed, she kicked off her shoes and let the breeze cover her. It was a habit to gaze up at his beautiful, beautiful face with the high-bridged nose and luscious lips. He had the most alluring mouth on the planet, a mouth she wanted to kiss all the time. He wore a goatee, which she thought was gilding the lily. It was so unnecessary to —

A knock on the side of the trailer shook her out of her reverie. "Hey, sweetheart," Lavender said. "I brought you a bowl of fruit and some saltines. I've never been pregnant myself, but my sisters used to say saltines saved their lives."

Ruby sat up, blinking. "Thank you," she said, and put her hands over her heart. "That's so kind."

"And this is the wireless password." She handed over a lime-green sticky note. "Noah put in a super-duper router four or five months ago, so it should be fine even with all of us accessing it."

"Thanks! I can get online through the phone, too, so no worries."

Lavender gazed around the camper. "This

36

is so you, kiddo. Love it." She slapped the side of the door. "You rest now. I'll fix us some supper."

"Oh, you don't have to do that! I was planning —"

"Don't be silly. I can cook vegan, you know. Not like your generation invented plants."

Ruby chuckled. "Thank you, then."

Propped against a pile of exotically embroidered and mirrored pillows, Ruby slid her laptop out of its special padded shelf and fired it up. She entered the network name and password into the settings, made sure the connection worked, and then checked her blog quickly for any spam. It was still the cherry blog from a few days ago. She'd need to get something up tonight or tomorrow. Some bloggers wrote every day, but Ruby never liked to be pinned into anything too tightly. Of the Foodie Four, only Ginny blogged every day, and she'd been doing so for almost seven years. Amazing.

The four had come together nearly five years ago, over the course of a few months. Lavender had found a series on herbs that Ruby had written and contacted her, asking to use it on her blog, and they started to chat back and forth. Valerie contacted Lavender about wine and lavender pairings, just brainstorming, and she joined the group. Ginny had been the last addition. Her blog had barely begun to capture attention, and Ruby stumbled over it one night and invited Ginny to join the conversation with the others.

At first they spoke mainly of the technical and marketing issues of blogging — how to manage "backbloggers," the regular responders, who might try to take things over or stir up trouble; how to deal with the vagaries of blogging software; how to maximize views. Ruby and Ginny shared a love of good photos, though Ruby just liked to scour the Internet for hers. Valerie was their droll, worldly-wise voice. Lavender kept them laughing.

Funny, Ruby thought now, yawning. Funny that they were so different and had become so much a part of one another's lives across so much time and space. Three of them — Ruby, Lavender, and Valerie — had met only once in person. Ginny had not come to that gathering, and none of them had met her face-to-face.

But it didn't matter. The friendships were true and strong.

She lazily clicked on Ginny's "Cake of Dreams" and caught up on a couple of posts she'd missed. Valerie had not posted anything since her husband died two years ago, and Lavender still had the Blue Moon Festival posted. It would take place next weekend.

Then, sleepy and with her guard down, she clicked on Google Maps and zoomed in on a Seattle address, then took the little man from the map and put it down on the street view, so she could admire the house. It was a two-story brick with a peaked roof and plenty of windows, some of which overlooked the Sound and the Olympic range in the distance. It was, she knew from her research, a prime Seattle neighborhood, so even though it was one of the smaller houses in the area, it was worth nearly a million dollars. Zillow told her that it was 4 bedrooms, 3.5 baths, with 3,540 square feet. Azaleas and boxwoods grew in front, and there was stained glass upstairs.

Really, it was just creepy how much information you could get between Zillow and Google Maps. Stalker heaven.

Ruby was not actually a stalker, however, because the house belonged to her mother. Or, rather, to her mother's husband, because her mother was a stay-at-home mom to three soccer-playing kids, two girls and a boy, the youngest. She drove a minivan, which was sometimes parked in the driveway in the photos. Once, electrifyingly, the satellite photo had captured Cammy herself, in lean blond perfection, carrying groceries into the house. The picture was so detailed that Ruby could read the Whole Foods Market logo on the recyclable grocery bags.

That photo was long gone, but this one seemed pretty new. The lawns were green.

Eased, Ruby exited the program and slid the laptop back into its place. She closed her eyes and imagined living in that back bedroom with corner windows overlooking the water, with the smell of food cooking in the kitchen and her mother's voice talking on the phone.

She slept.

CAKE OF DREAMS

A Good Cake for Travel

This is a homey little recipe, super-easy, that makes a sturdy coffee cake you can easily take with you on a picnic or in your trailer when you travel.

Yes, EEEK! I'm leaving on my big adventure in the morning.

SUPER-EASY STREUSEL CAKE

2 cups flour
1/2 cup sugar
2 tsp baking powder
3/4 tsp salt
1/2 tsp baking soda
1/3 cup butter, very soft
1 beaten egg
1/2 cup buttermilk

Topping

1/2 cup brown sugar
2 tsp cinnamon
2 T melted butter
1/2 cup chopped walnuts

Measure the dry ingredients for the cake and mix well in a bowl. Mix together wet ingredients and stir into the dry. Pour into a greased 9×9-inch square pan.

In a separate bowl, mix together topping ingredients. Sprinkle on top of cake.

Bake for 30 minutes in a preheated 350-degree oven.

87 Comments

Hilda12

Have a great trip, Ginny! Jealous, jealous, jealous!

Nancyb

I used to make that little cake for my children after school. Brings back such great memories of autumn afternoons and the smell of cinnamon in the air!

CrochetPeg

Have a total blast, sis! I'll be reading along every day. Love you!

Pippin987

Nancy, me, too! I love streusel, even though my WW leader would throw a fit over it. Just can't imagine making it with Splenda. LOL!

TinaR

Ginny, I'm so excited to meet you!!!!!!!!!!!!! We are going to have a blast.

Nancy, that's so sweet that you made those things for your kids. Did you bake every day? Do you still?

Berniebright
  Have fun!

READ MORE COMMENTS >>>>

CHAPTER 3

Dead Gulch, Kansas

The trailer Ginny would be driving to Oregon was the first thing she had purchased with her blog money. For a thousand years, she'd been in love with vintage Airstream trailers, and when her friend Valerie, who had written a wine blog for years, inherited one from her next-door neighbor, Ginny nearly died of envy. She must have given herself away, because the Foodie Four finally urged her to go looking for one.

It seemed like a fool's errand, honestly — where would she take it? She'd never gone anywhere and drove only a Taurus, which would not pull a trailer, that was for sure.

Lavender had asked, *Where would you want to drive it?*

And, right away, Ginny thought of Colorado. Only one state over, not even that far away, but she'd always wanted to go, to see the mountains that looked so sharp and cool and pristine in pictures. She imagined herself in her little Airstream, a Bambi maybe, parked beneath a big pine tree, looking at a mountain. A blue mountain with a blue sky over it like a tarp.

It turned out a lot of people loved retro trailers as much as she did, and she started to connect with them online. At first she was shy about it, saying only that she'd been thinking about getting one and asking what should she look for.

She had looked online at probably five hundred Airstreams from the fifties and sixties. The ones from the forties, she decided, were a bit too old, while the seventies were too modern. She stuck with her window of time, and even then it was a lot of looking.

It was Lavender who led Ginny to Coco, the 1964 Bambi that she had known instantly was her trailer. It was not exactly traditional, painted as it was with a garden of cabbage roses along the bottom and all kinds of custom restorations inside. It had belonged to a woman artist, a friend of Lavender's from their Pan Am days, who had towed it all over the world. The woman's daughter had lovingly restored everything that didn't work, such as the toilets and the axles, and anything else that was rotting or in trouble, preserving as much of the art as possible.

Ginny bought it on the spot, for full price — which, from that day to this, she had never told a soul. No one actually knew how much money she made, so it was hers to spend as she liked. She lied to Matthew and to her family, telling them she'd paid $21,000, and even that infuriated them. Her sister Connie told her she was selfish — that with that much money she could have put a down payment on a house for her daughter or helped out some of their farmer cousins who were hurting in this economy. Her other sister, Peggy, had been thrilled. She still told Ginny they should drive it some- where, maybe to Las Vegas.

Matthew didn't mind, exactly. It was one of the things they'd set up early in their marriage — that they wanted to keep money separated. She didn't want to be dependent on him. You never knew what might hap- pen. Even in their small town, people fell in love with other people who were not their spouses, and some poor woman was always getting divorced and struggling to make ends meet.

Nope. That would never be Ginny. She started work at the supermarket only six weeks after Christie was born — another thing that got her in trouble with Connie, working when her baby was so young — and moved up into the bakery by the time Christie was three.

When Ginny brought the Airstream home from the show in Kansas City where she'd picked it up, Matthew told her that he wasn't going to be camping in it. He didn't like camping, fishing, hunting. None of that stuff. He liked his creature comforts, his meals without dirt, his breakfast served on china, not paper. That suited her fine. She didn't actually want him in it, although she was wise enough to keep that to herself.

Ginny honestly had not cared one bit what anybody thought of her trailer. She loved it and spent the whole winter making it her own in little ways — with linens and Fiesta ware and photos she'd shot specifically to put up on the walls.

Now, on this mid-June Saturday evening, she carried a load of supplies from the house into the trailer. Paper towels and matches; tea and coffee and powdered creamer; a box of sugar cubes, which wouldn't be as messy as regular; mustard and mayo and salt. In her imagination, she poured coffee into a turquoise Fiesta ware mug and stirred in some creamer, then carried it to the door and stepped out into nature.

"There you are!"

The voice of Ginny's mother startled her out of her pleasant reverie. "Hi," she said.

Ula hauled herself up the steps. She wasn't stout, but her fitness could never be called anything but piss-poor. Standing just inside the door, as if tigers might be caged within, she said, "Colorful, isn't it?"

"That's one of the reasons I liked it."

"Looks like a Victorian whorehouse to me, but I guess we all have our different ideas of what's pretty."

Ginny squinted, but even blurring everything immensely, she couldn't get whorehouse. "More Art Nouveau than Victorian, I'd say."

"Whatever. Why do you always have to do that, make me feel stupid?"

"I didn't mean to." Or maybe, in some small, mean way, she had. "Sorry."

"You knew what I meant."

Ginny nodded. That it was a whorehouse. A house for a whore. A waft of *tomorrow* moved across her throat, a promise of cool air blowing from the open road.

Ula dug in her purse and brought out a small package. "I brought you a present."

Surprised and touched, Ginny opened it

to find a whistle. "You can blow that if somebody tries to rape you," Ula said. "Which you might think wouldn't happen at your age, but it's not just young pretty women who get raped, you know."

"I know. Thank you." She hung the whistle on a hook by the sink. "I am bringing Willow with me, you know." Willow was her dog, a mixed-breed border collie–shepherd–Newfoundland, who was smarter than most people and had a reassuringly deep and ferocious warning bark. She was mostly black, with gold ears and a white patch on her chest, and she had the broad nose of a Newfie and the pert beautiful ears of a shepherd. The brains were all border collie.

"How are you going to carry a dog?"

"She'll ride in the car with me, Mama," Ginny said mildly. "Do you want to come in and have a cup of coffee or something?"

"No, no. I have to get to the market. When are you leaving?"

"Bright and early tomorrow morning."

Ula stepped forward and gave Ginny a hug. "You know I think you're crazy, but you stay safe, now, and check in regular, all right?"

Ginny smelled Johnson's baby powder and Suave hair spray as she hugged her mother, a smell that seemed much too old for a woman in her sixties. "I will," she said. As she straightened, she said, "You can follow my blog, you know. I'll be posting every day."

Ula nodded. "I'll try to remember," she said, as if it was some crazy-hard task, and lumbered down the steps.

FROM: Ginny@cakeofdreams.com
TO: FoodieFour@yahoogroups.com
SUBJECT: Surprise!

Hey, girls. Remember how I thought that no one cared if I was leaving? Hahahaha. I was so wrong. They gave me a surprise going-away party. Only it wasn't a surprise, because Matthew told me before we left home (it was pretty mean to spoil Peggy and Christie's surprise like that, but he did it to hurt me, not them. I guess he's not as happy about me taking this trip as he has been saying). I pretended that I didn't know anyway, because the two of them went to so much trouble to plan it — Peggy did most of the legwork, but I guess they were on the phone every day. Christie came in from Chicago just for the night, and you could tell that it was her brainchild from all the special little touches and good taste. Which makes it sound like my mom and sisters don't have good taste, and that's not true. My mom had a cake made to look like an Airstream, from one of my blog posts (and here I thought she'd never even read it!), and Peggy, my younger sister, specially ordered a messenger bag she thought I'd like to sling over my shoulder.

I felt scared and sad in that room, I have to tell you. All the people who love me and I've known all my life — just about everybody came. My cousins and aunts and uncles and my snotty brother-in-law and all of our friends, and I was getting all emotional, thinking about leaving them all behind. I've never done anything like this in my life, and it's like some wild thing has taken hold of me, flinging me forward almost without me thinking. I feel homesick for everybody and I haven't even left yet! Christie told me that was normal. She said it happened when she went to college, then when she headed to Georgetown for med school, then again when she left for Chicago.

She made me a travel playlist for my iPod. Now I guess I need to get myself going. I can't believe I'm finally going to

51

meet you guys. Wish you could be there,
Val!!!!!

Ginny

FROM: Valerie@winedancer.com
TO: FoodieFour@yahoogroups.com
SUBJECT: re: Surprise!

I am so proud of you, Gin!! Wish I
could be there, too.

xoxoxoxox V

FROM: Ruby@flavorofabluemoon.com
TO: FoodieFour@yahoogroups.com
SUBJECT: re: Surprise!

Whenever I am going to leave one
place for another, it is as if every corner
and light switch and scent of the old
place suddenly becomes unbearably
unique and precious beyond measure.
And of course they are. Every moment
of our lives is precious and unique
beyond measure.

But there is a point when the home-
sickness gives way to anticipation, or
sometimes I feel them both, swirling
together. Sometimes I think what I feel
is about what I label it. So, tomorrow
morning when you get that blast of dry

mouth and butterflies, tell yourself it isn't fear — it is anticipation.

Love,
Ruby

FROM:
Lavender@lavenderhoneyblog.com
TO: FoodieFour@yahoogroups.com
SUBJECT: re: Surprise!

You get your bottom here, missy, hell or high water. You bought that trailer to go have an adventure, and you're going to have one.

CHAPTER 4

In the soft purple time before dawn, Ginny and her dog, Willow, padded silently back and forth between the trailer and the Jeep she'd finally bought. They loaded up the last of their things, Willow's soft dog bed for the cargo area, Ginny's sweater, and a pile of snacks and treats and the spare leash for potty breaks.

It had been a fitful night. Ginny had awakened at 11:45 and 1:32 and 3:10. Finally, when she woke up again at 4:02, wondering what in the *world* she was doing, she slid as silently as possible out of bed and went downstairs to start the coffeepot. While it brewed, she fired up the laptop she was taking with her, the private machine she didn't share with anybody. She dashed off an email to the Foodie Four, knowing that no one would see it until later. She was a notoriously early riser, and only Valerie was in a time zone behind her, in Ohio.

In the quiet darkness, she sipped her coffee and read the comments on her blog. This morning there were already eighty-nine comments, all wishing her luck, some extending more invitations, some offering tidbits of advice, like a good roadside café in Frisco on her way through the Rocky Mountains.

The comments made her feel better. She had accepted the invitations of two different backbloggers in different places along the road. The knowledge that they were out there, waiting, friendly, made it easier.

In some ways, the community she'd discovered in the blog was more real to her than her own family. They were certainly a lot more encouraging.

She posted a cheery response: *Getting dressed now! Can't wait!* Then she headed upstairs, Willow trailing behind.

Her traveling clothes were laid out in the spare bedroom, clean and pressed and ready to go: a pair of khaki capris with plenty of pockets — Lavender had pointed her to a hiking website for quick-dry travel clothes — a simple red sleeveless blouse that made her eyes look much bluer, and, her old standby, tennis shoes with ankle socks. Willow lay in the doorway, paws neatly stretched out in front of her, and her tongue lolled out in an easy pant. She watched Ginny with her bright gold eyes, curious and alert, knowing that something was up and she was a part of it.

Ginny knelt and kissed the dog's nose. "I'm so glad we met," she whispered, mindful of Matthew sleeping in the other room. He had not been thrilled with the puppy Ginny brought home from Walmart four years ago. A rescue group had been trying to find homes for the animals, and Ginny had spied Willow sitting in tidy puppy sweetness near the back, her ears up. When Ginny asked to see her, the girl hesitated. "I was thinking of keeping her."

"Oh," Ginny said, weirdly embarrassed. "I'm sorry! I thought they were all for adoption."

A woman turned and gave the girl a hard look. "They are, honey, don't you worry." She picked up the pup and placed her squarely in Ginny's arms. Willow sighed against Ginny's chest, and her fur was as soft and thick as a bear pelt. Ginny bent her nose into the puppy's fur and smelled sunshine and grass. She was lost.

"Hello!" she said quietly.

Willow licked her chin, a thoughtful, un-slobbery greeting. Her golden eyes studied Ginny's face. This was a dog who took her

56

responsibilities seriously, something Ginny could relate to.

Ginny took her home. Matthew had thrown a fit, but Ginny pretty much ignored him. It wasn't that she was unfeeling, just that she needed some company now that she'd quit her job and worked on the blog from home.

"Let's get you some breakfast," Ginny said now, and they went downstairs, where Ginny opened a can and poured the contents into the ceramic dish she'd ordered online. There were, she discovered, a lot of high-end items for dogs these days. As Willow ate, Ginny drank coffee and watched more light leak into the sky. Her stomach leapt again, right up under her ribs.

She was really going to do this!

Her plan had been to fix Matthew some breakfast and then head out afterward. But he'd been so irritable at the party last night that she had decided to simply give him a kiss and be on her way.

On her way! Bubbles of giddiness fizzed right below her skull as she headed up the stairs. In the doorway, she stopped, a buzz bolting down her spine.

Matthew was sitting on the bed, fully dressed in knee-length cargo shorts and a camp shirt and his always too-white tennis shoes, a suitcase at his feet.

"I'm coming with you," he said.

For one long minute, she stared at him. The buzz spread over her jaw and into her ears. His feet were settled side by side, exactly even, his white socks pulled to the exact same height on each side.

In a whirl, she thought of the Foodie Four, of Valerie, who had lost so much, and Ruby, who was young and intrepid, and Lavender, who had spent her whole life without a husband and seemed just fine without one.

"No," she heard herself say. "I'm going alone."

The words shocked her, but saying them aloud made her draw her spine up tall, as if she were Lavender, five foot ten in her bare feet.

Some men might have gone mulish or bossy. That was never Matthew's way. "It's ridiculous that you're driving that far when you've never even left the state," he said.

"I'll be fine," she said, but the words stirred up some worry, pulling it out of the dark pot of accumulated insecurities. "I have Triple A, and I've practiced driving all over with the trailer. It's not that hard."

"Not on Kansas roads, but what about the mountains? How are you going to drive in the mountains? You're a Kansas girl."

Again, the splash of acidic worry. "I'll be fine," she repeated.

Now he glared. "No, you won't. You'll be crying and lonely in two days flat. I know you, Ginny. You're not the kind of woman who goes out there on her own."

Tears pricked her eyelids, but she blinked hard. No way he'd see those tears. "Why are you being so mean at the last minute? We've had lots of time to talk about it."

"Maybe I didn't really think you'd go."

"It's only three weeks, Matthew. Maybe a month at the most. I'll be with friends —"

"Friends? Friends are the people who've been there for you your whole life, people who'd bring you a casserole if I died or who'll help you out when you're old." The skin beneath his left eye quivered. "You don't even know those women. And you're not in their class, anyway."

That one landed, right in her solar plexus. It was true — Ruby's father was an inventor and millionaire, while Valerie had once been a famous dancer, married to a pilot. Only Lavender, living on her farm, had a life Ginny understood, and even she had been a stewardess for years and years, flying around the world until they stuck her in an office and she returned to the farm.

Ginny was nothing but a college dropout

who'd been a supermarket baker. The others probably liked her only because they'd never actually *met* her.

What was she doing?

But something rose in her heart, gently, as she stood there stinging. She remembered evening after evening sorting through Internet sites of Airstreams. Remembered the exact instant Lavender had sent her the link to Coco, her trailer. *You and me,* the trailer said, opening doors and windows to let Ginny come in.

"I'm going," she said to Matthew. "And I'm going alone. There's a fresh pot of coffee, and I'll have my cell phone so you can call me."

He stared hard at her, visibly trembling. "If you walk out that door, Ginny, don't come back."

"Don't say things you don't mean."

"Oh, I mean it. You've made me a laughingstock in this town. Mr. Cake. The husband of the famous blogger. I've been patient, but this is going too far. Not one of my friends can understand why I'm letting you go."

"You're not *letting* me, because I don't have to ask permission! We've never had that kind of a marriage."

He stared at her for a long time. That

quivering spot under his left eye intensified. Between them were all the conversations she'd tried to have, all the things she'd tried to get out in the open — why aren't we having sex? Are you gay? Are you having an affair? What?

All at once, he seemed to hear those conversations. "Is this about the sex, Ginny?"

She sighed. "Not all of it."

"I don't understand why you keep making such a big deal out of it. It's not like we're kids. We have a good marriage."

Carefully, she softened her voice. "I came in to give you a kiss goodbye. I need to get going."

"I don't want a kiss. Just go."

It stung more than she expected, but Ginny turned on her heel, whistled for Willow, and headed outside, sure that Matthew would follow. The sun was coming up, pink and gold, and it burnished the top of the Airstream, as if promising good things ahead. Ginny opened the door to the backseat to let Willow inside. The dog settled down on her bed, ears alert.

Ginny glanced back at the house. It already looked like a place she used to live, a long time ago. One deep-red peony was blooming. Ginny walked over, pinched it off, and put it in her hair.

Then she climbed into the driver's seat, put a hand over the butterflies in her belly, and turned the ignition. The iPod was set to the playlist Christie had made for her, and as she pulled out of the driveway, Ginny turned it on.

"Born to Be Wild" blasted into the car, and Ginny cracked up. Leave it to Christie to set exactly the right tone. Heartened, she sent a mental tip of the hat toward her daughter and pointed the car in the direction of the highway. She decided to name the fizzing in her blood and somersaults in her tummy "exhilaration."

It was only as she looked in the rearview mirror that she thought to wonder: *Am I leaving my husband?*

CHAPTER 5

Sunday afternoon

She made it to Rocky Ford, Home of the World's Best Melons, by just after three. One of her readers, a backblogger who commented almost every day, had invited Ginny to stop in and have tea with her and some friends when she came through.

It had sounded like fun, finally meeting some of the people she had been talking to online for years, but shyness swamped her now. Tina had directed Ginny to drive to the Tastee Freez and park in the vacant lot behind it, and she managed to do that much without any fanfare. She turned off the car and sat in her seat, holding her phone.

What if she didn't make the call but drove on to what was supposed to be her first stop — Manitou Springs, which she had wanted to visit since she was nine and Marnie had brought back copper bracelets and candy rocks from there — and made some excuse?

Would Tina really mind that much? Ginny was probably overestimating her own importance, imagining that some stranger was eager to meet her just because she had some dumb blog. And everybody said blogs were dying anyway. And —

She took a breath. Blew it out.

What would Lavender say? *Get your butt outta that car, girl, and find some adventure.*

Ginny dialed the number Tina had given her. A bright voice answered, much younger and more cultured than Ginny had expected. "Hello, Ginny!" the girl/woman said. "I've been waiting on pins and needles for your call. I'll be there in two minutes."

And she hung up before Ginny had a chance to say much of anything. She tucked her phone into her pocket and got out of the car, smiling in spite of herself. Leashing Willow, she walked toward a stand of tall old elm trees, where Willow squatted in relief, then sniffed along the weeds.

It was a pretty little nothing town. The Tastee Freez was busy, with both tourists and locals in shorts and ponytails. A small downtown area built of stone in a style popular around the turn of the twentieth century housed a clothing shop and a couple of diners and a hardware store. Just like Dead Gulch.

A woman drove a newish black pickup truck into the lot, waving madly at Ginny. She was slight and thirty-something, and she jumped out, slamming the heavy door behind her, and put her big round mod sunglasses on her head. "Ginny?" Her teeth sparkled.

Ginny was suddenly self-conscious of her travel clothes, her ordinary hair. Tina wore a crisp red and white polka-dot blouse and white capris and wedges that tied around her slender ankles. Her hair was expensively cut and streaked, with auburn highlights woven into the long dark mass.

Her mother always told her to focus on others when she was feeling shy, so that's what she did now, putting a big smile on her face. "Tina? You are so young! And beautiful!"

"Oh, no, I'm not." She laughed and hugged Ginny. "What a thrill it is to meet you! My friends and I have a big spread for you over at my house, so let's get you over there. Your trailer and car will be fine here for a little bit — my cousin owns it and I told him you'd be coming, so just lock up and let's go. You must be famished and exhausted! How far did you drive?" Without waiting for an answer, she squatted in a somehow ladylike, pinup-girl way and greeted Willow. "You're a beauty, aren't you? I've got goodies for you, too, and you can have a nice run out in the backyard to stretch your legs." She opened the door to let Willow into the narrow backseat in the cab. "Go on, I'll get the air conditioner on."

Ginny blinked and headed back to the Jeep, trying to equate the Tina of her imagination — a forty-something, maybe plump and ordinary housewife — with this vivacious ball of energy. She grabbed her camera bag, locked the door, and double-checked the trailer.

At least she wouldn't have to talk much.

Tina drove them down a farm road, going quite a bit faster than Ginny would have, chattering, fiddling with the music. A long bank of cottonwoods lined the fields in the distance, marking the path of the Arkansas River, and in between were thickly planted fields — some cottonwoods, but mostly the cantaloupe for which the region was famous. "I hope you'll find something to take pictures of this afternoon. We have all been baking our heads off. We used a lot of your recipes. Have you ever done this before, met any of the people who go there, to the blog, I mean?"

Ginny started with the first question and moved through the comments, as if she was online. One at a time. When the comments first began to multiply, she'd been overwhelmed — forty per day, then a hundred. How could she answer all of them? And yet the commenters had each taken the time to come to her blog and say something in response, so she did her best.

"I'm sure I'll have so many choices that it will be hard to decide which one to use," she said. "I'm thrilled that you've used some of my recipes — and, yes, this is the first time I've met any of you." As she spoke, she found that the Ginny of the ordinary world was slightly overtaken by the Cake Ginny, a more confident person who could make witty asides and genuinely loved the watering hole she had inadvertently created. She smiled. "Thank you so much for inviting me."

Tina smacked her palm against the steering wheel. "I'm just so honored! Ginny, from 'Cake of Dreams,' right here in Rocky Ford!"

Her house turned out to be a large, beautiful modular plopped down beneath a copse of elms in the midst of a vast expanse of fields. A vegetable garden spread out in a green checkerboard behind the house, and a clothesline stretched between two tall trees. Brave pots of red geraniums were stationed on the porch, as if to stave off the loneliness creeping in from all directions.

"Did you grow up on a farm?" Ginny asked.

Tina nodded. "And I swore I wouldn't live here when I grew up, but you know how it happens — I fell in love and got married, and, sure enough, he was a farmer from right here in town."

"Were you high school sweethearts?"

"I knew him in school, but, no — I actually managed to get away for a while." She opened the back door to let Willow out and looked toward the horizon. "I went to school in Fort Collins, got my teaching degree, and I was going to live in Denver, but I came home for the summer and that's when I met Tom." Her shoulder twitched in a shrug. "He's a good man." Her smile was wistful as she added, "He'd never let me do what you're doing, drive across the country by myself."

Ginny met her eyes steadily. "You might be surprised."

A woman slammed out of the house to the wide porch. "Tina, stop hogging her!"

They all went inside.

Later, Tina drove Ginny back to the trailer. "Would you mind — would it be too imposing to ask if I could see inside?"

"No, not at all. She's my pride and joy!" Ginny pulled her keys from her pocket. "I love showing her off!"

"It was so much fun to follow the journey on the blog — the search, then when you found it. Was it Lavender who helped you find it?"

"It belonged to her friend." Ginny opened the door and waved Tina in ahead of her. "Ginger Holmes was an artist in Carmel-by-the-Sea. She died just last year, and her daughter was trying to get rid of the trailer, so I got lucky."

"Oh, it's beautiful." Tina sighed, putting her hands on her heart. "Look at all the decorative wood and the special touches. Do you call it Art Nouveau style?"

Ginny nodded, seeing the space with fresh eyes. She heard faintly the sound of some tinny music, caught a waft of ocean-scented air. She imagined sitting on the beach at dusk, a mai tai in her hand, watching the sunset.

Tina moved, touching the stove and the little sink, peeking her head into the bedroom. When Tina turned around, Ginny could see she was close to tears, and she impulsively hugged her.

"I am so envious," Tina whispered. "I'd

give up a lot to be doing what you're doing."

Ginny pulled back and looked her in the eye. "I'm scared out of my mind," she confessed, and they both laughed. "But I'm also very glad I'm doing it."

"I'll be following along."

"And maybe imagining what your adventure will be?"

Tina squeezed her hand. "Maybe."

THE FLAVOR OF A BLUE MOON
a blog about great food . . .

Comfort Food

We all need comfort food now and then — fat and carbs in some luxurious combination. I woke up with that hunger in my heart at 3:00 A.M., after driving a couple of days to get here to Lavender Honey Farms.

My answer is a cheesy fettuccine, made with cashew cream, greens, and beans. I use whole-grain noodles, though if you have a yen for the usual semolina variety, no one will judge you. I love the creamy taste of the beans, contrasted with the greens and the fettuccine. A hearty meal.

Cashews are a rich source of heart-healthful fats and are chockful of minerals, including iron, magnesium, and zinc. They're high in fiber and protein and . . . as you know already, they taste delicious.

FETTUCCINE WITH CASHEW CREAM, GREENS, AND BEANS

Serves 4–6

Start with the cream, and the rest should go easily — pasta, greens, then combine. If you are not using canned beans, they will need to be prepared the day before, too. This is a very, very nutritious dish, but if you don't tell your friends, they'll never know.

Cashew Cream

1/2 cup cashews, soaked overnight in 2 cups water, or boiled for three minutes, then drained
1/2 cup nutritional yeast flakes (not powder!)
2 cups water
1 tsp dried mustard

Blend until smooth. If you don't have a monster-style blender like the Vitamix, strain the mix through a sieve. Heat on low, adding salt to taste and soy or plain almond milk if it gets too thick.

1 lb. fettuccine

Cook it according to package directions, approximately ten minutes. While the water is getting ready to boil, prepare greens, below.

1 cup white beans, any variety, cooked or canned (I love butter beans and have lately been using a lot of mayocoba beans, which are a beautiful color).

If cooking them, start the day before. Check out the basic recipe **here.**

Greens
2 T olive oil
1 yellow onion, roughly chopped
3 cloves garlic, minced or pressed
4 cups fresh baby spinach or collards, washed and picked over

Heat the oil in a heavy skillet and cook onions on medium heat until translucent, then add garlic and stir for two minutes. Add the greens and cook until wilted. Add beans.
Place hot fettuccine (warm it under hot water if you like) in a large bowl, add greens and beans, then stir in cashew cream. Serve!

CHAPTER 6

When Ruby awakened, it was dark. Not just evening dark, but the kind of full, silent dark that falls after midnight. She had to pee, which was not so unusual these days, but when she stretched out again on her bed, nestled into the three pillows she most liked to have — one under her head, one to hold, one between her knees — she realized there was no way she was going back to sleep. Her mind was cheerfully awake.

It happened sometimes. With a shrug, she tossed off the covers and stood in the doorway. Her view in daylight was a row of blue mountains on the horizon and rolling green fields in between. Now there was only velvety darkness, broken here and there by a lone light shining over a barn or a porch, maybe, far away.

The air was soft and cool. Ruby slid her feet into a pair of waiting flip-flops, took the key to the trailer from a hook by the door, and stepped down, turning her head up to look at the unclouded dark sky, lit by millions — no billions! — of stars. The Milky Way swayed down the middle. The moon hung low to the west. Wonder swirled through her.

And hunger. She was absolutely starving, her imagination dancing with visions of bread and sun-dried tomatoes, or maybe some fruit, or maybe even more than that. Maybe she wanted to cook and play and enjoy this beautiful moment, with her baby in her belly and the stars shining and night like an enchanted cloak over the land.

She pulled open the screen door to unlock the trailer and stepped up, turning on the light by the door. Gleaming stainless steel greeted her — all the accoutrements of a professional kitchen, only mini-size. She and her dad had scoured the city and the Internet to get the fittings just right. The base was a 1968 Airstream Bambi, easily hauled by her camper.

With a loan from her father, Ruby had the trailer gutted, the axles and floors redone, and all the minor refurbishments for the frame completed. Then her father jumped in. He fancied himself good at most creative tasks and loved helping her find efficient ways of refitting the trailer. He was the one who'd found the storage units with shelves that slid out. He found the stove, a six-burner in a miniature size, from a company in Europe, and helped choose the materials for interior safety and beauty. There was a double oven, since vegan baking was all the rage these days, and a bank of refrigeration along the back, divided into sections for energy efficiency, so Ruby could run some or all at a given moment. At the other end were a table and two bench seats, where she could sit to prep food.

On a long shelf over the pass-through window was her collection of cookbooks. Tonight she reached for a favorite, *Moosewood,* spattered and waffled with use, and flipped through it for ideas, testing her body for what it wanted. Which also had to correspond with what ingredients might be available in the cupboards. She'd stocked up on the staples — pastas and nuts, dozens of spices and herbs, grains, flours, dry and canned beans, and bouillon. The fridge was nearly empty, since she'd planned to shop when she arrived, just to keep the weight down in the trailer. There was a large carton of soy milk and some fresh parsley and her ever-present lemons, onions, and garlic. She let her imagination swim toward what she wanted, seeing fettuccine, garlic . . . cashew cream. Just right. She began to hum to herself.

There were a few luxurious items her father had installed to surprise her. One was a dock for her iPhone, which he paid for so they could stay in touch. She plugged it in and pulled up a playlist she'd been adding to for years, then slid the volume down low. Glancing out the open door to the farm beyond, she clicked it down another notch. The chickens were probably sleeping.

The other luxury item her father had installed was a restaurant-grade food processor fitted into its own cabinet for safety. She slid it out and assembled the bowl and blades. Even preparing to cook settled something in her, and she felt tension slide away, down from her neck and shoulders, through her spine, into the floor. A breeze blew in through the door, ruffling her hair.

Cooking had been her refuge for nearly as long as she could remember. She'd begun with cookies and cakes as a child, then moved to main dishes. When it was time to go to college, she knew she wanted only to study cooking at a respected vegan school. There were not that many. She headed for New York and studied vegetarian cuisine, trying to find a way into the industry in the city.

She poured two cups of cashews into a small saucepan and brought them to a boil for three minutes. It wasn't the ideal method — it would have been better to soak the nuts overnight — but she was hungry now.

Into the food processor she poured the nuts and a little more water. The recipe was something that always made her think of Liam, and she'd been avoiding it for that reason. But she couldn't avoid it forever. Tonight her body ached for the creamy goodness, the sense of comfort that fat and solid carbs lent.

She'd met Liam at the Green Table, a high-end vegan restaurant on the trendy Lower East Side. The chef, Kevin Morrell, had studied with Alice Waters and a handful of other sustainable-food advocates and had won a cooking show, which gave him the cash he needed to open a restaurant the right way. The food was entirely vegan, entirely perfect, but from a work perspective Kevin was known for his intensity. Liam was his sous chef, as calm as Kev was fiery.

The first time Ruby had seen Liam, he was peeling curls of carrot into a bowl. He worked cleanly, quickly, and he was whistling to himself. His hands were works of art, long and powerful and impeccably clean, the fingernails perfect ovals. The skin was tanned, and his wrists were covered with golden hair. She wanted to paint those hands — they made her think of a monk cooking in some medieval monastery, an idea that seemed ridiculous considering she'd never even been to Europe, so how would she know what that looked like? But it was clear, the picture: Liam in a rough brown robe, his sleeves rolled back on his forearms, herbs hanging to dry behind him, a skinned rabbit on the wooden table beside the cutting board.

It made her dizzy. She even smelled the dill and the blood. She was wondering how she, the lifelong vegan, would know that skinned animal was rabbit, when he caught sight of her. "Hey," he said in his low voice. "You must be Ruby."

She looked up, still feeling disoriented, and was snared in his pale-green eyes. She fell in love just that fast, at first sight. It was as if she'd known him forever, as if she only had to remember his name. Her heart did not beat faster, but it filled with a sensation like sunlight, like music.

He gave her a quizzical expression. "Where do I know you from?"

A laugh fizzed right up through her throat. "I don't know! The fourteenth century?"

He gazed at her for a long time, looking at

her eyes and mouth and breasts, and that giddiness danced through her. If she could have, she would have kissed him right then, right there, but she would wait for him to realize they were in love.

Which he did, by the end of the day. It was fast and clear, their beginning. He brought her to his tiny rooms over a nightclub that sent pulses of sound and beat through the floor, and they made love all night, barely pausing to eat. It was as magical as anything she had ever known in her life. By the end of the month, they found an apartment together and were inseparable for six years.

In her food trailer in the middle of the night, Ruby boiled water for fettuccine and chopped onions and garlic to brown in olive oil. The scent filled the air.

Liam, Liam, Liam. Her monkish lover. That part had proved to be achingly all too true. He was sometimes difficult to live with, hard to please in his shunning of pleasures. He gave up wine or bread. He fasted. He ran, for miles and miles and miles. He sometimes would not make love because he was giving that up for a stretch.

But he loved her as insanely, as possessively, as unmistakably, as it was possible for a man to love a woman. That was one of the things she loved most about him — his fierceness, his intense passion when he let himself go, his undeniable, romantic, jealous love. He hated when other men looked at her, always feared one would catch her eye. He worried that he was too old for her, twenty-eight to her twenty when they met. He worried that she would drift away.

Nine months ago, he had announced out of nowhere that he was leaving. He moved out of their apartment into the apartment of another woman. Ruby had been absolutely shell-shocked. It made no sense. It was *anti-sense.* She'd had no inkling whatsoever.

Whatsoever.

She'd been a nutcase, sure there was some mistake, that he would come to his senses, that something was playing out on a karmic level, maybe, and he'd come back. They were working together still, and he sometimes seemed as if he could not resist her — taking her in the walk-in, fiercely, or as if he was angry. She allowed it, gave in to it, hoping something would jolt him, wake him up to the reality of their union. Once, breathing hard after they fucked in the tiny service bathroom downstairs, she put his hands on her face and held them there. "It's me," she said. "Me."

He kissed her so hard it was like a punch, then ran away.

The whole thing began to take its toll on Ruby. Her friends started worrying about how much weight she'd lost, how much she was drinking, how — well, how badly she was falling apart. She was their rock. They tried to be hers in return.

At last she'd found enough courage to leave the job and ask her dad if she could head back to San Francisco for a little while, just until she got her head together. Paul Zarlingo was an eccentric, an inventor who'd made millions on an invention during the dot-com boom. He spent his days puttering around his glass-fronted ocean-front mansion, inventing all kinds of things. He had patents on more than seventy inventions.

Of course, Paul told her to come home. Ruby packed up her life in the apartment she'd shared with Liam for six years and cried her eyes out. He was supposed to pick up his things after she left, then turn the keys back to the landlord, but he showed up early.

Ruby had built up some resistance, but not as much as she wanted. He stood in the doorway, his pale eyes blazing. There were blue shadows beneath them, as if he had not slept for days, and she felt a pain go through her. "Why is this happening?" she asked, breaking again.

He pushed into the room and held her. "Don't cry, Ruby," he said. "Please don't cry. I'm so sorry. I can't explain, but it has to be this way."

She hit him then, the only time in her life she'd ever hit anyone. She slammed her fist right into his ear and cried out when he grabbed her wrists and yanked her to him, and they kissed so hard, banging teeth and lips, that her mouth bled and was bruised for days after. They fell to the bare wooden floor and *fucked* right there in the middle of the empty apartment. Her back was burned from the intensity of it, and his knee was bleeding by the time they were finished. Her shoulder showed a bruise where he'd bitten her, and he had a bloody hickey on his neck and long scratches down his back.

Without a word, he stood up, put on his clothes, and left.

Now, at the lavender farm in the middle of the night, Ruby gently stirred fettuccine, those loveliest of long noodles, into boiling water. She put her hand over her tummy, which rose in a softer arch than she had expected, a pillow tucked beneath her apron. Conceived in fury, in anger, but nonetheless conceived.

A miracle. Against all odds, she was carrying a child. She had not let them tell her yet whether it was a boy or a girl. Maybe she wouldn't ever let them tell her, and it would be a surprise. Not very practical but fun.

When the pasta was finished, she tossed it with sun-dried tomatoes soaked in herbed oil and white beans sautéed with onions and garlic, and sprinkled it all with coarse grains of cracked pepper and Himalayan salt, then poured the cashew cream over it, stirring it all together. Some greens — spinach or kale or collards — would have added the right note of earthiness, but this was great. Brilliant, even. She took off her apron and settled in the open door with the plate in her lap.

She inhaled, then tasted her creation and sighed with happiness. Overhead, the Milky Way still shone. The moon had moved toward the horizon, illuminating a stand of trees. An animal skittered through the bushes close by, then peeked out through the leaves. Only its bright eyes floated in the dark. Ruby took another bite, watching.

The animal slid from the cover of leaves and slunk toward her, body close to the ground. A cat, Ruby realized, and the muscles in the back of her neck let go. "Hey, kitty. Want some?" She tossed a tidbit on the ground. After a minute, the cat crept forward and sniffed it.

"No good, huh?" Ruby said, and smiled. The animal, a very small black cat with a blaze of white down its chest and white paws, settled a few feet away, perfectly calm, and watched with round yellow eyes. "I guess cats like a little more blood."

Ruby tossed some more food on the ground and nonchalantly continued to eat her pasta. The kitten crept forward a quarter inch at a time, until close enough to sniff, then carefully lapped up a bit of the food.

It was then, as she contentedly shared the night sky with a tiny cat, that Ruby felt the baby move. At first she didn't realize what it was, and then it came again, a fluttering, then a longer swooping sensation through her middle. In wonder, she curled a hand over the spot, but she couldn't feel outside what she felt from the inside.

"Hi, baby," she said. "I am so glad you're here."

When she looked up, the kitten had disappeared, but it didn't matter. The night was filled with wonders. Stars and food and babies moving.

"Wow," she said, looking up toward the sky. And again, "Wow."

From the woods nearby came a snuffling sound, and a growl, and a scuffle. Ruby stood up, peering into the blackness, fearing for the kitten's life. The cat shot out of the trees, racing right toward her, and past her, into the trailer. Another animal followed on the cat's heels, a ragged-looking dog that halted, head down, eyes glowing, when it spied Ruby.

Ruby froze, the food in her hand. It was not a dog. It was a coyote, with a gold ruff and a long tail and nose. It stared at her for what seemed like years, then abruptly turned and loped into the cover of the forest.

Ruby looked behind her. The kitten crouched beneath the little table, eyes wide with fear, hair puffed out to double its previous size. Moving excruciatingly slowly, Ruby stepped into the kitchen and closed the screen door behind her. "It's okay, sweetie. I promise. You can stay here for tonight. You don't want to go back out there with that guy, for sure."

When Ruby approached, the kitten hissed, backing up as far into the corner as possible. "Okay," Ruby said, raising her hands in surrender. "I won't touch you." She sat down on the floor in front of the stove and carefully pulled the dish towel down from the hook by the sink. She ruffled up the fabric a bit, then put it on the floor. She wished she had some food a cat would like.

After a while, with Ruby sitting there cross-legged on the floor, the cat settled into a more comfortable position, paws tucked toward its chest, eyes starting to slant closed.

Ruby yawned. She stretched out on the floor, tummy full, and closed her eyes for just a minute. Across her imagination drifted Ginny's itinerary. Where was she now?

CHAPTER 7

As Ginny got back on the road after the stop in Rocky Ford, her belly was full of potato salad and fried chicken and pieces of three of her own cakes — one of which was the Black Forest cake that was one of her early hits, a version that took out a lot of the sugar in order to showcase the cherries. It was the one she'd chosen to shoot, asking if she could move it to the counter where indirect light flooded in from a skylight. She also shot group photos and many of the groaning table and set a timer so that she could stand with the others and have her photo taken with them. In the back of her mind, as she ate and talked and listened to the women tell stories of the blogs they'd have if they had one, and the books they'd read recently, and their own wishes for a good camera, Ginny composed a simple blog post.

Her first from the road.

As she headed down Highway 50, she felt triumphant and excited, rejuvenated for the last leg of her drive today. It was only five-thirty — plenty of time to get to Manitou before dark. She had a campground picked out, and tomorrow she'd spend the day exploring the little village and go to the top of Pikes Peak.

She yawned, glanced in the rearview mirror at her home on wheels. Tonight she would sleep in it for the first time.

The clouds caught her attention twenty minutes later. She glanced up at the mountains on the far horizon, thrilled that the landscape was changing. They were blue and sturdy against the western line of sky, but the tops were hidden in low dark clouds. She frowned.

"Hold off until I get parked," she said aloud. But she and the storm raced toward each other, and by the time she reached Pueblo, the sun — and the mountains — had disappeared. She wondered briefly if she ought to pull over, wait it out, but there was no wind, no lightning, and Manitou was only another fifty miles or so, on I-25, a major highway. The radio warned of thunderstorms, but a traffic report said nothing about dangerous road conditions. No tornado watches.

Just do it.

She headed north, butterflies dancing. She was almost there! Her first leg done!

Five minutes later, she drove into the rain. It was the most bizarre thing she'd seen on the road — on one side of the line, the highway was completely dry, and then she drove right into a heavy downpour complete with hail, so heavy it made the entire world dark and created a cacophony of sound, hammering on the roof and body of the car, sluicing off the Airstream behind her. Ginny put on her headlights and slowed down, her heart pounding as other cars rushed by, sending plumes of water arcing over her windshield.

A midsize sedan whooshed by. She clutched the wheel so tightly that her hands ached, but she kept her speed at forty, no lower. Ahead of her was a pickup truck going roughly the same speed, and behind her was a little bug of a car, using the protection of the Airstream to stay on the road.

Any minute now, she told herself, she would drive out of it.

But mile after mile the rain poured, turning the highway into a river. The Airstream felt as if it weighed a billion unstable pounds, but there was no wind to speak of, so that was her own fear speaking.

No fear. She chanted it to herself: *No fear, no fear, no fear.* Her shoulders began to ache, then burn with tension, and her neck hurt, and her eyes.

When a rest stop appeared out of the gloom, Ginny aimed for it with tears streaming down her face. She couldn't spare a hand to wipe them away, so she just let them flow, relief and terror mixing in some crazy combination as she pulled the car and Airstream into the big lot, along with a half dozen semitrucks and a couple dozen cars. The unceasing rain soaked her as she yanked her camera bag and purse from the seat, let Willow out, and they both dashed for the Airstream. She unlocked it, hustled them both inside, and sat down on the bed, shaking in reaction.

Then she bent her head into her hands and cried some more. What had she let herself in for?

At some point much later, Ginny woke up to Willow nosing her hand repeatedly. It was dark and still raining, though not with the force it had been earlier. The sound now was a soft patter on the roof of the Airstream.

When Ginny moved, sitting up stiffly, Willow backed away with her tail wagging and jerked her head toward the door. "Oh, sorry, sweetie. Let me get a jacket."

She fetched her jacket and put it on, pulling the hood over her head. She leashed the dog and they went out in the heavy drizzle. Most of the other cars and trucks had driven on, but a couple of semis were still parked, their engines idling. On the highway, cars roared by, one after another. The heavy clouds pressed down from above, and Ginny could only keep her head down. Willow did her business, then shook the rain off her fur.

"My turn," Ginny said, and headed for the ladies' room. There was a toilet in the trailer, but she might as well make use of this one while she could.

No one was in there, so she brought Willow with her. Willow sat politely while Ginny used the toilet and then stripped off her jacket and shirt and hung them on a hook. She washed at the sink, drying off with paper towels. In the mirror, she looked gray and withered, with circles under her eyes.

"Such an adventure," she said aloud, feeling the weight of it in her gut. This had been a stupid idea.

As if Willow heard her thoughts, she made a soft whine.

"I'm only kidding," Ginny said, slipping back into her clothes. "Once we get to Lavender's farm it will be a lot better."

As she finished, a young woman came in, her long red hair braided away from her face. "Hi!" she said in an Australian accent. "Raining enough for you?"

Ginny rolled her eyes. "Pretty crazy. Were you driving in it?"

"Yeah." She headed to the sink and turned the water on, soaping her hands and face, then scrubbing them vigorously. With eyes the color of a shallow lake, she peered at Ginny through the mirror. "Are you driving that Airstream?"

"Yes! My first trip."

"That's a brilliant trailer. Bambi, yeah?"

"That's right. I looked for a long time for the right one."

The girl splashed water over her face. "I'd love something like that."

Something real and true eased in Ginny's throat, as if she might be able to speak without screaming. "When the time is right, you will, I bet."

"Right." She dried her face and opened a little makeup bag.

Ginny whistled for Willow to follow her out. "Take care," she said to the girl.

"Right, love. You, too."

Back in the trailer, Ginny turned on some lights over the table, put on her sweats and heavy socks, and opened her laptop, which was fully charged. There was an email from Valerie.

FROM: Valerie@winedancer.com
TO: Ginny@cakeofdreams.com
SUBJECT: My daughter has gone
   native
LOCATION: back of beyond, SD

Hi, Ginny. How's your journey going so far? I keep thinking about you driving through the mountains at long last and wonder if that's as thrilling as you thought it would be. Are you into the mountains yet? I can't remember which day you were leaving, I'm sorry to say. That's because my teenage daughter has sucked the brains right out of my head.

We've been on the road six and a half days. Six days in the car with my darling girl. Six days of touring Native American sites, like Tecumseh's grave and Sitting Bull's birthplace and the site of Crazy Horse's murder.

Hannah has taped postcards of Sitting Bull and Red Cloud to her walls in the trailer. She takes hours to straighten her hair every morning, then weaves in braids and feathers. The effect is startling, I have to admit — she has her father's cheekbones and my dark eyes, so she could easily pass for Native American. But that's been the story of biracial people all through time, hasn't it? They can blend in, become someone new. Not like me, blackest woman in six counties. Not like you, Freckles. Or Miss Ruby Slippers, with her big blue eyes.

I'm rambling, sorry. I wish we were coming to the farm instead of making this tour of powwows and battlegrounds. It's all so wretchedly depressing, and I have had enough of depressing. I need to find a new life, a fresh start, but what does an aging, widowed ballerina do for the rest of her life? Is forty-seven too late to start over? Are we over the hill, my friend? I honestly don't know.

Sometimes I even feel guilty for that, for *wanting* to start over. Young (okay, young-ish) widows do it, but maybe mothers who've lost children don't. Except that I just don't see the point in staying stuck at the moment of loss. I don't see how it serves my daughters for me to stop living, too. I don't see how it makes my life mean any more. My father used to say people get over unimaginable things, and as a black man from Mississippi, I guess he had more insight than most.

The biggest reason to get unstuck and find that new life for myself is for Hannah, who is stuck back at the moment when those officials in their uniforms showed up at our door to tell us what we had suspected. She can't move on, because none of her friends will let her. I can't move on, because I am The Woman Who Lost Her Family in That Horrible Plane Crash. It cages us in, both of us. In San Diego, we can start fresh. Live by the ocean.

In some ways, the trip is working. Hannah is turning herself into a Native American, but at least she isn't trying to squeeze herself into her sisters' clothes anymore. Now she's not exactly being Hannah, but at least she's not them.

I honestly thought that after two years we might be further along this road. I thought *I'd* be further along. I miss them all so much. Maybe that's not something to be avoided. Maybe it's just going to be a piece of me forever.

Ugh, sorry! I'm whining again, and I will have to move the bracelet on my arm to the other and start over.

Please tell me about your adventures.
I'm dying to hear.

Love,
Val

FROM: Ginny@cakeofdreams.com
TO: Valerie@winedancer.com
SUBJECT: re: My daughter has gone
  native
LOCATION: back of beyond, Colorado

Hi, Val. First, big hugs. I'm going to
say again what I have said a dozen times:
You are doing the right thing under very
challenging circumstances. I'm proud of
you for taking action instead of staying
stuck.

Where am I? I honestly don't know
exactly. It's raining really, really hard.
I'm exhausted from driving and still
have to post a blog. I'll write more
tomorrow night.

But, yes, I'm on the way, and it's
exhilarating and terrifying and a thousand other things I can't pick out completely.

Can't you just keep driving and come
to the farm? Why not?

I don't know how you can escape missing them — and maybe you wouldn't want to, after all. I'm glad the trip seems to be helping with Hannah. You are a great mother, and they do grow up. I admire you so much.

And I know this sounds canned and like I'm not really reading/responding, but, I swear, even my eyelashes are tired. More tomorrow.

Please come to the farm with the rest of us. Please, please, please?

Love,
Ginny the demolished

Email sent, Ginny uploaded a handful of photos to the blog, wrote a quick post, and shut it all down. Willow hopped up on the bed with her, taking the space by the wall as Ginny had been training her to do — a big warm comfort when she felt lonely.

Drawing her quilt over her body and plumping up the pillows, she closed her eyes, imagining a big circle of protection around the trailer. Next to her, Willow snored comfortingly. Rain pattered down on the roof.

And, just as Matthew had predicted, a sense of vast loneliness crashed down on her like a blanket of ice. The distance she had traveled, so many, many miles, seemed insane, and where was she? In a beautiful campground by a river, or in the mountains? No, at a rest stop on the interstate, with trucks running their engines.

Back home, Matthew was tucked into bed, reading a mystery. She pictured her kitchen, the swath of counter that her sisters envied, the new range and oven, the flower vase on the windowsill filled with a selection of roses from her garden. Why had she left her roses? Matthew would never take care of them. They would die.

She imagined a gentle hand smoothing the hair from her brow. Just before she fell asleep, she could have sworn that music began to play, and there was the distinct sound of ice clinking into a glass.

LAVENDER HONEY FARMS
yamhill co., oregon

Home   Shop   **Blog**   Directions   Philosophy

At the lavender farms, this stretch of June is one of our favorites. The bees are happily drugging themselves on the fields of lavender, lambs are tumbling through the grass, and we're making cheese to take advantage of the season.

Our lamb Pilar came to us as a rescue from a local commune. She was battered and worn out, but our resident magician, Noah, managed to get her back into happy shape. This is her first lambing season, and she's taken to it like the champ she is. Sometimes survivors are the most sensitive of all.

Sheep cheese is not as common in America as cow's milk cheese, but don't let that stop you. Here are a few of our best cheeses, available only in limited amounts:

Rosemary manchego
Pecorino wrapped in walnut leaves
Malvarosa (one of my favorites!)

CHAPTER 8

Monday morning, after her tour of the perimeter, Lavender cut behind the house to follow a path through the woods behind the farm. It was a sunny morning, promising to be hot later in the day, and the bees were hungrily gathering pollen and nectar from the throats of the millions of lavender blossoms. It was a sight she loved as much as any, the bees so certain of their place and purpose. She fancied she could smell the honey from hives as she passed by.

Her destination was the manager's small house, which crouched at the edge of the stream that looped around the farm in almost too picturesque a manner. It ran fast this time of year, still fed by clear melting snows.

Noah sat on the steps of the porch in his stocking feet, drinking a mug of coffee. His hair, too long as always — a rebellion against his soldier days, she thought —

hadn't yet been brushed, and his eyes were swollen with sleep. Or what passed for sleep with Noah Tso. He was known to get by on an hour or two, snatched from the maw of his nightmares.

That's what happened when you sent men to war over and over. It sucked something out of them. She'd been a teenager during World War II, and those men fought a long time, too. Years on end, most of them. Noah had spent three tours in Iraq and one in Afghanistan and wanted only a place where he didn't have to pretend he still had the usual small talk and foolishness of everyday interactions. He just wanted to be left alone, to spend time on the land. Lavender could practically see the ghosts who followed him around, and, having known some ghosts herself, she'd taken pity on him.

Good thing, too. He was the best manager she'd ever had and was devoted to the principles of the farm that she'd laid out twenty-five years ago, long before it was hip: organic, whole, integrated, natural.

He ignored the women who angled for his attentions, with such aloofness that he was labeled arrogant, stuck-up, too good for himself — all those things people said when they didn't know what to make of a body. Because he was beautiful, they wanted him to see them in return; when he didn't, they felt embarrassed.

" 'Morning," Lavender said now. "You have a minute?"

"Always." He wiped a hand over his face. "What's up?"

She sat down next to him on the step, grunting a little. Her knees were creaky, no matter how much ginger she imbibed.

"Any more trouble along the fences?"

"Fixed a little breach yesterday afternoon, but it could have been anything." Noah turned his copper eyes, as penetrating as a laser, on her. "You're being paranoid."

Lavender shook her head. "Nope," she said, pushing her lower lip out. "Wade is after this land, mark my words, and once I'm gone, those nephews of mine will sell it to him so fast it'll make your head spin."

Noah nodded.

"He'll ruin it, Noah, every bit of it. He'll just turn it into another Wade Markum Enterprise, and everything I've been working for all this time will be lost."

"You keep telling me this, but I'm not sure what you want me to do. Sell it now. Rewrite your will."

She raised an eyebrow. "You're the one I want."

"No can do," he said, shaking his head.

103

"Sorry."

"Mmm." She took a breath. "Well, that's what this party is about, then. One of these gals might be my heir."

He frowned into his mug. Took a sip. "What makes you think any of them could do it? Running a farm like this isn't a little thing."

Lavender eyed a trio of hens who had wandered down the path behind her. One fat girl with wheat-colored feathers clucked under her breath, eyeing the ground. "I've known all three of them for years. Each one has something that might make her a good fit." She held up her thumb. "Ruby is devoted to the organic movement, and she's young and looking for her place in life." She poked her index finger into the air. "Valerie and her daughter need a fresh start, and Val's as smart as anyone I've ever met. She's spent a lot of time studying wine, which takes a knowledge of the soil."

Noah gave her a skeptical look. "She's the ballerina, right? City woman."

Lavender shrugged. "She's a stretch but worth a try." She stuck up her middle finger. "Ginny was raised on a farm and is so miserable where she is that I think she'd move to Mars."

"You do what you need to do, I guess. I'll

be here."

She patted his shoulder. "Fair enough." She got to her feet. "How is the dancing platform coming along?" Her vision for the night of the Blue Moon Festival included a party like the ones she'd enjoyed in her youth, with lights strung around a platform and everyone dancing to a band.

"It's good. Come on over later and I'll show it to you."

"Will do."

As Lavender was heading back toward the house, Noah called after her, "Lavender, I am sorry."

She only waved a hand. He thought he knew what he wanted, but she saw him better than he did himself. She hadn't given up yet.

Lavender found Ruby drinking a mug of tea on the porch of the cottage. Ruby didn't see her, so Lavender caught the pensive expression before Ruby could mask it with her eternal smile. She reminded Lavender of a Russian farm girl, with her straight blond hair and curves and the round apple cheeks. Before they'd met in person, Lavender imagined that Ruby would be a whirling dervish, thin and leggy and exuberant.

The exuberance was there, of course, the

zest that brought people to her blog in such numbers. But how did a person stay so cheerful all the time?

"Good morning," Lavender called out now. "Would you like some breakfast?"

"I'd like to make you some breakfast if you'll let me," Ruby said. "It's my turn, you know."

"Better be something hearty. I'm starving."

"Pancakes, then. How's that? Do you have any bananas?"

"Yes, ma'am, I do. I also have some fresh blueberries we collected down by the creek. We can run down to McMinnville later this afternoon and get groceries if you want."

"I'd really like to do that. I need to stock up on a bunch of fresh food."

The kitchen was tiny, just about enough room to turn around three times. "I need coffee," Lavender said. "You want some, too, or does it upset your stomach?"

"I'm going to stick with my mint tea." Ruby gave Lavender a wan smile. "The doctor gave me anti-nausea drugs, and I broke down and took some this morning."

"Sometimes medicine is a good thing."

They moved companionably around the small space, back-to-back, side by side. Ruby assembled her ingredients and heated a griddle Lavender had dug out of the back of a cabinet, a cast-iron beauty that covered two gas burners. It had belonged to her mother and showed the depth of time.

Ruby squeaked when she saw it. "This is so cool!" She made a kissing noise toward it. "I've wanted to get one for ages."

"My mother used it nearly every day of her life."

"I can imagine." She spread oil over the heavy iron, then lovingly heated it until water skittered over the surface. As she ladled the batter into evenly sized pools, Ruby bloomed with that beneficent, glowing smile. She half lit up the room with it. "Can we go to the meadery today?"

"You bet."

"And . . . uh, do you have cat food?"

Lavender frowned. "Cat food?"

"A little black cat showed up on my doorstep last night. She was being chased by a coyote, and I took her in. She slept on my tummy all night. Oh! And speaking of *that* . . ." She put her hands on her hips and gave Lavender a big grin. "Guess what? I felt the baby move last night!"

Lavender blinked, trying to sort out the threads of that paragraph, but what she was really thinking was what a pretty thing Ruby was, all that shine to her. What the heck was wrong with that man of hers, anyway? It made no sense.

"Congratulations! That's a big moment, I understand." As Lavender spoke, she sorted through the emails from Ginny. "As for the cat, I'm sure she's one of the barn cats. There is a feral colony around, too, but they're not inclined to sleep with humans."

"Feral cats? How do they live if there are coyotes?"

"They're quick and smart, and not all of them do."

Ruby blinked, her hand frozen, then said, "Oh." She put the pancakes on two plates, turned off the burners, and carried them over to the table.

"Nature is cruel," Lavender said. The pancakes were light and fluffy, steaming with hot huckleberries. "These are gorgeous, girl."

Ruby poured maple syrup over hers and passed the bottle over. "I know that, about nature. But if a kitten shows up hungry and hiding from a coyote, a woman doesn't have to be as cruel as nature." She popped a bite of pancake into her mouth, raising her eyebrows as if to challenge Lavender.

Instead, the older woman nodded. "Fair enough. I've got some tuna around here. She'll like that, I betcha."

Just then Ruby's face crumpled and she covered her mouth with her hand, raising a finger at Lavender before she ran for the toilet.

While Ruby threw up, Lavender prepared a cup of chamomile tea and sweetened it with a touch of honey from her own hives. When Ruby returned, she said, "Try that."

Ruby nodded, pulling the pancakes and tea over to her. "Maybe I can eat now."

I'm writing this from my cozy little trailer, on the road. Outside, rain is pattering on the top of my roof, and, inside, my good dog Willow is snoring softly.

Today I had the great good fortune to meet one of the community here, Tina Romero, from Rocky Ford. She was kind enough to invite me to her home, where she and some of her friends had made several cakes from "Cake of Dreams." Thanks, Tina! I had such a great time.

This is my Black Forest cake, which some of you might know was the very first cake I posted to this blog. Isn't it pretty? Find the recipe *here.*

107 Comments

9:17 TinaR

Ginny is so gracious! We were so excited to meet her, and she was just as nice in person as she is in her blog. I'm going to just say that her picture here doesn't do her justice. She's a very pretty woman.

9:18 Young Girl

So jealous! Wish I could have been there.

9:32 Glenna

I have baked that cake many times since the first time I read the recipe here. It's a family favorite now.

10:10 Hilda12

You're on your way!

CHAPTER 9

Ginny awakened to the sound of car doors slamming and the shouts of children. The air in the trailer was stifling, because she hadn't opened any of the vents or windows, and her body was covered in a thin sheen of sweat. Willow was sprawled out in the longest stretch of space in the trailer, on the tile between the stove and dinette. She was sound asleep. Peeking out the window, Ginny saw a family piling into the rest-stop bathroom. Although she couldn't see it, she heard the rumbling of a semitruck engine somewhere close by.

Her mouth was dry. Her neck was stiff. She had to pee.

Some adventure.

Still, she stood up, finding her back and knees stiff from the long drive yesterday, and hobbled into the bathroom. It was a tight fit, but she loved the birch on the walls and the Art Nouveau glass mirror. The shower had been detailed with four tiny rows of glass tile inlaid in a chevron pattern, and it was big enough to stand up in. Some of the trailers she'd looked at made the bathroom and shower a single room, and she'd decided right away she wanted better than that. A morning like this was a good reason why.

Slipping back out to the main area, she pushed open the roof vents to let in some cooler air, then made sure the curtains were closed good and tight, stripped naked, and stepped into the shower. Quickly, she rinsed away the sweat of the long night, feeling some of her depression sluice away into the drain with it. It seemed slightly wicked to be showering in a big parking lot on the side of an interstate, and she suddenly liked being a person who could do it.

She considered splurging on washing her hair but, since the campground was only a little ways up the road, decided against it. A person who could shower in her trailer in a parking lot could also put her hair in a ponytail for the rest of the morning.

Buoyed, she dressed and thought about making a cup of coffee on her little stove. Willow yawned and wagged her tail, however, so Ginny took the dog out for a morning pee.

And stopped dead. The temperature couldn't have been more than sixty degrees. The air smelled like grass and fresh morning, the feel of it on her skin as whispery as the sky, stretching overhead in bold, bright blue. She breathed it in, deeply, and let it go, astonished. Who knew the air could be like that in the summertime, especially the day after a heavy rainstorm?

Willow was less impressed with the quality of the air and pulled Ginny to the grass. A couple with a fussy little dog waved at her, and she waved back. The kids who had awakened her raced around an open area, no doubt burning energy before they headed on their way.

Back home, Matthew would be getting ready for work. Something about that comforted her, but she didn't stop to examine why. Last night she'd been homesick, but now she was on her way for real. In Colorado, a state she'd wanted to visit her whole life. Criminal that it had taken so little time to drive here.

Willow snuffled along the edge of the field that bordered the rest area. Ginny made herself *just be* right there with her dog, on this singular morning in June. The hour was early yet, so the light was new and pale. It limned the edges of grasses and a handful

114

of walkingstick cactuses with buds sitting in readiness on their fingertips, revealing each needle on each arm of those severe-looking plants. Beautiful.

It was a stand of grass with curlicue tops that made her decide to go back to the trailer for her camera. Willow loped along happily, waited with a cheerful smile, then trotted back. Ginny took several dozen pictures, zooming in and out, playing with depth of field, trying to capture the mood of fresh, delicate morning light, that sense of beginning and hope.

She finally realized she needed to be at ground level for the shot she wanted. Glancing over her shoulder, she saw only one truck left in the lot, so she lay down flat on the grass on her belly, aimed her camera upward at the circlets shining in the sunlight, and took some more pictures. Once she began, she found that the whole world looked different from this angle, as ever, and she made a mental note to talk about this with her students. She shot the cactus and the edge of the building's roof looming over everything, then rolled over and captured a long series of Willow's jaw and nose and ears, all from this intriguing, ground-level angle.

When she stood up, there was a man

watching her as he filled up a water bottle from the drinking fountain. He was around her age, probably, wearing jeans and boots like a rancher. The only thing left in the parking lot was a semi with a metallic-blue cab and an unmarked trailer. Must be his.

Embarrassed, Ginny looked down and brushed dirt off her jeans.

"That's a fine-looking dog you've got there," he called out.

"Thanks."

He capped his bottle and came a little closer. "You mind if I pet her? I've just lost my dog, and you know how that ache is."

One part of her mind warned that he was a *STRANGER* and *POSSIBLY DANGEROUS* and it might be a *BIG TRICK*. Her heart, however, was pierced. "Oh, I'm so sorry. What was his name?"

The man knelt by Willow, who wasn't friendly or unfriendly but waited with dignity for the admiration that was her due. "Her name was Miz Cedar. She died just last week." He moved his hands on Willow in the way that told you he was somebody who knew and loved dogs. "Cancer." He cleared his throat. "Best damned dog I've had in my life."

"I can't even stand to think of it. Willow's only four."

"Border collie and what?"

"Newfie and shepherd, my vet thinks."

"Bet she's as smart as most politicians."

Ginny chuckled. "At least." The man had wavy gray and black hair and strong hands. "Is that your rig?"

"Yep." He half-grinned as Willow stretched her neck up so that he could scratch under her chin.

"Did Miz Cedar travel with you?"

"She did," he said gruffly. He stood. "Thank you kindly. You have a safe driving day, you hear?"

"Thanks," Ginny said. "You, too." She watched him walk away on long legs and couldn't help noticing that he had a very nice behind. It made her feel young, and she headed for the trailer with a jauntiness in her step. "Come on, girl," she said to Willow.

Ginny secured the interior, tucking away loose items and making sure nothing would rattle around or get broken, then took a moment to examine the exterior for hail damage from the storm last night.

There were a few dings in the smooth surface, and she ran her hand over them, as if kissing a child's skinned knee. Hail had been one of the things she worried most about — in the tornado country of Kansas, it was realistic — but research had revealed that the aluminum in the Airstream's skin was very high quality and thus resistant to damage in the first place. More intriguing was the fact that if the metal was allowed to sit in the sun, many of the dents would dissolve by themselves. She hoped it was true.

The dog hopped into the Jeep, and Ginny started up the engine. One day accomplished.

Onward ho!

FROM: Ginny@cakeofdreams.com
TO: FoodieFour@yahoogroups.com
SUBJECT: !!!!!!!!!!

I'm in Colorado, just over the Continental Divide!!!!!!!!!!! It is even more amazing than I expected. I'm kicking myself that I've never been here in all my forty-six years and it was only one day away. This morning I took a cog railroad to the top of Pikes Peak, America's mountain, and you can see practically the world from up there. Miles and miles and miles and miles, all the way into Kansas and across the Continental Divide, and it's so high and craggy that I felt dizzy. (Or maybe that's the altitude. One lady got sick from it, and they had to take her down in an ambulance. Did you know that altitude sickness is a real thing?)

You guys know I'm not the writer you all are, but I have been taking a million pictures, and some of them are really great.

It's pretty impressive, but then you keep driving, and there are more and more and more beautiful mountains. Once, I had to pull over and rest because I was getting all teary-eyed over them.

How come I never came to Colorado before this? Why did I just think about it and never DO anything about it? I get so mad at myself for things like that sometimes, like for how many things I haven't done. Next to you guys, I feel like oatmeal. Kansas oatmeal. How would that be for a blog title? Hahaha.

Kind of rough driving last night, but today was much better, even though I got into the mountains proper. As long as you take your time, it's not bad, even on the passes, though I wouldn't like to drive them in the rain or snow. Yikes!

I'm done for the night. Gotta get some sleep!

Love you all, can't wait to see you.

Ginny

FROM:
Lavender@lavenderhoneyblog.com
TO: FoodieFour@yahoogroups.com
SUBJECT: re: !!!!!!!!!!

Sounds like you're having an adventure now, toots. Enjoy every second.

FROM: Ruby@flavorofabluemoon.com
TO: FoodieFour@yahoogroups.com
SUBJECT: re: !!!!!!!!!!

Dearheart,
You are making my heart sing. I love to imagine you sleeping in your Coco, with Willow snuggled up next to you and the rain falling down on the roof. It makes me want to come cuddle with you both. Does Willow snore? Can't wait to give you a big victory hug when you arrive!

Love,
Ruby

THE FLAVOR OF A BLUE MOON
a blog about great food . . .

Recipes   Appetizers
Main dishes   Sides   Sweets
Sort by Name   Sort by Category
About Ruby

The Elixir of Honey

Honey is a magic elixir — made from the tiny drops of nectar taken from hearts of flowers, carried by little bee feet to a secret cave where it is transformed by time into thick gold sweetness.

Not all vegans eat honey, but many do, and I am one of them. When I was so very ill as a child, my father tempted me with bread smeared with thick local honey he purchased from a neighbor, thinking it contained some alchemical healing sparkle to it.

Perhaps he was right. Every batch of honey is different, miraculously woven of the local flora — perhaps columbines or clover, roses or bee balm or buckwheat, which is so thick and dark and pungent. (It is also my favorite pancake!)

I am here at Lavender Honey Farms, exploring the lovely business of bees and lavender and honey and dancing in wonder at the alchemical delight of it all. Lavender honey is delicate in color and ever so faintly floral.

Honey has well-known antibacterial properties, and some studies have shown it to be an effective way to reduce C-reactive protein, which might be what my dad instinctively knew when he gave it to his very sick daughter.

CHAPTER 10

Ruby had expected something different from the meadery, which proved to be a sterile room with three big metal stills. A bloom of disappointment covered her heart and she touched it, wondering what in the world she had been expecting —

A cool room with walls made of gray stone. Light shining through thin rectangular windows, dust motes dancing in the beams, making them look practically solid. On a wooden table, amid a pile of greenery (dill, some voice in her mind said), stood an enormous jar of honey the color of hawk feathers. Her own slim white hands — her hands but not her hands — setting down a wooden cask with a stopper on the side . . .

Ruby blinked, and the vision disappeared, leaving her once again in the utilitarian meadery of the present. Stainless-steel counters and sinks lined the room, which Lavender explained were used for washing produce. "And other things."

"Other things?"

Lavender took the stopper from the still and drew out a measure of golden liquid. "Blood, sweetie. This is one of two places where we can slaughter the chickens."

Ruby looked around the room in alarm, a buzz filling her ears as she imagined animals being slaughtered, blood pouring out into the drains —

"Ruby, taste this," Lavender said firmly.

The buzzing halted, and Ruby realized the room had no sense of being haunted. It was as straightforward as any restaurant kitchen she'd ever worked in, with the easily sterilized surfaces required by modern hygienic standards. She knew that the chickens were held in someone's arms, killed individually, and maybe that —

Her head buzzed again. To distract herself, she reached for the cup. "It's alcohol, isn't it?"

"A sip will not deform your child."

Ruby smelled the alcohol before the cup reached her lips, but she also smelled something else — golden afternoons, sunlight and flowers, the faintest, maybe even imaginary, scent of lavender. She let a few drops fall onto her tongue. It was strong, fiery, but, again, she could taste something

124

more, that gilded depth of honey.

"Mmm, that's wonderful!" Ruby sighed. "I'm enchanted!"

Lavender took the cup and tossed the rest back, rolling her tongue against the roof of her mouth, making a smacking noise, moving her mouth back and forth. "This might be the best batch yet. I've been working on mead for fifteen years."

"Isn't this wine country?"

"Yep."

"Why not wine, too?" Ruby's father loved wine, all the little notes and stories of it. When Valerie had been writing her blog, he'd followed it religiously. Ruby always thought he might have something of a crush on Val.

"Above all things, know yourself," Lavender said. "I like fussing with mead because it's made of honey, but I wouldn't have the patience to make good wine." She put the cup down. "Do you want to see the hives?"

"Am I going to get stung?"

"Shouldn't. We'll keep our distance this time. You're not allergic to bees?"

"No. I'm kind of afraid of them, though."

"Most people are. But I think you'll like it."

"Okay."

Ruby ambled out behind Lavender, taking

pleasure in the sunlight on her head. A big black chicken walked along with them, feathers glossy in the sun. "Can you pet chickens?"

"Some are friendly. This one just likes to talk."

"Do they have names?"

"Not official names. Some have nicknames. I call this girl Martha, for no particular reason."

"Hi, Martha." The chicken clucked in a busybody sort of way, and Ruby laughed. "How are you this morning?"

Cluck-cluck, cluck, the chicken said, *cluck-cluck.*

"Really?" Ruby asked. "And then what happened?"

Cluck-cluck-cluck. Peck. Peck. *Cluck.*

They emerged through the doorway in the shrubs, and again Ruby was taken aback by the stunning view of the lavender fields, spread out like giant purple pincushions over the hillside. Lavender led the way down one row, and Ruby followed, brushing her hands over the tops of the flowers. Bees bounced along the rows, feeding.

Lots of bees. The sound of them, bustling and full of purpose, was a fizzy note in the air. Ruby paused, enveloped in the landscape, surrounded by flowers, the smell of the lavender wafting over them, the bees buzzing, the sunlight tumbling down over the hilly landscape. She stretched out her hands and closed her eyes, trying to focus on just the sound. Then she let that fade and breathed through her nose, inhaling deeply the sweet fragrance of lavender, so intensely pleasurable that it could almost make a person levitate.

Then she opened her eyes and let in the visual: the mounded shape of the plants, stretching out in dark purple and light, white and pink, every single one covered in a head of blossoms, as round and regular as Chia Pets.

Lavender had turned to watch her. Ruby gave her a beaming smile. "Wow," she said. "Wow, wow, wow. This is fantastic."

"It is, isn't it?"

If Ruby was a photographer, like Ginny, she'd take a photo of Lavender standing there against the sky, up to her knees in lavender. As if you could go swimming in it!

She started to walk again, fizzing right along with the bees. As if the baby felt her exuberance, it did a slow, mellow flip, and Ruby laughed. "Do you actually make money from the lavender?"

"You bet." Lavender gestured toward the two-story farmhouse, near the road. "That's why I moved out of the farmhouse and into the cottage, so we'd have plenty of room for the shop and the distillery. We can explore that, too, if you like."

"We can wait for Ginny. Then you don't have to show it twice."

"I think she'll like it." Lavender pinched a single blossom, crushed it in her fingers, and passed it over to Ruby. "This is Royal Velvet. It doesn't produce as much oil per plant as Grosso, which is the most common form of lavender. Velvet is much purer. Smell that?"

Ruby inhaled gently, letting the scent fill her sinuses a little at a time. It did seem quite strong, a most lavender-like lavender, but she wanted a comparison. "Do you also grow the other one?"

"I do. This way." They waded to the end of the row and down into another patch, this one with alternating colors of blossoms. The plants were sturdier-looking, taller, more vigorous, and when Lavender pinched off a flower, she said, "Grosso has a fairly strong note of camphor, which lessens the quality, in my opinion."

Ruby smelled the blossom, and she could definitely pick out the camphor, an astringent note that undercut the sweetness of lavender. "That's amazing," she said. "I've

128

used lavender now and then in cooking, and it's a very strong purple color."

"Right. Provence is the queen of culinary lavenders. The shape and color of the flower is what you want there."

"Provence," Ruby repeated. "Grosso. Royal Velvet." She held the other blossom to her nose, and the difference was so dramatically clear that she exclaimed, "Oh! I see!"

Lavender smiled. "Good girl."

"Did your mother name you for the fields?"

"Oh, heavens, no. These were hazelnut orchards." She swallowed, peering into the distance, then sighed and swept a hand down to brush the plants. "I didn't want to run the place back then — I ran away to be a stewardess the minute I graduated high school. Wanted to see the world, and I did. That's how I met Ginger, the one whose daughter sold Ginny the trailer."

"The artist in Carmel who was your friend from the airline days?"

"Yep." Lavender half-grinned. "She was an Aussie. We had some good times, she and I."

Ruby blinked. The smile, so ripe with wicked memory, made everything she knew about Lavender rearrange itself to include a young woman in a tidy uniform having adventures around the world. "Those are stories I'd love to hear."

"I'm better telling them after a glass or two of mead."

"I get that. How old were you when you came back here?"

"Fifty-seven. I was in admin at the airline by then and getting pretty bored with it. Then my nephew who ran the farm died unexpectedly, and it was time to come home. I poured my savings into turning it into an organic and lavender farm. I knew that was what Glen would want. He'd worked so hard on the place, I couldn't let him down." She paused, again looking out toward the horizon. She rubbed the center of her chest, as if rubbing the ache of a broken heart, and Ruby knew just how that felt.

"You miss him."

"He was the closest thing to a child I had." Abruptly, she started to walk. "That's before you were born, isn't it?"

Ruby laughed and nodded. "It is. Kinda weird to think about that."

Lavender gestured for Ruby to follow, and she made her way toward the other end of the fields. Looking back over her shoulder, Ruby admired the tidy rows of smeary plants. Maybe this could be her work, this magical plant. Maybe Lavender would apprentice her, and she could raise her baby in a place like this one —

"Did you hear me?"

Ruby swung back. "What?"

"How did you get your name? I never have heard that story."

"My dad used to like to listen to this radio show about Ruby, the Galactic Gumshoe."

"No kidding! I remember that."

"Really? Nobody else has ever known what I was talking about! That's so cool."

They swished through the lavender in silence for a moment, then Lavender asked, "And your mother? You never speak of her at all."

Ruby thought of the Google Maps view of her mother's house in Seattle. "I don't really remember her. She left when I got sick."

"When she found out you had leukemia?"

"It sounds terrible, I know it does, but she was young and . . ." Ruby shrugged. It always made her feel vaguely ashamed, as if she should find some true reason, but she never did. It *was* terrible, leaving a seven-year-old who was that sick.

She felt Lavender's strong, broad hand sweep around her own, the palm papery. Lavender gave her hand a squeeze. "She

131

didn't deserve you."

"I agree." She squeezed back and put a hand on her tummy, a silent promise that she'd never be that kind of mother. Ever. "Luckily, I got a great dad."

"He sounds terrific." A slight pause, then, "I assume the baby is Liam's?"

"Yeah." Ruby sighed. "It was foolish. The very end, right before I came home."

"Does he know?"

"Um . . . actually, no. I haven't told him yet."

"Are you going to?"

Ruby shrugged again. "I guess I have to, right? That's the only answer. But that means I have to talk to him or have contact, and, honestly, it's really hard."

Lavender nodded. She led the way through a diagonal shortcut and stopped. There, sitting in rows at the end of the fields, were four white bee boxes, so perfectly recognizable for what they were. "There are the lavender bees. I have some others on the other side of the farm, but these are close so they can just gather lavender nectar for now."

"What about when the lavender stops blooming?"

"I'll harvest the honey and put the boxes closer to the forest and the other fields."

Ruby rubbed a gentle hand in a circle over her belly. Lavender's question had brought Liam's face to mind so vividly that she felt the wild grief welling up again. Even thinking of talking to him made her want to cry. "I know it's just a bad breakup and everybody goes through it," she said, and once she started, the words tumbled out, one after the other after the other, "but sometimes I really feel like Liam was the love of my life and I won't love anyone like that again. I mean, I'm still so raw, after all this time! I miss him like crazy, every single day, and so much! And I can't stop pining. It's crazy, right? But that's the honest truth. He was my soul mate and something terrible happened, but I don't know what it is, and I feel like I'm going to go insane trying to figure it out."

Lavender didn't say anything for a minute. She swooped down and tugged a long feather of grass from its mooring and began to dissect the seed head with her thumbnail. "It did seem very abrupt."

"I know, right?"

"The thing is, it also seemed very certain. He didn't waver. He left you and he went to live with someone else."

Ruby made a small noise, putting her hand over the place that had just been gutted. "That's harsh."

"No, it's a fact. If you can look at the facts, maybe it will make it easier to start feeling better."

"Maybe." Ruby bowed her head. "It is true, exactly what you said. But it's also true that we fell in love practically on sight and were together for six years."

"Maybe he fell in love with the other woman on sight, too."

"Maybe," Ruby whispered. It felt as if an anvil were sitting on her chest. "So why did it feel so fated?"

"Because maybe it was fated. Maybe it was to bring you that baby."

Ruby looked up. "Right! Maybe it is. It's pretty amazing." She nodded. "I'll send him an email in a few days, tell him the truth."

"You probably need to get that out of the way."

A little blossom of hope, buzzy as a bee, suggested that it might be the way back to him, back to *them,* if he knew they'd made a child.

"C'mon, let's get to town and do some shopping," Lavender said. "We've got a lot more to do for this festival. You can help me cook over the next few days. We can use the extra space in the food truck."

"Cool." Ruby skipped ahead, thinking

with pleasure of breaking in the trailer for real, of serving people. Her father would be happy.

The drive to McMinnville took them on country roads that looped through soft yellow and green fields and past all kinds of houses — trailers and cottages, modern buildings and stately old farmhouses. There was a tiny strip of town dominated by a giant silo and splendiferous gardens of roses. Ruby saw black-and-white cows, wide plantings of crops she couldn't identify, and wineries and more lavender farms. "Are there a lot of lavender farms around here?"

"Oh, yeah," Lavender replied. She drove her truck with the confidence of a lumberjack, her big, aged hands strong on the steering wheel. "It's a big draw in the midsummer; there's a lavender festival that brings in a lot of tourists."

Ruby thought about that. If there were a lot of farms, there was a lot of competition, and maybe this wouldn't be the best work for her. Maybe her food truck was still the best thing. She could get a permit, drive around the Bay Area, find the best parking spot.

It sounded exhausting, which in turn made her feel guilty, because she'd talked her dad into lending her the money. Her stomach started to bubble, so she tried to focus on something happier, like the pretty view of mountains in the distance, but they went over a hill, swooping down the other side, and Ruby blurted out, "I need to stop!" She put a hand over her mouth, breathing as evenly as she could, holding on until Lavender swerved into a driveway. Ruby flung open the door and puked into a ditch, only afterward looking to see if anyone was around. There was an old man in overalls and a straw hat staring at her from his tiny patch of green lawn across the street. "Sorry!" she called. "I'm pregnant."

He glared and muttered something, then stomped away in boots that were not tied, the laces trailing behind him in the grass. A cat dashed out from under the bushes and tried to grab them, leaping again with each footstep.

Ruby wiped her mouth. "Sorry. It's gross, I know it is."

"It's not gross. It's just how it is for some women. Have you had a physical?"

"Of course. My doctor said it should get better soon. Most women get over the worst of it by four or five months."

"I'll look up some more teas this evening."

McMinnville was a normal-looking small

town, with houses laid out in tidy blocks and a strip of downtown with a restaurant called the Blue Moon Tavern, which Ruby had to take a picture of for the blog. Down the street a little ways, Lavender pointed out an old hotel. "That's a place worth visiting when Ginny gets here."

Suddenly she slowed, peering into the window of a café. "Well, I'll be damned. Those bastards."

"What is it?"

"My goddamned nephews are talking to Wade Markum." She pointed toward the café. "He's the farmer I was telling you about."

"I don't think you were telling me. Maybe Ginny?"

"Maybe." She pulled over, parallel-parking the big truck as easily as if it were a smart car. With narrowed eyes, she peered over her shoulder at the window, which had a reflection of trees and sky bouncing off it, so Ruby couldn't see what Lavender saw. Lavender tapped her fingers on the steering wheel and her mouth worked, lip in, lip out. Finally she swore again, softly. "Damn it."

"Will it help to talk it out?"

"Wade has about a thousand acres of land catty-corner to mine. He's been farming for forty years and wants my land, too. He's made me some offers, but he's not interested in the lavender, or the organic produce, or the chickens. He'll mow it all under to make pasture for sheep and, more specifically, lambs."

Ruby made a noise of protest.

"Portland eats a lot of lamb these days," she said matter-of-factly. Again the lower lip, in and out. In and out. She tapped the back of her thumb on the plastic wheel. "And it's not like I have anything against lamb, but I've worked my ass off to build that business, and I'm not going to stand by and let it be mowed over."

"So what can you do?"

Lavender flung open the door. "C'mon."

Ruby hurried to catch up as Lavender strode across the street. Ruby had to wait for a car, and then another, and then someone stopped for her. She ran across, raising a hand in thanks. As Lavender pushed the door open, she thought to turn around and look for Ruby. She waited there, every bit as wrinkled as you'd imagine an eighty-four-year-old to be but still straight, as powerful as a wizard.

Or a witch, Ruby thought, but "wizard" sounded more powerful.

Whatever. That powerful woman moved into the room and paused by the table.

"How you doing, nephews? Couldn't wait till I was dead?"

"Lavender!" One of the men stood up. He was tall and stout, like a football player who'd turned to real estate. "We're on our way out to the farm, as a matter of fact. We just stopped for a late breakfast and ran into Wade here."

"Bullshit," Lavender said.

All three men looked prosperous, in a Western-casual kind of way. Jeans paired with expensive shirts. The city men wore loafers, but the farmer wore boots that were a little muddy. Ruby felt smug being able to pick out that detail.

The farmer stood up. "Why don't you join us, Lavender? We are talking about your farm and the potential it offers."

Ruby's eyebrows shot up. Bold!

Lavender crossed her arms and addressed her nephews. "I know you're waiting for me to kick the bucket so you can hand over the farm and upgrade your mini-mansions —"

"That's not true!"

She continued without acknowledging them. "But, as you see, I'm as hale and hearty as I've ever been. I'm having a party this weekend for my eighty-fifth birthday. Why don't you all come? You can see for yourself that lavender is just as viable a product as lamb."

"Lavender —"

"Have you met my apprentice? This is Ruby Zarlingo. She writes a famous blog called 'The Flavor of a Blue Moon.' You should check it out."

Ruby lifted a hand, but Lavender was already hustling them out of the restaurant. "Bastards," she muttered under her breath. They strode down the sidewalk, Ruby hurrying to keep up with Lavender's long-legged stride. She finally slowed after two blocks and peered around, as if emerging from some dream. "C'mon. Let's get some coffee or something. A pastry, maybe?"

"Maybe some toast," Ruby said. People who weren't vegan often didn't realize that pastries mostly had eggs and/or butter.

They found a different café, the Wild Wood, which was an absolutely adorable retro-looking place. The hipster waitress had black hair with short bangs and red lipstick, and she smiled as she gave them menus. "Hi, my name is Tiff. You ladies want something to drink?"

"Hot tea for me," Ruby said.

"Coffee," Lavender barked. She glared at the menu as if it were her nephews and the farmer.

Ruby smiled apologetically, and the server winked.

The place was magical, Ruby thought. Retro signs for Maytag washers and Hires root beer and potatoes and broccoli and cauliflower hung on the walls, and there were old-school kitchen utensils of every variety hanging from the ceiling — eggbeaters and potato mashers and spoons and spatulas. Her restaurant side was charmed. She wanted to be the owner of this place, with its Formica tables and vinyl dinette chairs in pastel colors. She'd make it a vegan restaurant, of course, with wholesome pastries and treats and breakfasts, like Sticky Fingers in D.C.

A ripple of excitement touched her. Yes, that could be so fantastic! Maybe restaurants really were her work.

The menu was fairly standard diner with an upscale feel. "This doesn't feel like a small-town café," she said aloud. "The other one didn't, either, now that I think about it."

"It's wine country." Lavender slapped the menu down and folded her big hands. Knots showed at some of the joints, and brown spots speckled the skin. "Everybody thinks they're gourmets these days. Truffle oil this and foie gras that."

"They don't call themselves 'gourmets' anymore," Ruby said. "They're 'foodies.' "

"Right. Like us." Her eyes unexpectedly twinkled. "There are a couple of celebrated chefs in town if you're interested in exploring."

Ruby lifted a shoulder. "Maybe." It made her feel tired.

Maybe restaurants *weren't* her work.

The server brought their drinks. Ruby ordered toast with strawberry jam and no butter. Lavender, who never seemed to stop eating, wanted a cinnamon roll.

"So those were your nephews, I gather?" Ruby asked. "And they stand to inherit?"

"That's right. They're not bad men, they just don't want to run a farm, and I get that."

"Can't you put something in your will that will make sure the whole thing stays the way you want?"

"It is supposed to be handed down to the next family member in line."

"That seems shortsighted. You took over in the eighties, right? By then they must have realized that times were changing, that not everyone wants to farm."

"At the time, it was expected that my brother's boy, Glen, would inherit. He was a devoted farmer, and he ran the place like a general, raising profits by fourteen percent in three years. But, as I told you," Lavender's voice cracked, and she took a sip of coffee, "my nephew died — killed in a car accident. That was when I inherited. It was god-awful."

"I'm sorry," Ruby said.

"He was a good man. We'd talked a lot over the years about him turning the hazelnut orchard into lavender, so I went ahead with it after he died. His life insurance, combined with my savings, ended up paying for nearly every bloody penny of it."

"Can you encumber it somehow? Make sure that they can't sell it to that guy or something?"

"I have to do something," Lavender agreed. "You and Ginny can help me brainstorm."

Ruby leaned forward and touched Lavender's hand. "I bet there's a way."

Lavender grunted, pushing away her coffee as she rubbed a fist over her diaphragm. "They gave me indigestion, the rats. Guess I'll have to have some namby-pamby milk."

CAKE OF DREAMS

This little cake is the first that I've made in my Airstream oven. It's a cold night in the mountains, even though it's summer, and I had to bake something to feel normal again. Not a fun day driving, my friends! I had to pull off early, thanks to wind, but it gives Willow and me a chance to have a good night's sleep.

Halfway there!

Comments [119]

Pippin987
Stay safe, Ginny! The candle I lit for you is still burning strong.

nobodyknowsnuttin
That cake sounds like something my mom used to whip up after school. Yum!

justbake
The gang in Idaho can't wait to meet you, Ginny! We're preparing a big feast. Let us know if you're running behind. There have been fires around here.

READ MORE >>>

CHAPTER 11

Ginny wrote her cheerful blog sitting at the table in her trailer, peering out into a storm that flung lightning bolts like arrows. It had just sprung up, noisy and furious. Rain pounded on the roof, as loud as an entire drum company. Her hands ached from gripping the steering wheel like a vise to keep the trailer on the road as it snaked down through the mountain passes. The wind had been a plague all day.

She supposed she was due a challenge. The previous two days had been easy, despite the mountains.

There had been no rain today until just a little while ago, only that blustery, buffeting wind. She was less than sixty miles from her planned stop on the Great Salt Lake, but there had just not been another hour of driving in her. When she'd spied this truck stop perched at the end of a small town, she grabbed a spot with relief. A handful of semis were parked along one end in a wide lot, their engines rumbling in the cold afternoon.

Her simple little cake scented the air with sugar and comfort, and her empty plate attested to the fact that it had been a better-than-decent experiment. She had worried a lot about being able to bake on the road, to keep the photos going for the blog. She hadn't known how it would be to bake in such different circumstances.

But she'd also decided the blog was hers and she made the rules. If she took photos of other people's baked goods on the road, it was no big deal. It wasn't as if she was a genius of a cake baker, anyway — the appeal was her photos.

Overhead, rain pounded on the roof. Willow dozed on her foot.

It was very cozy knowing there were eggs and milk in the fridge, along with some cherries she'd picked up at a farm stand in western Colorado. The romance of the road was not exactly present at the truck stop, but that was part of the game, too, she supposed. She'd hoped to spend the night on an island in the Great Salt Lake, but now, to stay on time, she'd have to scrap that idea. She pulled out her map and spread it flat, trying to figure out her next leg.

It had been a bit optimistic to plan for four hundred miles every day. Pulling the trailer up and down the passes was a slower process than she had expected, for one thing. It was slower driving, period. Sometimes it was embarrassing to be the slowest vehicle on the road. Cars and trucks roared by her, impatience winking in their taillights.

At least they could pass like that. It was harder for Ginny, pulling the trailer, but sometimes she, too, was impatient, plodding behind a farm truck loaded with hay or an RV'er ambling down the road. This morning she'd seen a couple she met in Grand Junction, and the old man waved as she passed. She tooted her horn. It made her feel known, part of the community.

Now she plotted out her next leg, then carried a book back to her bed and propped herself up on the pillows. It was so gloomy she had to turn on a lamp, and that gave an even richer sense of coziness to the day. Willow padded down the minuscule hall and jumped up on the bed with her. Ginny buried a hand in the dog's thick fur, propped her glasses on her nose, and began to read.

Happy. This was what happiness felt like. She hadn't realized you could feel it when you were all alone.

She must have dozed off, because she woke up hearing music and the clink of glasses. A woman's throaty laugh wafted through the trailer, and she could have sworn she smelled onions cooking in fat. Her stomach growled. She popped open her eyes, blinking.

There was nothing, of course. Just a dream. Willow stretched, her claws touching the far wall with a soft snick. No onions. No woman laughing.

Her stomach, however, was definitely growling.

One thing about parking at the truck stop was that she could have a hearty, hot meal that she didn't have to cook. It was still pouring rain. Leaving Willow curled up in a deep sleep on the bed, Ginny grabbed her umbrella and dashed across the parking lot, splashing through puddles that soaked her jeans up to the knees. She dove through the glass doors of the diner and shook herself and her umbrella.

A woman in a retro-style uniform, pale brown with a ribbon of pink stripes down one side, came over. "How ya doing, hon?" she asked. "One?"

"Yes, please." Ginny followed, head down.

There were lots of other single diners in here, but it still made her feel awkward in a way. Across the room, she spied the red-headed Aussie, her braid hanging over the shoulder of her plaid shirt. The woman waved and Ginny waved back.

"Here you go," the server said.

Ginny needed to be able to eat by herself, in public. "Thanks," she said, sliding into the booth.

The menu offered home-style cooking: meatloaf and mashed potatoes, and country fried steak, and biscuits and gravy. She studied it luxuriously, rubbing her growling belly.

Someone approached the table, and Ginny looked up, expecting the Aussie or a server. Instead, it was a man, who said, "Hey. Aren't you the lady with the dog?"

His face came into context. He was the guy who'd petted Willow at the rest stop back in Colorado. The man whose dog had died. "Oh! Hello. Yes, that's me."

"How's the trip going?"

"Good." She frowned, turning the menu side to side on the table between her two index fingers. "Today was a bit challenging, but I guess that's to be expected."

"It definitely happens."

"I must not be doing too terrible if I

caught up to you."

His eyes twinkled. "Well, I live in Grand Junction. I had a layover. Fresh load now."

Ginny laughed. "Okay, that makes more sense."

"Mind if I join you?" He pointed at the empty spot across from her. "As you might have discovered by now, a person can get a little tired of their own company."

She hesitated, more because she found herself sitting straighter, admiring his rich voice and good-looking face, than because she thought he was dangerous. "Uh —"

"No, no. Don't worry." He stepped back. "I'm not offended. But they know me around here. They'll tell you that my name is Jack Gains and I run loads from Grand Junction to Portland about twice a month."

Ginny flushed. "I didn't think you were dangerous," she said. "I'm just kind of new to all this." She gestured, including everything. The restaurant, the road, the trailer outside.

He nodded. "I thought so."

For one more minute she hesitated, a voice in her head blaring, *HE IS A STRANGER.* The voice sounded suspiciously like her mother's. "I'd love to have you join me, Jack Gains," she said, and indicated the other side of the booth. When he slid in, smiling, she said, "I'm Ginny Smith."

"Nice to meet you. Where's your dog?"

"Sleeping. It's been a boring afternoon. We pulled in here around two and have been holed up in the trailer ever since."

He rubbed his face. "Yeah, that wind was no fun. I was stopped on I-70 for nearly three hours. I heard over the radio that a truck jackknifed south of here on I-15."

"It's a relief to know even an experienced driver was rattled by those winds." She stretched out her hands, feeling the ache in the joints and tight tendons. "I was afraid we were going to end up in a canyon a couple of times."

"No, it was bad. I heard it's whipping up some forest fires up north."

"Seems like the rain would put them out."

"If they get it. Weather patterns in the mountains are unpredictable."

The server came over. "You want your usual, Jack?"

"Yes, ma'am."

She scribbled on a pale-green tablet. "Are you ready to order, sweetheart?"

"Meatloaf, please. No gravy on the potatoes, just some extra butter. And coffee."

"Got it." She winked as she picked up the menu. "Don't let him sweet-talk you, now.

This one is a charmer."

"Oh, it's not like that," Ginny said, showing her wedding ring. "We just met."

They both chuckled, and Ginny realized that it had been teasing. A flush roared through her cheeks, over her ears, down her neck.

"It's all right," Jack said, leaning over the table. "She's got a little crush on me and was staking out her territory."

Ginny still couldn't look at him. "I see."

"I'll be right back, folks."

The woman ambled away and Ginny became acutely aware of the placement of her feet under the booth, her hands on the table, the shine of her wedding ring. The silence around them seemed alive, buzzing.

"So, where're you from, Ginny?"

Stop being so missish, she told herself, using a phrase from the historical romances she loved to read. She was also partial to memoirs about cooks and women who had been brave for their times. She looked him right in the eye. "A little town outside Wichita, Kansas."

"I'm familiar with Wichita. I do a run to St. Louis once every coupla months. What's the town?"

"Dead Gulch," she said, and it sounded funny to her, a made-up name for a dusty

152

western town. "Do you know it?"

"I've been through it once or twice. Right on Highway 50, right? There's a grain mill on the edge of town on the north."

She smiled. "That's it."

"Farm country. Not much to it, is there?"

"You don't choose where you're born."

"True enough." He nodded, tapping a sugar packet against the table. He had long thumbs, with clean oval nails. "You grow up on a farm?"

"I did," she admitted. "My daddy grew soybeans, mainly. My mom kept chickens and sells eggs, produce, that kind of thing, from a stand alongside the road. It wasn't the most glamorous life, I can tell you. I hated it."

"A pig farm is worse," he said, half-smiling. The waitress brought big mugs of coffee and hustled away, calling out to somebody coming in the door. "That's where I grew up."

"Really?" Ginny winced. "They do stink."

He opened the sugar packet and poured it into the cup slowly, watching it. "I hated it, too. Thought about a million ways to escape, and you know what I did? I ended up taking agriculture classes at school. Thought maybe I'd grow peaches."

"Not all farming is equal," Ginny said.

"Peaches sound like a good option. Did you try it?"

"Nope. Got married right out of school and had to figure out a way to make a living quick, so I was a farmhand instead of the boss, then a truck driver headed for divorce."

"Sorry." She watched him open one plastic creamer and pour that into the cup, stir, and pick up another. "It's not exactly a good life for a family man, is it?"

"No, that's true." He seemed to get his coffee precisely right and took a sip. Made a soft noise of approval. Ginny felt the sound at the edge of her jaw, down the side of her neck. She found herself watching his mouth.

She looked away, alarmed.

"I say something wrong?" he asked. "You've gone all flushed on me again. Does that strike a nerve? You know a truck driver who done somebody wrong?"

"Um, no," Ginny said, and laughed a little. "I'm just —"

"New to all this, right?"

She leaned over the table, her cup clasped between her hands, opened her mouth, hesitated, and decided to just be herself, whole cloth, for once in her life. "What if I told you I'd hardly ever left Kansas before last Sunday?"

"Ever?"

"Once, to go to a wedding when I was a teenager. We drove to Minneapolis." She pressed her palms against the cup, taking comfort in the solidness of ceramic and heat. "I have never been on a plane, or seen the ocean, or been to the mountains, before this week."

Tenderness turned his mouth up at the corners, gentled something in his gray eyes. "And now you're driving yourself and a trailer across the country." He inclined his head. "What brought that on?"

And keeping with her decision to be honest, Ginny said, "My friend invited me to come to Oregon and celebrate her eighty-fifth birthday with her," she began. She told him about Lavender — "another farm!" — and the Foodie Four. "We're kind of an odd bunch, honestly. Kansas housewife, a hipster foodie, Lavender, and Valerie, who was a prima ballerina in Cincinnati. She used to write about wine."

"But if there are four of you, why are only three meeting at the farm?"

"Valerie is doing something else," Ginny said, and paused. "Two years ago, her husband and two of their three daughters were killed in a small-plane crash. Her

155

daughter is not handling it all that well, and Val is taking her on a tour of Indian country. It's her big passion."

"That's bad luck. How old is the girl?"

"Fourteen now."

"Don't get over that in a hurry, do you?"

"No," Ginny agreed. She thought of the frantic emails at the time, the looming horror of it. Both Lavender and Ruby had flown to Cincinnati for the funerals, but even though Valerie and Ginny were the closest, in terms of both friendship and distance, Ginny had not gone. She hadn't found the bravery.

Then.

Tonight she was braver. "I was mad at myself for not going to the funerals, for being so afraid." It was maybe the most honest thing she'd ever said out loud. "And I decided I didn't want to be that person anymore."

"So you bought that fancy trailer and took yourself on a road trip?"

"Pretty much." She took a sip of coffee, feeling a different version of herself reflected in his eyes. It was odd — and weirdly freeing — to tell her story to a stranger, a person who hadn't known her for the whole of her life. "I write a blog about cakes, and

I'm meeting some of my readers along the way."

"Blog?"

"You don't know what a blog is?"

His mouth twitched. Amusement? Annoyance? "Of course. I was just asking more about it."

"Sorry."

"It's all right."

Ginny said, "I used to be a supermarket baker." She gave him a rueful smile. "Glamorous work, I know, but it was pretty creative and I liked it. Then one day I just decided to start this blog about cakes, and I took a photo of a German chocolate cake I had baked and posted it." She fell silent, thinking about how that single decision had shifted her life so massively. The woman she had been that lonely afternoon could not have imagined this moment.

Across the table, Jack watched her over the top of his mug. His eyes were clear, the corners creased with laughter and squinting for hours into the sun.

"It changed everything," she said. "Have you ever had that happen — done some small thing and it ended up changing your life?"

"Couple times," he said. "The first time, I fell out of a tree and shattered my shoulder.

It never was quite the same after, which meant that my plans to be a professional ball player went right out the window."

"Ow!"

He looked down, plucking at the edge of a napkin. "The other time was when I stole my wife from my best friend."

"Wife." The word felt heavy between them, even though Ginny had a husband, too, waiting at home. In a way it made it safer, and she breathed a bit deeper. "Were they married?"

"No," he said. "We were all in high school. She moved to town when we were juniors, and Carl flipped for her. They dated for almost a year, and then he went on vacation with his family, and we ended up at an inner-tubing party at the same time, and she looked so damned hot in a yellow bikini that I decided I had to have her."

Ginny smiled. "That's kind of romantic, actually. Especially as you ended up married."

"I guess." His voice was raspier. "Except Carl never forgave me. Lost him for good over it, and then Debbie and I ended up being just about as miserable together as two people could be." He lifted a rueful eyebrow. "Bad fit."

"Kids?"

"You don't know what kids are?"

Ginny laughed.

"I do have a couple. Grown now. A daughter who lives in Texas, and a son who can't get his act together and still lives with his mom in Denver. How about you? Got any kids?"

She told him about Christie. "She is so smart. She's a resident at a hospital in Chicago. I'm very proud of her."

"You should be."

Somehow, it was easy to talk to him. They kept talking. And talking. And talking. He told her about a dog he'd had when he was a teenager, a daring and irrepressible Lab. She told him about the goldfish she won at the county fair that ended up living for twelve years. They touched on movies and books — she liked dramas and romances, and he liked science fiction and action adventure. He said he listened to a lot of books on tape — currently it was *A Game of Thrones,* which made her revise her estimation of his brain. "That's a pretty dense series," she said, folding an empty sugar packet into an accordion.

"You read it?"

She nodded. "My daughter insisted, and although I don't always listen, I was intrigued by this one. It's really romantic and

159

magical and all that, you know?"

He nodded, smiling. "I do. I love it. Who is your favorite character? No, wait. Let me guess. Daenerys."

"I love Daenerys," Ginny said, thinking of the dragon queen and her bravery, "but I love Tyrion the most. You?" She smiled. "Wait. Let me guess."

He leaned back, waiting. Ginny studied his face, his wide mouth and the crow's-feet around his gray eyes. Something shimmered between them, soft and pale and ethereal, as if the time–space continuum had suddenly been rearranged.

Silly.

"I think," she said, "that you like Tyrion, too."

He grinned.

Rain kept falling. They kept talking.

It was almost four hours later that Ginny spied the time. "Oh, my gosh! I have to go. My poor dog must be crossing her legs by now." She jumped up and stuck out her hand. "Nice to meet you, Jack."

"You, too, Ginny." He shook her hand gravely. From this angle, she could see the silver strands in the waviness of his dark hair. "Take care, now."

"You, too."

She forced herself to turn and walk away.

As she was about to open her umbrella and dash through the rain, she heard him call her name. "Ginny!"

He jogged over and gave her a piece of paper. "My cell-phone number, in case you have any trouble on the road."

"Thanks." The paper felt hot in her fingers, and she pushed it deep into the pocket of her jeans. "See ya."

He saluted. She felt his eyes on her all the way to the trailer.

CHAPTER 12

Willow met her at the door, tail wagging urgently. "Come on, baby," she said. "I'm so sorry. I just got to talking."

Her dog leapt down, blinking sadly at the rain. Ginny tried to cover her with the umbrella as they headed for the edge of the parking lot, and both of them got soaked, but Willow squatted in the dark, peeing on a wildflower for what seemed like five minutes. She shook herself, looked at Ginny for direction. "Let's get out of this rain, huh?"

They jogged back and Ginny backed into the trailer, holding the umbrella over the dog. "Shake it out here, Willow." She shook herself to illustrate, but Willow only gazed up at her with a doleful expression. *Why are you making me stand out here in this mess?*

"Oh, all right. Come on." She backed into the hallway to let her dog come in, looking around urgently for something to drop over Willow.

There, sitting at the table, was a woman. Her hair was swept away from her face, and she drank a martini from a perfectly shaped glass. "What are —"

Willow shook, hard, sending water everywhere. Ginny flung up her hands. "Argh!"

Heart pounding, Ginny dived for the afghan draped over the sitting area, looking back over her shoulder at the woman.

Gone.

Willow shook again, head to toe, splattering Ginny's face and mouth. "Stop, stop, stop!" She dropped the afghan on Willow's back, trying to minimize the damage, then wiped her muddy paws with a dish towel and rubbed her down with the afghan. Willow slid out of her grip and shook again, this time without damage to the surroundings. Ginny realized her heart was racing.

She frowned at the table. The light glowed softly from an overhead spot, faintly blue. The woman must have been a trick of the light, some strange imaginary dream.

A ghost, Ruby would say.

A wish to have company, Christie would say.

Her imagination, that's what Ginny would say. She grabbed a roll of paper towels and wiped down the surfaces splattered with

Willow's rain shake — the front of the fridge and stove, the legs of the table, the floor; even the window got a few splatters. She wiped it off, closed the blinds, made sure the door was locked.

Shivering, she threw away the paper towels, gathered up the dish towel and afghan to be washed, and stripped out of her clothes to shower.

But for a moment, standing naked in her trailer, she thought of Jack's hands, his seasoned mouth. She touched her breasts, her belly, wishing . . .

When she realized what — or, rather, *whom* — she was thinking of, she snatched her hands away and turned on the water, scrubbing her skin to warm it up, forcing herself to think about Lavender's farm, about the next leg of the trip.

Afterward, snuggled into her pajamas, she made a cup of tea, curled up in the kitchenette, and dialed home.

Matthew answered on the fourth ring, groggy, and only then did Ginny realize that it was eleven o'clock at home. He would have been in bed for an hour. "Hello?" he said. "Ginny, are you hurt?"

"No, I'm sorry. I just mixed up the times. I'll call tomorrow."

"Christ, I've been asleep for an hour."

"I know, I'm sorry. Really, go back to sleep."

A rustling on the other end. "I'm awake now. You might as well tell me where you are. Is everything going all right?"

She imagined him sitting up in bed, shirtless. He slept in his boxer shorts only, which was sometimes torturous since his body was in good shape from regular workouts, and he rebuffed any of her attempts to touch him or cuddle up when he was next to her in bed. "So far so good. I ran into weather a couple of times but got through it."

"Where are you now?"

"Utah. I was trying to get to the Great Salt Lake, but it's been really windy today, and now it's raining like Armageddon, so I finally gave up and pulled in to a truck stop."

"That's smart. I heard about the weather on the news and worried about you a little bit."

"You could have called."

A long silence. "I guess my feelings were hurt."

Ginny stretched out her toes, feeling the pull along her calves and ankles. "That was never my intention."

"I know. Are you having fun?"

"Um . . . sometimes, yes. Sometimes it's a little lonely, but I have Willow and the

165

people on the blog, commenting. I'm hoping to get to Idaho and one of the bloggers tomorrow, then probably the farm on Friday morning."

"Well, that's good."

"How are things there?"

"Nothing new, Ginny. The same old things. I get up and go to work and come home and eat a TV dinner and watch some TV and go to sleep."

"You could go have dinner out, you know."

"I will, probably. Just expensive."

"Right." Something that had been puffing up a little like a balloon as she listened to his familiar voice suddenly deflated. "Well, I'm sorry I woke you. I just thought I'd check in so you wouldn't worry."

"Try not to call so late next time. It'll be hard to go back to sleep."

She sighed. "I'll make sure. Good night, Matthew. Tell my mom I'm fine."

"Wait, Ginny. I'm sorry. I didn't mean that like it sounded."

"It's fine. Good night."

"Good night."

She pressed the off button and sat with the phone in her lap, staring toward her bed, where a lamp on the wall cast a warm pool of yellow light. Tears, quite surprising, ran down her face, unchecked, and the yearnings of two decades seemed to well up all at once, making her skin burn. She loved her husband, or at least she had at one time, but she couldn't go on like this.

Twelve years ago, Matthew had given up sex. He didn't actually come out and say that. He just stopped having sex with her. Ever.

At first she'd been bewildered — until then their sex life had been healthy, if a bit routine. It was never quite *enough* sex for her taste — she'd rather have indulged a couple of times a week, where Matthew preferred once a week, or even once every other week sometimes — but it was good when they tangled themselves. He was a good-looking man, the envy of her friends, and worked out with his old football buddies at the local cinder-block gym, giving him that chest that looked so sexy when he stripped off his staid insurance-man shirts. He had just the right amount of hair and strong pecs, smooth, muscled shoulders. Once upon a time she had enjoyed surprising him in the shower and running her hands all over the rounds of flesh. Arms, shoulders, chest. So sexy.

One December he slipped on the ice at work and fell, hard, breaking his right arm so badly it required surgery and rupturing two disks in his back. The arm healed over time. The back gave him trouble for years. It could still give him agony now and then.

Somewhere during the healing period, Ginny realized they had not had sex in several months. Understandable, considering, but she was hungry for intimacy, for the connection and pleasure and everything of sex.

Matthew turned away.

And he had been turning away ever since. She had tried everything. Sexy nightgowns, of course, and surprising him in the shower, which ended so badly that she never tried it again. He refused to see a marriage counselor. He refused to talk about it at all. Said he just didn't feel like it.

She tried reason. She tried anger. She suspected he might have developed some impotence with his back injury and suggested Viagra, which infuriated him.

She wanted to talk to her friends about it, but mostly they complained about how often they *didn't* want to have sex and how their husbands were always chasing them around, suggesting scandalous acts. She could not face their pity.

There were two choices after that: accept it or leave him. She was thirty-four years old — which in her world was pretty old —

with a teenage daughter and a job as a supermarket baker. What could she give Christie on her own?

So she stayed. She closed off that part of her life with a sigh of regret and spoke to no one about it. No one knew. Not her mother or sisters, none of her friends, not the Foodie Four.

No one.

Sitting in her trailer with the phone in her lap, she became aware of her body, her skin. She thought of the trucker and wondered how it might be to kiss a mouth like that, a stranger's mouth. What it would be like to have sex again, after all these years.

Ashamed, she pulled her camera over, plugged the cord into the laptop, and started to upload photos. It was this pursuit and the blog that had saved her. After a time, she forgot the sound of the new man's voice and lost herself in the world of light and color and shape that was photography.

What would she have done without it the past few years?

A gentle knock sounded at the door, so quiet she was sure that the knocker — and she knew exactly whom it was — was being careful not to wake her.

For a long moment, she made no move at all, except to look at the door. Willow growled softly in warning, her usual response and one Ginny appreciated. She thought about the way Jack had laughed when she made a joke and the way he looked at her. Directly, and as if she was something worth looking at. Her restless skin said it would be dangerous to have his breath in here, rustling over her, and she knew it was not appropriate to let him in when she was wearing only her pjs.

Faintly, she heard the sound of that jazzy song, and with half of her mind she tried to place it while she stared at the door, wondering whether to open it. A World War II dance tune, maybe. But where was it coming from?

The very, very quiet knock on the door came again. Ginny pressed a palm against her throat, feeling her heartbeat flutter unevenly against the pad of her index finger.

Should I?

Shouldn't I?

One thing that did not cross her mind was that he was dangerous. Somehow, she knew in her deepest gut that he was not. He was aging and a little weary and maybe opportunistic, but not dangerous in the sense of killing her in her sleep or raping her if she decided she didn't want to have sex with him.

If? Did that mean she was considering it? Because what else did a man really want if he showed up at your door at ten-thirty at night?

Ginny stared at the door. When she thought she heard him leave, she crept to the door and flicked the curtain aside. He was walking away in the rain, his head bent, his shoulders hunched and wet.

She let him go.

THE FLAVOR OF A BLUE MOON
a blog about great food . . .

Recipes   Appetizers
Main dishes   Sides   Sweets
Sort by Name   Sort by Category
About Ruby

Summer!

At the market this morning were piles of small dark-green watermelons, tumbled together like basketballs in cardboard bins. I drifted over in answer to the little cries they sent out, rolling them to find the sugar marks, the bleached yellow spot where it sat against the earth, face toward the hot sun of Mexico. These were crisscrossed with rows of paler green, and I picked them up one at a time, weighing each by balancing it in my palm, until I found the heaviest for its size, and then thumped it, listening for the watery reverberation that tells you it's ripe and ready.

Three more I chose this way, and I have just cut the first one open. It made a thwacking, sucking sound before it cracked in half, revealing deep-red flesh. With the edge of my knife, I slivered off a paper-thin slice from the very center of the fruit and popped it into my mouth — and, oh, readers, it was like diving into a cool river in the heat of a long hot afternoon, like splashing into a lawn sprinkler when you're five, like watching fireworks explode overhead.

It is sweet, it is summer, it is watermelon.

Facts: Watermelon is not only delicious, it is astonishingly good for you. Low in calories, packed with vitamin C, beta-carotene, lycopene, magnesium, and B1 and B6. It is also a mild diuretic, which is helpful if your ankles swell in summer humidity. Try some with a sprinkle of salt, or use a melon baller to mix up cantaloupes, watermelon, honeydew, and whatever other fruit catches your eye.

But here is my favorite recipe for a watermelon salad. The nutrition here is off the charts, and it is also enormously delicious, because there is absolutely no point in nutrition without delight.

AVOCADO AND WATERMELON SALAD
Serves 4–6

Dressing
1/2 red onion, very thinly sliced and separated into rings

2 T peach white balsamic vinegar, or champagne vinegar if you like

1 T mixed peppercorns, crushed

1 tsp coarse salt

1/2 cup olive oil

Mix together and let stand at least one hour.

Salad
2 ripe avocados, skinned and cubed
1/2 single-size watermelon, cubed
Spinach leaves, stems and spines removed,
  chiffonaded or torn into bite-size pieces

Toss all the bits together; serve with a garnish
of basil or mint leaves. Feast!

Chapter 13

After two full days of cooking with Lavender, Ruby was wiped out. Her arms were tired and her back ached slightly, and, of course, her belly swished and swashed, making her feel vaguely ill.

She needed a nap.

The kitten slept on her head, purring. Ruby closed her eyes and let that sound of richest contentment rumble through the casing of her skull. It lulled her to sleep.

She dreamed she was in a room with an IV drip attached to her arm; she could hear a beeping somewhere and the watery sound of the PA system. She knew it well, this room, with its falsely cheery sheets and the monster in the corner. In her dream, she scowled at it, a dragon-looking being with slanted pupils in red eyes, and the fire of pain licked at her feet, her joints, her hands. As she stared, the monster began to lumber toward her, breath fetid and dead with the children it had already consumed. *No!* she cried in the dream.

The force of the cry shook her back into her bed. Her cozy, soft bed in her camper, full of colors you never saw in a hospital — gold and silver and copper and rose, patterns swirling over everything. Extravagant, comforting.

The kitten made a tiny mewing noise as Ruby stretched, the cat's heart beating with fragile teeniness into Ruby's ear. Peaceful.

Ruby turned her face to nuzzle the kitten, letting the nightmare go. It was an old one, a dream she'd had a thousand times as a child, the monster creeping forward to steal her away.

No surprise that she was having the chemo dreams. All this throwing up was quite reminiscent of those days. At least she wasn't miserably nauseous all day every day, for weeks on end.

The kitten roused herself suddenly, jumping off the bed to go to the door of the camper. Ruby had found a harness in town, and she rolled off the bed, attached the leash, and opened the door.

The kitten rushed for a butterfly lifting up from a wildflower, flipping madly to grab the beautiful creature right out of the air. Her body was as graceful as the wind, her claws extended, paws wide, and she flew back to earth with her prize.

"No!" Ruby cried. But it was too late. The kitten swaggered along the grass, so plainly strutting that it seemed evil and funny at the same time.

"Dang it," Ruby said under her breath.

"What in the name of Zeus are you doing?" Noah said.

He'd come up the path from the distillery, carrying a shovel and a rake in gloved hands. His hair was covered with a hat, and his worn shirt had rolled-up long sleeves.

"This kitten showed up the other night. A coyote was chasing her."

"So you're going to keep her on a leash, are you?"

"Why not?"

"Have you ever met a cat, of any kind, anywhere?"

"Of course I have." The kitten dropped the butterfly. It fell on the ground, dead, and the kitten poked it with a white-tipped paw. It fluttered slightly, and she pounced again, hard. Part of a wing broke off. Ruby felt slightly nauseous. "I can't keep watching this." She made a move to take the butterfly away, but Noah grabbed her arm.

"This is what cats do. They hunt. They kill things. Sometimes they eat them, but sometimes they just torture them. They like to race around and leap high and swish through the grass, like little Ninja Girl here."

"Little Ninja Girl," Ruby said, laughing. It suited her, with her sleek black body. "How old do you think she is?"

"I know exactly — eight months. She was born in the barn. Her daddy is a big feral guy who paces the woods like a panther."

Ruby realized this was as much as Noah had ever spoken to her, and, curious, she tossed out another question. "Is the daddy a black cat, too?"

"No," he said, and his eyes scanned the woods as if the tom might appear. "He's a dark-gray tabby, with one notched ear. I've seen him take down squirrels like they're moths."

"Wow." The kitten tired of trying to revive the butterfly and rustled through the grass. Only her tail and the leash, trailing out, were visible.

"Let her off the leash, Ruby. That's not how cats live."

"But what if something happens to her?"

He looked at her. "Things happen to people and animals all the time, but you can't force her to live a life that isn't natural to her."

Ruby thought of the darkness, the kitten

178

dashing toward her, and the coyote's eyes glowing. "This kitten came to me," she said, "specifically me, in the middle of the night, and my code of honor says I am going to protect her."

"Fair enough."

He started to turn away, but Ruby asked, "Don't the feral cats eat the chickens?"

"They do," he said, pausing. "You can always tell a cat's been at the chickens by the parts they eat — the breast and thighs."

Ruby laughed. "Kentucky Fried Chicken."

"Right. Other animals leave different calling cards." He tugged off his gloves and tucked them into his back pocket, pulled off the hat, and wiped his sweaty forehead. "Skunks like the head and stomach. Coyotes leave no trace." He warmed to his subject, eyes glinting. "Raccoons, though, are the worst. They stick their hands through the slats in the cages, and when a chicken comes close to see what it is, they grab the chicken by the throat and yank it right out of the cage." He used his hand to illustrate. "Then they take it down to the river to wash it."

"Ugh," Ruby said, feeling her belly roil. The urge to puke was vivid and urgent. She raised a finger, dashed to the edge of the meadow, and barfed. Instantly, her belly felt better. "Sorry," she said as she returned, wiping her mouth.

Noah stood with his arms crossed. His waist was narrow, his forearms corded with powerful muscle, and his hair gleamed in the sun. For the first time in about a hundred years, she thought about what a man other than Liam might look like naked, or at least shirtless.

He raised an eyebrow. "Pretty delicate, aren't you?"

She waved a hand. "It's not that. Just pregnant."

"Ah. That explains a lot."

She gave him a frown. "Like what?"

He grinned, and it was the first time she'd seen him smile. It wasn't that it was dazzling but the opposite — it was crooked, offsetting the intimidating perfection of his face. A blast of pure female hormonal appreciation rushed right through her middle.

"Just things," he said.

Seriously? she thought. This was what Lavender talked about, that he was so beautiful that women constantly threw themselves at him, then got mad when he didn't see them or acted aloof.

The kitten, weary of butterflies, came ambling out of the grass and rubbed against Ruby's legs. She scooped her up and the kitten butted against her chin. "There's my sweetheart," Ruby cooed. "I bet you want more tuna fish, don't you?"

"You gave her tuna? Aren't you vegan?"

"Cats aren't vegan, silly. They'll die if they don't get protein."

He laughed softly. "Good to know."

"Will you take a picture of me and the Ninja Girl?" Ruby pulled her phone out of her back pocket and passed it over, posing for the camera by holding the cat up to her face.

He held the phone sideways, stepped forward, and clicked, then waited for it to come up. He looked at it for a minute, then frowned. "Let me try again." Ruby smiled, kissing the kitten, who only endured it. This time, Noah gave a nod. "Good one." He passed the phone back. "For your blog? Your boyfriend?"

"More boring than that: my dad. He worries." Holding the cat easily on her shoulder, she messaged the picture to her father. **Me & Ninja Girl at the farm. Pretty, huh?**

"That's what dads do, I guess."

A truck rumbled into the driveway in front of the shop, pulling a shiny retro Airstream. "Ginny!" Ruby squealed. She put the cat down, then dithered about whether to put her in the trailer. The kitten had settled down to lick a paw, and Ruby picked her up, kissed her hot, shiny side, and put her in the camper. "I'll be back, sweetie."

She glanced at Noah, but he didn't say anything, only gave her that unreadable gaze. Ruby turned and dashed down the hill, feeling a stitch in her side almost immediately. She slowed to a walk. The truck pulled around the circle, the navigation excellent and practiced.

It was only as she grew closer that she realized that this Airstream was not a little Bambi but a solid, tour-the-world size, with two doors and a lot of windows. Ginny had worried about the towing capacity of her Jeep, which was not this big red Ford truck that looked as if it could haul twice again as much. The angle of light made it impossible to see into the truck, even when Ruby shaded her eyes.

Lavender came from the direction of the cottage, her hands still gloved in green cotton. She carried a spade and lifted it to shield her eyes. "That can't be Ginny."

Ruby shook her head, conscious of Noah joining them, too. They all waited as the truck doors opened and a very tall, long-legged girl leapt to the ground. Her dark hair was braided away from her face and high cheekbones, and the braids were wrapped with leather. Her arms were circled with beaded bracelets and she wore moccasins on her feet, but, even so, Ruby didn't put it together until a woman came around the truck. She was as petite as the girl was tall, her skin much, much darker, the glossy color of pecans. She moved with the effortless elegance of the prima ballerina she'd once been. "Surprise!" she cried. "We decided to make it after all."

"Valerie!" Ruby exclaimed, and looked back to the girl, who was nearly unrecognizable in her Native American guise. "Hannah. I didn't recognize you."

The girl gave a nod beneath hooded eyes, but Ruby saw the exact instant she laid eyes on Noah. Her nostrils flared, she cocked her chin sideways to hide her gaze, and she tossed her head. "Hi," she said with enormous ennui.

Ruby glanced at Valerie with one eyebrow raised. Valerie gave a subtle roll of her eyes — *I told you, guys!* — and said, "Give me a hug, beautiful girl. And tell me how you are."

They all hugged and kissed, and Valerie stood back. "Where's Ginny? I thought she'd be here by now."

"Not until Friday."

Ruby felt an inexplicable wave of worry

wash over her, a wave that ended up — of course — in her belly. And of course she had to barf. She dashed over and puked in the weeds. She was also sick of that part — the way it came on so fiercely. "Damn it!" she cried, wiping her mouth. "I'm so tired of throwing up!"

"Are you sick?" Valerie asked with alarm.

"No," Lavender said, looping a gentle arm around Ruby's shoulders. "Let's head inside and get some food for some lunch, shall we? We'll tell you everything." With a gentle nudge, she set Ruby free in the direction of the cottage and gathered Hannah under her long arm. The girl was nearly as tall as she was.

"Very glad to see you. I can't wait to hear about your travels through the reservations."

"Nations," Hannah said, easing away to walk ahead of them.

Valerie sighed. Under her breath she said, "It's been a long trip."

"Never mind," Lavender said. "You're here now. And we are thrilled."

Noah hauled the table and chairs out to a flat grassy spot dotted with tiny daisies. A big willow tree stretched its arms over the cottage and yard, and a circle of daisies bloomed at the foot of it.

Valerie and Lavender sliced cucumbers and pickles and tomatoes, arranged plates with turkey and hard-boiled eggs, hummus and celery and fresh red peppers. Hannah was forced into service, her feet in the soft leather shoes slapping against the wooden floors to underscore her huffy protestations. Ruby made a watermelon and avocado salad from the produce they'd picked up in McMinnville, and when Hannah raised an eyebrow in disgust, Ruby said, "You'll see. It's great."

Ruby found herself watching the girl. Whenever Noah came into the room, Hannah straightened almost haughtily, showing off a profile as sharp and clean as the face on a coin. Endearingly, she kept her slim shoulders hunched over a bustline that was much too large for her size. Ruby remembered those days, the sudden, inexplicable stares, the sometimes flattering, sometimes dismaying attention.

Once they were all settled around the table outside, Valerie said, "So you are not sick, Ruby? It's not chemo throwing up?"

"Oh, my God! No!" Ruby said. "I'm so sorry. I didn't realize you might jump to that conclusion. I'm just pregnant."

Valerie raised her eyebrows. "Really?"

"Confirmed. Due October second." She

leaned back to put her hands on the round of belly, thinking it seemed bigger than it did yesterday. With some satisfaction, she said, "I'm afraid I'm going to get as big as a house."

Valerie leaned over and squeezed Ruby's hand. "That's beautiful, Ruby. Absolutely wonderful."

"Thanks."

Valerie gave a sidelong glance at her daughter. "Miracles happen."

Hannah wiggled her foot and practiced her aloofness.

"And what about Ginny?" Valerie asked. "I haven't had an email or a text in a couple of days." She leaned forward and slid a celery stick through the bowl of hummus. "I was worried that she'd get stuck behind the fire lines or something."

"Fire lines?"

"Big fire in Idaho. It wasn't causing a lot of trouble when we passed through yesterday, but they were worried about some windstorms in the forecast."

"I saw her blog post last night, but she was only in Utah."

"I haven't been online for a couple of days." Valerie patted the pocket of her cargo shorts. "Hannah, will you go get my phone off the dash?"

Hannah rolled her eyes and heaved a long sigh.

"Now, child," Valerie said.

The girl hauled herself to her feet and headed toward the driveway. Valerie waited until she thought Hannah was out of earshot, then said quietly, "She's driving me crazy."

Hannah turned around. "I heard that. Just because I don't want to be all Kunta Kinte."

"Nobody said anything to you, Hannah. Go get my phone."

Ruby watched Hannah scuffle across the gravel circle drive, thinking the pebbles must hurt through the leather moccasins. "I went through an Indian period," she said.

Noah snorted.

"What?" Ruby said, keeping a straight face. "I'll have you know I am 1/120th Cherokee."

His nostrils quivered. "I can see that."

"I'm just saying that girls go through things sometimes. I thought if I was Indian, I'd be more in touch with the land, and I loved the culture of the Plains tribes."

"Nations," Valerie said.

Ruby chuckled. "Right."

"I know," Valerie said, and sat back in her chair, turning her glass in her long brown hands. "It's just a stage, a passion or something, but I would like her to explore the heroes of her own culture. Tecumseh and Sitting Bull are great men of history, but so are the Chevalier de Saint-George and W.E.B. DuBois. And on her dad's side there are all those heroes of Scottish culture — William Wallace and . . . whoever."

Lavender snorted. "Hype." She put her glass of tea back on the table. The ice cubes clinked. "Give her time. A passion is a good way to get through something."

"I know. That's why we did the trip."

Noah said, "Tecumseh and Sitting Bull?"

She smiled. "Yeah. She's crazy for Sitting Bull."

"Good taste."

"How are you holding up, gal?" Lavender asked. She narrowed her eyes. "You look good."

"Thanks. I'm okay." She reached for another celery stick. "Why am I the only one eating here?"

Ruby laughed. "I was trying to let everybody else actually get some before I turn into Wolverine Ruby."

"Eat!" Lavender plunked some fruit and a single piece of bread on her plate. "I've been plagued with indigestion for a couple of weeks now. Never know what'll set it off."

"Have you had it checked out?" Valerie asked.

Lavender waved a hand. "If you start treating me like an old woman, I'll start treating you like a widow."

Valerie held up her hands. "Wouldn't think of it." She glanced over her shoulder to see if Hannah was still gone. "That's the best part of leaving Cincinnati. Finally we can just be invisible, ordinary tourists. That was hard to do in Cinci."

"I bet." Ruby dug into her salad, savoring the cold sweetness of the watermelon, the depth of fat and creaminess in the avocado. "Do you know where you'll end up?"

"Not really. We're going to spend the summer with my parents in San Diego, but who knows after that. Maybe we'll just keep wandering for a year."

Hannah returned, long arms and legs moving as if she had no joints. Really pretty girl, Ruby thought. She wanted to play with her hair. "Here's your phone. Can I *eat* now?"

"Of course." Valerie flipped open her phone. "No messages. And" — she touched another spot on the screen — "no emails from her, either. I'm sure she's fine."

"Hope she's having an adventure," Ruby said, eyeing a ring of red onion.

189

"No doubt about that," Lavender said.

Ruby's phone buzzed. A message from her father said, **Cute pic! I can see your tummy showing. How's my baby growing?**

She smiled and texted back, **Which one? I hate texting. Call me, will you? One second.**

Ruby looked up from her phone. "Excuse me a minute, please. My father is anxious for news."

She swished through the long grass toward the lavender fields. "Hey, Dad," she said when he answered. "What's up?"

"Not much. Everything going all right?"

"It's beautiful here." She inhaled the fragrance of lavender, baking under the sunny skies. "Isn't Oregon supposed to be gloomy?"

"Not this time of year, I don't think. The summer is good in the Northwest." She could hear him cooking, a utensil clicking against a pan. "So you have a cat now? You know you can't change the cat litter when you're pregnant, right?"

"No. Why?"

"There's a parasite that lives in cat feces. You can't touch it."

"Good to know. And, anyway, she's a barn cat, so I guess she might hang out with me, but she's really not that tame. She likes to eat mice."

"She's cute. You're feeling good?"

She thought of the throwing up, the endless, endless throwing up, and her grouchiness, and the not sleeping, but the only thing he could do was worry, and she could manage this. "I'm fine, Dad. Lavender and the others are going to take good care of me."

"All right. I won't keep you, then. Keep me in the loop, sweetheart."

"Will do. Love you, Dad."

"Love you, too, Ruby."

She touched the screen to turn off the call, brushing her other hand over the lavender standing up to her hips on either side, and absently tapped the email icon. Her in-box came up, populated with the usual junk mail, a couple of notes from friends, and last — electrifyingly — a message from Liam.

The header was **Thought You Should Know.**

A tangle of cold things wrapped around her throat, and she clicked on the email. The body of it hadn't yet arrived via cyberspace, so she had to stand there for long seconds with her phone in hand, watching a little circle spin to tell her the program was working.

Still working.

Still working.

She made a small noise, and, as if the machine heard her frustration, it filled in suddenly. Short and to the point.

Dear Ruby,

I wanted you to hear it from me rather than from our friends or somewhere else. I am getting married to Minna in two weeks. I'm sorry if this hurts you. That was never my intention.

Be well,
Liam

Ruby cried out, and a sharp, ripping pain went through her middle, as if a monster had reached into her chest and torn out her heart, leaving blood vessels and arteries hanging, pouring blood out onto the ground. She fell to her knees, nearly buried in lavender, and felt the impact shudder upward through her body.

Liam!

FROM: Ginny@cakeofdreams.com
TO: Valerie@winedancer.com
SUBJECT: Waving from Utah

Thursday morning at my little table, looking out at the beautiful, beautiful mountains.

Hi, Val. How are things going in Custer Land? ☺ I can't remember where you were supposed to be by now, either, so fill me in.

I'm in Utah, outside Provo. Had to stop yesterday because of the winds, and then it rained last night. Somebody said the rain was good and the wind is bad, because there are fires somewhere in Idaho. Are you headed through there? Seems like the path to Boise would be pretty safe. (Shrug.)

Had the most interesting conversation last night! Ran into the truck driver who admired Willow the first day out. He got sidelined by the same storm that finally made me stop, which actually made me feel better — if a trucker pulls over, the weather is probably not great, right?

Now that I'm doing this, I'm really even more disappointed in myself that I was too afraid to travel alone to Cincinnati and missed the funerals. I know you've said you understood, but it was cowardly. I should have been there for you, and I was too afraid to go by myself. I don't even remember now what I thought would happen.

Never mind. All water under the bridge.

Now I guess I'd better get on the road. Miles to go before I sleep, hahaha.

Ginny

[ADDED TO EMAIL QUEUE TO SEND . . . NOT MAILED]

CHAPTER 14

Ginny was awake at six, roused by Willow nosing her under the covers, blowing hard, ever so gently rattling the tags on her collar. Clear morning daylight poured through the windows, promising a good day on the road, and Ginny flung on her sweats and a sweater.

The minute she stepped out of the Airstream, she saw that Jack's big blue rig was gone. Of course it would be. A pang of regret pushed through her chest.

On the other hand, the sky was absolutely pristine, a color of blue that almost hurt to look at. Not a single cloud marred the sheen of that sky, although she could see a ribbon of clouds to the north, low and thin. Nothing to worry about. She ought to be able to make Boise today with no problem, and then — Lavender's!

She ate a simple breakfast of yogurt, toast, and coffee, sitting at the table and looking out through the generous window at the craggy blue ridge of Rockies. Pleasure hummed beneath her ribs. She drizzled honey over the toast.

Willow probably needed a walk, and Ginny probably needed to post a blog, but she felt no urgency to do either one. Maybe they could stop at a more attractive spot along the way for Willow's walk, and maybe her readers would forgive her this once if she didn't post a blog. She'd posted last night, so maybe she'd get one up tonight, and, anyway, she'd be seeing a group of backbloggers later today.

On the map, she blocked out her route, calculating distances and stops, leaving some wiggle room to arrive in Boise by four or five. The group of backbloggers would pick her up at six-thirty.

That finished, she dressed and turned the hot water on for dishwater. Her phone started to buzz on the table, so she turned off the water, dashed over, and grabbed it. Her daughter's number showed on the screen. "Hey, you," Ginny said with pleasure. "Aren't you supposed to be working right now?"

"I have been working, but I took a break to call my mother and find out how the big adventure is going."

Ginny couldn't help it, she laughed. "It is not easy," she said with some emphasis, "but I am having the time of my life."

"I've been reading your blogs. It sounds like a blast. Have you met any interesting people?"

A flush washed over her, forehead to breasts. "Not really. There isn't much time to hang around, honestly, and I'm headed for the lavender farm to see my friends."

"Mom, you should get out and mingle! You'll enjoy it. Promise you'll try to do more of that."

"I'll try." She put her cup and spoon and bowl into the dishwater. "Have you talked to your dad?"

"I have," she said. "He is not happy with you, but you already knew that."

"Right."

"He'll be fine, Mom. Just remember, you're having an adventure, and you'd never want me to give up something like that because a guy got mad at me over it."

"He's not really some guy, Christie. He's your dad."

"He can still be my dad if he's mad at you," Christie said, and paused. "Kinda interesting that you said my dad and not your husband."

Ginny halted in the action of dropping a

197

dishrag into the water. It hung over the water in points, the edging blue and yellow, crisp and clean because she'd bought them for the trip. She felt something ripple through her, a sense that these details would always stick with her. Steam rose from the water. "Hmm," she said.

"Don't worry about that right now," Christie said. She murmured to someone over her shoulder. "Sorry, Mom, I gotta go. They've got some charts I need to sign."

"No problem. Love you, honey."

"Love you, too. Call me when you get to Lavender's farm. I want lots of pictures!"

"I will."

She ended the call absently, staring out the window over the sink with her phone in her hand. Willow barked suddenly, and, startled, Ginny jumped. The phone sailed out of her hand and right into the water.

"Oh, my God!" She stuck her hand into the steaming water to retrieve it, but the water seared her skin and she jerked it out instantly. "Dang it!"

The seconds swooped by in a wild rush as she mentally scrambled for a way to get the phone out of the water. Gloves? No, she didn't have them here. A spoon! She yanked open the drawer, ended up yanking too hard, and the whole thing spilled on the floor. "Crap!"

Plucking a serving spoon from the pile of utensils, she swept across the bottom of the sink, bringing up the spoon, the cup, and finally her phone.

Her dripping-wet, soaked-to-the-microchips smartphone. The screen was blank. Water poured from beneath the case and the various openings — speakers and plug-in spots. Her heart sank.

But she didn't give in. She pried the cover off and dried it thoroughly. What dried out electronics? Was it oatmeal? No, rice.

Which she didn't have.

Willow cocked her head as she watched Ginny wring her hands, and something about her whiskey-colored eyes, the patience and simple curiosity there, calmed Ginny down. "It's only a phone, right? Not the end of the world. I'll get some rice and we'll try to dry it out, but what's the worst that could happen? It's a dead phone. No big deal."

Willow wagged her tail.

For a minute, Ginny held the dead phone in her hand, feeling strange. How long since she'd been out of touch, *completely* out of touch? Of course, she could always fire up the computer if she needed to, but that was not an issue this morning.

She put on a light jacket and walked over

to the truck-stop diner. It was pretty slow now, at almost eight. The truckers had all moved on very early, no doubt trying to make up for the lost time from yesterday. A girl with long black hair was separating receipts at the cash register. "One for breakfast?"

"No, thanks. I have a request. I soaked my phone and need to get some rice. Would your manager let me buy a couple of cups?"

"Whoa, that sucks." The girl grinned. "Let me go find out. Just ordinary rice, right?"

"I guess."

The girl went into the kitchen, and Ginny spied the waitress from the night before sitting in a booth, eating. Long night. The woman spied her, and her eyes turned to slits. She waved Ginny over.

As Ginny crossed the room, the woman took a piece of paper out of her pocket and slid it across the table. "He left this for you. I don't know why he didn't give it to you himself."

"He?"

"Jack."

Ginny ran her finger along the fold of the paper, thinking of him walking away with wet shoulders last night.

"Careful there, sweetheart." The woman had two tiny, identical smears of mascara under each lower lid. "He's not exactly the settling kind."

Ginny tucked his note into her jeans pocket. "I'm married."

"So you say." She picked up her toast with work-reddened fingers. "Just a friendly warning."

"Thanks." In her peripheral vision, Ginny caught sight of the hostess coming back from the kitchen. "See you."

The note poked her thigh as she headed to the front, as if the corner were a knife. The girl handed over a plastic bag of rice. "Two dollars."

Ginny passed over the money.

"Good luck!"

Dead phone, she thought, pushing out into the sunny morning, *but a note from a guy.* Why had he given it to the server? Why hadn't he just left it on her windshield or tapped on her door?

She waited to read it until she had tucked the phone into the bag of rice and finished securing the trailer. Willow leapt up into the backseat of the Jeep. Ginny stood at the driver's side door and pulled out the folded paper. Sun fell unobstructed on the back of her neck and hit the paper with such strong reflection that she had to squint to read the blue ink.

His handwriting was strangely elegant, all triangles and points, not at all what she was expecting.

Dear Ginny,

I'm leaving this up to fate. If you go into the café this morning before Veronica leaves, and if she really wants to give you the note, you'll get it. If not, we'll just be ships that passed in the night.

I tried to stop by last night, but you were already asleep, or maybe you weren't too keen on letting a strange guy into your trailer late at night, which is smart, I guess. I'm probably ten kinds of fool for writing this letter like a schoolkid, but it was easy to talk to you, like we were old friends who finally got to meet again.

I'm not gonna lie, either — I like looking at you. The freckles on your nose, and your shy smile, and . . . other things, too, which I'm too much of a gentleman to say.

You're probably thinking I'm a nutcase now, and I don't blame you, but I felt like I had to write this down and give it a shot. You said you're married, and I respect that. You have my number. My email is hghgains@intertime.net. If you get a chance, drop me a line.

                                    Jack

Ginny touched her nose with its freckles and thought for one hot second about his gray eyes, his kindly smile. As she stood there in an ugly truck-stop parking lot, under a vast blue sky, holding the first note a man had ever written to her, she felt a sense of opening, as if there had been mountains standing between her real life and the false one she'd been living and she'd suddenly spied a road through them.

She wouldn't call him, of course. That was how affairs started, and she was a better woman than that. But she gave herself a minute to think about him admiring her freckles and breasts or maybe her bottom when she walked away. The air smelled of cotton candy and rumpled sheets and all the things she'd been missing for so long.

In her neat way, she folded the paper exactly as he had, then tucked it into the glove box, where it would be safe but out of sight.

Then, with deliberation, she turned her thoughts to her friends waiting for her in Oregon. Only one more night on the road, and she'd be with them!

■ ■ ■ ■

Ginny skirted the Great Salt Lake and headed north into Idaho by late morning. The traffic thinned considerably, not surprising for a Thursday. She saw other RV'ers like herself, and single people in Subarus on long-distance drives, and the odd trucker catching up and overtaking her.

The day was very hot. Even with the air conditioner blowing full blast, Ginny sweated down her back and under her hair. She stopped to water and walk Willow twice as often as usual, worried that she would get dehydrated, and finally rolled the windows in back down halfway so the dog could get some strong air.

Something made Ginny start to sneeze, but she left the windows down anyway.

More worrisome were the clouds on the horizon, now stretching over the mountains from east to west as far as Ginny could see. They were low and thick, but sun poked through them here and there, so maybe it wasn't anything to worry about. She didn't want to start getting paranoid about rain.

If she'd had her phone, she could have checked the weather. Instead, she turned the radio dial, trying to find a local station.

She picked one up out of Salt Lake City, then got a scratchy country station from Boise that never did give the weather or anything else, just inane patter she thought might be canned elsewhere, paid for by the radio station.

She flipped it off. If the weather got bad, she'd stop.

But as she came closer to Boise, the clouds boiled closer and deeper across the road, as if a dragon were breathing, and she caught a hard whiff of smoke.

Was it a *fire*? Jack had mentioned the winds whipping up forest fires. She slowed down, peering over the windshield at the slate-colored clouds, but she didn't really know if they looked any different than regular storm clouds. In a way, a fire would be less daunting — she wouldn't have to drive through rain and lightning, worried sick that she'd slide off the road. The highway ran alongside the mountains, not through them.

And at least the clouds blotted out the sun, letting things cool off a little. She turned the radio back on, just in case she could pick up weather reports as she got closer to Boise, and sang along.

Her mind wandered as the Jeep gulped down the miles. A thousand things rose up in her mind and then drifted away — memories, possibilities, recipe ideas. A collection of ranch buildings, all roofed in green metal, made her think inexplicably of a bicycle she'd had as a child, which she rode on the gravel roads through the country, wind in her hair. She'd skinned her knees and elbows and eaten dirt a thousand times falling off that bike. She'd begged for a little motorcycle as a young teen, but that idea had been nixed.

The memory made her wrinkle her brow. Once, she'd been bold. Mighty. What had happened along the way to change that?

Trying to get out of Dead Gulch, maybe. Almost succeeding, then failing in such an ordinary, boring way. Pregnant. Married too young.

She wouldn't trade Christie, of course. Her daughter had ended up being a great blessing. But if she had it to do again, would she marry Matthew?

Once upon a time, she had not been indifferent to him. She thought of seeing Marnie's husband grabbing her ass at a barbecue one night. Ginny had been in the bathroom and they thought themselves unobserved, and it was a real grab, his fingers digging into her cheek, one sliding down between. Ginny nearly melted in pure envy. Bobby was not a good-looking man, with his balding head and big nose, but he'd always been lusty like that. You had the sense that he'd just take you hard and holler loud and make sure you came just as he did.

It wasn't until she was nearly upon it that she realized that the cloud had changed, deepened. It billowed downward, cascading over the front of the mountainside.

Fire.

She pulled to the side of the road, astonished and oddly giddy. Bright orange flames burned in a serpentine pattern against the hill — up one, down the next, and up the next and down.

Without even thinking, she grabbed her camera from the backseat. Willow whined, but Ginny said, "Stay, baby. I'll be right back."

She dashed down the slope from the road and ducked between two strands of barbed wire, checking only in a cursory way for bulls that might charge. The fire was some distance away, but the animals would be running away from it, not toward it.

As if to emphasize that, a knot of antelopes, small and fleet, dashed into her line of vision. Ginny trained her lens on them and shot a fast series of photos: the darkness behind them, the orange line of fire,

207

the animals fleeing. Great shots! A swell of artistic pleasure swam through her.

She trained the camera on the flames, which were burning downward at an amazing rate, gobbling up trees and shrubs like an angry dragon. Cars raced by on the highway, and she heard sirens somewhere.

She had no idea how much time had passed when she heard Willow barking frantically in the car. She lowered the camera and froze. The flames roared over the mountain right in front of her, breathing and moving like a live being, licking out, spilling over the top, then disappearing.

She could not breathe. Her legs wouldn't move. Her camera was halfway to her chest, held out like a shield.

Ash and blackened debris fell like snow through the air, some still carrying fire on its tail. She saw one ember catch the grass near her feet, and still she could not —

"Lady, what the fuck are you doing? Get out of here!"

She whirled, body loosened, and saw a young firefighter, grubby and smeared with ashes, waving her away. She glanced over her shoulder — a wall of fire was roaring down the mountain.

Her paralysis shattered. She ran, feeling cinders sting her face and arms, praying her hair would not catch. Diving between the strands of barbed wire, she cursed herself for putting Willow in danger like this. She'd never forgive herself if anything happened to her dog.

A barb caught her shoulder and shirt and ripped deep. Ginny cried out, ducking lower, but the shirt tore as she pulled away. It made her stumble, and the camera banged against her knee. Willow was barking frantically, and a horn blared somewhere nearby, and Ginny heard herself panting and sobbing like an animal. She caught her jeans on the wire, extricated herself, and bolted up the hill, actually hearing the fire that licked at her heels.

She opened the door to the Jeep and flung the camera inside, then jumped in and started the engine, only to realize that the fire had crossed the highway in front of her. A ripple of primeval horror made every hair on her body stand straight out. As if that would protect her.

Willow howled.

"Oh, baby, it's okay. I promise. I promise." She roared into action, seeing a flat area just ahead where she could turn around. The trailer bumped behind her, and a row of fire trucks and emergency vehicles roared by, headed for the fire line. Ginny's hands shook as she turned the truck around and forced her way back into the traffic fleeing the fire. A woman ahead of her had a Subaru packed to the gills with household goods. A guitar leaned against a stack of books.

In the rearview mirror, she saw the billowing black cloud backlit with hellish pink light. The smell of the fire filled the cab, clung to her hair. Willow whined and panted, pacing from one side of the car to the other, panicked.

"Sweet Jesus," she breathed. "Get me out of here alive. Please. I'll never be such an idiot again, I swear."

LAVENDER HONEY FARMS
yamhill co., oregon

Home Shop **Blog** Directions Philosophy

Lavender Tea for Soothing an Emotional Meltdown

We have a pregnant woman and a teenager in the house at Lavender Honey Farms. Either of them is likely to fall to hysterics over anything at any moment. Once they finish sobbing, there will be a nice tea and a hot bath for them. This is a great decoction for the bath, calming and sleep-inducing.

1 oz. lavender flowers
1 oz. hops
1 oz. sage
1 oz. thyme

Mix dried herbs together and loosely pack into a muslin square tied with string (or one of our reusable bath sacks, which you can order *here*). Run a hot bath and let the herbs soak, along with the tired/cranky loved one for as long as necessary.

Have you checked out our selection of *loose lavenders*? There's something for every purpose!

211

Chapter 15

Lavender saw Ruby fall to her knees. Drawing on almost four decades of airline emergency management, she cast a quick glance at the others and settled her cup carefully on the saucer. "I'll be right back."

She found Ruby bent over, hands wrapped around her belly, but she wasn't throwing up. A keening noise came out of her. Lavender touched Ruby's shoulder with an open palm. "Are you all right, child?" She didn't want to say what worried her, that it was the baby, that Ruby was miscarrying, in case that *spoke it into existence,* as her mother used to say.

"No." Ruby raised her head. Her nose was running, and her eyes were red and awash with tears. "Liam is getting married in two weeks."

Only a man. Lavender let go of a breath and pulled a clean hankie out of her pocket. "I'm sorry, honey. Is that what he said in response to your news of being pregnant?"

"No, I haven't told him yet." She held up the phone, cradled in her palm, her wrist bent backward in a languid position. With her free hand, she wiped her nose, but the tears kept falling, as if from a river. "He just emailed me so that I wouldn't hear it from somewhere else."

Lavender bent with some difficulty and drew Ruby to her feet. She wanted to say, *It's only a man. . . . There are others. . . . You'll get over him. . . .* "I'm sorry about your broken heart," she said instead, "but you're here with us. The only thing you have to think about now is the baby."

Ruby let herself be led through the thin row between plants. Her legs brushed blossoms on either side, sending a faint waft of lavender through the air. Calming. Ruby hiccupped a little, wiped at her nose. "Do I still tell him now? I don't know what to do about that."

"You probably still have to tell him. It's only fair to let him know." Lavender wondered if he would turn his back on the baby. That would be best overall, of course.

"Are you okay?" Valerie asked, standing as they came up to the table.

"I'm fine," Ruby snapped. "I wish everyone would just leave me alone." She plopped

213

into her seat and made a face. "Wow, that was so not me."

Valerie chuckled. "Welcome to motherhood."

A pinch worked its way through Lavender's chest, persistent, then gone. She coughed, then rubbed the spot for a minute. Into memory floated the face of a swarthy man with beautiful lips, almost too full. Lavender had not been able to get enough of kissing those fat, luscious lips, and he was not like a lot of men, who found kissing to be only a prelude. He kissed for ages at a time, the two of them pressed against a wall in a dusty hallway, his body against hers, mouths firm and wet and succulent, moving and pressing, sucking and supping, tongues tangling. Absently, she touched her mouth.

"That was a faraway expression," Valerie said, smiling faintly. "Will you share?"

Lavender glanced at Hannah and gave an inward shrug. If the girl had not already ripened, the time wouldn't be far off. "I was remembering a man who broke my heart once upon a time. I was twenty-two and I met him in Cairo. He was a pilot, and so beautiful." She shook her head. "For over a year, every time we could manage to be in the same city, we" — she realized that not only Hannah but Noah was listening, and she picked through the words — "got together." Lavender thought of the hot joinings, the frantic heat, the long lazy days in air-condition-less hotel rooms, windows open, cigarette smoke curling up from their hands. She leaned back luxuriously. "He was really something."

"Those pilots," Noah said. He winked at Lavender. "The pilots always got the women when we were on deployments. Every time."

"My dad was a pilot," Hannah said haughtily. "He wasn't like that."

"Oh, honey," Valerie drawled. "How do you think I met him?"

"You were on a plane. That's not the same."

Valerie laughed, but Lavender saw the sharpness in her eye. "Your father was a silver-tongued devil, Hannah my dear, which is where your sister Kalista got it." She addressed the others at the table. "Both of them could talk the wings off an angel."

"But he wasn't a player."

"No," Valerie said, and touched her daughter's hand. "He was a very good family man."

Hannah yanked her hand away. "I hate talking about them." She left the table.

"Liam isn't a silver-tongued devil," Ruby

said with some misery. "He was so devoted to me, you wouldn't believe it. I mean, girls were always coming on to him, and he just never even saw them. He only had eyes for me."

"Not a pilot, I guess?" Noah asked, tongue literally in cheek.

Lavender laughed at the startled, confused expression on Ruby's face. "What?"

Noah held Ruby's gaze steadily, easily, until Ruby got it. "Oh." Reluctantly, she half-smiled. "No, he was a cook, but, believe me, chefs can be players, too."

Valerie ladled watermelon salad and more crackers onto her plate. "What happened to your pilot, Lavender?"

"Oh, Khalid." She sighed. "He was married. He would have continued on forever, but I was idealistic then and wanted to find a husband of my own. I let him go."

"Did you ever marry?"

Lavender sipped her mint tea. "No. After a few years, it was pretty clear to me that it didn't make the girls happy. I'd run into somebody and they'd gotten fat or they were divorced or stuck in someplace like Dead Gulch, wishing they were back in the sky. Ginger and I decided we were going to stay single."

"Ginger is the one who owned Ginny's

trailer, right?" Ruby asked.

"Yep. She eventually did marry a good man — a pilot, as it turned out — when she was thirty-seven. Late in those days, and pregnant, so it was a happy ending. She became an artist and still traveled in that Bambi. We stayed in touch."

The table went quiet. Lavender thought of her recent sighting of Ginger when she toured the farm in the morning. Maybe it was because Ginny was bringing the trailer out here.

"I guess I'd better get back to work," Noah said. "Want me to walk you back, Ruby?"

The girl had been staring at her fingernails, phone loose in one hand. She raised a pale face, those Dresden eyes blinking in exhaustion. "Sure," she said, and let him help her up. "Thanks."

Lavender watched them walk away. "I guess I'm ready for a nap."

"I'll pick up," Val said. "And I'll see if I can get a reply from Ginny, so Ruby doesn't worry. She's a little mother, isn't she?"

"Born to it." Lavender touched Val's lean shoulder. "Rest yourself, gal. Don't get worn out, now."

CAKE OF DREAMS

Pilgrims are poets who create
by taking journeys.
— *Richard R. Niebuhr*

This was not the easiest day of my life. I'll be late posting this, too, since I have no connection to the Internet. So sorry, my friends.

CHAPTER 16

By the time she made it to her evening stop, Ginny was weepy and absolutely exhausted. Something she'd eaten at lunch disagreed with her, and her stomach was upset and gurgling. The fire had closed the highway toward Boise, which meant she would have to take a long detour through the mountains of Idaho and Montana, then loop back down toward Portland. It added hundreds of miles to her route, and she wouldn't make it to the farm tomorrow. She hadn't made the backbloggers' party, either, nor could she call them to let them know. The telephone numbers were in her phone, of course, and that was still not working.

She'd hoped to stop in Idaho Falls, but because of all the rerouted traffic from the fire, every campground in the area was filled. One of the attendants at the last place she stopped to inquire had pointed her to this lake. She realized as she pulled up that he was probably a fisherman, and the lonely lake was perfect.

For him.

For her tastes, the area was quite isolated, with only a handful of campsites taken. Ginny dithered in the parking lot by the unmanned ranger station, tapping her thumb against the steering wheel. This was not what she'd been expecting, and it added to her sense of isolation and dread. Maybe she should keep driving.

Her hands ached. She desperately wanted a shower. Her stomach roiled and pitched, and every bone in her body ached. Driving farther seemed like a punishment.

Make a decision.

She made camp by the lake. Ginny let Willow out to explore the area, knowing she wouldn't wander far. The dog padded into the water up to her ankles, took a drink, smelled a log, stared off into the distance. There were probably bears out there. Coyotes and raccoons, maybe.

She really did not feel well. Her head ached, and shivers were starting along her spine. Maybe the best idea right now would be to just get some sleep.

First, she leashed Willow and took her for a walk along the edge of the lake in the twilight. The water was still and a cool breeze blew off it. A man walked toward her, hunched and frowning, and didn't speak even when she said, "Good evening." A bristling unease crossed her body, and she couldn't help looking over her shoulder at him.

STRANGER!

She shook it off. Again her mother's voice.

On the way back, she saw a campfire burning not too far away from her own camp. A whirl of men's voices rang out, laughing, hooting, as if they were having a party. As she approached her trailer, it looked frail against the big twilit sky, silver and delicate, as easy to rip into as the foil wrapping on a Hershey's Kiss.

Maybe she ought to move on, forget about this.

But her body protested. Everything ached. Her stomach kept roiling, and her shoulder hurt where the barbed wire had torn it earlier. Who even knew how much farther it was to the next stop?

Friendly lamplight spilled from the kitchen window of the Airstream, the trailer so ardently female with its cabbage roses and winding vines. Why hadn't she realized that? That she'd be advertising her femaleness by driving a flower-painted trailer?

She stopped, taking in the scene, trying to

talk herself into a more reasonable state of mind.

A terrible vision spurted across the peaceful scene — her body bloody and violated, sprawled on the narrow floor of that beloved little kitchen. The roar of a gang of men having their way with her, the terrible pain —

She swayed dizzily and put a cold hand against her forehead, pressing fingers against her eyelids for a minute. Her skin was very hot, and her stomach was beginning to really *hurt.*

Whatever it was, she couldn't drive this way. With a sense of resignation, she climbed into her turtle shell, secured the door carefully behind her, and drew all the curtains. Willow woofed and settled down on the floor.

Right. She had a dog. Willow wouldn't let anyone in to hurt her.

Feverish, cramping, she curled up on her bed without even taking off her jeans. A ribbon of reason wound through her mind. In a little while, she told herself, she would take some Advil. For right now she desperately wanted to lie down. Just for a minute.

She dreamed of a green chrysalis built around her, seeming fragile but really very strong. The colors were extreme — purple

222

and green and bright yellow — and seemed to pulse and beat. Even in her sleep, even in her dream, she thought there was something wrong with that, and if she wasn't so hot, she'd open her eyes.

A woman with a martini glass bent over her, whispering, *Wake up, wake up. You're in trouble.*

She jerked into wakefulness, the fever making everything seem light from within. Willow licked her hand. Ginny crawled to the bathroom and looked for something to take, but her vision was so blurry, she couldn't figure out which bottle was which. She struggled back to the bed, kicked off her jeans, and crawled under the covers, shivering and shaking.

Willow leapt up on the bed with her, and Ginny gratefully buried her face in her dog's fur, ashamed to be weeping, unable to stop.

What if she died of E. coli or something? How would Willow get out? Her dog would die, too, a slow and terrible death of dehydration. She should open a window or something. Willow was smart enough to claw her way through the screen.

She felt herself being dragged under by the fever.

A bright burst of orange exploded. Ginny bolted upright, realizing that it was Willow barking savagely at someone at the door of the trailer. She raised a hand to her aching head, felt the clamminess all over her skin. Indistinct voices came from the other side of the door.

The door handle rattled, and Willow renewed her furious, savage barking. Someone said, "Fuck it," and the voices drifted away. Carefully, Ginny swayed toward her dog, sinking down beside her.

"Thank you, baby." She pressed against the thick fur, and Willow turned and licked her face.

She would have to get moving again. She had to get the hell out of here. In a few minutes.

She'd get up and take some ibuprofen. In a minute.

In a minute.

CHAPTER 17

In the quiet before dawn, Ruby opened her laptop, careful not to disturb the kitten curled up beside her. She'd slept the hectic, overheated, restless sleep of the broken-hearted, waking too often to think of Liam in a tuxedo, saying vows, thinking of him with his arms around someone else. Lavender's words haunted her: *Maybe he fell in love with the other woman on sight, too.*

But how did you fall out of love so fast? How did you do it at all? That was the thing she couldn't figure out.

She needed to tell him about the baby. Instead of going to email, she went to Google Maps and clicked on her saved searches. The map zoomed to Seattle and then to the neighborhood. She zoomed and zoomed and, when she got close enough, she clicked on the little yellow man to go to street view.

And there was her mother's house. Electrifyingly, the photo had changed. The lilacs around the yard were blooming, clearly, and there, in the backyard, was the family: Mom, Dad, three children, and a dog in the grass. It made her think of a dollhouse family, so tidy and balanced.

Stupid ritual, this one. She was hardly ready to be anyone's mother if she was still such a child herself. Who did this, anyway? Her mother had walked away from her when she was seven. And sick. Why wasn't Ruby furious with her?

A burn settled under her diaphragm, and she immediately cut off that line of thought. She had forgiven her mother over a lot of years. She forgave herself now for having a quirky little habit.

She opened her email program. There, saved with an orange arrow beside it, was Liam's last email, about getting married. Before she could chicken out, Ruby hit *reply* and wrote:

Liam,

Married! That's really something. I'd say congratulations, but I wouldn't mean it.

I have news, too. I'm pregnant, five and a half months. If you count back, you'll know when it happened — right there in our empty apartment just before I left. Yes, it is yours, conceived in fury, but conceived nonetheless. Since I was sure I'd never have a baby, I'm keeping it, of course.

I don't need anything from you. I did feel as if I should tell you, however.

Ruby

She hit *send,* then, heart pounding, gently moved Ninja Girl and got dressed. The kitten stood, stretched, and settled back into a tight little ball on the bed.

Ruby left the camper door open, in case the kitten needed to get out, and headed for the lavender fields. It was not quite dawn, but muted light spread along the top side of weighty clouds that had settled over the farm. A pair of chickens joined her as she walked up the path alongside the laying shack. Many of the other chickens were pecking around in the dirt, their voices a soft, burbling sound. She didn't recognize the two who'd fallen in step with her. One had red feathers layered with cream and a cream-colored chest. The other was black and gold, very pretty. Both were placid and sturdy and very sure of themselves, clucking in low tones as if discussing the local gossip, swaying along as if they were two old biddies with their hands behind their backs. Their company eased her.

So did the fresh, cool air. The low clouds were full of rain, though it hadn't yet begun to fall. She breathed deeply, in and out. *Finding her center,* her dad had called it when she was so ill from chemo, finding a place that was calm and right and beautiful, no matter what was going on outside or in her poisoned body. The technique had seen her through a lot of bad hours, and it helped now.

All night she had tossed and turned over Liam's news, over what to say to him about the baby. She slept in tiny snippets, reviewing their passionate love affair, flashing on things she'd struggled to stop thinking of — his long, beautiful hands, scarred by his years in the kitchen; the sound he made when he nuzzled her first thing in the morning, a long, satisfied groan that made her feel enveloped every single time.

It was the worst kind of sleep, haunted and restless.

She crossed the threshold into the lavender fields, but the chickens paused behind her, as if they did not have the password to enter the magic garden.

Ruby halted, aching. The sight caught her right in the throat every time, the tidy rows of giant pincushions with tiny purple flowers floating over the green, the small pink fairy roses edging the rows — purely for beauty, Lavender had told her. Ruby knelt now and plucked a few roses carefully, pinching them free with her sharp nails. She twisted them into a bouquet and raised it to her nose. The scent was sweet, rose and lemon and morning, and it unrolled against her sinuses, rubbing fragrance over the bridge of her nose and the taut space between her brows.

She waded into the lavender, breathing that, too, into the mix. The pain she'd been carrying since yesterday let go, as if she'd dropped a backpack. In her belly, the baby moved, tumbling in a circle, and she covered it with her hand, filled with wonder that such an impossible thing should have transpired.

A baby! *Her* baby. "What's your name, little one?" she asked. "I can't wait to see you."

Finally, she could stop and just be. Breathe. Head into the everythingness that always existed. At seven and eight and nine — struggling through her illness, finding hope, only to be devastated over and over again — she and her father had often walked down to the beach to sit on the sand

and touch everythingness in the sound of the waves, whispering, crashing, rippling, fluttering.

Behind her, the chickens conversed in hushed tones, as polite as if they were in church, and it made her laugh. She turned around to thank them and saw Noah standing between the banks of shrubs, watching. She waved the hand with the roses.

"I didn't want to disturb you," he said. He was dressed for a workday — jeans shoved into battered leather boots, which had seen plenty of mud and muck and time, and a simple checkered shirt beneath a green hoodie that made his tanned skin look warm. "You're up early."

"I couldn't sleep."

He hesitated, then came down the row next to hers, a hen waddling behind him. The hen paused in a grassy spot, pecking, and he shooed her back through the natural gate. She fluttered and squawked but obeyed.

Again Ruby let go of a soft laugh. "I never knew they were so interesting. They were chatting away, walking with me like they were a couple of dogs."

"They have a lot of character, all right."

He joined her, reaching down amid the lavender to pinch off three blossoms. "Has

Lavender talked to you about the varieties?"

"A little. Some are for perfume, some for culinary, some for decorative purposes, right?"

"Yep." He bruised the blossoms and held them out to her.

Ruby tried to remember her discussion with Lavender. "This is Grosso, right? And it yields more but has a less pure lavender scent because of . . ." She frowned, inhaling, then caught the scent of it. "Camphor?"

He gave a nod, lips turned down in approval. "Good."

"How do you get the oil out?"

"We have a lavender distiller. It extracts the oil from the blossoms. Takes about fifty gallons of blossoms to produce a half cup of oil. And that's with Grosso, not Royal Velvet."

Rolling the lavender and the roses together, Ruby sniffed. "I'd love to see it sometime."

"I'm sure that could be arranged." He plucked another trio of buds, bruised them with his thumbnail, and breathed them in, almost meditatively. "It's a good crop this year."

"Why don't you take over the farm for Lavender?" Ruby asked. "You seem to like it."

He bent his head. "No, that's not my goal. I'm here to take care of the animals, to help her out."

Something about the slant of his jaw, the set of his shoulders, told her there was much more there than that. She used a trick she'd learned long ago, of simply being quiet to let someone talk, but he could out-quiet just about anyone.

"Why farmwork, Noah? Did you grow up on one?"

"Not really. My parents were farmworkers, and I grew up in that world, mostly in the Central Valley in California."

"So all kinds of farming." She rearranged her history of Noah, seeing him as a young man in the lettuce fields. "Are they from Mexico?"

He gave her a half grin. "Is that who works in the fields?"

"Oh, don't do that." Ruby met his gaze. "It's a legitimate question, not racist."

"I'll let you off the hook." He started walking down the row and gestured for Ruby to follow. "They are not from Mexico. My mom was half Mexican, half Anglo. My dad is Cheyenne and Ute with a little bit of Navajo thrown in for good measure."

"Ah." She flashed him a sideways grin.

"Brother! Did I tell you I am 1/120th Cherokee?"

His sun lines crinkled faintly, almost into a smile. "You did. I can see it in your sense of humor."

The baby swirled again, and she touched the place, smiling to herself.

"So that'll make the baby, what — 1/240th Cherokee?" Noah asked, straight-faced.

She snorted in laughter. "That's right. If it were true, which it isn't."

"I kinda guessed that."

"Be sweet to Hannah, will you? She's already got a big crush on you."

He nodded. "Poor kid. That's a rough story. Maybe she'll want to help me around the farm a little bit today. Her mom seemed like she could use a break." At the end of the row, he stopped. "Are you feeling better?"

The kindness, the way he stood there looking at her with concern, made her eyes prickle. She ducked her head. "I guess." She shrugged, tucking a lock of hair around her ear. "We've been broken up for nine months. I should be over it by now."

"Or not," he rumbled. "It takes as long as it takes. But you've got good friends, and everybody is really happy to help you with your baby."

"I know. I'm lucky."

"Cute, too. Hope you know that." He looked toward the treetops, the gesture of a shy person.

"Oh, yeah? Pregnant, throwing up, and now crying?"

"Still cute," he insisted. "Come on. I want to show you something." He held out his hand, and Ruby took it in the friendly way it was meant. His palm was calloused and hard. It felt like a hand you could trust.

"Did you come looking for me?" she asked.

"I went to your camper first." He didn't let go of her hand, and Ruby liked how much bigger he was next to her, tall enough that she had to look up to see his face. "You seemed upset yesterday."

A wash of grief moved over her, head to toes. "Yeah."

"It never seems like it when it happens," he said gruffly, "but when something breaks, there's usually a good reason."

Liam's face floated in front of Ruby. "I can't talk about it."

He nodded, tugging her through the break in the shrubs and down the hill toward the chickens. Their beds were made of hay, and a roof covered the wide, open space. Chickens wandered through, waddling to and fro, some busily, some lazily, all colors — white and gold and black and mottled variations of all sorts. A slight, dark woman of about twenty collected eggs carefully, yellow eggs and blue, pale green and the usual white and brown.

Noah spoke to her in Spanish, and she flashed a smile over her shoulder, shooting back something saucy and aloof. He laughed but didn't share it with Ruby. She peered into the basket at all the eggs.

"Over here," Noah said, and led Ruby to a nest where two tiger-striped kittens, eyes still closed, curled together with a pair of eggs.

"Oh!" Ruby cried. "That is the cutest thing ever. Can I touch them?"

"It's better not to handle them when they're so young." A chicken fluttered over, complaining loudly, and pecked at Noah's foot. "As you see."

They stepped back, and the chicken leapt up to the nest and settled protectively over the kittens and her eggs.

The girl raiding the nests said something arch, and Noah shot something back without looking at her. She wandered up the hill.

Ruby watched the girl's hips swaying exaggeratedly. "She's teasing you?"

"She says you are a woman with some curves, that's good."

"Great." She rolled her eyes. "Just what a jilted girl wants to hear."

"Women worry too much about being skinny," he said abruptly.

Ruby put her hands on her tummy. "I don't. I love this body, whatever shape it's in. Being sick teaches you that."

"I guess it would."

"I figured you for the silent type," Ruby said. "You're very talkative, actually."

"Not with everybody."

Ruby smiled.

A cell phone buzzed, and Noah slipped it out of his hoodie pocket. He glanced at the message. "Gotta go."

"Thanks," Ruby said. "For everything."

"De nada."

LAVENDER HONEY FARMS
yamhill co., oregon

Many of our lavenders are coming into full bloom as we head into the height of the season. We are beginning to harvest blossoms for a variety of uses, and we will be filling up our gift shop for the Lavender Festival, coming up in July. That's a glorious time to visit Yamhill County, so if you haven't done it, grab your husband or your daughter or maybe your best girlfriends and come tour the glories of lavender country.

We will be hosting more than a dozen workshops — some on culinary arts, some on decorative uses of lavender, some on photography and plein air painting, and even one on making perfume. Space is limited and these workshops fill up fast, so take a look at the full calendar and sign up today! A refundable five-dollar deposit will hold your place.

Lavender Honey Farms Schedule of Events

For the full description of the Lavender Festival, check out: http://www.oregonlavenderdestinations.com/festival.php.

CHAPTER 18

As she walked the perimeter of the farm at dawn on Friday, Lavender saw her old friend Ginger again. This time she sat on a wooden folding chair facing the blooming fields. A canvas was propped on an easel before her, and she had a palette in her right hand, a paintbrush in her left. Even at a distance, Lavender could see that the canvas was a blur of purple and blue.

Twice in life, Ginger had come to do this very thing, paint the lavender fields, so Lavender first thought it was a memory rising up out of the earth, as they so often did these days.

But then she noticed that Ginger's hair was long, spilling down her back in red curls. Her dress was airy and pink, a dress from another time. Lavender whistled for the dogs, compelled by something to walk up the hill toward the specter of her friend.

As Lavender approached, Ginger dipped

her brush into a small pool of color and dabbed it on the canvas. She wore a white apron over the front of her dress, but a little paint had stained the sleeve. It had always been that way with Ginger: She was one of the great natural beauties, but her dress was always a bit askew, her shoe had a grass stain, a hem was coming undone, and paint showed up everywhere — under her nails, in an eyebrow, in a smear on her elbow.

When Lavender saw her the first time, Ginger had behaved like the other ghosts — she didn't seem to know Lavender was there. This time, she looked up and smiled.

Her skin was translucent and unlined. Lavender had forgotten how startlingly clear her eyes were. How young they once had been!

"Are you coming for me?" Lavender said, without knowing she would.

"Are you ready?"

"Not today."

Ginger nodded, dipped her paintbrush, and again stroked color on the canvas.

"When?" Lavender asked.

Ginger smiled, the expression ever so slightly sad. "Soon, my friend."

A quick clutch of emotion seized Lavender's throat, and she looked away, overcome by a wild sense of loss. She took in the view of the flowers, the hills in the distance, the diffuse light of the cloudy day.

At the top of the hill, not a ghost but a solid human being was wading through the fields: Ruby. Surprisingly, Noah stood at the opening of the bushes. He had the most curious expression on his face, somehow hushed, as he watched the girl in the flowers, her light-blond hair caught beneath a kerchief, her curvaceous figure clasped by a T-shirt and jeans.

Not yet, Lavender thought. Not now. She turned her head to say so, but Ginger was gone, dissolved like a breath of mist into the day.

Not yet.

But, just in case, there were things that had to be done. Whatever attachment she felt to this earth belonged to the lavender and the chickens and the farm. She had to find an heir. Would it be Ruby? Or Ginny? Could it be the thing that would draw Hannah back from the moment she'd lost her father and sisters? Could Valerie stay here long enough to find her new place?

Lavender strode quickly toward the workshop and her office, filled with a sense of urgency the questions aroused. She had to get this settled.

CHAPTER 19

Ginny awakened in her bed, at first thinking she was at home. A breeze blew over her face and the bed was enormously comfortable. It was the gently moving ribs of her dog, panting quietly, that drew her into reality. The food poisoning, the guys at the door —

She bolted up, eyes flying open, and a pain stabbed the base of her neck.

"Whoa, there, girl," said a rumbling, rusty voice.

Ginny jumped practically out of her skin, a move that made tremors radiate through her limbs. A big hand landed on her shoulder. "Sorry, I didn't mean to startle you."

She peered at him, the face slowly coming into context. Gray eyes, that wavy salt-and-pepper hair. "Jack?" Her voice came out as cracked as an antique dish. "What —"

"How do you feel about a glass of water?"

She remembered then how sick she'd

been, the vomiting and diarrhea and terror and fever. She put a hand to her forehead, feeling that the fever had broken. "Maybe. What time is it? What day is it?"

"It's Friday, around seven-thirty, I guess."

"Wow." She felt dizzy, unable to fit the pieces together between last night and this morning. "Water is a good start. There are bottles in the fridge."

He fetched one, twisting the top off before he handed it to her. "Go easy."

Folding a hand over her tender belly, she sipped gingerly. The water was cold and poured down her parched throat in a welcome stream. "Whew."

He perched at the edge of the bed. "How are you?"

"Better, I guess." She realized that she was wearing a nightgown, and that had not been what she was wearing last night. A flush covered her neck. "Did you change my clothes?"

"Yeah, sorry. I thought it would help. You were soaked with sweat, completely delirious, when I got here. Was it food poisoning?"

"Pretty sure. What else comes on like that, right?" She sipped the water again and looked at him. "But how did you know to come help?"

"You texted me."

She frowned. "No. My phone is dead."

"Well, I got a text. Maybe it's okay now." He pulled his phone from his shirt pocket and punched a couple of icons to bring up a text: *From Ginny Smith: Urgent. Very sick at Grizzly Lake. Please come.*

A ripple of something unholy washed down Ginny's spine, completely out of proportion to the situation. She couldn't actually remember much past curling around Willow on the floor — maybe she *had* texted him.

She pointed to the counter by the sink. "There's a bowl of rice over there. My phone is inside. Will you get it for me?"

He followed her instructions, pulling the iPhone out of its nest. Ginny pressed the buttons to try to bring it up, first the home button, then the power button on top, just in case.

But some part of her knew it wouldn't work. The camera was blurry and dotted with water. The screen showed condensation beneath the glass. "No, this phone is absolutely dead."

"I don't know," he said with a shrug. "I got the text. I came. You were in bad shape, and I wasn't too happy about some boys over there having a big party."

A bolt of memory shot through her brain. "They tried to get in." She clutched a fistful of Willow's fur in her hand. "Willow barked like a crazy savage." She bent over and kissed her dog's nose. "Thank you, baby."

"Maybe it was Willow who texted me." He reached over and scrubbed the dog on the side of the face, and Willow gave a big smile, lifting up her chin so he would scratch her chest. "She wasn't too happy about you being so sick."

"How did you get in?"

"The locks aren't all that tough on something like this, sweetheart, which we're going to have a conversation about. Right now let's get you something easy to eat."

"Can you look up something for me on the Internet first? I need to call my friends and let them know what's going on."

"Sure."

She gave him the website address for Lavender Honey Farms and asked him to connect to the phone number. It went through and a woman answered. "Hi, I'd like to talk to Lavender Wills if possible."

"I'm sorry, she just headed out for supplies and won't be back for a couple of hours. Can I give her a message?"

"Yes, please. Tell her that Ginny Smith has run into a couple of delays, but I should be there late tonight or early tomorrow. My phone is not working."

"Hold on, let me write this down." The woman repeated key words aloud. "Ginny Smith. Delays. Phone out. Anything else?"

"Yes. Will you ask her to post something to my blog so my readers won't worry?"

"Oh, is this Ginny of 'Cake of Dreams'?"

"Yes."

"I read your blog every day! I love it. We have all been worrying about you since you didn't post yesterday. Has that ever happened before?"

"No. It's a long story, but if you wouldn't mind telling them that I'm safe, I'd really appreciate it."

"I'd be honored. I can't wait to meet you."

"Thank you." Ginny punched the exit button and handed the phone back to Jack. "I need a shower desperately. And I know you must need to get on the road, so I'll be fine now."

"I'm good," he said. "I called and let them know there was an emergency."

A sweetness swirled around her heart, colored pale green. "Really?"

"It's your freckles," he said, and winked. "Let me give you some privacy and you can get dressed, then we'll go get some easy-to-digest food in Butte. How's that?"

"Good," she said. "Really good."

She was very shaky but functional as they caravanned into Butte. It was a small town on the edge of the Rockies, the peaks still showing dirty white snow in some places. *Would that be a glacier?* Ginny wondered, pulling the trailer into a long space at the back of the parking lot. Jack parked his rig beside hers.

"How are you holding up?" Jack asked as they headed inside.

"Okay." Ginny scanned her body, feeling the weakness left over from the violence of the attack on her system. "It will be good to get some food."

The diner was clean and bustling, and they settled into a booth by the window. The seats were red leatherette, the view worth a million bucks — sharp, high mountains against a sky so blue it nearly hurt to look at.

Ginny shook her head. "I keep looking at the mountains and wondering what took me so long to get here. I feel like I was born in the wrong place."

Jack held the menu loosely in his hands, gazing out the window. When the light hit his eyes, the pupils contracted so much that the irises looked as if they were made of silver disks. Beautiful and, considering the weird text situation, creepy. Maybe he was a being from the other side, an angel sent to accompany her on this wild journey, or some kind of a ghost.

But his hands were those of a man. A raw cut marred the middle knuckle of his index finger. The nails were mostly even, but one looked as if it had been torn off too short some time ago. The skin was weathered and brown.

He shifted his gaze away from the window and settled it on her face. "What?"

"Nothing."

She looked over the menu carefully, asking her stomach what it could tolerate. *Nothing much,* it replied. *Tea and toast or Cream of Wheat to start.*

Jack asked, "If I order eggs and bacon, will the smells bother you?"

"I don't think so." She smiled. "No promises."

"Understood."

When the waitress had taken their order and headed away, Ginny said, "I'm feeling guilty about all this. You had to have been quite a ways down the road. Did you have to detour because of the fire?"

"I did. And don't worry about any of it. I called and made everything all right, and

I'll follow you into Portland."

"No," she said with a scowl. "I'll be fine."

He measured her. "I don't mind."

"I do." She met his gaze steadily. "I appreciate you coming back for me, appreciate everything you did, but I need to make this trip on my own."

He leaned back as the coffee and tea were delivered. "I swear I won't pressure you to do anything, if that's the problem. You're married, I get that." Ducking his head, he reached for a packet of sugar. "Did you . . . uh . . . get anything from Veronica?"

"A note, you mean?"

"Kinda silly, I guess."

"Not silly. Really touching and . . ." She found herself looking at his mouth, wondering what it would be like to taste it, how he would kiss. How he would touch her. How she might touch him. What it might be like to have a man inside her after all this time.

Her long-starved nerves rustled to attention. "I liked your note, Jack, and . . . I like to look at you, too. But I'm not the kind of person who has an affair."

"What if it's not an affair?"

She raised her eyebrows. "What does that mean?"

"What if we're just friends, Ginny? What if we stay in touch because we like to talk?

And maybe sometimes we can hang out."

She had a sudden flash of memory, his gentle hands washing her face and neck with a cool cloth. She had reached for his face, touched his cheek, and felt the whiskers on his jaw. The memory brushed every nerve in her body into full alert. "I don't know."

"We don't have to talk about it right now." He gave her a sideways smile. "I just finished listening to *Stranger in a Strange Land,* the old Heinlein book. You want to borrow it for the rest of your day?"

"Maybe I do," she said, accepting the shift in conversation. "I definitely do."

After breakfast, they walked out to their vehicles, slowly. Ginny let Willow out of the backseat and leashed her so they could walk along the side of the grass. "I bet she's going to be happy to get to the farm finally."

"She probably just likes to be with you, wherever that is," he answered, reaching down to scratch the scruff of Willow's black neck and her gold ears. He moved both hands over her, rubbing, stroking. "Her fur is great, so thick."

"She molts, though. *Giant* hunks of hair."

He stood. Brushed his hands off. Looked at his rig, then back to Ginny. "You going to be okay now?"

"Yep. The food did the trick. I'm a little tired, but I'll take it easy."

"Guess I'd better get a move on, then. You still have my phone number?"

"I do." Earnestly, she looked up. "Thank you so much for everything you did, Jack. I don't know how I got so lucky to have met you, but it was good luck for me." She hesitated. "Is it all right to give you a hug?"

"You bet." He opened his arms and Ginny moved forward, wrapping her free arm around his waist. His arms fell around her, and their bodies touched.

Time expanded, stretched, somehow turned upside down. As her chest touched his, as their arms locked around each other, she closed her eyes and turned her head so that she could press her cheek into his shoulder. His body was both harder and softer than she had expected — a little soft in the middle, very strong in the shoulders and arms, and she let herself really feel that, feel the body of a man against her own body. Her skin rippled faintly, up and down, and she caught another flash of memory, of him turning her away from him so he could take off her shirt and wash her back, protecting her privacy as much as possible. She thought of his hands on her skin and shuddered faintly. He held her closer, making a low sound in his chest.

But it was the scent of him that was her undoing. He smelled of himself, of man and bacon and the sugary essence of cake baking, and it cut through every inhibition she carried, as if it were a magic spell, as if he could change her just by being so close. His hand moved on her back, and Ginny raised her head, not letting him go. He looked down into her face, and she saw that he was not young, that there was loose skin around his jaw, those deep creases beside his eyes. Yet as he bent to kiss her, she could only think he was the most beautiful man she'd ever seen.

His lips touched hers and her knees literally went weak, buckling her closer to him. It was gentle, his mouth full and exploratory against her own. Only lips. Lips touching, pressing close, releasing, a series of small, then longer kisses. His hands moved on her back, and she found herself arching, wanting to rub her body back and forth across his.

His hands made their way into her hair, and she tipped her head backward into the clasp of his palms. "You smell like peaches," he said gruffly, and kissed her for real.

For real.

At the touch of his tongue, Ginny's body burst into flames and she could see the fire points: blazing nipples burning away her shirt, fire shooting from between her legs, melting her jeans, her fingertips burning away his clothes, searching for his skin, his bare skin, his —

She broke away. "I — uh —" She put her flaming fingers to her blazing mouth. Licking her tongue over her blistered lips, she took a step back, shaking her head. "I'm not that person. I'm sorry."

"Ginny —"

Shaking her head, she turned away, pulling Willow along. She felt the truth blazing down her spine, and some part of her — the biggest part of her, if she was truthful — wanted him to come after her, put his hands on her again, take away her clothes, and . . .

Dizzy with desire, she yanked open the car door and let Willow back in. The dog gave a soft whine, looking over her shoulder, but Ginny couldn't allow herself that last glimpse, lest she turn to salt like Lot's wife or, worse, a whore flinging herself at him, begging for just one night.

She closed the door and put her head on the steering wheel, breathing deeply to bring her soul back from wherever it had gone.

The smell of him lingered on her palms, maybe in her clothes, and she couldn't stop trembling.

After a minute, she heard his rig fire up and the gears moving. It eased past her, but she didn't look up until the sound of it had gone so far down the road that she couldn't hear it anymore.

Only then did she take a deep breath of relief, start the car, and get on the highway herself. After a few miles she even turned on the CD player, realizing that she'd forgotten to pick up the book he promised to lend her.

FROM: Ginny@cakeofdreams.com
TO: FoodieFour@yahoogroups.com
SUBJECT: checking in from Missoula, MT

I have had the weirdest twenty-four hours! Detour for a fire, food poisoning, ghostly visitations (not kidding!), help from strangers.

I am posting this from an Internet café in Missoula, Montana, and the place is grimy and filled with kids with backpacks who haven't bathed, so I'm not going into detail. Just wanted to let you know that my phone is dead and I can't get on the Internet without it, so don't worry. I had a nasty case of food poisoning, and I'm a little on the peaked side, so probably won't get there until morning.

Weird, weird stuff has happened. Good and weird, and weird and not so great, and just plain weird weird. Can't wait to tell you. Can't wait to SEE you all!

Will one of you go by the blog and post something? I've been trying and trying to get on and I can't access it. It's Wordpress — ginnycake and pwd frosting.

Love,
Ginny

FROM: Valerie@winedancer.com
TO: Ruby@flavorofabluemoon.com,
  Lavender@lavenderhoneyblog.com
SUBJECT: DON'T SPOIL THE
  SURPRISE!!!

Lavender and Ruby — don't let Ginny know I got here. I want to surprise her!!!

FROM: Valerie@winedancer.com
TO: FoodieFour@yahoogroups.com
SUBJECT: re: checking in from
   Missoula, MT

Thank goodness you're okay! It's not like you to be out of touch.

All is well with Hannah and me, except she's turning into a Lakota Indian and will run away from home when she turns sixteen to go on the powwow circuit.

Wish I could be there with all of you.
                                    Valerie

FROM: Ruby@flavorofabluemoon.com
TO: FoodieFour@yahoogroups.com
SUBJECT: re: checking in from
   Missoula, MT

Ginny! Ghostly visitations??? I cannot wait to hear about that.

We are eagerly awaiting your heralded arrival, *ma cherie.* They are building the dancing stage for Sunday night's festivities and stringing little tiny white lights, and we're all praying there will be no rain, only a big full blue moon.

The lavender is astonishing, Ginny-girl. You're going to have a field day (snort!) shooting it. I keep imagining you up to your ears in it, shooting, shooting, shooting. I was going to snap a pic on my cell phone for you, but that would spoil the stunning surprise of it!

Hurry, hurry, hurry. (But also be careful!)

Love,
Ruby

FROM:
  Lavender@lavenderhoneyblog.com
TO: FoodieFour@yahoogroups.com
SUBJECT: arrival

We have your parking spot swept and ready for you. We can't wait to see you and Willow, and Coco, the trailer!

Sounds like you found adventure, just as you hoped.

xoxo
Lavender

THE FLAVOR OF A BLUE MOON
a blog about great food . . .

Recipes   Appetizers
Main dishes   Sides   Sweets
Sort by Name   Sort by Category
About Ruby

A rainy day here at Lavender Honey Farms. We all want to be outside, dancing in the sunshine with the bees and the scent of lavender in the air like the promise of happiness and calm, but we are stuck indoors. Knitting, reading, looking up appropriate goddesses for one another. (It would spoil the surprise to tell you who is who, but check back Monday for a full report on our Blue Moon Festival, also known as Lavender's birthday.)

This kind of weather always makes me want comfort food. Lots of omnivores think that comfort food and veganism are incompatible terms, but here is a dish you could happily serve to any meat eater, and (shhh!) they'll never know the difference.

KINDLY SHEPHERD'S PIE

Serves 4 generously

Olive oil, 2 T, plus 1 T

2 ribs celery, 1 monster onion, 2–3 carrots, all diced

5 cloves garlic, smashed, peeled, roughly chopped

1 medium parsnip, diced (optional. Some people don't like the sweetness of this vegetable, but I really, really do)

1 cup fresh or frozen peas

1 T tomato paste

1 qt. high-quality vegetable broth

1 bottle heavy red wine, such as zinfandel (the deeper the body, the better)

2 T tamari

Splash of Worcestershire sauce

1 T fresh thyme

1 cup porcini mushrooms, cleaned and sliced

1 cup button mushrooms, cleaned and sliced

2 cups ground-meat substitute, such as Quorn or MorningStar Farms crumbles

4 large red potatoes, peeled and diced (or, for a more rustic dish, leave the skins on)

1/2 cup margarine

1/2 cup soy or coconut milk

Salt and pepper to taste

Prepare all vegetables except potatoes and

have them ready. In a Dutch oven or heavy, large saucepan, heat 2 T olive oil (or more — this is not a high-fat dish, so using 3–4 T would not be amiss). Add onions, garlic, celery, carrots, parsnip, and cook over medium heat until softened. Add tomato paste and stir into vegetables.

Open the wine. Pour one generous glass for yourself, then pour the rest in the pan.

Add vegetable broth, spices, and tamari, and bring to a boil. Lower heat and simmer until liquid is reduced by at least half.

Meanwhile, peel (or don't) the potatoes, cut into chunks, and cover with water.

Bring to a boil, then slightly lower heat. Simmer until potatoes are tender.

Taste broth, correct seasonings. Add peas and mushrooms, and ground-meat substitute if you are using it, and let simmer on low heat while potatoes cook.

Heat oven to 400 degrees.

When potatoes are tender, drain the water and add margarine. Mash or whip until the potatoes are smooth, then add milk to make a slightly soft mash.

Taste the stew. Liquid should be thick and velvety, with a rich, deep taste. If it needs more flavor, add salt or a little more tamari, or one cube of veggie bouillon. If it is not thick enough, remove some liquid from the pan, stir together with two tablespoons of flour until very smooth, then add back into the stew and let thicken.

When the stew is right, pour it into a 10-inch glass pie pan or cast-iron skillet and top with mashed potatoes until it is covered completely. Using a spoon or fork, make peaks in the potatoes so they will get brown and beautiful in the oven.

Place under broiler for five minutes or so, just to brown the top. Let cool for five minutes; serve in generous portions.

CHAPTER 20

It started to pour down buckets of rain around lunchtime. The women huddled in the tiny living room of the cottage, arranged on the deep couches and overstuffed chairs with fading tapestry patterns. Ruby draped her legs over one side of her chair and settled her laptop on her thighs. She refreshed email every so often, but so far there had been nothing from Liam. Maybe he wouldn't even acknowledge the email.

That would be terrible.

Valerie knitted a sweater from soft wool the colors of a harvest table, her reading glasses perched on her perfectly straight, elegant nose. Hannah, hair simply braided out of the way, slumped in a corner of the couch, reading a Western romance novel with an old-school cover of a bare-chested Native American man with feathers in his hair. He looked, Ruby thought, a bit like Noah. That aggressive nose, the strong shoulders.

Lavender sat at the table shoved up against the wall, going over paperwork of some kind. She fiddled with her pencil, flipping it back and forth.

"I wish it would stop raining!" Hannah growled. "This is so boring!"

"You're reading," Valerie said mildly. "There are other books in the trailer."

"I'm kinda sick of reading, all right?"

"You want to play a game or something?" Ruby asked. "I saw a backgammon board over there."

"No." Hannah caught her mother's sidelong glance and added, "Thanks."

Ruby was bored, too. Hours of rain were no fun for anyone. She hit the refresh button again, then, tired of herself, typed in "mead." A long list of websites scrolled open, history and supplies and legends and lore. She clicked on one at random and found a medieval-looking site, dark as an oak barrel. *The drink of Vikings and medieval kings!* it proclaimed. In the back of her mind, a lute played a lively tune, and she had a vision of a woman in a red and gold dress dancing on a stage. "Maybe we should all dress up for the Blue Moon Festival," she said. "Like in costume or something."

"*Now* you tell me," Valerie said. "I have

three tutus in various styles in boxes somewhere on the way to San Diego."

Ruby hooted in delight. "Tutus! That
would be so cool, wouldn't it? We could be
barefoot ballerinas."

Lavender grinned. "You girls would look
lovely. I'd look like a silly old bat."

"No, no, no!" Ruby cried. "You would be
the Snow Queen! We could put you in a" —
she narrowed her eyes — "a silver tutu, with
lavender flowers in your hair."

"A Snow Queen with flowers in her hair?"
Lavender said with a snort.

"Maybe it's not a Snow Queen, then, but
I'm right about the flowers and the dress.
And, Hannah, I see you in orange, or maybe
red — Persephone." A shiver ran over her
arms at this, seeing it in her mind.

"Who is Persephone?"

Valerie, without ceasing her knitting for a
single moment, said, "She is Demeter's
daughter, who was stolen by Hades and
taken to hell. It is a myth about winter and
the renewal of spring."

"Eww. I don't want to be her."

Ruby rubbed her hands on her thighs.
"Her mother saves her, and she becomes
the queen of the underworld, very powerful."

"Who would you be, Ruby?" Valerie asked,

again not skipping a beat. "Demeter?"

"I'm not wise enough. I would wear blue, I think. Who wears blue?"

"Demeter," Lavender said.

"Who else?"

Hannah tapped into her phone. "How about Ariadne? She is a moon goddess, which we would need, right? And she's called the high fruitful mother."

Ruby pointed at Hannah. "There you go. That's me. Ariadne."

"Isn't she also a storyteller?" Valerie said. "The weaver of tales."

"Whatever. I love the fruitful-mother part."

Hannah, still scrolling through her phone, added, "And she's blond."

"Okay," Ruby said, wiggling in her chair. "Lavender is the Snow Queen. Hannah is Persephone. I'm Ariadne. Who are you, Valerie?"

"Oh, I don't know." Her voice was droll and she looked over her glasses. "The queen of something, I expect."

Ruby laughed. "With rhinestone sparklies, right?"

"And a crown."

Hannah laughed, too. "And a — what do you call the thingy they hold, with jewels on the end?"

"A staff?" Ruby guessed.

"Scepter," Valerie said.

The back door slammed and Hannah sat up hurriedly, smoothing her T-shirt. Sure enough, it was Noah, carrying his beauty like a heavy weight, head down. What must that be like, Ruby wondered, to be the man in a room for whom all the women straightened? She wanted to put him at ease. "Noah! We are thinking we should be barefoot goddesses for the Blue Moon Festival. We will need some gods."

"Come again?"

She gave him her best dimple, raising an eyebrow and a shoulder. "What god would you be if you could be any?"

"Not god material, I'm afraid. Lavender, we have some issues with the ice machine. Can I talk to you about it?"

"Again the ice machine?"

"It's giving out."

"Hmm." Lavender put down the pencil and took her reading glasses off. "Let me think about it."

"All right."

She gestured to the last empty chair in the room. "Sit a minute, why don't you?"

"Nah, I've got —"

She pointed at the chair, tapped her finger in the air. *Sit.*

He settled gingerly on the very edge. Scratched his temple.

"What god would you be, Noah, my dear?"

He scowled. "I don't know. I don't know any gods."

"Hannah," Ruby said. "Look up some gods that suit him." She turned back, smiling. "I'm going to be Ariadne."

"How about Hades?" Hannah/Persephone piped up. "He's the god of the underworld."

Lavender grinned. "Well, that fits, doesn't it?"

"Sure, whatever. I'll be Hades. But I'm not dressing up and I'm not going barefoot."

Ruby laughed, the sound emerging from somewhere deep in her chest. People had always commented on her husky, robust laugh. "No toga, no sandals?"

He looked at her a beat too long, his eyes full of sleepy suggestions. "A sheet, maybe."

"We vote for that," Ruby replied evenly. "Just you in a sheet."

Slowly, he rubbed his hands together. "What are you wearing?"

"I don't know. We have to find tutus now, don't we, girls?"

"What's a tutu?"

"It's what dancers wear onstage," Hannah volunteered. "My mom was the first black

266

prima ballerina in Cincinnati."

"No kidding." Noah gave Valerie a genuine smile, and Ruby swore the lights in the room started to short out. "That's cool. That must have been a lot of hard work."

She gave an elegant shrug. "Dancing is hard work, period. I was lucky to have a lot of support."

"And she's going to be a queen of something," Hannah said.

"How about you, hon?" he asked.

"Oh," she ducked her head, toed the edge of a rug. "Not quite sure."

Ruby raised a brow toward Valerie, and Valerie sucked her top lip into her mouth. "Can we actually get tutus somewhere, do you think?" Ruby asked. "Like, rent them? We only have one day."

Lavender said, "I'm not wearing a tutu. I'm too old."

"Oh, yes," Ruby said, "you so are. You're the birthday girl."

"What about Ginny? What would she like, do you think?"

"The cake queen? Who would that be?" Ruby pointed to Hannah. "Goddess seeker, find us a cake goddess."

"Looking." She punched in a phrase, frowned, tried another. "I'm getting a bunch of blogs and cake shops."

"Hmm."

"Artemis," Lavender said. "Ginny is Artemis."

Inexplicably, Ruby wanted to cry. "Oh, that's beautiful."

"Who is Artemis?" Valerie asked. "I can't remember all this stuff. It's been a long time since college."

"I'll look it up," Hannah said.

In her pocket, Ruby's phone started to play a song. Jason Mraz's "I Won't Give Up."

She slapped her hand over it. "Crap. Crap. Crap! It's Liam. What do I do?"

"Answer it," Lavender said firmly. "It's got to be done."

With a shard of ice sticking through her heart, Ruby stood and answered the phone, heading for the back porch. "Hello?"

"Hey, Ruby," he said, as if he were a westerner, not a New Yorker. The sound of his baritone voice, dark and honeyed, flowed down her neck. She hunched her shoulders, using an arm to cover her ribs.

"Hey, Liam. I guess you got my email."

"Yeah." Silence rocketed down the line. "I don't know what to say."

"I don't know. I just thought you should hear the news."

"I thought you couldn't get pregnant,

because of all the chemo and shit."

"Radiation. It's chemo and radiation." She peered through the screens around the porch at the rain obscuring everything with a blurry gray. "I thought it was impossible, too, but I guess it wasn't."

"So we had sex for six years and you got pregnant the very last time?" Only now did she catch the hostility in his voice. "Is that right?"

She took a breath. This was the side of him she hated, the cold-bastard side, the inquisitor who could turn off all emotion and make her feel like a foolish, stupid child.

Not this time. "Yep," she said.

"It sounds like bullshit to me. Like you're just trying to fuck up my wedding to Minna. Your timing is —"

"Stop." Ruby took a breath. "I don't need anything from you. I don't want anything from you. I wouldn't have told you at all, but my friends thought you deserved to know. So — have a nice life, Liam. I don't need you."

"Ruby! Don't hang up!"

She waited, her throat as tight as if she had drunk poison. Hearing his breath through the line made the fine hairs on her neck rise, as if in readiness for his lips. She had a vision, a sudden, shocking, disturbing

269

vision, of his naked penis, red and crooked, as he came toward her on the bed, once upon a time. How she had grown to love it, like his voice, like his hands with their rough calluses!

Where had he gone, her lover? "Liam, it's like . . . a miracle."

"It's like a lie, Ruby. You can't really expect me to believe you."

The words splatted against her face, cold and whole. "Have you ever known me to lie? Ever?"

"No. But you break up pretty bad."

"Gosh, I can't imagine why, after we were the couple of the century for six years."

"It's over."

"I know that!" she yelled. "I got it." A sharp pain burst over her eyebrows, and she put her hand over it. "Speak your mind, Liam. I don't have all day while you think of a posture — but you know as well as I do that I would not lie about something like this."

The line hummed. "I know."

"Look, I'm going to hang up. Talk to me later or don't. It's up to you."

A half beat of silence. "Minna doesn't want me to talk to you. She'll be pissed as hell that I called you today."

"So we don't have to talk at all. I just

270

wanted to do the right thing."

"I want to. I want to send you money."

"You know I don't need any money, Liam." It had been such a sore point between them, his alternating jealousy and delight in her father's extreme fortune. "Don't worry about any of it. I'm fine."

"It *is* a miracle, though, isn't it?" His tone was hushed. "The baby? Like what if I never have another one? What if you don't?"

This was how he swayed her — not the swagger or the charm. His genuine bewilderment at life sometimes, his desire to find the numinous in things. "I can't tell Minna. It will destroy her."

The dagger-shaped icicle in her heart twisted. "Right."

"I'm really sorry, Ruby. I did love you, you know."

"Don't," she said, and hung up.

CHAPTER 21

After the phone call with Liam, Ruby paced the porch for fifteen minutes, trying to pull herself together, to calm her racing heart and shaking hands, to erase the lingering spill of his voice. In her belly, the baby swooped, but Ruby didn't feel even slightly nauseous.

Huh. She'd thrown up only once today. Maybe it was getting better.

She needed to cook. Popping her head into the other room, she said, "I'm going to my trailer for a while."

"Everything all right?" Lavender said, looking up.

"Not really. I just need to cook. I'll be back later."

"Take an umbrella from the foyer."

Noah had settled on the floor on one side of the coffee table. Hannah sat on the other. A backgammon board was open between them. "Your move," he rumbled to Hannah.

She picked up the dice and rolled. Valerie watched the game over her reading glasses, needles clicking along.

"Don't stay gone forever," she said. "We have some planning to do."

Ruby nodded and ducked into the rain. It pattered softly on the umbrella, enveloping her in a soft quiet that eased the back of her neck very slightly. Out in the rain, with no one watching, she could let the tears fall down her cheeks, embarrassing, stupid tears that showed her weakness.

What was this craziness with Liam, anyway? She sliced through the long grass of the meadow, getting the hems of her jeans soaking wet. It wasn't as if she'd never had a boyfriend before him. She'd had plenty. She'd slept with some of them, too.

Why was she hanging on? It didn't make any sense. It was making her miserable. She had to find a way to get over it.

As she approached the Airstream kitchen, she heard a little mewp. From the shelter under the trailer, a pair of gold eyes peered out of the darkness. They looked as if they were floating, then her black face disappeared in the shadows. Ruby blinked, once. Mewp.

"Oh, poor baby!" She reached down and scooped the kitten up. Ninja Girl wiggled up to Ruby's shoulder, her fur wet and cold against her neck. Ruby stroked her, turning her face to kiss the kitten's soft side. "See," she said, adding aggrievement to the yeasty brew of her emotions. "This is why humans sometimes need to intervene. Why aren't you in the barn?"

As soon as the trailer door was open, Ninja Girl jumped inside and delicately ran over to the licked-clean saucer on the floor by the table. "Mewp!" she said, blinking over her shoulder at Ruby.

Ruby allowed a chuckle to break up some of the craziness in her chest. "You're a hungry thing! Luckily," she said, opening one of the cupboards, "I stocked up on the yucky stuff you like. How about salmon with greens?" She held up the can. Ninja Girl twirled around her ankles.

This was why old ladies had too many cats, Ruby thought. She scooped the food onto the dish, and the kitten delicately ate one tiny bite at a time, chewing each three hundred times, like a proper lady. When Ruby ran her fingers over the cat's spine, she arched upward, purring between bites. Her fur was as soft as a powder puff Ruby had as a little girl. Someone once brought scented talcs to the hospital ward, and the girls all smelled like sweet musk and baby powder for months after.

The feeling of Ninja Girl's fur, the sound of her little purr, eased the wild craziness of Ruby's mood. She settled on the floor with her laptop and checked her email, thinking maybe Liam would have followed up, but there was nothing, of course.

She wished she had a mother or a sister to talk to, someone to whom she could confess her incredible foolishness and finally hear an answer. She wanted advice, a map to follow, a drug to take, something that would sever her connection to a man who did not love her anymore.

As she mulled it over, Ruby suddenly realized it was classically calm Ginny to whom she could unburden herself. She opened an email and wrote:

FROM: Ruby@flavorofabluemoon.com
TO: Ginny@cakeofdreams.com
SUBJECT: JUST TO YOU

I'm falling apart and trying not to let anyone see it, but I know you have a daughter my age, and maybe you'll have advice. I can't talk to my dad, because he worries SO MUCH, and Lavender is great but she's never really been all mixed up in relationships, you know?

She poured out everything that was weighing on her, asked for advice, and sent the email. Then she leaned back against the cupboards. Ninja Girl licked her paw, black tail curled around her other feet, the white socks peeking out from beneath it.

After a few minutes Ruby got to her feet, feeling the dampness of her clothes. She could change in a little while. The edges of her tongue fluttered with flavors — onions and garlic, rich broth, peas and carrots. She would make a shepherd's pie for their dinner, for everybody. On the counter, she lined up her ingredients: olive oil and potatoes, a good boxed vegetable broth since time was too short to make her own. She lacked a bottle of red wine — of course, she didn't buy it now, because she was pregnant — and she knew from long experience that it made a big difference in the depth of the dish. She called Lavender's cell phone. "Hey, do you have a bottle of red wine?"

"Of course. I bought some yesterday. But you're not drowning your sorrows, are you?"

"No! No way. I'm making dinner for everybody, and I need some wine for it."

"Ah. I'll send a bottle over, then. What time is supper?"

Ruby glanced at the Felix the Cat clock

on the wall, which reminded her that Felix was a tuxedo cat. She grinned at Ninja Girl. "Around six. I'll bring it over when it's finished."

"What can we add?"

"Bread and salad — fruit or vegetable, it doesn't matter."

"Done."

When she hung up, Ruby pulled up a cooking playlist and set it to *play* on the speakers. Humming along with Pink, she smashed garlic cloves and peeled them, slid the wrapper from an onion and set it aside. The carrots and celery were slightly limp, so she put them in a bowl with ice water to crisp up.

A knock at the door sent the kitten skittering for a hiding place. She scrambled in one direction, tried to get under the stove, streaked behind the table.

"It's me, Ruby," Noah called. "It's raining out here, you know?"

She yanked open the door. "Sorry! Come in. I was making the world safe for a certain Ninja Girl."

His head and shoulders were soaked, and he leapt up the steps and into the trailer with a bottle of wine in hand. Water dripped down his nose, and Ruby laughed again. "I am sorry." She gave him a dish towel and he handed over the wine.

"Oooh, good one," Ruby said, reading the label. "Thanks for bringing it over."

Noah rubbed his face and shoulders. Then, in a move that took her completely by surprise, he leaned in and shook his curls, sending water all over her.

Ruby shrieked and held up her hands. "Ick! Stop, stop!"

He grinned, the curls falling around his face in black ringlets. His teeth were not quite perfect but they were very white, and his tanned skin glistened with the rainwater. "You gonna drink that whole bottle yourself?"

"I'm not drinking any of it," she said. "I'm pregnant!"

"How about pouring me a glass, then, and I'll be your sous chef." He lifted his chin at the unchopped veggies.

Ruby smelled him over the onions — cloves and sweat and a note like the breeze over the ocean. It made her think that his skin would taste like the ocean, like the tang and salt left after a wave swept over your body. "There's not a lot of room in here."

"You mean you want to be alone to brood."

She shrugged, touched the swell of her belly. "More like think things over."

"What things, sweetheart?" He took the bottle out of her hand, opened a drawer and then another until he found the corkscrew. "How bad you feel?" Expertly, he sliced the foil, slipped the cork from the bottle, waved it under his nose, and gave a small nod. It surprised her somehow. She would have said he was a beer man, or maybe whiskey. Most soldiers weren't big on wine. "Is that thinking making you feel better?"

She sucked her top lip into her mouth, let it go. "Not exactly."

He opened a cupboard, finding glasses on the first try, and poured a substantial amount into a highball glass, then gave her the bottle. "Let me help you."

His eyes were almost copper colored, like a river in late summer, and when he looked at her, she almost thought she could see the rippling currents. "There really isn't room for two," she repeated.

"It's fine." He tasted the wine, a very small sip. "Mmm. That's good."

Ruby gave him a knife. "Chop the onions." She took out another cutting board and stood beside him. "Where did you learn about wine?"

"I worked vineyards a lot as a teenager. Napa, Sonoma. You learn a lot."

She nodded. "Did you know Valerie was a

wine blogger before her husband died?"

"Huh. Quite a Renaissance woman — maybe I should talk to her. I keep thinking it would be a kick to try some vines here. With the bees and the lavender — could be interesting." His hands were deft and strong, with long fingers and good technique. "She quit?"

"Yeah. She says she's not sure she wants to write about it anymore. It makes her think of her old life."

"I can see that." He scraped the diced onion into a bowl and plucked a celery stalk out of the water. "How much celery?"

"Couple ribs. Thinly sliced." Ruby poured the onion into the olive oil and stirred it. The heat was not high. She added the garlic, stirred again, sprinkled in a little bit of sea salt, then took a carrot from the bowl and began to trim it. "When I think about her life and everything she's lost, it makes me feel like a stupid little girl for all my whining."

"It's not a contest." Painstakingly, he sliced the celery, making sure each piece was the same size as the next. "And you haven't had an easy time, either."

"I know. She's just so together, really, so brave. Even at the funeral, she was dignified." Ruby made a face. "Not my forte, I guess."

"You're not a drama queen, though. You're a very cheerful person."

"Am I?" She looked up at him, suddenly vulnerable. "I want to be. It seems like a waste to be grouchy if you have a single new day on this earth, but since I broke up with Liam — or, rather, since he broke up with me — I've had a lot of days of wallowing."

He pulled another rib of celery out of the water, cut off the end, and took a crunching loud bite, then offered it to her. To her surprise, Ruby leaned forward and snapped off the next bite. "I love celery," she said.

"Me, too."

He was really very close, those heavy ringlets asking to be twined around her fingers, that triangle of throat asking for lips. To her absolute amazement, she reached for a curl. "You have the prettiest hair. But I guess you hear that from all the girls."

"None as pretty as you."

A red-tinted glow filled the air as they stood there. Noah looked at her mouth, and for a minute she thought he might kiss her. She thought she might kiss him.

But a new love affair wasn't the answer. Not until she was over the old one. She turned back to the onions and gave them a stir, added the carrots. "I sometimes use parsnips in this dish, but they are a little sweet."

"I am pretty sure I've never had a parsnip in my life."

"They look like giant white carrots." From the corner of her eye, she spied a black nose sticking out from the cupboard. "Don't look now, but Ninja Girl is slipping out of hiding."

He shifted with great care, and they both watched the kitten ease very, very slowly out of the closet and into her potato-box bed. She settled, paws turned under her chest, and blinked at them. "Wow," Ruby said, "she's just got me."

"They do that. Kittens and cats, puppies and dogs. I love that pack of dogs that follows Lavender around."

"Do you have any cats or dogs?"

"Two cats at the moment." He sipped the wine, put his knife in the sink. "I had a dog in Iraq, but he got killed."

"Oh, dude. That sucks."

He swallowed. "Yeah. It's been a while now, but I miss him. His name was Duke, and he was a beautiful black German shepherd. Smarter than most people, and loyal as hell. And you know, it's just good to have a dog in that world."

"I can't imagine that world, not even a little. I can't imagine why anybody wants to go."

"I was eighteen and didn't have a lot to look forward to. Not like somebody was going to send me to college, and I wanted out of the fields in the worst way. Army gave me an out."

"You were in Iraq?"

"Three times; once in Afghanistan."

"You never got injured?"

"Yeah, but never bad enough to get sent home. They send you to the hospital, give you a break, and then you go back."

"Hand me the vegetable broth, will you?" She popped it open and poured it into the pot, along with the wine. "Oh, crap. I just realized I don't have mushrooms! What was I thinking?"

"We can run down to Gaston. It won't take ten minutes."

"Yeah? Let's do it." She pulled off the apron she wore, hung it on a hook, and turned the heat off beneath the pot. She eyed the glass, from which he'd taken only a few sips. "You drive."

He tugged his keys out of his pocket. "I can do that."

In the truck, she said, "I didn't mean to cut you off. About Iraq."

"It's all right. I don't really talk about it that much."

"But *I* am a good listener." She gave him a sideways grin. "You probably want to tell me everything."

He laughed softly. "Do I?"

"You do. Everybody does. I get the most amazing stories from people. Once, on a ferry, this man told me about coming out to his wife and every single thing that happened that night."

"Ugh. Why didn't you stop him?"

Ruby propped her elbow on the window ledge, thinking about that stooped little man in a very expensive suit, his thin hair brushed carefully over his pate. His eyes were watery and brown and kind, which was why she'd sat down next to him. "I didn't want to stop him. It was an honor to listen. Now I can carry it with me, right? And somebody heard him."

Noah glanced at her, then had to focus on the left turn onto the county highway. Once he got on the road, he flipped on his lights to guide them through the gray afternoon, the windshield wipers slicing back and forth, back and forth. "Who do you tell your stories to?"

"I don't."

"To your boyfriend?"

284

"Sure, some of them."

"The cancer stories?"

"No." She shifted, wiggled a foot, crossed her arms. "I don't like to be defined by that."

"I get that. But, you know, as much as I don't want to be defined by my years as a soldier, there's no getting away from it. I came to the farm to sort through it."

"Like Duke the dog?"

He glanced in the rearview mirror. "Yeah. Like the dog. Like the guys who died, and all the little kids, and all the things you do and wish you hadn't in a war."

Ruby watched his face for a long minute. "When I first found out that I was sick, I told my best friend, and she told her mom, and then we couldn't play together anymore."

"Dude." He looked at her. "That sucks."

She nodded.

They hit the outskirts of a very small village. She saw the lights of a grocery store shining through the rain. Noah parked in front, turned off the car. "When I got my orders to deploy the fourth time, I seriously thought about wrecking my car into a lamppost and hoped that I would just get injured, not killed."

"Dude," she said, and smiled. "That sucks."

Again she made him laugh. "Come on, let's get your mushrooms."

When they got back from the grocery store, Noah carried the bags into the trailer — they'd picked up more than just mushrooms — the weight of them showing off the veins and cords in his forearms. He settled everything on the counter and said, "Now what?"

He took up too much space, that was what. "I'm fine, Noah," she said, taking mushrooms and more onions out of the bags. He lined bottles of Pellegrino on the counter.

"But I have wine to drink, remember?" He picked up the glass and took a sip, a wicked smile on his mouth.

"You're in the way." She turned the heat back on beneath the pot.

"I'll make myself useful." He grabbed the porcini mushrooms. "These need slicing, I guess?"

She felt sparks along the side of her body that was close to him. They were sharp and pointed, like the pricks of sparkler stars. "Fine," she snapped. "Slice them." She whirled around to put the bottles in the

286

fridge and had to slide them in on their sides.

When she stood up, he was a bit too close again, and she had to duck around him, her hip grazing his hip. It was like this, cooking. She'd grown used to it, learned how to ignore the accidental brush of a hand over a butt or a breast or any number of other intimate combinations that could occur in a kitchen.

To drown her thoughts, she slapped her iPhone into the dock. Florence and the Machine poured out, "Kiss with a Fist." "What kind of music do you like?"

He settled the washed mushrooms on the counter and dried his hands. "I'm just your basic boring guy. Little bit of everything. Hip-hop and rock. You're probably much cooler than me, seeing as how you've been living in New York City and all." A slow sideways glance. "And you grew up in San Francisco, right?"

She glanced her own sideways way. "Are you teasing me?"

"Would I do a thing like that?"

"You might be trying to cheer me up."

"Maybe." He brushed her elbow with his own. "Is it working?"

She nudged the place where Liam lived and found it less raw. "Yes."

"Good." Neatly, he sliced the mushrooms. "I like you, Ruby."

"I bet you say that to all the girls."

"Well, I do. But it's not usually true." He settled a mushroom slice on the back of her hand. "I can be myself with you."

She laughed and popped the mushroom into her mouth. "I'm not sure whether that's a good or bad thing."

"You're stuck now."

"Am I?"

He nodded, those eyes glinting with summer flashes. "You like me, too."

CAKE OF DREAMS

Why would I give you anything but this?

Sorry to be out of touch, friends, and sorry for all the worry! All is well, just had some technical problems.

Pippin987

We were so worried!

READ 268 MORE COMMENTS >>>>

CHAPTER 22

It was impossible to speed while dragging the trailer, but Ginny came close. As she drove through the mountains and into Washington State toward Oregon, she gunned it as hard as she could, fleeing the idiotic spectacle of herself kissing a stranger.

"Kissing" him didn't even begin to describe it, really — she'd flung herself at him, rubbing against him like a cat in heat.

Tears stung her eyes as the scene played itself out over and over and over again. Tears of humiliation, tears of longing, but, mostly, tears of fury.

If Matthew had not been so mean-spirited as to withhold all sex, she wouldn't have been in this position in the first place. She would never have driven alone across the country, inviting trouble and attention. She wouldn't have been tempted by the craggy voice and tender kiss of another man.

She wouldn't be so horny right now that

her skin was about to combust all by itself. They would find her car at the side of the road, her body a pile of ashes in the seat.

Everything she'd been thinking spilled out, as if that kiss had knocked down all the walls she'd built around herself. She was furious with her husband. Furious with him for getting her pregnant in the first place so she had to quit school — and it had been calculating on his part. He hadn't wanted her to go to Wichita, to be on campus with all those other boys. He kept pestering her to transfer to community college. She swore he'd put a hole in a condom to make sure she didn't run away.

Or maybe that was too mean. Maybe it had been an accident, but that didn't change what happened. She'd dropped out of school, just like he wanted. She had her baby, her darling Christie, and that part she wouldn't trade for all the money in the world, but when she suggested that the baby could go to day care and Ginny could go to school part-time, Matthew had thrown a fit.

And then — *then!* — he stopped having any kind of sex with her at all, refused to go to counseling, refused to try medication or even to satisfy her ever, and expected her to take it.

Which she — doormat of the century —

had done.

Crossing over a bridge, she slammed her hand on the wheel again. "Why have I been such a wimp? Why did I let him do that? Why did I let my friends treat me like I'd done something wrong when the blog did so well? I made that blog!"

Willow leaned forward and licked her ear.

"I know. I'm not mad at you. I'm really mad at myself."

But all of that evaporated as she found herself, at last, driving along the Columbia River. It was as different from the mountains as the mountains were different from the plains, but just as beautiful, maybe even more so. It was lush and green and . . . quiet-seeming as any landscape she'd yet seen. It eased her, that green, that shining water beneath a sky filled with puffy gray clouds.

She stopped at a campground on the banks of the river. It was fairly full and boasted a little store at the center with — she gave a silent cheer — Wi-Fi. She picked up some fresh bread and made a supper of a grilled cheese sandwich, which she ate sitting in her camp chair, looking up at the bluffs.

I am never going back to Kansas.

The thought was so clear and direct and

whole that she knew it was true.

"I am never going back to Kansas," she said aloud, and laughed, feeling as buoyant as if she were a suddenly untethered balloon, as if she could float up into that gray sky and never look back.

It made her dizzy.

Never going back. Never, never, never.

Willow sat watching the river, alert for stray lambs that might need rescue, and looked up at Ginny's laughter. Her tail swept across the dirt. *I'm happy if you're happy.*

Ginny carried her glass and plate inside, hearing the faint sound of old-fashioned music again. Her ghostly music. "Thanks," she said aloud.

No one said, "You're welcome," but it was in the air, dancing on the music.

She sat down at the laptop, realizing that the past couple of days without Internet were the longest she'd gone without being connected in years. It was weirdly liberating, but she was also craving contact. Desperately.

The first note she wrote was to Matthew.

FROM: Ginny@cakeofdreams.com
TO: msmith@greatinsurance.com
SUBJECT: I'm fine & something else

Matthew,

If you tried to call, you know that I haven't been answering my phone, because I dropped the darn thing in the dishwater.

I have realized on this trip that I am not happy. I'm not happy with Kansas. I'm not happy with my friends. I'm not happy around my family.

And I am not happy with you, which I am pretty sure you already know very well. We have not had sex in twelve years, Matthew. TWELVE YEARS! That's ridiculous, and I'm not putting up with it anymore.

I am not coming back to Kansas.

I am filing for divorce.

This is final, and I don't want to have a big discussion about it. The time for discussion was ten years ago. Or five years ago, or maybe even last year.

I'm telling you first, and you have a head start of two days. Then I'm telling Christie, my sisters, and my mother. I probably won't bother to tell the girls, except Karen.

Sorry to do this by email, but the phone is dead and you'd just throw a big fit. The easiest thing is to do this fast, sharp, and clean.

Ginny

For a long moment she stared at the screen, nudging her heart and liver and belly to see how they felt about this. She remembered, in a flood, all the small humiliations of the past twelve years. His rejection of her, his annoyance when she walked around in her underwear — or, God forbid, naked. His fury at her when she had joined him in the shower that last time, shoving her away in utter disgust.

She thought of how it felt to drive this trailer, to make herself meals, to continue the important parts of her life now — her dog and her friends and her work — even when she wasn't at home.

Last, she thought of the blasting, burning fury of her desire this morning, a normal response to a normal stimulus, the healthy response of a healthy woman who wanted to have a normal sex life like a normal fortysomething. Tears stung again.

But instead of *send,* she hit *save.*

Courage fail.

FROM: Ginny@cakeofdreams.com
TO: Justbake@git.com
SUBJECT: SORRY BEYOND BELIEF

Sweet Mavis,

I hope you can forgive me for not showing up. Three things happened:

#1 I drowned my phone in the dishwater first thing yesterday morning.

#2 I had to turn back when the fires crossed the highway, routing me away from Boise and up through Montana.

#3 I ate some bad food and had a serious case of food poisoning.

#2 meant I couldn't get there. #1 meant I didn't have access to your phone number or email address, and #3 meant I couldn't even get to an Internet café to email you.

I promise I will find some way to make it up to you. I am so very, very sorry.

Ginny

The next step was to get a blog posted quickly, using the materials she had at hand — that incredible view and her camera. She scrolled upward to read the comments from the last post, the one she'd written from Utah, before the fire.

Ginny answered every one in turn, a

laborious task, since there were more than two hundred, some of them repeats as people returned and posted again after she didn't show up this morning.

Toward the end was a post from Ruby: *Just heard from our darling Ginny, my dears. She's had some technical issues, but she'll be back online very soon. Don't worry about her. In the meantime, come talk to me at my blog. We're partying at Lavender's farm.*

The very last comment was from Just Jack. It said, *What about a microwave cake? Peach, maybe.*

She took a breath, her memory flashing back to that kiss — which shamed and aroused her in equal measures. How foolish she was!

To distract herself, she set about dumping the black and gray water in her tanks and refilling the freshwater tanks, grateful there were facilities here for it. Afterward, she showered the nasty task away, made a cup of tea for her still-tender belly, and returned to her email.

Amid the floods of spam and blog-related mail were three that caught her eye. The first was from the backblogger in Boise.

FROM: Justbake@git.com
TO: Ginny@cakeofdreams.com
SUBJECT: re: SORRY BEYOND
     BELIEF

Ginny,
   It was embarrassing when you didn't
show up or call or anything. I don't think
I'll be following your blog anymore.
Sorry.
                              Mavis

   Ginny didn't blame her, but it was a blow
nonetheless. She clicked on the next email,
from Ruby.

FROM: Ruby@flavorofabluemoon.com
TO: Ginny@cakeofdreams.com
SUBJECT: JUST TO YOU

   I'm falling apart and trying not to let
anyone see it, but I know you have a
daughter my age, and maybe you'll have
advice. I can't talk to my dad, because
he worries SO MUCH, and Lavender is
great but she's never really been all
mixed up in relationships, you know? Or
at least it's been a really really long time.
   First of all, the big surprise I was going to keep until you got here is that I

am miraculously, amazingly, joyfully *pregnant.* (Joyfully, that is, when I am not throwing up, which I do *constantly.*) The baby is due in October, and I am madly hoping for a little girl.

The baby is Liam's, which is also kind of weird, since we had sex a zillion times and I never got pregnant, and then after we'd broken up and had angry sex, I get a baby???

Anyway, Lavender told me that I had to tell him, and I was about to and instead I got an email telling me that he was going to marry Minna. Honestly, if you saw the two of us standing side by side, you would be shocked at the difference. She is as lovely as a white asparagus, with a long neck and long limbs and barely any curves to her, and when you see me, you will see that I'm more of a tomato, or possibly now a watermelon. How could the same man have loved us both?

I need to pull myself together and learn to be happy again for the sake of my baby. I want to be the mother to her that my mother could not be to me. I want her to feel loved and adored and wanted, because she is.

If your daughter were in this situation,

what would you tell her?

Can't wait to give you a big hug in person.

Love,
Ruby

P.S.: Wait until you see Noah! Holy mother of God. He has really rare good looks, every little thing designed exactly right for maximum male allure. Not perfection, because we don't really love male perfection, do we? It's his mouth, and the angle of his nose, and the dismissive way he deals with people, and his hands, and his sexy, sexy hair. Maybe I should just jump his bones and be done with it. Ha!

Before she opened the third email, delaying it like a special dessert, Ginny wrote back to Ruby.

FROM: Ginny@cakeofdreams.com
TO: Ruby@flavorofabluemoon.com
SUBJECT: RE: JUST TO YOU

RUBY!!!!!!!!!!!!!!!!!!!!!!!!!!!!!!!! I'm so happy for you. That's just wonderful, wonderful, wonderful news. I can't wait to see you and hug you and give that baby a pat. Have you started showing a lot yet? People will pat your belly in public, as if that tummy doesn't belong to you at all.

I wish I were the writer you are, so I could write something elegant to you. Instead, I'm just going to write what I'd write to Christie.

The questions you are asking are at the heart of a lot of our sorrows, all the things that make us worry and make us sad and make life so inexplicable. Why did Liam fall in love with Minna? Why did he fall out of love with you? Why did you get pregnant now (instead of earlier, before he fell in love with someone else, which sounds like the underlying question)?

There aren't any answers, I'm sorry to say. We make things up to explain people's actions, but that's all it ever is, making things up, making excuses, trying to create some understanding. So what do you say about it all? What would make it easier to bear?

But, mainly, the question of Liam will resolve itself. Eventually you're going to get over him, if you allow it. If you don't talk to him, his memory will start to fade. Focus on getting ready for the baby and the happiness you feel over that. (A baby, a baby, a baby!!!)

And, honestly, if Noah is that hot, maybe you *should* have a fling. Maybe it would help. Just don't break his heart. I've seen pictures of you, sweetie, and however gorgeous he is, he can't be more gorgeous than you are.

We can talk about this as much as you want when I get there. I have some things on my mind, too, about my marriage and my life in Kansas, and a lot of other stuff. I feel like I'm becoming someone else, right before my own eyes. This has been an incredible few days.

Love,
Ginny

Finally, she took a breath, gooseflesh rippling over the back of her arms, and opened the last email.

FROM: hghgains@intertime.net
TO: Ginny@cakeofdreams.com
SUBJECT: (blank)

Ginny,
Your lips tasted like peaches. Like dawn. I haven't felt like that in about a hundred and fifty years, which is to say, ever.

On Sunday afternoon, at two o'clock, I will be at the Blue Moon Tavern in Mc-Minnville.

Please come.

Jack

She closed her eyes and let herself travel back to this morning, to the taste of his mouth, the violent hunger sparked by his tongue sweeping into her mouth, the feel of his hands on her body.

Today was Friday. On Sunday he would be in McMinnville.

No. She swallowed and closed the email, as if not looking at it would make it go away.

She was not leaving her husband for the attentions of another guy. There would be no purpose to that. She had to find her own place, her own way, figure out who she was and what she wanted.

So just have sex, said a traitorous little voice that came from somewhere low in her gut. *That's all he wants, you know. He's not falling in love — get real. He's a trucker on the road. He probably does this all the time.*

Aching, she stepped outside into the gloaming and sat down next to Willow, who watched with alert purpose for invading squirrels. Purple shadows eased in over the opalescent ripples of the river, darkened the

303

ravines. On a bluff overlooking the water, she saw the tiny figures of people, and she imagined the view from that high spot, wonder pushing away the dark knot in her chest. It was as if the landscape was a character in itself, as if the land had magical powers, the ability to heal. The air was cool and damp, rising off the water, and it touched her face with moist kisses.

The urgent need to act left her. She didn't have to send that email to Matthew today. There was time. A part of her felt the urgent need to put it in writing to her friends, and maybe she would do that later, but for the moment what was in front of her was enough. The landscape, her dog, her chrysalis home allowing her the freedom to become . . . whatever might be next. For now she had no idea, but this was good, just as it was.

Now, with her dog.

Now, with the night.

Now, alone and free.

CHAPTER 23

Ginny awakened at six and got on the road in a half hour, anxious to get to the farm. The day was clear and bright, and she made good time through Portland since it was Saturday morning and traffic was mild.

It was barely ten A.M. when she drove through Yamhill County, down Highway 47. The sun was a tender glaze over the hills and soft green landscape, the air still moist with last night's rain. She'd gone to sleep listening to it.

Not that she'd really slept. The rain had begun not long after she went to bed, a steady patter on the roof of the Airstream, and Willow was a warm, softly snoring body next to her. But Ginny had stared out through the window at the sky, her mind tumbling with the journey she'd nearly completed, with the food poisoning and the kind strangers on her path and the conversation with Matthew and the fact that she'd missed a blog for the first time ever.

Maybe that was what happened when you had a life.

And of course she thought of Jack, of the little blips from Thursday night that filtered through the feverish mask over her memory, the way he had turned her away to preserve her modesty, the way he washed her neck and back. His hands on her arms as he pulled the shirt over her head.

Tossing and turning, tossing and turning.

So it was a relief to get up and on the road early, while everyone else slept. It was a relief to get off the main roads and follow the directions through the rolling landscape west of Portland, to follow the directions to the farm.

And it was an absolute delight to see the sign and the two-story white house she recognized from Lavender's blog. She pulled in, an expert at tight turns now, and bounced a little down the gravel road. She spied a camper and an Airstream painted with Frida Kahlo–style foods — it had to be Ruby's. She also spied another, longer Airstream, a twenty-six footer she recognized from the pictures she'd seen of it.

Valerie!

She pulled over and leapt from the car, letting Willow out without her leash. The dog trotted behind as Ginny jogged over to the door of the trailer and knocked. "Val! You scamp! Get out here!"

A teenage girl hauled open the door, her loose hair a frizzy tumble. She scowled. "My mom's over at the house."

"Sorry. I didn't mean to wake you."

Hannah — obviously this was Hannah — shrugged and closed the door.

Ginny looked over her shoulder, trying to decide which one was the house — the two-story? Or the cottage at the edge of a field of vegetables?

She didn't think it was the two-story, which she knew housed the distillery and the shop. Two cars were parked there.

Whistling for Willow, she headed for the cottage and then spied a chicken. Would Willow chase them? She hadn't shown signs of it, but some dogs did. Some dogs killed chickens.

But Willow stuck close, heeling as she always did, and Ginny rounded the cottage to find three women sitting at a table covered with a cloth and cups and the remains of breakfast. They had moved their chairs into the sunlight to offset the chill. Ginny paused, wondering if she should just dive in or —

"Ginny!" A blond woman wearing a scarf

over her hair leapt up and ran full throttle toward her. Ginny barely had time to brace herself before the young woman flung her arms around her, engulfing her in a powerful hug — strong arms and soft curves and ferocity. "Oh, I am so glad to see you! We worried a lot!"

"Ruby!" Ginny hugged her back, then pushed away to take a good look at her. China-doll eyes in a porcelain face, that thick blond hair, a smile like a starlet. "You are even more amazingly beautiful in person than you are in your pictures."

"So are you!"

"Let me in on this," said a strong voice, and there was Lavender, rangy and tall, her face powerful and old. "Give me a hug, child."

Ginny laughed and hugged her friend and mentor. Hard. Lavender's arms clutched her just as fiercely in return. "I have had such an adventure so far! Thank you."

"I'm so proud of you, Ginny-gal." Lavender patted her back robustly.

"My turn."

The other two stepped aside, and there was Valerie, with her obsidian eyes and slender figure and impossibly straight shoulders. "I can't believe you're here," Ginny said, and tears sprang to her eyes.

She leapt forward and gave Val the hug she'd held on to for two years. They rocked back and forth, transmitting the thousands of unsaids they needed to offer. Happiness, comfort, relief.

"I couldn't miss this," she said, and kissed Ginny's cheek. "You are so much prettier than your pictures!"

"Thanks," Ginny said, rolling her eyes, "but it's probably just the journey." She spread her hands. "I escaped!" she told all of them, and laughed. "I'm outta Kansas, ladies. Can you believe it?"

Ruby gave a hoot, and Valerie did a little dance, and Lavender put two fingers in her mouth and whistled so loud it would bring down a 747.

For the first time in her life, Ginny was home.

Someone fetched her a mug and someone else filled her cup from the pot on the table, and Ginny dropped a sugar cube into it. "So tell us all about it," Lavender invited. "Did you meet anyone on the road? What happened to your phone?"

Ginny laughed and began to give the highlights — the hailstorm the first night, the phone in the dishwater, the fire and the antelopes, the heart-stopping beauty of the

Rockies, the food poisoning.

And that was where she stopped. She still wasn't sure what had happened to send a mysterious text to Jack, and she didn't exactly want to talk about him, either. Not yet. Maybe not ever. She knew they wouldn't judge her, but it all seemed like something from a dream.

She did ask, "How far is McMinnville from here?"

"Twenty minutes. Maybe a half hour," Lavender said. "We go there for shopping all the time. But if you need only a few supplies, we can go to the village up the road. Why?"

Ginny found herself picking at a hangnail. "Just wondering."

"Hmm." Ruby poked her with a toe. "That's a funny expression."

"Don't be silly. What I do need to do is get a new phone, like . . . pronto. Where would be the best place?"

"We're going into Portland to try on tutus for the party," Valerie said. "I'm sure we can find somewhere to shop there."

"Tutus?"

Ruby said, "Valerie has a connection at a theater in Portland. They're going to lend us tutus so we can all be barefoot goddesses at the party. Won't that be a blast?"

There was almost a halo of light around Ruby, an aura so bright and cheerful that it made her skin shine.

"I don't know. What kind of a goddess? What kind of a tutu?"

Valerie winked. "We'll make sure we're in something flattering, I promise."

"I'm not going," Lavender said, standing up. "The farm won't run itself, and I've got a mountain of work to do before the party."

"Do you need help?" Ginny asked.

Ruby inclined her head, studying Lavender. "You need to come with us. The farm will look after itself for a day, and, besides, you're the one who knows how to navigate Portland."

"No, ma'am. I've got Noah to help. You girls all go have fun. We'll cook dinner when you get back."

"I'm taking us *out* to dinner," Valerie said. "There are a dozen places in Yamhill County alone that are famous for their chefs and wine, and I want to try them. We can cook on Monday."

"Fair enough." Lavender picked up a dish and a clutch of flatware. For a moment she paused, frowning, then put a fist to her chest.

"Are you all right?" Ruby said, jumping up.

Lavender let go of an enormous burp, and all of them laughed. "Fine, child. Get out from underfoot, now, and find me a goddess outfit."

Ruby flung her hands up. "Yay!" She looked at Valerie. "Can you eye her size all right?"

"Got it." Valerie stood, too. "I'd better go roust my girl. She's got to get herself ready."

Ginny rose to her feet, as well. "Do I have time to take a quick look around? Maybe Ruby can show me?"

"Oh, yeah." Valerie waved a slim hand. "She'll be a half hour or better."

"I remember that stage," Ginny said. "My daughter could spend six hours in the bathroom."

Ruby cleared some of the dishes, Ginny grabbed the rest off the table, and they carried them inside. Then, with a little leap of happiness, Ruby said, "Let's go! You won't believe how beautiful the lavender is. And the chickens are so cute!"

"Cute chickens?" Ginny rolled her eyes. "You aren't naming them, are you?"

"These are laying hens, silly. They aren't going in the pot."

Ginny met Lavender's eyes. The older woman winked. "Okay, show me," Ginny said, allowing herself to be tugged along.

The lemony glaze still clung to the sky and intensified all the hues of the morning. Ginny wished she had her camera, but sometimes shooting meant she wasn't really looking, so she and Willow allowed the exuberant Ruby to lead them around the barn and up the hill, past the chickens, where they gathered a couple of tagalongs. Willow seemed completely uninterested in them — a relief.

"Ooh, here's Noah now," Ruby said. "See what I mean?"

Ginny smiled. The man coming down the hill with a pitchfork in his hand had a headful of black curls, too long, that fell around an extravagant face — full lips and cheekbones like bird wings. Not her type at all, but definitely beautiful.

"Good morning!" he called out.

"Good morning." Ruby tossed her head ever so slightly. "Our Ginny has finally arrived!"

He joined them and held out a longfingered hand. "How are you? Noah Tso."

"Ginny Smith."

"You missed Ruby's great shepherd's pie, you know." He swiveled his gaze toward her, and everything in his demeanor shifted, as if he were shaped of iron shavings drawn irresistibly to the giant magnet of Ruby, who

313

stood there glittering and glowing and smiling secretly at him.

"Sorry to hear that," Ginny said, hiding her own smile. "Maybe I'll get another chance."

In the end, Lavender was convinced to drive them to Portland. They all piled into her van: Valerie up front to help navigate, Ginny and Ruby in the middle seat, Hannah in the very back, earphones and cell phone effectively insulating her from everyone. Her appearance was less aggressive this morning — hair straightened and hanging down her back, eyes lined to emphasize their tilt, and beaded bracelets, feathered earrings, a choker made of wooden beads and shell.

It was a relief not to drive after so long a trip. She and Ruby chattered all the way in, about Ginny's blog and the reaction to her absence, about Ruby's blog and her ambivalence about it lately. All the while, Ruby held her hand over her belly, protectively covering the baby inside her. Ginny remembered that feeling. For all that she'd given up, Christie's arrival had been worth it.

She also remembered that Ruby had asked for advice about Liam. Touching Ruby's hand over her belly, she asked, "How are you feeling? Still throwing up?"

"Not since yesterday morning! But look at my face." She gestured to a zit on her chin. "It's like I'm a teenager again." She glanced back over the seat. "No offense, Hannah."

Hannah pulled the earphone away from her left ear. "What?"

"Nothing." Ruby moved her hand out and pressed it lightly on top of Ginny's. "Do you feel her?"

The faintest sensation of movement fluttered under Ginny's palm. "Yes. Isn't that the most amazing thing?"

Ruby put her other hand on the other side of her belly, her gaze focused inward. "It really is." She gave Ginny a sudden, winning grin, revealing dimples. "I tend to be all about amazing, anyway, but this takes the cake. Honestly, I've been grumpy and strange, for me. Do you think that's just being pregnant? Or having a broken heart?"

"Maybe both. Pretty soon, I bet, you won't be thinking as much about your heart and more about the baby. That's kind of how it works — the baby will insist you focus here."

"That's helpful."

Hannah leaned forward over the seat. "You have a broken heart?"

From the front seat, Valerie said, "Hannah! That's none of your business."

Hannah popped her gum. "She said it. I was only asking."

"It's okay." Ruby turned sideways. "I broke up with my boyfriend nine months ago and he's getting married to someone else."

"How long were you guys together?"

"Six years. I met him in New York."

"And he doesn't even want the baby?"

Ruby half-smiled, looking right at Hannah. "Apparently not."

Hannah studied her face. "Are you the one who had leukemia when you were a kid?"

"Hannah!"

Ginny couldn't help it — she smiled and reached for Valerie's hand over the seat. *It's okay.*

"I'm curious!"

"Val, we're good. Just watch the road and leave us alone, all right?" Ruby turned her attention back to Hannah. "I'm the one."

"What if you get it back and the baby has no mother?"

"That would totally suck for me, but I have a dad who is the greatest father in the world, and he'd take care of her."

"It's a girl?"

"I hope so. I'd like that. I never had a

sister, and it would be fun to have girl energy."

Ginny carefully kept her eyes on the road outside, feeling the air around them grow cold suddenly. *Moment lost,* she thought.

But Hannah said, "I had two sisters. You know that, right?"

Ruby nodded. "I knew your mom when it happened. I went to the funerals. Lavender and I both did."

"Not you?" Hannah poked Ginny's shoulder.

"No, I didn't go." A waft of something moved over her chest — regret, maybe. Shame. Or both. "My husband was very much against it, and at the time I didn't —" She broke off. "Never mind."

Hannah chewed her gum. "It was terrible. Not as terrible as having leukemia, though. At least it only lasted one day. Leukemia lasts a long time, right, and you have to have chemo for ages and lose your hair?"

Valerie turned around in her seat, but before she could say anything, Ruby repeated, "Val. We're good."

"Let them talk," Lavender said quietly.

"I was sick for seven years, off and on," Ruby said. "I lost my hair and once I had to be in the hospital nearly all the time for about three months."

Ginny had a vision of a tiny, frail Ruby, all blond hair and big eyes, and her heart ached.

"And now you're okay completely? How do you know?"

Ruby lifted her shoulders. "You don't ever know, I guess, but I haven't had any cancer for twelve years, so that pretty much says they finally got it all. I had a bone-marrow transplant when I was fourteen, and that did it."

"Did you know kids who died?"

"Yes," Ruby said simply. "Lots of them."

"Does it really hurt to die that way? I read that it did, that cancer chokes your whole body so that everything hurts a lot."

Ruby paused, her crystally-blue eyes on Hannah's face. She didn't flinch away from the direct eye contact but instead gave it all of her attention, something Ginny would have found difficult. Hannah stared back, popping her gum as if she didn't care.

Clearly holding Hannah's challenge, Ruby said, "Yes, it hurts. Sometimes for a fairly long time before you finally die. It's a pretty cruel way to go."

For a long moment, Hannah was silent. Her hands hung over the seat, her nails painted with black polish that had chipped in several places. "I used to worry that my

318

sisters hurt a lot at the end, but somebody told me it happened so fast that they probably didn't even know it happened." She paused. "That they died."

"I don't know about plane crashes, but that sounds true to me," Ruby said.

Hannah shrugged. "I guess we'll never know." She flung herself back into her corner and plugged in the earphones.

Ginny glanced at Ruby, who also met Ginny's gaze without guile. They both leaned back in the seat. Ginny could see the side of Val's face, where tears dripped silently from her jaw.

CHAPTER 24

The first stop was the phone store, where Ginny replaced her drowned unit for a hefty fee. She carried it to a bench outside the store, and while she waited for the others, who were browsing in the shops along the strip mall, she checked her voice mail.

There were twenty-seven messages, which for her was a tremendous number, even for a couple of days. When she clicked on them, thirteen were from Matthew.

She frowned. He hadn't called her at all before she lost the phone. Had something gone wrong?

A heat of resistance welled up against listening to the messages. Even if it was trouble, she just didn't want to talk to him, didn't want to ruin the day with his voice.

The other messages were a mix — a handful each from Valerie, Lavender, and Ruby, two from her daughter, one from her mother, and one from a Boise number she knew would be the backblogger who now hated her.

There were also three from Jack. One was from two days ago. "Hey, Ginny." His voice was deeper, richer on the phone, pouring right from the speaker into her ear, as intimate as if he'd licked her earlobe. The sound struck her so hard that every inch of her skin turned a bright hot red, the color steaming invisibly into the air, and she had to close her eyes to hide the lust boiling in them.

"Listen," he said, "I looked up your phone number from the contact information on your website. There is a big fire up here in Idaho. They've closed the interstate and there's a traffic jam that's causing all kinds of trouble. Hoping maybe I've caught you before you get too far down the road. You can detour up through Idaho Falls and Montana, which is what I'm doing. Maybe I'll see you along the way. Take care. Give me a call when you can and let me know you're all right, will you?"

The next was clearly a response to that crazy text she had not sent. "I got your text and I'm headed back to find you. Wish you'd pick up — pretty worried."

For a moment she looked over the parking lot, frowning. How could she *possibly* have sent a text from a dead phone when she was passed out on the floor with a fever of God-only-knew what? She'd have to throw this puzzle out to the others and see what they made of it.

The third was from right after breakfast yesterday, after the kiss. "Jesus, Ginny. I know you can't get this message right now, but maybe you'll hear it eventually." A pause. She could hear him breathing quietly. Could hear some sounds in the background, maybe his engine.

Ginny bent around the phone, as if to create a private room. His voice rolled down her skin, the ragged edges somehow rousing every cell in her body, pricking elbows and wrists and throat and belly and the soles of her feet. She pressed her finger against her other ear to shut out everything else and closed her eyes.

"I'm having trouble thinking of what to say," he said at last. "I just keep replaying that kiss, the way you tasted, the sounds you made, and all I want is to do it again. Kiss you. For about ten years without stopping. That's probably a totally idiotic thing to say and you probably think I'm a crazy stalker, but, I swear, nothing like this has happened to me in twenty years on the road."

Another pause. Long, with the engine and a song playing in the background. "I want to see you again. Please."

Ginny pressed *end* and held the phone in her hand, feeling it burn her palm. Her skin itched as if it were about to sprout vines and flowers.

And yet.

There were those thirteen messages from a man she had promised to love, honor, and cherish forever. He cherished her, or at least he wanted to keep being married to her, which might or might not be the same thing.

"Wow, that's a pretty intense scowl," Ruby said, sitting down. She had a bag in her hand. "Bad news?"

Ginny looked at Ruby. On impulse, she said, "Listen." She pushed the message from Jack, the last one.

Ruby bent her head and a twitch touched her lips, then her eyes widened. "Whew," she said. "That's one killer voice." She handed the phone back. "Do you want to tell me more about it?"

"He's a trucker I met the second morning. He was at the rest stop and wanted to pet Willow. And then I kept running into him. And then — this weird thing happened — which I haven't figured out yet, but I want to get everybody's feedback — and he kind of rescued me when I was sick, and then the next morning . . ." She took a breath, trying to keep the kiss safely corralled, away from the incendiary points in her body. "I kissed him. Or he kissed me. Or something. And I want to feel guilty, but I don't, Ruby. I don't! What's wrong with me?"

"You have a bad marriage, that's all."

"Why do you say that?"

Ruby made a quizzical face. "You're not really asking that?"

"I didn't think I talked about it all that much."

"Oh. Sorry. Maybe I misunderstood."

Ginny sighed. "No, you're right. It's miserable." The word weighed a thousand pounds, and she bent over to put her face in her hands. "Miserable. I have been miserable for ten years. Twelve. More! That's why I started the blog. That's why I bought the trailer. That's why I'm here. I really, really, really want to leave him, start over, find out what the rest of my life should look like."

Ruby put a hand on Ginny's back. "And that's why you kissed a man who has a voice like a rock god."

"This isn't about men or sex or falling in love. I need to figure out who I am, without being somebody's wife or girlfriend." Ginny shook her head. "But I'm very, very, very attracted to him. It's wrong. I know that."

Ruby's hand moved in a circle, smoothing the prickly skin. "I have faith in you. I know you're going to make the right decisions."

Ginny looked up at her young friend, into her serene expression. "Thank you."

"Anytime."

She straightened. Looked at her phone and the thirteen messages from Matthew. "I have to make a couple of phone calls. I'll be done in a few minutes."

"No problem." Ruby dropped her hand back into her lap. "I think we're going to grab some lunch as soon as we finish at the theater, so you don't have to get all wrapped up. Just let them know you're safe."

Which was the easy way out. Ginny called her daughter, whose voice mail picked up. "Hi, sweetie. I wanted to let you know I'm safe and all is well in case you tried to call me. I dropped my phone in the dishwater and ruined it, then got caught in the Idaho fire and had to detour around it. But I am now safely in Oregon with my friends."

She paused, her eyes focused on the tree-covered ridge directly to the west of where she sat. "Thanks for the encouragement, Christie. I have discovered so much about myself on this trip, and, honestly, I never

325

want to go back to Kansas again."

The messages from her friends she could skip, and she'd listen to the one from her mother later. There was only one thing left to do, so she clicked on the first voice mail from Matthew, left Thursday afternoon at 3:12 P.M.

"Hey, Ginny, we have a problem with the air conditioner. Do you know where the paperwork is?"

At 5:04: "Hoping to get in touch with you today about that paperwork. You're probably driving. Call me later."

At 8:45: "I'm going to bed. Don't bother to call me."

At 6:00 A.M. yesterday: "This is getting weird, Ginny. What are you doing that you can't answer your phone at six o'clock in the morning? This is crap."

At 7:00 A.M., 9:42 A.M., 11:23 A.M., 1:50 P.M.: "Call me."

At 5:25: "I'm going out with the guys. Don't bother to call me, not that you've bothered. Jeez, Ginny, I keep hearing that there's a fire in Idaho, and you're being so independent. How the hell do I know if you're okay?"

At 7:21, slightly tipsy: "I'm here at the White Horse with Joe Kim and Grange, and I was just thinking how long we've been together, me and you. Remember that game against the Duke Dogs when I threw a sixty-seven-yard pass and we went to eat at Sizzler afterward and the waitress snuck us drinks? Those were good times, babe. Good times."

Ginny remembered. They'd been giddy with triumph and youth. They ate steaks and drank margaritas served in lemonade glasses because the waitress, all of twenty-two, was hot for Matthew and had listened to the game on the radio. Ginny got drunk and three hours later threw up in the bathroom at Grange's house, because his mother worked the greyhound tracks outside Wichita and never got home until three or four. Nobody had been available to drive Ginny home, so she'd slept on Grange's plastic-leather couch, huddled beneath a coat because everybody else was passed out.

Good times. She'd given him a blow job in the bathroom while he played with her nipples under her shirt.

Suddenly weary, she didn't know how she could listen to the rest of the messages. He'd left three more that night, the last at one in the morning, when he'd no doubt been well beyond slightly high and into full drunk. He didn't do it often, but there was

327

no way he'd been up at one and not been drunk.

Instead, she listened to the voice mail from her mother, left early this morning. "Ginny, I don't know what nonsense you're up to, but you can't just leave your husband. He's a good man and a good provider, and you're out of your mind to divorce a man who loves you when you're middle-aged. Kelly Lambrusco got away with it because she's built like a brick you-know-what, but that's not you. You want to spend the rest of your life alone?"

As she listened, she shook her head. "Mother, what in the world are you talking about?"

And then, with a sense of doom, she remembered the email she had written but *not sent* to Matthew, about never returning to Kansas and wanting a divorce. Had she accidentally hit *send* instead of *save*?

With a shaking hand, she scrolled past the earlier voice mails from Matthew to the ones left this morning. "Ginny, I just got your email. What are you talking about?" He sounded irritated but not angry. "Is this about all those phone messages I left you last night? You know I was drunk. It didn't mean anything, and it's sure not worth a damned divorce. You've gone crazy on this trip, and I don't understand a thing you wrote. Call me."

She pulled the phone away from her ear. He thought *his* messages were making her crazy? She started to scroll back, but Lavender was striding toward her. "Trouble at home, gal?"

Ginny couldn't decide whether to laugh or frown, so she did both. "I don't know what's going on."

"Will it keep?"

She'd been out of touch for three days so far. Another few hours wouldn't kill anybody. She stood. "Yes."

"Good. Let's go."

CHAPTER 25

Ruby instantly loved the smell of the local theater's backstage area. They were meeting a wardrobe mistress who a friend of Valerie's had put them in touch with. The place smelled of dust and time and wax, and she felt she could almost see the ghosts of dancers from performances past swirling around, their toe shoes tapping with authority against the wooden floorboards.

A willowy woman in her sixties met them at the back door. "Oh, my gosh," she said, touching her throat. "Valerie Andrews. I'm so thrilled to meet you."

Ruby thought, *She's famous!* Which she'd sort of known, but it was funny to see it like this. Ruby knew Valerie through her wry, down-to-earth, also-famous blog on wine but had never known her as the dancer she'd been.

"Hello, Mrs. Tinker. I'm so grateful to you for this." From her bag, Val pulled a wrapped gift. "Just a small token of appreciation."

"Oh, thank you! Call me Bette." Her fine skin showed a high blush over her cheeks and down the sides of her neck. She was obviously so happy to meet this famous dancer, and it made Ruby want to squeeze the wardrobe mistress tight. "Would you mind signing a program for me? I saw you dance twice, and I saved one of the programs."

"I'm so touched, I can't even tell you!" Val exclaimed. "Of course I'll sign it." She tugged Hannah forward, and for once the girl put on her manners instead of an attitude, holding out her hand and smiling politely as Val said, "This is my daughter Hannah."

"How do you do," Hannah said.

"I'm pleased to meet you," Mrs. Tinker said. "Are you a dancer, too?"

"No. That was my sister Louisa."

"Oh, yes. Right, the one who — er, well, I'm so sorry for that loss. For both of you."

Hannah's spine went rod straight, making her taller by two inches, and Ruby stepped forward, grabbed her hand, and squeezed it with a bright smile up at the girl.

Lost in the awkwardness, the woman wrung her hands, looking for a long moment between Valerie and Hannah, then back to Val.

Gently, Valerie said, "You have set aside some tutus for us to try?"

"Yes. Oh, yes. Come this way."

Ruby held on to Hannah. "She meant well."

"I know. I wasn't going to say anything." She tugged her fingers away. "I'm not an idiot."

Ruby leaned in and nudged her with an elbow. "This is going to be such a blast. Don't you think?"

"I guess."

The woman led them to a door that she unlocked with a key attached to her wrist. "This is the storeroom," she said, and they followed her into a room lined with tutus and costumes in every imaginable style and color and length. "What kind of things were you thinking of?"

"Goddesses," Ruby said. "We want to be barefoot goddesses."

"Ah." Mrs. Tinker's eyes narrowed and her lips pursed, the computer of her brain sorting through the options. "Mrs. Andrews, I'd love to fit you first. What were you thinking?"

Valerie shook her head. "I have no idea.

Will you choose something beautiful for me?"

"May I?" She pressed a hand to her chest.

Ruby said, "She wants to be queenly. Can you come up with that, maybe with a crown?"

"Odette!"

"*Swan Lake,*" Valerie said to the others. "That would be perfect, Bette. Lead the way."

"The rest of you can take a look if you like. Handle things carefully. We'll be right back."

Ginny and Lavender just stood there. Ruby swept forward, grabbing their hands. "C'mon, Hannah! You, too."

"I don't know what to look for," Ginny protested, yanking back to avoid being swept into Ruby's scheme. "This is weird. Maybe I don't want to wear a tutu!"

"Oh, it'll be fun."

"For *you,* Ruby." Ginny's alarm was scribbled over her forehead, on her mouth. "I don't like dress-up games."

"You don't?" Hannah echoed with incredulity. "I love them. You don't have to be yourself."

Ruby seized a skirt made of endless varieties of blue with a silvery overskirt. "Or maybe more yourself than you could be in real life." She held it up, disappointed to discover that the waist was tiny, tiny, tiny.

Of course. She smoothed the fabric over her belly sadly, knowing it would never fit in a million years. "Nothing in here is going to work for me, is it? Even *not* pregnant, I'm not small enough." A sudden vision of everybody else dancing in tutus, their feet bare, while she swayed in her ordinary clothes made tears well up in Ruby's eyes. She ducked her head, smoothing a palm over the dress, and tried to blink herself back to an even keel. Again she touched the skirt. "It looks like a blue moon," she said with longing, and a sense of tragedy swamped her. Her tears flowed like a fountain. She couldn't stop them.

"Oh, sweetie," Ginny said, sliding an arm around her shoulders. "If we can't find something here, I can make this for you in about an hour." She looked over her shoulder. "Lavender, do you have a sewing machine?"

"I don't sew," Lavender said, tugging out one after another of the skirts, "but there are a couple in the workroom." She frowned, rubbed her belly. "We need to get some food sometime soon. I'm starving."

"Me, too," Hannah said, walking down the aisle and flipping through the dresses.

"You could do this in an hour?" Ruby asked, her tears drying up as fast as they'd arrived. She ran her fingers over the fabric. "This sparkly stuff and everything? It's the silver and blue that I really like."

"We would buy it like that, with the sparkles on it. I'm sure Portland has plenty of places to buy good fabric."

"You would do that?"

Ginny gave her a quizzical smile. "Of course."

Ruby abruptly settled her head on Ginny's shoulder. "You're the best."

Ginny chuckled.

"Let me find you something, please, please, please?"

"I don't think so, Ruby. I feel so —"

"You don't have to wear it if you try it on and feel bad. What could it hurt to just try it on?"

Ginny hesitated, and Ruby suddenly saw her deep shyness and remembered how far she'd come in the years they'd known her, from a wallflower to a star.

Ruby grabbed Ginny's hand and hauled her down the row, looking for a color that popped out at her — not that tepid blue or the screaming yellow. No, no, no. About three rows over she finally saw it, the very shade of the flesh of a perfectly ripe peach.

"This," she said, pulling it out. The construction was simple, too, just the floating skirt and a sleeveless bodice adorned with sequins.

Ginny reached for it, brushed her hand over the bodice. "This color," she said with a sigh. A stain of bright red burned over her cheekbones.

Intrigued, Ruby said, "What are you thinking to have that blush on your face?"

"Do I?" She put her hands on her cheeks. "It's just that . . . well . . ." She looked over her shoulder. In a near-whisper, she said, "Jack said that my lips tasted like peaches."

"So try it on! It will be perfect on you."

Ginny agreed. "Where?"

Ruby laughed, looking around. "Here, I think. Just take off your shirt and pull it over your head."

Ginny felt self-conscious, but she did it. Her shoulders were slim, her waist small, and the tutu fit her with a little bit of snugness over the bust, which actually made her breasts swell up over the bodice in a very nice way. Ruby tugged it slightly. "Will it stay on?"

"I can't wear this!" Ginny put both hands over the upper swell of her breasts.

Ruby brushed her hands away. "Look at me, Ginny." She smiled. "You look amazing. I swear. Walk around in it for a minute, see how it makes you feel."

She did, wandering down the aisle away from Ruby, her head down as she brushed her hands over her skirt, palms open like a little girl. Ruby smiled and swung around with the blue one against her body, thinking inexplicably of Noah trying to cheer her up yesterday. Maybe they would dance together at the festival. She imagined the dark starry sky and the lights strung around the platform, which a crew was finishing today, and Noah's thick, too-long curls falling around his face. It was only a flash, a sense of his hands on her sides, his smiling mouth close, their bodies —

Rebound, said a voice. *Don't do it. Not for you, not for him.* She knew he was vulnerable. She could feel it in him, deep and hungry, a yawning need for union.

For healing.

Ruby attracted men like him by the platoon, men broken by a thousand different things, hearts shattered, hopes smashed, souls shredded. She gave them kindness. Sometimes she had given them kisses. She gave them laughter and high regard, and that was often just right.

Ambling up the aisle, aimlessly pulling out a gown or a tutu or a costume, her fickle mind fluttered and settled on Liam. He had not seemed broken, not by anything in this life, anyway. It all went back to that weird vision she'd had of him in the very beginning, of his monkish self in a medieval world. And who was she to say — maybe they were memories of another life. Millions of people all over the world believed in reincarnation, and it would certainly explain a lot. Liam's monkish current self, her own sense of connection to him. Maybe this life, this broken heart and the baby, were corrections to karma — punishment or reward.

Who knew?

Which ducked the Noah question. She prided herself on being real with other people. She was so ripe for a rebound lover, and he would probably be very willing, but she was adamantly not over Liam, and Noah deserved the full-throated focus of a woman who was ready to love someone.

Too bad, really. She could like him. She just wasn't ready to love anyone else yet.

A pale silvery tutu caught her eye, and she pulled it out. The sleeves were long and sheer. Iridescent beading swirled over the bodice and tea-length skirt. It was perfect for Lavender, and Ruby pulled it out to carry with her.

Ginny stood at the end of the row, swinging back and forth to make the skirt sway. Her hair fell down around her face, showing her pale white neck. From this distance, she looked about seventeen.

Jack said that my lips tasted like peaches.

Half of Ruby wanted to protect Ginny from the possibility that this guy was a player who made time with lonely women. The other half wanted to see Ginny let her miserable marriage go, by whatever means necessary. As if she heard these thoughts, Ginny looked back at Ruby. Ginny's glossy, uncolored hair was in her face, and her shoulders were bare, and Ruby realized that she had absolutely no idea that she was stunning.

"I think I like it," she said quietly.

"It's right for you."

Ginny pulled the dress over her head and put her shirt back on. "Let's go find the others."

Lavender and Valerie stood with the wardrobe mistress, arrayed in a half circle around Hannah, who admired herself in a long mirror. Her hair was loose on her shoulders, and she wore a red tutu, strapless, that showed off her tiny waist, impressive bust, and delicate shoulders in a way that was slightly astonishing.

"Well, girl," Ruby said, giving a catcall.

She lifted one corner of the skirt in her hand. "I guess you found your dress."

"Oh, I don't think so," Valerie said with lips pursed. "It's much too old for her."

"She's fourteen?" the wardrobe mistress asked, cocking her head. "That's perfect for Persephone."

Hannah put her hands on her waist and swung the skirt slightly. "I think it's the most beautiful thing I've ever seen." She met her mother's gaze in the mirror. "Please? It's not like I'm going to wear it to a high school dance or something. It's a grown-up party."

For a long moment Valerie was silent, looking at her daughter. Ruby eased over and put a hand on her shoulder. "She looks like *herself* in this."

Valerie nodded. "All right."

Hannah clapped her hands. "Yippee!"

CHAPTER 26

After lunch and a bit more shopping, they drove to the ocean, at Ruby's insistence. She had discovered over the meal that neither Ginny nor Hannah had ever seen it. "It's only seventy miles from here!" She opened her wide eyes wider. "Lavender! We have to take them!"

So Ruby drove, with Valerie beside her. Ginny and Hannah rode in the middle seats, both of them peering out with excitement, eager to be the first to spot the sea. Lavender stretched out in the far backseat, taking a little nap. Ginny looked at her a couple of times, slightly worried. Lavender had not eaten much of her lunch.

But she was sleeping easily, her color good, and Ginny told herself that because someone was old was no reason to think they were about to get sick.

In the back of her mind, Ginny fretted over the phone messages she had not finished listening to. She also kept mulling the question of whether she would meet Jack tomorrow in McMinnville.

She didn't think so, but a part of her kept imagining him in a booth in a café, facing the door, looking up hopefully every time a new person came through the door. She didn't have to kiss him again or anything like that. She could just have a nice glass of iced tea and go back to the farm.

Maybe.

Maybe not.

"I see it!" Hannah shouted. "Right on the horizon!"

Ginny peered hard, and she gave a little whoop when she saw the line of blue against the sky, darker, definitive. "I see it, too!"

They traveled down a bluff to the sand, and during the whole journey Ginny kept dipping her head, trying to keep the water in sight. The ocean!

The van had barely stopped when she pulled open the door and dove out to the parking lot. A stiff wind swept over her face, sending her hair back in a flag. She closed her eyes, wishing Willow was with her, that the two of them could be running on this beach together, seeing the water for the first time.

She bent over and took off her shoes and

socks, leaving them in a pile beside the van, and jogged toward the sand, forgetting everything and everybody as the water lured her, a dark blue-gray and endless, restless, under the clouds gathering overhead. She walked through the sand, feeling it shift beneath her feet, and stopped only when she arrived at the edge of the water.

It didn't matter that a lot of other people were there, that people walked behind her, that some children were squatted over buckets and small orange shovels, making roads in the sand. It didn't matter that an almost certain promise of doom hung over her life.

Nothing mattered except the fact that, by some miracle, she — Ginny Smith from Dead Gulch, Kansas — was standing with her feet in the Pacific Ocean, and she'd made it here almost entirely on her own will.

For a long time she stood there, watching the waves undulate, little caps here, big waves there, a breaking edge of foam, then a tube of clear water that looked like glass as it rolled toward her, coming from who knew where. Japan. Russia. Vietnam. That water had touched lands and feet in the vast far away. She imagined she could hear echoes of them, carried on ghostly water radio waves.

She closed her eyes and breathed in the smell, which was like and unlike the coppery notes of a river or a lake. It was denser, deeper, woven with dead flesh and living sea beings and the approaching rain.

But the best of it was the sound, the sibilant ruffling of the water over the sand, the splash and roar born of constant movement. It was vast and incomprehensible. It made her feel tinier than a single molecule in the foaming waves and, conversely, so much a part of all things, everything. For a moment she nearly slipped away into the ether, dissolving into sky and sound and scent.

She realized that tears were streaming over her face. How was it possible she was standing here?

Whirling around, she flung her arms out and whooped. "Woo-hoo!" she cried at the top of her lungs, and then Ruby was there, grabbing her hand, the scarf gone from her head, her hair blowing around her face. They danced in a circle, leaping when the waves covered their feet. Hannah ran up and each of them grabbed her hand, and her hair, too, blew in the wind.

They danced and Ginny cried out, "I am never going back to Kansas!"

When they returned to the farm, Valerie

volunteered to make dinner for everyone, since they had decided not to go out. "I promise I won't poison you all."

Lavender, looking pale, headed upstairs to take a nap. Ginny wanted to make Ruby's gown. She'd found pale-blue organza dotted with silver sequins at a big-box store in Portland.

She sewed the simple costume in the workroom of the farmhouse, thinking of her daughter and all the costumes she'd sewn for her over the years. Sticking spare straight pins into her sleeve, Ginny thought she probably ought to try Christie again. Had Matthew said anything to Christie about the divorce letter?

It all seemed so far away.

As Ginny stitched up the seams and put in a simple hem, the smell of lavender hung thickly in the air around her. Many of the products sold in the store were assembled in the very same room. A long table stood against a windowless wall, lined with baskets of thick-ribbed corduroy and flannel, all in shades of purple and gray and the thread of gold that marked the farm. Canisters of lavender blossoms were nearly empty. Eye pillows, neck wraps, and even gloves were carefully stacked in tidy piles, ready for ticketing or stickering.

In the other room were screens covered with lavender blossoms drying on racks, and in another was the distillery, a big copper teapot that looked like a shrunken still from Prohibition. Ginny had walked around it, curious to see steam circling in a glass tube and lavender oil dripping out of a spout into a jar with a narrow neck. She bent close to the spout and nearly swayed with the power of the oil. It almost seemed she could feel it entering her pores, little purple fingers massaging her temples and chest.

It was quite a large operation, and Lavender hadn't started it until she was in her late fifties. That was encouraging: Ginny had lots more time to build a sustainable business of her own if she so chose.

Was the blog a business? Did it count, all by itself?

When she finished the gown, she carried it outside, intending to take it to Ruby right away, but she spied the shiny blond head walking amid the chickens, clearly talking to them.

So she took the gown with her to her own trailer, hung it up, called Willow to come sleep with her, and they curled up in the familiar comfort of the Airstream's bed. It had been quite a busy day. As she settled down, pulling the quilt over her, the phone rang. She sighed and reached for it, knowing who it would be.

Matthew's number flashed on the screen. She let it ring again, and then one more time, debating whether to answer. Only the fact that she owed him a report of her safety made her answer. "Hello?" she said, as if she didn't know it was him calling.

"Ginny, is that really you?"

"Yes, Matthew, I'm so sorry — I dropped my phone in the dishwater the other day and drowned it. I'm —"

"You couldn't call from a phone booth?"

"They don't really have phone booths anymore, in case you haven't noticed. You could have gone to my blog."

"I did, and it wasn't all that clear what was going on until last night, and then there was that email from you."

"Matthew, we can talk about that —"

"I don't want to talk. You're just mad about the voice messages, but you know how I get when I'm drunk. You had a right to be mad, but I didn't mean it. You know I didn't. I was just lonely and horny and a little out of control, I guess."

Ginny sat up. "Horny? You?"

He paused. "Have you listened to the messages I left?"

"No, I haven't had a —"

"Jesus fucking Christ. Then that email was for real?"

"No, I mean, yes, I mean —"

"You want a divorce, Ginny?"

Her heart clutched, cold, condensing down down down to a tiny pea of terror, then she took a breath. "I didn't mean to send the email —"

"Thank God for that."

"— but, yes, Matthew." Her heart swelled with blood and heat and pulsed with new possibilities. "I want a divorce. I'm not coming back to Kansas."

"That's the stupidest thing I've ever heard of. You're having a midlife crisis. You'll come to your senses."

"No, Matthew —"

"I'm not talking anymore, Ginny. Erase all those messages from me. They don't mean a thing."

"You can't just" — a click on the line — "hang up on me!"

The line was dead. Ginny stared at it, her head buzzing with the clearest fury she'd ever felt in her life, like a thousand wasps ready to rise up and —

She roared aloud, "Argh!" Willow jumped, tail thumping nervously against the bed. "Oh, I'm not mad at you, sweetie. Never you." She rubbed her vigorously, turning the fur into a crackling static field.

Unable to bear the tight space of the Airstream, she flung open the door and carried the phone outside, shaky with fury. A brisk wind was blowing up, the same rainstorm they'd been fleeing since they left the ocean, and it didn't cool her in the least. She punched in the messages he'd left while he was drinking.

At 8:52, his voice considerably more boisterous than in the previous one: "I'm just sitting here with my bros, thinking what bullshit it is that you're out on the road like this. Why would you do that, Ginny, huh? I'm a good husband. I know you're all pissed off about the sex, but not everybody cares that much about all that. I'm a good catch, God damn it!"

Ginny pulled the phone away from her ear to see how much more of the message there was, and she was only a tiny bit of the way into it. Without a qualm, she moved on to the next message.

The next one was short, at 10:05 P.M.: "You know what, wife?" His voice was definitely slurred now. "You're a cunt. Thass right. I said it."

Ginny rolled her eyes, the anger settling somewhere along her shoulder blades, hot burning spots beneath her skin, both painful and buzzing. She thought of the Rockies, pointed and bold against a blue sky. She thought of the Columbia River, shimmering in the dusk. She thought of the ocean today, roiling and dancing.

She clicked the next message. Very drunk now, 1:00 A.M. He was sobbing. "Ginny, I love you. Don't you know that? You are the only woman I've ever loved, ever in my life. I should have been listening, and I wasn't and I'm sorry. Really sorry. I screwed up tonight and I really am sorry, and I hope you'll forgive me. You'll hear all about it, I'm sure, from that crazy friend of yours, Marnie. You know she's not really your friend, she never has been, she's always coming on to me, grabbing my privates, and trying to get me to feel her up, and I just got mad tonight, honey, I'm sorry, I really am. I really love you. Only you, all these years." He started to sob again, and Ginny couldn't stand it. She hung up.

Had he had sex with Marnie? She couldn't decide which part of that sentence made her angrier. Sex? Marnie? Both?

In her hand, her phone rang. It startled her so much that she nearly dropped it, and she was about to answer it with sharpness, thinking it was Matthew again.

Jack's number came up on the screen.

Her heart slammed into her ribs, but she did not answer, letting the ring pulse against her palm. It finally went to voice mail, and Ginny stood staring at the phone, wondering if he would leave a message.

What if he said he had changed his mind and wanted to forget about meeting her tomorrow in McMinnville? She had not responded, after all. What if he took her reticence as rejection and she never saw him again?

That would be best. She might not be in love with her husband, but she was married, after all. No matter what foolishness he'd indulged in the night before or how he had treated her, she had her own integrity to consider.

The voice-mail signal ticked against her skin. She pressed the icon to listen.

"Hey, Ginny. Sorry to have missed you again. I was hoping you might have replaced your phone by now. And I'm hoping you've made it safely to your friend's place. I got my truck unloaded and I'm headed over to a buddy's house for supper."

For a moment, she thought that was it. Then he said, "Look, I don't want to be a nag, so if I don't get an email or a phone call from you, I'll leave you alone. Take care, now."

Before she even knew she'd do it, she clicked on the callback number. A shiver ran up and down her neck, electrifying the burn on her shoulder blades as she listened to the phone ring.

"Hello?" he answered, and the sudden fact of his living voice in her ear paralyzed her for a second, long enough that he said, "Is that you, Ginny?"

"Yeah. Yes." She cleared her throat. "Hi, Jack," she said, and couldn't think of what else to say. Her cheeks burned as the silence hung between them. Finally she said, "I got your message," at the same time that he said, "I'm glad you called."

They both apologized and then they both fell silent again, and Ginny couldn't help it, she started to laugh. "Sorry, I'm being an idiot," she said.

"Not at all. I think you're flustered, which is what I am."

"You are?"

He let go of a rueful laugh, rough and low. "Hell, yes. You've got me totally rattled, Ginny Smith from Dead Gulch, Kansas. I've read about a hundred of your sweet blogs."

"There are a lot of them." She thought of the blogs, so many, each one chronicling a day in her life before she met him. How much would he know about her now?

But of all the people in her life back home, who had read any of them, even when she made *Martha Stewart Living*? She thought her mother and Jean might have dipped into them, but not far. Karen and her sister Peggy had read them, still read them, but Matthew made a point not to, making fun of it with his friends — her girly blog, as if it was a teenager thing she indulged in inappropriately, like hip-hugger jeans or blue streaks in her hair. Christie read it most days, as did the Foodie Four.

And now Jack. "I'm touched," she said. "And a little embarrassed."

"Don't be embarrassed," he said. "I love the way you look at the world. Upbeat. Beautiful. Even ugly things are beautiful when you look at them."

"Thank you," she whispered, closing her eyes, pressing the phone against her ear. She wanted to smell him again, to press her face into his neck and —

Stop. Ginny focused on Willow, who'd followed her out of the Airstream. She sat on the trailer step and threaded the dog's ear through her fingers. "I think you know me better than I know you now. You should start a blog."

He laughed. "Not happening."

"You can't have liked everything," she said.

"I do, actually. It's for women, I get that, but I like it anyway."

"That sounds fairly honest."

"I don't lie. It was a resolve I made when I got into that big mess with my ex."

"Me, either," she said, and realized that she was sort of lying. "Usually."

"Am I causing problems for you?"

"No. It's my life that's been causing problems for me. But I don't do things like kiss strangers when I'm married to somebody else. That's not me."

"I'm not a stranger, though, am I?" There was a smile in his voice.

She had no idea how to answer. She suddenly wanted to see his face so badly, to be looking into his eyes, as if she had a nutritional deficiency that would lead her to eat rocks or get rickets if she didn't correct it immediately. "I saw the ocean today."

"And what did you think?"

"It was — more than I can put into words. I'm not a word person, really. I had to close my eyes and let it wrap me up and fill me up, and then I could stand to look at how beautiful it was. I could look at it for a thousand years."

"That's a nice poem from somebody who

isn't a word person."

"I guess."

"Are you going to meet me tomorrow in McMinnville?"

She let go of a breath. "Are we going to be friends, Jack, or something else? This doesn't feel like friends, and I'm kind of afraid you're using me."

"I don't think we're going to be friends, Ginny. I think we're going to be lovers, and I think it's going to be good. I might be worried a little, too, that you're going to play with me and never leave that husband who makes you so miserable."

"I never said he makes me miserable." It bothered her that the phrase had come up twice today.

"You didn't have to say it, exactly."

She wanted to say, *This feels wrong.* She wanted to say she was married and didn't cheat. But both of those would be lies. "I want to see you tomorrow. I'll meet you at the Blue Moon." She laughed. "One of my friends is a blogger with that name. 'The Flavor of a Blue Moon.' "

"I'm glad, Ginny. I'm so glad. I won't so much as hold your hand, I promise."

She didn't believe him exactly, but aloud she said, "That's good. I'll see you then."

She hung up without waiting for his

answer and pressed her face into Willow's shoulder, the thick fur soft against her forehead. Willow groaned and settled one paw on Ginny's arm, in case Ginny should care to scratch her belly. With her fingers aimlessly scratching the dog's belly, Ginny let her heartbeat slow.

Adulterer, said a voice, and this time it didn't sound like her mother's but like some version of her own. Her conscience, maybe.

Lavender Honey Farms
yamhill co., oregon

Home   Shop   **Blog**   Directions   Philosophy

We've started distilling the new season of oils this week. It is quite a process, so if you haven't seen it, stop by the shop sometime soon and join one of our tours. We have two on Saturdays and Sundays, and you can usually talk one of our clerks into showing it to you during the week. (Please don't ask for special tours during the Lavender Festival! You'll have to join one in progress.)

In honor of the new pressing, all of our oils are 10 percent off on the website or 20 percent off at the shop. While you're here, pick up some fresh organic eggs from our free-roaming chickens (you can see them wandering the farm anytime) and check out the organic produce available. This week we have a wide variety, including red and gold beets, spinach, green onions, and many others.

See you soon!

CHAPTER 27

Lavender posted her blog, then stretched out on her bed, gob-smacked by an exhaustion that had plagued her all day. One of the dogs, Junior, padded into the room and settled down on the floor beside her, keeping guard and company, and Lavender let her hand fall over the side of the bed to the dog's back.

She'd had indigestion all last night, so badly that she had to get up for Tums six or seven times, and it still bothered her now. Eating eased it a little, though the McDonald's lunch they'd indulged in hadn't helped. Foolish old woman.

A breeze came through the window, fluttering a curtain so threadbare and faded that it was hardly cloth anymore. She watched it sail up and fall back, the light pouring through it, tiny holes showing along the hem. It made her dizzy, almost faint, and she closed her eyes.

She was profoundly exhausted, as if she'd had the stomach flu for a week or hauled hay for three days straight. Back in the days when she was flying, there had been times when she crossed so many time zones over a week that she'd gone slightly batty with it and slept sometimes for twenty-four hours straight. It felt like that now, like she needed to sleep for two solid days and start over.

The breeze played on her nose and cheekbones. Those were the days. Ginger and Helen and Lavender, the flying three, wandering to Morocco or London or Buenos Aires. It was elegant then, flying; people dressed up for it. Not like now, when people were packed in like anchovies, all wearing sweats and glitter on their butts. She didn't have any desire to fly anywhere nowadays.

But it was the farm that had done that. The first half of her adult life had been spent wandering, playing, experimenting with the limits given to women in those days. She'd had the chance a couple of times to step out of the game, settle in with a man and have some babies, but each time the lure of the next destination held sway. She'd never regretted it.

The second part of her life had been this farm, building this business she was so very proud of. She'd worked sometimes eighteen, twenty hours a day at first, sleeping four hours, then shoving food down her throat and getting back to work for another fourteen or sixteen. There had been a host of disasters, large and small, and each one nearly brought her to her knees. If she had not had the basic organic methods and established chickens and sheep flocks, she would never have survived. God bless Glen. She hoped he'd be proud of her.

Ginny's freckled nose floated over her imagination. Ginny was doing it in reverse. She'd spent her childhood on a farm, too, and had stuck with that life as a mother, but now she was wandering out into the world to see what else she could do. It wasn't easy, not at nearly fifty. Lavender was proud of her.

But it was plain that Ginny would not be the heir. Her eyes were pinned on some far horizon, and she couldn't possibly stick anywhere right now. It made Lavender a little sad, but that was that.

Who would take the farm? Her belly protested the worrisome thought, and she made a concentrated effort to let it go. Things worked out. She'd just have a nap, then get up and have dinner with the group and make an early night of it. Tomorrow was her birthday!

THE FLAVOR OF A BLUE MOON
a blog about great food . . .

Recipes   Appetizers
Main dishes   Sides   Sweets
Sort by Name   Sort by Category
About Ruby

The McDonald's Edition

The Golden Arches are synonymous with junk food, blamed for everything from childhood obesity to women giving up stockings. But here we are, the Foodie Four (plus one daughter), at McDonald's this afternoon. We were afraid you would judge us, dear readers, but I am here to tell you:

You don't have to feel guilty about eating McDonald's anymore!

First of all, I believe there is a place for a little junk food in every diet. I'm a fiend for French fries, in whatever form I can find them, and they have pretty much no redeeming value. Salty, full of fat, high in calories.

And I don't care! How about that! I love French fries!

Here's the other thing: McD's has come a long, long way in recent years. They dumped the trans fats, are paying attention to sourcing for meats and eggs (though let's face it — this is a big corporation; they're probably not

361

perfect), and they offer a lot of healthy choices. Salads, apple slices, bottled water. Even a vegan can eat well at McD's these days, and that is not the case with a lot of fast-food places.

We had a blast indulging our junk-food jones today. Here we are:

Comments:

Granttime:

Ruby, are you *pregnant*?

CHAPTER 28

Ruby reclined in the harem bedroom of her camper. The rain had stopped, but there were still heavy clouds overhead, and the air left behind carried a damp chill. Wrapped in a sweater, laptop open in front of her, she admired the photo from this afternoon. It was so great to have everyone together. As she admired it, a comment popped up: *Looking good, Mama.* It was from her dad. Grinning, she picked up the phone and called him.

"Where are you?" she asked without preamble.

"Tom and I just made it to Sydney this morning. You look great, kid. Really healthy and happy. Are you having a good time?"

"It's a blast. I love this farm, Dad! You should see the chickens. They are so adorable, and they take care of kittens in their nests, right along with the eggs. Isn't that cool?"

"It really is." She could hear him doing something in the background, probably unpacking. "What else?"

"Let's see . . . I'm in love with the lavender fields. They're astonishingly beautiful. And there are beehives that Lavender harvests honey from; it's made from the flowers. And — oh, ick, ick, ick!" Ninja Girl had leapt into the camper, a butterfly flapping against her lips. Proudly, she jumped up on the bed, blinking her bright yellow eyes, and put the butterfly down. "The kitten has a butterfly! She just put it on my bed! What do I do? Ick!"

"She's showing you that she's a solid hunter, sweetheart. Praise her. Tell her thank you."

"Ewww, it's still fluttering!" Ninja Girl pounced happily and grabbed it again in her teeth, clearly quite proud of herself. "Okay, I see, baby. Take it outside now."

Ninja Girl looked at Ruby, shifted weight on her front paws, but didn't move. The butterfly, a big yellow thing almost bigger than the kitten, gave a sad, dying flap.

"Okay, thank you." She petted her kitten's back, careful not to touch the insect. As if that was what she'd been waiting for, Ninja Girl dropped it and leapt down, sauntering to the door, tail high. Ruby had to laugh.

My job here is done. "Dad, she's so cute."

"Good to hear. And how 'bout you? How are you feeling?"

"Never better, and" — she snapped her fingers — "I have actually stopped throwing up. Miracle of miracles."

"Told you it would get better."

Ruby eyed the now-still butterfly. She would have to take it outside in a minute. For now she scooted her feet away from it. "I told Liam about the baby."

"And he didn't give a damn, right?"

"Yeah. I guess you were right about him all along." Her father had never liked Liam, thought him a spoiled rich kid.

"Are you okay with it?"

"Getting better, I guess. It's really great to be with my friends, and, honestly, I think I might want to live here on the farm for a while."

"How far away are the hospitals?"

Ruby scowled. "I don't know. Not that far. We are right outside Portland."

"You need to be sure you have high-quality medical care, kiddo. There are —"

"Okay, don't." She brushed hair away from her face. "I've been cancer-free for a long, long time, and it's not coming back. Getting pregnant isn't going to make me sick."

Her father paused, and when he spoke, his voice was a little hushed. "I know. I'm sorry. It'll make more sense to you when the baby comes. You'll understand why I'm so overprotective."

"I know why, and I love you for it. Just don't bring it forward, all right?"

"It's a deal. Keep me posted, huh?"

"You know I will. I love you, Dad. Be careful out there."

"Always."

She hung up and glared at the kitten, then the butterfly. It wasn't going to move itself, so she gingerly grabbed the very, very edge of an intact wing and carried the butterfly to the door. Ninja Girl eyed her prize, making Ruby feel guilty. "I know it was a prize, baby, but it kinda creeps me out. Can you play with it outside?"

"She doesn't speak English," Noah said, making her jump about a foot.

"Stop sneaking up on me like that!"

He chuckled. "I heard you were on the phone and stepped away to give you some privacy. That your dad?"

"Yeah. He's surfing in Australia."

"Rough life."

She sat in the doorway. "He is not hurting for money, that's for sure."

Noah settled beside her, legs swinging. "Is

he a dot-com guy?"

"Not really. He invents things. Lots of things. He invented one thing for the computer industry that made him super-rich at one point. That's all it takes, really."

"Unless you're a rock star and spend it all."

She grinned. "That's true. He's not really a rock-star kinda guy."

"Where's your mom?"

Ruby sighed. "She lives in Seattle. In this cute little house by the sound, with three kids who play soccer and a husband who must provide a pretty good living. She drives a minivan."

"You don't talk to her?"

Again that sense of sadness. "Nope. I haven't had a conversation with her since I was about nine, maybe. She left when she found out I was sick, but she kept calling for a while after that."

She felt Noah's gaze on her face, but she thought he would eventually say something. He didn't, and she looked up.

He took her hand into his, palm to palm, fingers laced. "I hate that."

"I'm over it."

He lifted her hand to his mouth, kissed her fingers. "No, you aren't."

Instantly, all the sex sensors in her body

stood at full alert. She could almost hear the bugle call. Using the same fingers of the hand he held, she touched his mouth, the fat bottom lip, and he captured the tip of her finger in his hot mouth. Meeting his eyes, she said, "I'm really not over my boyfriend."

"I know." He kissed her fingers again, eyes on her face, on her mouth. Abruptly, he stood. "Let's take a walk."

Confused, Ruby said, "Um . . . okay."

"I'm loading lavender into the still and I thought you'd want to see it."

"Ooh, yes! I'd love that."

His smile was slow and bright. "Come on, then."

On the way up the hill, he said, "Do you have names picked out yet for the baby?"

"I don't! I keep thinking I need to look at lists of names and come up with some, but at first I was too superstitious, then I was too sick, and I've been here since then." She had to hurry a little to keep up with his long-legged stride through the tall grass. He noticed and slowed down. "Maybe flower names for a girl. I like it that Lavender has a flower name. Maybe Rose or Daisy."

"And if it's a boy?"

"I don't know. I just don't think it is."

"But what if?" He held the door to the

shop open for her, waving her in ahead of him.

"You're right. I should think of something. But I have almost four months."

The shop was closed for the day, with everything neatly put away, the cash drawer open. The front room was very pretty, with lavender curtains and woven wreaths of lavender and bottles of various kinds of cosmetics. "Is everything made here?" Ruby asked, pausing.

"Not all of it. Lavender's main thing is her oil production, and there are some bulk culinary and decorative lavenders. They make some pillows and eye masks, that kind of thing." He waved. "But a lot of it is just pretty stuff, you know, for tourists. We sell a lot through the website, thanks to Lavender's blog."

"Profitable?"

"Surprisingly so." He gestured for her to follow him up the stairs, and as they reached the second floor, the smell of lavender hung like a fabric in the air.

Ruby took a deep breath. "That's wonderful. I want to drink it!"

"We do have tea." He grinned. "In here."

The room had once been a large bedroom, with lots of Victorian touches — long double-hung windows, now curtainless to show the expanse of green fields, the barns and outbuildings, trees, and, in the distance, the rolling hills bumping up against the cloudy sky. Cool light flooded the room, touching on a pair of copper kettles connected by a coil. "It's so cute!" Ruby said. Two more stills were in the room, and one made a soft hissing noise.

Next to the still were baskets of lavender blossoms, cut very evenly with a stem of about four inches. "Is this done by hand?"

"We do this with a small machine, but a lot of the rest of it is done by hand. We hire crews of high school students."

"Really?"

He shrugged. "Not much work for kids out here." He knelt by the baskets and hauled one up off the floor. The light lavishly brushed him, highlighting cheekbones and mouth, the cords of his arms, the shape of his thighs. She thought of his mouth on her fingers, and all the newly awakened bits of her stretched and poked — feathers over her throat, dancers on her breasts, soldiers of want marching up her thighs. He had a gorgeous butt, high and round, perfect for the loose old jeans he wore. She thought of what that back might look like, that rear end, all naked and —

He shook the blossoms and looked over

his shoulder. "Are you paying attention?" he asked, and a sleepy expression told her he knew the truth.

Inside her, the baby moved, sliding a foot or a hand from one end of her belly to the other. A welcome distraction.

"I am." She brushed hair off her forehead and stepped closer.

He took the lid off one side of the kettle. "This is the still pot," he said. "We leave the stems about four inches long and load them into the pot pretty tightly." He illustrated, grabbing fistfuls of stalks, then packing them into the pot, over and over. Each movement released the scent into the air, until Ruby was practically dizzy with it. "Steam will take the easiest path, so you want to be sure it's touching as much lavender as possible. Look."

He pushed a small step stool over, and Ruby stood on it to look inside the pot. "Can I add some?"

"Sure." He offered the basket, and Ruby gathered fistfuls of blossoms, as he had, and pushed them down, searching for holes in the stacks, sealing up gaps with more flowers. The texture of the filled pot was springy and dense.

"This is so cool," Ruby said.

"You think everything is cool."

She laughed. "It's true. I do. That's why I'm having so much trouble figuring out what to do with my life."

"I thought you were a chef."

"Technically, yes." She tucked stalks into the sides of the pot. "I love cooking, but restaurants are brutal. I don't like working that many hours."

"What about the food truck?"

She shrugged. "Where's the baby going to be? Inside the hot truck while I work? I don't really like that idea as much as I thought I would."

"And the blog?"

"It's fine. I've been doing it for eight years, though, and maybe I'm tired of it." She peered into the pot, nudged some more blossoms into place. "I just feel like I'll know the right place when I see it."

"Or maybe you'll know some other way. You'll realize you really like something you're doing. Things don't always show up as ringing gongs."

"That's kinda what my dad says, too." She stepped down. "There. Check it out."

He pressed the springy mass, then stood on the stool and added another few handfuls of blossoms. "Good." With an easy gesture, he set the basket aside, grabbed the lid, and fitted it to the top, connecting a tube to the other kettle. "This has to fit tightly so that no steam escapes," he explained, and pointed out the path of the steam. "It will rise up to the top here, go through the tube, and come into the condenser; then the lavender oil is separated and comes out here." He pointed to a small glass bottle.

"All those flowers into this?"

"Amazing, right? I love the chemistry of all this stuff."

"Like wine, right? You liked the wineries, too."

He looked at her. "You're right, I did. I do." He turned the machine on and pointed to one of the other stills. "This one," he said, "has been going for a while, so it has produced this oil." He stuck his nose in it, then offered it to her. "That's the real deal."

Ruby inhaled. "Can I feel it?"

He moved the bottle. "Catch the drops in your palm."

She put her hand beneath the spigot, and a heavy globule of oil, then another, fell slowly into her palm. "That's good," she said, and raised it to her nose. "Oh, my God, that's beautiful!" Again she inhaled, letting it fill the hollows of her nose and sinuses, letting it hang a little at the top of her throat. "There is no camphor in this one, is there?"

He had his palm beneath the spigot, too, and smiled. "Good job. This is Royal Velvet." He held his cupped hand to his nose and closed his eyes, and Ruby nearly swooned. His lashes were black and long, falling on his cheekbones in unexpected and ridiculous adorability.

She shook her head. Too much. His beauty was like something she'd made up, practically surreal.

"What?" he said, giving her a perplexed twitch of the eyebrows.

"Nothing. Never mind."

He stepped over and tugged on her blouse. "Lift up. It would be a shame to waste this oil."

"Oh, I don't —"

"Are you shy, Ruby?" He seemed genuinely surprised.

"Not usually. But nobody has seen my tummy yet, except me."

"I don't have to look. I'll just rub it on right quick."

Ruby's skin whispered, wiggled, got ready. "No, it's fine." She tugged up her top and there was her roundness, all fat and funny and beautiful. He poured the oil from his palm on her skin, and Ruby poured hers, too, but he did the rubbing, a firm, easy circle on her skin, round and round, hypnotic, even. His skin was dark against the moon-pale shine of hers, and it aroused her even more, and she wanted him to lift up her top even farther, to rub that oil on her breasts. She wanted to rub some on his skin.

He raised his head. "Okay?" he said softly, leaning closer.

"Yes," she whispered, and he leaned down all the way to kiss her, his hands circling her bare waist, one on her back, one on her belly, as if in protection. Ruby slid her arms around his shoulders, touched his hair, pulled him close, opening her mouth to him.

And there it was, the sorrow, all the ghosts coming to life around them, rustling and murmuring. She heard them as he suckled her lips, gently, gently, as his hands moved over her tummy, her back, as she pressed closer into the heat and solidness of his body.

She wanted him. Now, today, this very minute. She needed to get laid; she needed his hands on her breasts and that cock moving inside her. It had been way too long.

And yet there were the ghosts, pressing closer, whispering. Children, men, animals.

With more firmness than she knew she had, she pushed away, her hands against his shoulders. The whispering darkness halted.

"I don't think I can help you."

"What are you talking about?" He sounded half angry, half lusty, and she didn't blame him. Her own limbs were hot and liquid. "I don't need *help.* I've been half crazy with wanting my hands on you, Ruby." He stroked her back. "You're so juicy."

He bent in and kissed her again, hauling her closer, their bodies in contact from mouth to toes, and the kiss burned, and she tasted love and loss and hunger. His hands swept up her back, under her shirt, and she found his skin, too, hot, sleek, smooth. Without halting his kiss, he urgently skimmed her shirt upward, slid his hands over her breasts, and she made a soft, hot cry. She grabbed his ass, pulling it into her, rubbing hard against him.

The whispering, the murmuring, swelled around them, not so much evil as tortured and despairing. She tried to block them out, focusing on the feel of his silky hot back, on the electric nip of his teeth. She put her hands on his face and sucked on his lips and —

Not this.

The voice was simple and calm and clear.

Not this.

Mustering all of her will, everything she

had, she said, "Noah, stop. We can't do this."

"What?" He raised his head. "Why? I don't care about your boyfriend."

"No, that's not it." She swallowed, easing herself away from him slightly so that she could put her hands on his face. "I can't explain. I just know that this needs to be different. Something is —" She peered upward at him, swaying toward his swollen mouth, his naked chest. "I think you know what it is you have to say, to tell me." She narrowed her eyes. "Confess?"

For a long, miserable moment, he stared at her, hair falling down around that astonishing face, inky darkness covering his eyes. Light broke over his shoulders, and his hands rested on her sides.

He ran his hands over her arms, over her breasts. With a gesture of practiced nonchalance, he shook his head and stepped away. "I don't know what you're talking about." Ruby listened inwardly, waiting for the voice again, but she felt only a simple sense of rightness. She pulled her shirt down over herself as she waited for him to turn. He stood at the window, spine rigid. "Sorry," she said, and headed for the stairs.

He caught her arm. "Wait."

She stopped.

"That was disrespectful, and I'm sorry to

be an ass. Kinda hard to switch gears that fast." He skimmed his hand over her arm. "Friends?"

She tipped her head sideways. "You'd rather be friends than talk to me?"

He shrugged. "Not really. It's just —" He shook his head.

"Okay." She touched his face. "You know where to find me."

FROM: Ginny@cakeofdreams.com
TO: msmith@greatinsurance.com
SUBJECT: Divorce

Dear Matthew,

I didn't mean to send that email yesterday — that's not the way I wanted to do things. But when you hung up on me this afternoon, I had no way to express what I am feeling.

You were not listening. You have not been listening for years and years. Even now, when I'm trying to tell you something really important, YOU HUNG UP ON ME!

I am very unhappy in our marriage. I have been for a decade or better, and, what's more, you know it. You KNOW it! You just kept thinking that if you didn't listen, I would give up, and you know what, Matthew, I almost did. I tried to make this marriage work, to find ways to occupy myself and find other things to make up for the lack of intimacy, but in the end I couldn't.

All those other things gave me myself. The blog, my online friends, my dog, and my trailer. I am happier right now than I have been at any time in the past ten years.

So you can listen or not listen, but here is the absolute truth in two easy sentences:

1. I am divorcing you.
2. I am never coming back to Kansas.

I do not mean to cause you pain, but I am tired of swallowing my own pain to make other people happy. And, to tell the truth, I don't think you're happy, either. Let's be nice to each other and get a divorce.

Ginny

CHAPTER 29

When the rain began to fall, Ginny napped, luxuriously curled up with Willow, the drops pattering lazily on the roof of the Airstream, a warm quilt pulled up over her ears. Thankfully, she did not dream. Not about Jack, or Matthew, or anything else.

It was still raining off and on when she got up. She changed clothes for dinner, putting on jeans and a warm sweater. She covered Ruby's dress with a trash bag, tying the end to protect the hem from mud splatters as she walked up the hill. She opened her umbrella and whistled for Willow. "Let's make a dash for it, baby!"

And dash they did, keeping to the grass to avoid the muddy road. The chickens were all tucked in their beds. A light shone in Valerie's Airstream, parked beneath a copse of pine trees, and Ginny had to stop for a moment to admire it. Willow trotted on, head down miserably, and Ginny had to run

380

to catch up.

They entered the cottage through the screened-in porch. Ginny wiped Willow down, cleaned her feet, and took off her own shoes. She left the umbrella to dry. "Smells good in here!" she called.

"I'm baking a sweet potato pie," Valerie said as Ginny came into the kitchen. The windows were fogged over from the cooking.

"Mmm."

Ruby shelled peas at the table, holding the bowl in her lap. She had an efficient rhythm of cracking a pod, skimming out the peas with a thumbnail, tossing aside the empty pod, grabbing a new one. "Want to help?" she asked. "There are a lot!"

"Sure, but, first, do you want to see your dress?" She shook out the bag and pulled it backward over itself, revealing the two-layered gown beneath.

"Ginny!" Valerie exclaimed. "Did you do that *today*?"

Ruby leapt up, nearly spilling the peas. She grabbed the bowl at the last second and set it on the table. "Ooooh! It's beautiful! Can I try it on?"

"Of course. I want to be sure it fits."

Ruby carried it into the other room.

"Where's Lavender?" Ginny asked.

"Still napping. I popped in to talk to her a little while ago and she wasn't feeling well. Maybe a stomach bug."

"Or food poisoning!" Ginny touched her belly in memory. "That was awful."

"I never did hear the whole story."

"It's pretty bizarre, actually." She washed her hands. "What's next?"

"You can peel the potatoes."

It was a tiny room, but there was just enough space for the two women to stand side by side. Valerie chopped onions for what appeared to be a stew. The smell of sweet potato pie, squash and cinnamon together, twined through the air. Cozy.

The two of them had become close when Valerie had a crisis in her marriage. She suspected her husband of an affair — which turned out not to be true that time — and confided in Ginny, who confided her own unhappiness, though not all the details. That month-long exchange cemented their friendship from then on. When Val's husband was killed, she wrote endless, long, wailing emails to Ginny, who read every word, commented as needed to keep the healing flow going, and let it trail away when Valerie found her widow legs.

"So," Valerie said, smiling.

"So," Ginny answered.

Val washed green onions. "You're never going back to Kansas, huh?"

"Never." Ginny picked up a big russet and started to peel. "When I got food poisoning, I ended up at this lake where there were almost no people. I was too sick to keep driving, but it was a little dicey, you know? And I didn't have my phone and all that, but I was so sick I had to stop."

"Scary."

"Yeah." In her mind's eye, she was back in the trailer, with the drunk hunters — or whatever they were — banging on the door. "These guys tried to get in, but Willow scared them off, and the next thing I knew, it was morning."

"Oh, my God. You passed out?"

"I think I was running a very high fever. It had the feel of that kind of delirium." Ginny finished the first potato and dropped it in a bowl. "The weird part is that I'd made friends with this trucker on the road, and — this is the weird part — somehow I texted him from my dead phone. He back-tracked a long way to find me, and he took care of me in the night."

Valerie stopped chopping and rested her wrists on the counter. "How did that happen?"

"I don't know. It's like a completely weird thing."

"It wasn't just him saying that?"

"No. He didn't know where I was until I texted." She shook her head, carefully keeping the peel in a single strip around the potato. "And that phone was absolutely dead. You saw it."

"That gives me the creeps a little," Valerie said. "Maybe he's a ghost, your trucker. Like one of those teenage stories."

Ginny laughed. "Oh, he's real."

"What's going on?" Valerie said quietly.

"I don't know yet." She met her friend's eyes. "I have so much to tell you guys."

"Don't start without me!" Ruby swished into the kitchen, and they turned. She held out her arms. "Ta-da!"

Ginny let go of a delighted laugh. "You look amazing!" The blue offset Ruby's bright-blue eyes, and the bodice left her shoulders bare and revealed a voluptuous cleavage. The skirt swelled over the baby bump and swished outward, silvery and sparkling.

"I feel like the moon goddess in this," she said, spinning in a circle.

"It's appropriate, too, because that's your blog." Ginny tugged the skirt a little. "I'm delighted that it fits so well."

"I hope it doesn't keep raining!" Ruby spun one more time. "Okay, let me go change, and don't say a word till I get back."

They waited. Valerie wiped her onion-ravaged eyes. "I should have made my daughter do this."

"What's she doing? I saw the light on in the trailer. It looked very homey."

"Probably reading. That's her default mode. She is the biggest reader I've ever met, and I'm pretty serious myself."

"Me, too." Ginny finished another potato. "What are we doing with these? Chop or grate or slice?"

"Grate. I'm making hash browns."

Ruby swirled back into the room and settled at the table with her peas. "Okay, now talk."

Ginny said, straight out, "I think I'm getting a divorce."

"What?" Valerie said. "Because of the trucker?"

"The guy with the voice?" Ruby gave a little shiver. "I get it."

"No," Ginny said. "Not because of that. Not because of anything to do with this trip except that I never want to go back to Kansas again. I can't believe I finally got out of there."

"So, why? He won't leave Kansas?"

385

"No," she said again. And, slowly, "Because I don't want to be with him anymore. I haven't wanted to for a long time, but that didn't seem like a good enough reason to leave, you know?"

"I told you I knew you were miserable," Ruby crowed, throwing a pea that hit Ginny on the arm. "Ha!"

She picked it off the counter and tossed it back. "There is more, actually."

Valerie turned, eyes dark and still. "He didn't abuse you?"

"No." Ginny took a breath and told them what she'd never told another living being. "We haven't had sex in twelve years."

"Oh, Gin!" Valerie said softly. "Twelve years?"

"I know." She picked up another potato. "I tried everything. *Let's go to counseling, let's see the doctor, let's talk about this, for God's sake*, but nothing."

"Twelve years?" Ruby said. "That's half of my life!"

"I feel like an idiot that I put up with it for so long." She paused and met Valerie's eyes. "I just didn't know what to do."

"Is he gay, maybe?" Ruby asked. She nibbled peas out of her palm as if they were candy. "It happens a lot, you know."

"I've thought about that, but he didn't

seem like it before the sex stopped."

"Does he have any guy friends he hangs out with?"

"Yeah, they're all ex-football players. Married, guy's guys."

"See?" Ruby grinned. "You should ask him."

Ginny shrugged. "At this point, I don't care anymore."

Valerie touched her shoulder. "Have you told him that you want a divorce?"

"I didn't mean to," she said. "I wrote an email that I wasn't going to send, and then I sent it."

"No!" Ruby let go of her robust laugh, then covered her mouth with her hand. Her eyes glittered. "How Freudian is that?"

Ginny laughed, too. "I know. I feel bad that it happened like this, but it gets it out in the open. Only trouble is that he's not accepting it. He thinks I'm going to come to my senses." She put the quotes around the words with her fingers.

Lavender, coming into the room, said, "It sounds like you have come to your senses." She sat at the table with Ruby, looking wan but sturdy, and plucked a handful of peas out of the bowl to nibble one at a time. "I knew you were going to leave him the minute you bought that trailer."

"Maybe I did, too," Ginny admitted aloud. "I've been looking for a new life since my daughter left home ten years ago."

Ruby leaned over and pressed the back of her hand to Lavender's face. "You're still so pale. Are you feeling better?"

"Oh, I'll be fine. It's just a touch of something." She popped peas into her mouth. "I'm not going to hide in my room while you all are here."

Valerie stirred the pot. "Do you have any idea what you're going to do?"

"Zero. I only know I'm not going back to Kansas."

"You're welcome to stay here while you figure it out," Lavender said. She plucked another handful of pea pods from the bowl in Ruby's lap and split one open. "Are you comfortable enough in the trailer to live in it for a bit?"

"It's only been a week, but I think so." In her mind's eye rose a vision of herself camping on a beach somewhere, waking up to the sound of waves crashing on the shore. A sense of possibility swept her, smelling of morning. "Maybe I want to wander around a little. I thought it would be lonely on the road, but it wasn't."

"I'm heading down to San Diego to be near my parents," Valerie said. "If you like, you can caravan with us."

Ginny didn't want to say straight out that she wanted to be on her own, so she smiled and said, "I'll think about it."

The rain didn't let up, so they set the table in the tiny kitchen and crowded around it for dinner, just the five females. Noah was nowhere about. "He said he'd come for dessert," Lavender said, "but he's in a mood."

"He showed me the still this afternoon," Ruby said, dipping a chunk of bread into her stew. "It's pretty cool."

"I helped him with feeding the chickens," Hannah said, throwing a long look at Ruby. "He wasn't grouchy *then.*"

Ruby grinned. "Well, you know, I can be pretty irritating." She jumped suddenly, making a little squeaking noise, and put a hand on her tummy. "Yikes! That was a big kick!"

"That's a very active baby. He'll be running you ragged by the time he's one," Valerie said. "That's how it was with my Louisa. And she was a nonstop girl."

Ginny felt uncomfortable at this mention of one of the dead sisters. Hannah wiggled her leg under the table, making Ginny think she felt uncomfortable, too.

But Valerie's face was smooth and serene

389

as she continued. "Kalista was so lazy in the womb that I kept worrying about her. Hannah here" — she nudged her daughter with an elbow — "made me so fat I was afraid I would pop like a balloon."

Ruby said, "Was Kalista lazy when she was born?"

"Not really," Valerie said. "She was a quiet baby, an observer. I'd say she was like that as she grew up, too, wouldn't you, Hannah?"

She stared at her plate, gave a tiny shrug. "I guess."

"You're the middle sister, right?" Ruby said.

"Yep."

"And the reader. Neither of my other girls liked to read. It's as if Hannah is reading for the whole world."

"Why are we talking about them like this?" Hannah said, slamming her hand down. Spoons rattled.

"Why wouldn't we?" Valerie asked calmly. "We loved them. It's nice to think about them sometimes."

"I don't like thinking about them. It *hurts*! I wish I could forget they ever existed." She pushed back from the table and leapt to her feet, but by the time she was standing, Ruby was there, putting her arms on Hannah's

390

shoulders.

"Wait! I know something about this, I promise."

"Leave me alone!" Hannah shook free. "I don't care what you have to say." She stormed toward the door.

Ruby called after her, "What if you were the one who died?"

"What do you mean?"

"Would you want us to never talk about you again? Pretend you didn't exist?"

Hannah paused. Frowned. "I didn't die."

"Me, either," Ruby said. "I thought I would, about five times. Chemo makes you feel like you're going to die, and I was a little kid, only seven, the first time I started it." She took a breath. "Sometimes, Hannah, I was so afraid that I would die and disappear and no one would ever know I'd even lived."

Hannah's eyes filled with tears. "That's terrible."

"I'm alive. Some of the kids I was in the wards with didn't make it, and I love to say their names out loud. I love to think about their faces and what they liked."

Ginny had always loved Ruby, but right then she adored her even more.

Hannah eased back into the room and

perched on a chair, right at the edge. "Like what?"

"My friend Mona loved comets. She had them all over the place, on her notebooks, and her pajamas, and they put some on the wall for her. She had a scruffy little dog named BeBe, all black, with hair in its eyes."

"When did she die?"

"When I was eleven and she was ten. They thought she was going to make it, and right at the end of the five years she got sick again."

Valerie said, "Why don't you have some supper, Hannah? We'll keep talking."

"I don't want to talk about my sisters, though, or my dad." She gave her mother a challenging glance.

"You don't have to. I might want to, though. So you can go if you like."

As if summoned, right on cue, Noah came into the kitchen. "What are we talking about?" He ruffled Hannah's hair and sat down beside her, looking across to Ruby, who sat straighter, even though she didn't look at him.

Interesting, Ginny thought.

Lavender said, "Sometimes I see ghosts around this place. Maybe when you're as old as me, you'll see ghosts, too, Hannah." She slapped her knee. "Anyway, let's put on some music and get happy!"

She stood up with purpose, then doubled over, grabbing her belly with a moan. Staggering sideways, she grabbed for a chair and knocked it over. Ruby, closest to her, tried to catch her before she fell, but Lavender was already in motion and hit the floor.

CHAPTER 30

Ruby and Noah sat side by side in the county medical center ER. Val and Hannah had stayed behind at the farm. Ginny had gone in with Lavender, easily slipping into the role of capable mother/nurse, and they'd let her, taking seats in the cold waiting room. Overhead, the lights buzzed faintly, and somewhere a child cried, but mostly there was only the hush of worry hanging in the air.

Ruby stuck her feet out in front of her, studying the shape of her pink high-tops. They were proving to be highly impractical shoes in this wet place, but she still liked them. Inside her, the baby moved every now and then, as if trying to find a more comfortable spot to sleep. Ruby shifted, thinking that maybe if she slumped, the baby was squished. Absently, she rubbed her hand in a circle over her belly, then remembered Noah rubbing his hands over her this afternoon and froze, flushing.

He sat beside her, utterly still. One jeaned leg was propped on the other, ankle to knee, so that his right knee jutted out toward her. Along the internal seam, the fabric fanned in small, even lines all the way down his thigh. His hand was on his knee, and his sleeve was rolled up on his forearm. The shirt was fresh, not the same one he'd worn this afternoon. That had been a work shirt, worn soft, with pockets in which he stuck random things, like an invoice or a packet of seeds. The tools — wrenches and screwdrivers — ended up in his back pocket.

The shirt he wore tonight was crisp white cotton with tiny, wide-spaced red lines. The color pointed out how tanned his forearm was and how oddly hairless. His skin was very smooth, covering the cords of muscle with a buttery gloss. Again she wanted to touch him, just put her hand along that butter and feel the suppleness.

He said nothing.

Neither did she. Until she finally said, "Stop being so awkward, Noah. We were friends before this afternoon."

"Were we?"

"Of course we were. You were teaching me about lavender and chickens and trying to cheer me up."

He kept his eyes on the hallway. "Not sure friendship is exactly the right thing between us, Ruby."

"Why?" She flicked her fingers over his arm. "Because I'm so hot you can't stand to be around me?"

He glanced sideways at her. "I'm still thinking about kissing you today. You're not?"

She flushed again, looking away. "No." His tongue in her mouth, his hands on her sides. "Yes," she admitted.

"Right. So 'friends' is not the right word."

"You know, the thing is —"

He held up a hand, shaking his head. "I hate those conversations. We're not even involved."

Yet. Ruby heard the word clearly in her head.

"Okay," she said, and unconsciously nibbled a fingernail. "But I'm bored, and there is no one else here to talk to, so you might as well talk to me."

"You can talk."

"That's not fun. I'm worried and I want to take my mind off Lavender. I'm scared she's had a heart attack."

His jaw clenched and he shifted in his seat, leaning forward almost prayerfully. "Yeah."

Ruby took a long, cleansing breath and let it go. "So let's talk. Twenty questions. I'll start."

He groaned but sat up.

"What's your favorite color?" Ruby asked.

"Blue."

"Your turn to ask a question."

"Oh. Um . . ." He flung out his fingers. "What's your favorite food?"

"Cherries. Yours?"

He gave her a faint grin. "Steak. Rare."

Ruby shuddered for effect because she didn't want to disappoint him. "What is your mom's name?"

"Linda. Yours?"

Ruby flinched. It was unconscious and unstoppable. "Cammy," she said, voice thick.

Noah met her eyes for the first time. "Sorry, I forgot."

She nodded. "TV or books?"

"Books. I don't even have to ask you."

"Why, because I'd just naturally be a TV lover?"

"Uh, no. The opposite. Book fanatic."

She beeped like in a game show. "Wrong. I like to read, but give me television and I'm one happy girl."

"I don't even have one."

"Not surprised." She shifted so that she

397

was sitting with one leg up on the chair, facing him a little more. "All you brooding types give up television in your ennui."

That kindled a half smile. "What do you watch?"

"God, everything! My dad hates it, but I like sitcoms and dramas and news shows and those house-hunting shows. Love HGTV, full stop. Decorating, landscaping, all of it. I love it when they buy an old house and make it over. I love it when a couple is shopping for their first house. All of them." She pointed a finger in the air. "Oh, and all the food shows, of course."

He studied her for a moment. "You're a little housewife at heart, aren't you?"

Ruby couldn't tell from the tone of his voice if that was meant to be an insult, so she went with the truth. "I prefer 'homemaker,' " she said pertly. "I mean, somebody has to do it, right? Shake out the sheets, put some flowers around, make sure there are supplies — toilet paper and bread and whatever — cook a good meal, smooth everything for the day."

"Yeah." He swallowed, as if the litany hurt him. "Yeah," he repeated gruffly. Then he sniffed. "So maybe that's your work."

Tears sprang to Ruby's eyes. A life spread before her in possibility — a kitchen stocked with everything she could think of, all the special herbs and spices that took her fancy, star anise and lemon curry and tarragon, and special spoons and plates for every possible scenario. She would have sturdy pots for stock and very good knives. She could feed chickens and grow flowers and have a vegetable garden and hang pictures on the walls. "In New York, we lived in six hundred and ten square feet for six years. It was so crowded I couldn't keep it tidy, and there was no room for anything beautiful."

"Tidy?" His body language eased, too. "That's a prim word."

"I have a prim side, sir."

He full on grinned, and Ruby felt she'd scored points for making him loosen up. "Why do I doubt that?" He lifted a finger. "Oh, I know! Because you have a camper that looks like a sultan's den."

Ruby conceded with a tilt of her head. "But, honestly, I do like things to be right, to be appealing to look at, and if things are messy, it's not beautiful anymore."

"I bet your apartment was beautiful anyway."

"Really? That's a nice thing to say. Thank you. I tried."

He nudged her foot with the tip of his boot. "Lavender brought you guys out here so she could leave the farm to one of you."

"She can't! The nephews get it because of some weird deed thing."

"It's only money. That's all they want — money."

"Why not you?"

"I don't have the resources to buy it, and that would have to be done to keep it out of the hands of Wade Markum. And, anyway, I like what I do, managing the animals, looking out for crops, all that. I don't want to run a shop or do the marketing or anything like that."

"The mead?"

"You have a thing for mead, don't you? No, I don't care about that part, though I like the bees and the honey." He met her eyes simply, those long dark lashes making him look like an earnest three-year-old. "We'd be a good team, Ruby. A really good team."

A waft of lavender blew over her face. She imagined suddenly what she would do with the kitchen to make it work better, clear out the old butcher block so she could cook more easily. Lavender was hearty, but Ruby could care for her as she grew older.

"I don't have any money, either," she said. "And I've already asked my dad for a lot. He won't be pleased with this idea." She

400

widened her eyes, imagining. "At all."

Noah nodded. "Well, I thought you should know."

Under Ruby's ribs, the baby punched upward, and Ruby scowled, rubbing the foot down. "I didn't think babies were this active so early."

"Almost six months, right?"

"Yeah. I guess it could be." She stood up to walk it off.

"One more question," Noah said.

Ruby turned.

"How much have you thought about your boyfriend tonight?"

She smiled. "Not once. Thank you."

He fell back against the tan plastic chairs, looking insouciant and delicious with his black hair falling around that astonishing face. "You're welcome."

Two more hours passed before the ER doctor decided that Lavender had had a gall bladder attack, two hours during which Ruby and Noah played rummy and poker with a deck of cards they found on a table, using coffee stir sticks for points.

When Lavender and Ginny came out, Lavender looked waxy and tired. Ruby scowled, getting to her feet. "What did they say?"

Ginny shook her head, clearly not pleased, either. "They made an appointment for her to be checked out by her physician, first thing on Monday morning, and ordered her to avoid consuming much — if any — fat until then."

Lavender snorted. "I'll be damned. I'm eighty-five, and I'll do what I please." A charcoal bruise had bloomed on her left cheekbone, where she'd struck the ground when she fell. She settled on a plastic chair, hands on her thin thighs to prop her upright. She took a breath.

"Are you sure you feel okay to go home?" Ruby asked.

"I'm fine, I'm telling you. I've had these attacks before. Eventually it'll sort itself out."

"A good night's sleep will help," Ginny said. "And tomorrow is your birthday!"

"Lotta good it'll do me, if I can't celebrate properly. I want bacon for breakfast and cake for dinner."

"And by damn you'll have it," Noah said, stepping up to offer Lavender his elbow. "The queen of the lavender fields!"

CAKE OF DREAMS

Lavender Cake: Sugar and Spice and Silver Moons . . . oh my!

June 30, 20—

Shhh! I'm up much earlier than everyone else, to make this cake for Lavender, whose eighty-fifth birthday is today. It's a lavender cake, of course, and I had to think long and hard about how to make this work. I think you will agree that it's beautiful, and I can't wait to show you the photos from tonight.

Tonight is the blue moon. Enjoy the rare and magical energy. Send out a wish and see what happens!

(And who is writing this blog? Is it Ruby? ☺ Friends, you would love her.)

17 COMMENTS

CHAPTER 31

In her trailer, Ginny bent over the finished cake with her camera. The light on her table here was not quite the genius swath of light that came in on her kitchen counter, but it was pretty good. A lot would depend on how she parked, she supposed, straightening to decide which direction she faced just now. The light was coming from the east, edging over the horizon to glitter through pines. She'd draped a thin dish towel over the window to diffuse the bars of light, and the result was a bowl of goldenness.

Which was not what she was going for. The cake was white and silver and soft purple; the yellow was bringing out the wrong tones. She held the camera in one hand, looking around at the other surfaces, chewing on her inner cheek. Photoshop would make it possible to change that, of course, but she had a certain pride in her natural-light skills, and even if the conscious

404

mind didn't notice the difference, she always felt that the subconscious would know.

The light was much better coming in through the windows by the bed. What if she used a cookie sheet and a drape of some kind in that corner?

Outside the open door of the trailer, Willow made a squeaky noise, a yipping bark that meant play. Who was here? Ginny peeked out, and there was the kitten Ruby was so enamored with, tiptoeing through the grass to slide by the dog, who stood at full attention, ears up, pointed nose pointier, tail wagging high. "Willow," she said firmly. "Leave it."

But Willow's black tail kept wagging, and her face was a wide, cheerful smile. The kitten moved a quarter inch at a time, as if in slow motion, eyes focused full ahead, as if to make Willow invisible. Ginny covered her mouth when giggles threatened to come out, and impulsively she shot a series of the dog and the cat. Then, when the cat came in to the trailer, she settled the cake on the counter and put the kitten beside it. Black and white, so perfect.

Her phone rang as she was finishing, and the cat dived under the table. Glancing at the screen, she saw that it was her daughter.

"Christie!" she cried. "I'm so glad to talk to you!"

"How are you? You sound like you're having a blast."

Ginny paused, feeling suddenly as if it couldn't possibly have been only a week since she'd left home. "I'm great. So great. Did you worry when I dropped out of sight?"

"Honestly? No. I worked about thirty-six hours straight, then crashed for twenty. By the time I woke up, you were back in touch."

"That's handy." Ginny laughed. "We're having the birthday party today and I was just shooting the cake. It's lavender and —"

"Mom."

Hearing the seriousness in Christie's voice, Ginny took a breath. "You talked to your dad."

"Grandma, actually. She is pretty upset. She's sure you're ruining your life."

"I know. I should talk to her, but it's going to be . . ." She sighed. "Depressing."

"She thinks you're running away." Christie paused. "Are you?"

"Of course I am. Have you been to Dead Gulch, Kansas?"

"It's not so bad."

"As a place to be from." Ginny shook hair

out of her eyes. "You ran as fast as you could."

"That's true. But I didn't have a husband and a life and a garden I was crazy about."

Ginny watched the kitten slip out from under the table and walk along the seat, then to the counter. A thud of anxiety punched her rib cage. "Are you angry?"

"No, please don't think that. I just don't want you to make a rash decision, one that you might regret."

"Ah." Disappointment splashed her face, shocking and cold. She had expected Christie to have a different reaction. "I don't think I am."

"Maybe you only need a break, not a whole new life."

"Maybe." Ginny heard the stiffness in her voice, but there was a chant in the back of her mind: *Never, never, never, never going back.* "Enough about me. How's life with you? Doing anything besides work?"

"Not really. I wish I could offer something a little more interesting, but the truth is, it's just work."

The kitten had eased back to the cake. Ginny said, "Well, thanks for calling."

"Keep in touch, Mom, okay? Keep me in the loop."

"I will. I promise." She took a breath. "But

I need you to believe that I know what's best for me, okay?"

Christie gulped. "Yes. Okay. I'll try."

"Love you."

"Love you back."

She was already reaching for the camera as she hung up and waited for the inevitable. The kitten wiggled her nose around the cake, white whiskers illuminated in fine threads against her shiny black fur. In the light, it showed brown layers. Ginny clicked the shutter, *again again again again again,* and so she caught the instant when the kitten put a paw on the cake and pulled away a hunk of frosting, and when she licked the frosting off her paw. Ginny laughed. The kitten dashed away, and Ginny straightened to look at the sickeningly adorable pictures.

Leaning on the open door, she looked out at a view of the sun rising over a meadow blurred by a low mist. In the distance were mountains and trees and, closer in, the cabin and the big tree and the platform where they would dance tonight. She thought, *I am never going back.*

She repaired the damage done by the kitten, then carried the cake over to the cottage. Willow walked up with her, but when Lavender's bunch of cheerful mutts came running over, tags jangling, Willow leapt into the tumbling pack. They dashed off toward the field. It had made her nervous the first time they'd done this, but it mainly seemed that they ran and wrestled and practiced herding skills on one another.

Valerie was in the kitchen, trying to be quiet as she scrounged around in the cabinets for pans and bowls. "Lavender is still sleeping."

"She must not feel well," Ginny whispered back. "Doesn't she do a walk around the farm every morning?"

"It is her birthday. Maybe she decided to sleep in." Valerie came over to look at the cake. "This is brilliant, Gin. I love the tiny moons."

"Thanks," Ginny replied softly. "We got lucky — the sun is shining!"

"I was thinking we should set the table outside for breakfast. Wouldn't that be fun? And maybe have some mimosas?"

"That would be very nice. Do we have champagne?"

Valerie flashed a smile over her shoulder. "I do. What I don't have" — she extracted a big ceramic bowl from beneath the counter — "is orange juice. How would you feel about going to get some?"

"Of course! It's just a few miles down the

road, right?"

"I have no idea. I saw Noah outside a minute ago. Ask him."

"All right. Anything else we need?"

"A pint of strawberries and some raw sugar."

"Done." Ginny headed out and saw Noah working on the tent. "Good morning," she called. "Can I bother you for directions?"

"Sure." He jumped down from the platform, eyeing his handiwork. "What do you need?"

"Grocery store, for orange juice."

"You're going?"

"Yes, do you need something?"

He gave her a rueful grin. "I do — but feel free to turn me down."

"Why, what is it?"

"The ice machine is broken again, and I need about a hundred pounds of ice, if you can manage it."

"I can do that. Blocks or cubes?"

"Cubes." He reached into his back pocket and took bills from his wallet. "You'll need to go to McMinnville — about twenty minutes, a half hour. That okay?"

McMinnville. "Um, yeah, sure."

"Sure?"

"Yes." She'd scope it out, see where the Blue Moon Tavern was, where she'd meet

Jack later. *If* she met him.

When Ginny whistled, Willow came running and leapt into the backseat of the Jeep, panting hard. Ginny took a moment to bring her some water, then they drove out on the narrow highway in the quiet Sunday morning light. As the sun rose higher, it cast a buttery sheen over the world, the grassy fields and grazing sheep. She spied a winery high on a hill and passed innumerable small farms, often with signs in front offering produce or eggs.

If Dead Gulch had been this pretty, she wouldn't have wanted to leave it at all.

In McMinnville, she followed her phone's directions to Safeway and parked, rolling the window down halfway for Willow. It was a cute little town and, judging by the cars in the lot, prosperous. Ruby had told her there were a half dozen great restaurants along the main drag.

She picked up the orange juice, strawberries, and sugar, then wandered around the store a bit, trying to think of things she might need in her trailer or they might want for the party. Recalling Ruby's cherry blog, she filled a plastic bag with ripe red cherries and added some bananas and salad greens to the cart. For Willow, she picked up a bag of jerky treats.

At the ice machine, she filled up her cart. One hundred pounds sounded like a lot, but it was only ten bags, and they were compact. She paid and headed back out.

And halted.

A man stood by her Jeep, petting Willow through the open window. He had his back to her, but she recognized the long, lean limbs, the slim hips. She froze on the sidewalk, feeling everything heat up and shiver all at once — Fate, standing there in a pair of jeans and a long-sleeved blue Henley.

What if she just went back inside and waited for him to leave? Then this whole conundrum could be avoided.

But wasn't she supposed to be *choosing* her life and what she wanted in it? Her shoulder blades itched. With a firm step, she pushed the cart off the sidewalk and crossed the parking lot.

Jack turned as she approached, and at the sight of his weathered face, his kind gray eyes, she felt dizzy with relief, with the sense of almost missing something very important. "Hi," she said, and her voice was barely there.

"Hi. We have to quit meeting like this."

"I'm starting to think if I flew to Moscow and walked in to a movie theater, you'd be in the next seat."

His eyes twinkled. "When I saw Willow in your car, I couldn't believe it. Where are you staying?"

"About twenty minutes north of here." She gestured at the full cart. "They sent me for ice."

"Let me help you load it up."

Ginny pulled out her keys with a hand that shook, and she unlocked the back. Jack came around beside her, and they loaded the ice into the back without speaking. She was acutely aware of his arm next to hers, of her thigh close by his. The scent of his skin filled her head, and she couldn't think of anything except touching him.

Before she could do anything rash, she tossed the last bag on top and stepped away, reaching for the door over their heads.

"Ginny," he said — just her name.

She closed her eyes, feeling him along the back of her neck, a ghost touch. When he raised his hand to brush his fingers over her cheek, ever so gently, she raised her own hand and pressed his fingers closer. His scent, powerful, astringent, and sweet, made her head spin, and she had to hold on to something, and it was him.

When he bent down to kiss her, she met him with everything in her, with all the wishing and dreaming and hungry years that had dogged her. He tasted like peppermint, and his mouth devoured her with the same ferocity that she gave. His hand caught her face, and he tilted it up, hauling her body closer, and Ginny nearly swooned, literally, when their legs scissored together, his thigh pushing between her legs, her hip pressed against him.

She reached up to touch his hair, thick and wavy against her fingers, and he stroked her side, swept the edge of her breast, kissed her deeper yet. Everything in her burned, and she wanted to take him right there in the parking lot, and it was that need that made her raise her head, pull away slightly so she could look up at his face. "I have thought of you every other minute since we kissed. It's crazy."

"It is." He shook his head, touched her neck and her jaw. Her mouth. "I'm not even on every other minute. It's all of them. Every single one." He looked at her mouth. "And I want a lot of things. I want to talk to you all night and drink a margarita while we eat Mexican food, and I want to know what your favorite food was when you were sixteen, but until I get you naked and me naked with you, I'm not gonna be able to do anything else."

She melted, her body buzzing with the pictures that gave. She closed her eyes and he bent in, kissing her throat, pulling their lower bodies closer, and he moved himself against her, moved her against him, and Ginny was suddenly fearful that she would have an orgasm right there, in her clothes, without much stimulation at all. "I have to get back," she said, breaking away. "I don't know what to do about this."

He grabbed her hand. "Don't run, Ginny. There's something here. You know it."

"I have to think. And I can't think when you're right in front of me."

"That's a good sign, right?"

She ached to fling herself back at him, for once in her life to do what she wanted instead of what the rules said she should do or what she thought she should do. No shoulds. She wanted crazy hot sex with a man who made her feel alive. She took a breath and made a choice.

"I have to take the ice back to the farm, but why don't you come to the party tonight?"

"Yes," he rumbled. "Yes. What time and where?" He pulled out his phone. "Put it in the maps."

"Dinner is at seven or so, but it's pretty laid-back."

As Ginny typed in the name of the farm, he said, "This has never happened to me before."

She smiled up at him. "What? That you were crazed with lust at the sight of a middle-aged woman with too many freckles?"

"No," he said. "Just this crazy feeling. Like I know you, like I've known you always."

"Careful," she said, handing his phone back to him. "I might think you're nuts."

"You know I'm not."

Ginny studied his face for a long moment, allowing whatever she felt to simply be there. A swell of tenderness and gratitude mixed with excitement and with hunger. And, yes, that sense of recognition. Rightness. "I've gotta go. Come to the party at around six, I guess."

"Wait," he said, and kissed her again, slowly and gently. "I'll be there."

CHAPTER 32

When Ruby found out that Lavender was still in bed, she crept down the hall to the two small bedrooms and found Lavender's door open. The old woman was still buried in her covers, snoring lightly. Ruby left her alone and decided that she would walk the perimeter, as Lavender did every morning. She didn't know what she was looking for, but maybe the act of doing it would show her.

Two of the dogs peeled away from the porch to go with her, a golden retriever mutt and a collie/shepherd mix of some kind. Ruby didn't really know dogs; she'd never had one. But these two didn't seem to need any direction, and she liked the company, so she swished through the grass to walk along the fence line, looking for anything that looked out of place or — whatever.

She would just show up for Lavender, see what she could see.

The morning was perfect. The word "splendid" swayed through her mind, lit from behind with sunshine. The sky was clear as far as she could see, stretching over the rolling green fields like a Constable painting. Ruby started to sing a little, songs she remembered from her grandmother and from a short stint in Girl Scouts between bouts of chemo and from the camp she'd attended twice, full of sick kids who could be normal only with one another. The dogs trotted ahead, sometimes stopping to investigate some fabulous thing in the grass. Ruby strode along a path Lavender must have made over the years.

The direction gave her a different view of the layout of the farm. She passed behind two large greenhouses — not commercial-huge, but big enough for a lot of plants — and remembered when Lavender had lost one to a storm and the other was heavily damaged, about three or four years ago. It had been a crushing financial blow, but as Ruby walked by today, the doors to the first greenhouse were propped open, showing flats of seedlings at various stages of growth. She wondered why they were planted inside, when it was summer, and made a note to ask Noah.

The second greenhouse was devoted to

418

lavender. There were dozens of flats of green and gray-green plantlings, and Ruby wanted to wander over and take a peek but reminded herself the job was to make the rounds, and she kept going.

Her path led around the base of the lavender fields, looking upward to a stand of bushes she thought were lilacs. This would be a spectacular view in the springtime! She imagined armfuls of lilacs, big glass vases of them on every surface. Maybe because she'd been thinking so much about the notes of fragrance in lavender, she wondered if lilacs could be harvested, too. Of course they *could,* but to what purpose? Was lilac oil viable for perfume? Could you use the same stills for different plants?

The hives were alight with buzzing bee happiness this morning, and Ruby gave them plenty of space. She was still afraid of them. How did you get used to handling something that could, and probably would, sting you, hurt you?

The dogs rushed ahead suddenly, swerving into the trees, and Ruby called out, "Don't take off, you guys!"

Noah emerged from the forest, a tool belt clanking around his hips. Why was that so sexy? She shook her head at herself. Just horny.

"Good morning," he said cheerfully, and Ruby's baby danced inside her as if she was greeting the voice.

She laughed, touching her tummy. "Good morning. And my girl says good morning, too. She got all excited when she heard your voice."

"Yeah, well, what can I say?" His hair was tamped down beneath a baseball cap this morning. "What are you up to?"

"Um, well, Lavender is still sleeping, so I thought I would do the walk around the farm for her so she wouldn't have to worry about it later."

He didn't speak for a moment. "Really."

"I know, kinda silly, since I have no idea what I'm looking for, but it seemed like a good idea."

"Not silly at all. Mind if I join you?"

"Of course not. You can tell me what you see."

He whistled back over his shoulder and the dogs came bounding out of the trees. Through the trunks, Ruby spied a small cottage. "Is that where you live?"

"Yep. Me and my cats, Jericho and Babel."

"Whoa, seriously biblical." She narrowed her eyes, trying to see him as a conservative Christian.

"They're rescues, a pair of siblings whose

owner died. I got them at the pound."

Touched, Ruby only nodded.

As they walked, Noah pointed to various things. A place where foxes liked to hunt, a spot where murderous raccoons would rinse chickens in the stream. She'd never seen the pasture where the food chickens lived. She had never seen the ginormous compost heaps sheltered beneath a roof, tons of the stuff, rotting away. It didn't smell, to her surprise, but maybe it would on a hot day.

Noah carried a proprietary tilt to his head as he pointed out all these things, narrating the walk, the things he looked for. "I want to make sure everything is safe and secure, as much as possible. I want to clean up any damage, get rid of any dead animals or deadfall that's causing trouble. I'm looking at the fences."

"What's that?" Ruby pointed to a building much like the meadery, only a little bit larger.

"It's the slaughterhouse," he said matter-of-factly. "Just like the meadery — it's all stainless steel inside." He stopped, one foot stuck out in front of him. "We kill them as kindly and painlessly as possible. One person holds them, another slits their throats."

Ruby blinked at the tears in her eyes, and

she wiped them away. "Sorry. I respect that, but it's not my way."

He spread an arm out over the pasture, where the chickens wandered in the grass, chatting among themselves. "They have good lives and good deaths. It's the best path to meat on the table."

"It is," she said. "But this is not the path for me."

"I know."

As they walked on, Ruby realized that she'd been seriously imagining that she might be able to live here, that somehow she might find a good life here. Not an easy life, though it would be easier than the hours of a kitchen. As a mother, she had to consider that.

Not that she had any idea where she would procure the funds for such a buy. Her father had been quite, quite clear that he was tired of financing her whims. The vegan-food-truck idea was his last investment.

It was disappointing that her enthusiasm for that project had been particularly short-lived. Maybe she was as flaky as everyone said.

And maybe this was a flaky idea, too.

"Hey, I didn't mean to upset you. Are you all right?"

Ruby stopped. "No, you didn't. I'm upset with myself, with all my . . . inconstancy."

He smiled, then swallowed it when she scowled at him. "Sorry, but it's such an old-fashioned word."

"I'd love to buy the farm and keep it going the way it is, but I honestly can't imagine that I could do it, knowing there were animals being slaughtered right on the land." She shook her head. "I just can't. I don't mind the eggs, because I see the hens are happy and it's not as . . . visceral, maybe? And I can manage the honey with no trouble, but the —"

He raised a hand. "Can I interject something here?"

"Interject?"

"You could decide not to raise the meat chickens." He shrugged, hands on his hips. "Easy enough, right?"

"Just like that? Just decide?"

"It would be your farm."

Ruby looked around, turning in a slow, easy circle. Her hands were on her tummy, and her baby bumped against her palm. She looked at the sky, at the house with its shop and lavender presses, at a pair of hens waddling down the path as if in deep conversation, at the farm buildings, and finally at the lavender fields. "When I stand here, I know I could do this. I see myself with my baby in the lavender fields and collecting eggs and making sure everything is running right in the shops. I see myself making a home, a real home, here." She turned back sadly to Noah. "But what do I know about any of it?"

"Only you know the truth, Ruby."

She liked the sound of her name in his mouth, the ever-so-faint roll of the "R," the resonance of the "B." "I don't know where I belong."

"None of us do, until we find it. Come on," he said, putting his arm around her shoulders in a companionable way. "Let's go have some breakfast with everybody and try to enjoy the day. There's time."

(Recipes from Ruby, Ginny, Lavender, and Valerie. A celebration of the Foodie Four — running on all four blogs today)

A Blue Moon Menu

Lavender:
Barbecued chicken
Mixed salad from the organic gardens
at the farm
Deviled eggs

Ruby:
Seitan chicken wings
Blue moon cupcakes
Watermelon, fennel, orange salad

Ginny:
Lavender cake with moons

Valerie:
Wines from the Willamette Valley
Ales from local breweries

CHAPTER 33

Lavender took a long hot bath in the claw-foot tub that looked out toward the mountains. Soaking her bones in water scented with her own oils, she thought about being eighty-five. On the one hand, it seemed curiously idiotic that she should have ever grown old, and no one could argue that eighty-five wasn't old. In her heart, where the real part of her dwelled, she felt the same as always — perhaps not twenty, but not yet forty. Thirty-two or thirty-three, maybe, confident but young and adventurous. At that age, she'd been flying with Ginger, everywhere, all over, getting into trouble, drinking too much, sleeping with the wrong men. And sometimes the right ones.

Just now she sipped ice water, not wanting to muddle her head too soon. And, if she was truthful, the exhaustion that had been dogging her for two days was there in every bone. Her stomach had settled a bit, but she'd barely eaten anything, just in case. She honestly didn't think it was her gall bladder — she'd had those attacks and they didn't feel like what she'd experienced last night, that burning indigestion, the sense of exhaustion.

She heard her fretful thoughts and cackled. Taking another sip of water, she said to herself, "Face it, Lavender. You're old."

She'd rewritten her will after her nap yesterday. It had not been a difficult decision. Which of her lovelies would take the farm? Not Ginny, who was as filled with wanderlust as anyone could be. Not Valerie, who made do with roughing it but desperately wanted the life of clean elegance she'd grown to enjoy over the years.

Ruby. Ruby loved the land and the honey, and Lavender had the sense that she would care even more as time went by, but she'd been a bit of a flibbertigibbet. And she was still pining for that man, the idiot in New York who couldn't see what was right in front of him — a girl as suited to motherhood and family-making as a person could be.

Lavender wanted Noah to have the farm, and she'd like to see Ruby sign on, too, the pair of them healing each other's wounds and making a sweet family built on this good land. She could trust them.

But Noah didn't want it, or said so. And Ruby was unsettled.

The burn started again in her gut, and she hauled herself to her feet, toweling dry her long, lean body. A good body, one that had served her well for a long, long time. She braced herself on the wall and waited for a wave of dizziness to pass.

Into the buzzing came a sense of vastness and relief, a whisper of something new and familiar all at once. She smiled, pressing her hand to her forehead, as if to press it into her memory.

When it passed, she headed, naked, into her bedroom to get ready for her party. She combed her short hair away from her face and put on the silly tutu — honestly, only because the girls liked it so much, and they would all be such perfect flowers tonight. She might as well have a little foolishness herself. To that end she'd picked up a dime-store crown, and she tucked it into her hair now, then dabbed bits of red lipstick on her wrinkled mouth. When she stepped back from the mirror, she smiled, and her ethereal reflection smiled back. "Silly old thing," she said, pleased.

Pleased with everything.

CHAPTER 34

Ginny headed back to her trailer at around five, after spending the day cooking with her friends. The "Foodie Four" had never had such a strong meaning, as they chopped and sang and laughed together in the tiny cottage kitchen. Lavender seemed fine after her long sleep, and she basted chicken on a grill outside the back door, piles and piles of it. Ruby marinated seitan in a heavenly-smelling brew, readying it to be flash-fried in a batter just before being served. Ginny, more of a baker than a cook, did what they told her to do, tearing lettuce and spinach, shredding carrots, chopping pineapple for Ruby's blue moon cupcakes.

Ginny had not told anyone that she'd invited Jack to the party. She wasn't sure he would come, and how embarrassing would that be if he didn't?

No, she thought, opening the trailer door and letting Willow go in ahead of her, that wasn't true. She knew very well that Jack would arrive. She would be clean and dressed beautifully and she would have all of her makeup on, and he would, sometime tonight, make love to her. To tell herself any other story would be a lie, and whatever choices she was making now, she vowed that was one thing she would not do: pretend.

She showered luxuriously, washing her hair, shaving everything. Afterward, she lovingly spread lotion from one end of her body to the other, making sure to get the back of her thighs and her bottom, her rib cage and breasts. For a moment she looked at herself in the mirror, with her hands on her smallish breasts, which were covered with freckles. Would he find them beautiful? It wasn't as if there'd been a lot there to get saggy, but she was edging hard toward fifty. Things slipped.

She thought of him, what little she knew, and wondered if this was crazy. If she was a bad woman.

But her internal barometer said no. This was right. For tonight, anyway. She wasn't leaving home to find some other man to rule her life. She'd left to find herself, and that self wanted sex — hot, fierce, sloppy, vigorous, tender, scratching, luscious sex — in the worst way.

She dried her hair and piled it on top of her head, put on her prettiest underwear, and then donned the peach dress, so delicately colored. The bodice was tight and she had to pull her breasts into position, swelling very nicely above it but not in any kind of slutty way.

On her feet she put peach-colored flip-flops — well, technically they were orange. The sandals had been a gift from Ruby to each of them to match the colors of their dresses, so that they could get to the platform without hurting their feet. Lavender's were silver, Val's white, Hannah's red, and Ruby's blue.

When she was getting ready to head out the door, her phone rang. She stared at it for a moment, almost certain something bad was happening at the end of that line, something she didn't want to hear. If it was Christie or Jack, she would pick up. If not, she wouldn't.

The call was from Kansas but not from a number she recognized. As she held the phone, it clicked over to voice mail, and Ginny waited for the tone that signaled the message was ready to be heard.

She waited.

And waited.

And decided she wasn't about to take this

call or any other. She was going to be herself tonight, without obligations to anyone. Leaving the phone on the table, she slipped outside in her tutu and flip-flops, her dog in her wake. Faintly, she heard the *ding* of the voice-mail messenger.

Ginny and Willow ran across the fields, dashing toward the lights strung up around the wooden platform. It would be a long time until sunset, but a band had begun to play some bluegrass, Lavender's favorite, and the cheery sound danced on its own amid the lights and the tree branches.

Ruby was the first on the platform, swaying happily in her new dress, her tummy seeming to grow every day all of a sudden. She was so pretty, so dazzlingly illuminated, that Ginny leapt up and gave her a giant hug from behind. "I'm so glad we're all here!"

Ruby grabbed her hands and leaned backward, resting her head on Ginny's shoulder. "Will you be my baby's grandma? I mean, I know you're technically too young and all that —"

Ginny squeezed her around the shoulders. "Of course, of course, of course! We all will be!"

Ruby turned. "No, I mean specifically you, like a real grandma. My mom is" —

she shook her head — "selfish and far away, and she'll never even care that I have this baby. You'll take it seriously. Take her and me seriously."

"I promise," Ginny said, putting her hand on her heart. "I promise to be your baby's actual grandmother, for real, no questions asked."

"Good."

Looking over Ruby's shoulder, Ginny said, "Holy cow. Look at Noah. Hannah is going to keel over."

Ruby spun around, and her hand on Ginny's arm tightened. "He is stupidly beautiful. *Ridiculously* beautiful. *Absurdly* beautiful! It's not even fair."

Ginny laughed, watching Noah stroll through the long grass. He wore a crisp, long-sleeved white shirt, black jeans, and an embroidered red vest with a bolo tie.

"Deliciously beautiful," Ginny said. Noah's hair had been brushed back from his elegantly boned face and curled at his neck like that of a Spanish count.

"You know what I like best?" Ruby said, leaning close. "When he grins, all the angles go off, and it makes all that perfect perfectness just so normal."

Ginny looked at her friend. "What's up with you two?"

Ruby swayed. "Something." She swished her hands through her net skirt, inclining her head to shoot a coquettish look at him. "Nothing. And something."

He leapt up on the platform as easily as a cat and came toward them. " 'Evening, ladies. You both look beautiful."

"I'm not going to tell you that you look beautiful, because you already know it," Ruby said, still swaying back and forth. Her shoulders, smooth and clear, caught the light in swoops and swirls, and Ginny saw how Noah's eyes lingered across all that pretty skin.

"I'm going to see how things are in the house," Ginny said. "See you in a little while."

Tables had been set up all around the freshly mowed grass circling the big willow tree, and now Ginny set out plates, a big mix of colors and styles, from pottery to china, along with cloth napkins and silver in the same mishmash. The tables were rented, covered with pretty tablecloths. Valerie came along behind Ginny with candles in hurricane lamps, and Hannah, burning bright in her red dress, lit each one with a long match.

People started to filter in, a few at a time,

driving pickup trucks and sedans and a handful of sporty little cars in various styles. It wasn't a huge crowd — Lavender estimated it would be about twenty or twenty-five above their own core group.

Among them were the nephews, whom Ginny was interested to meet. When Lavender introduced them, Ginny was surprised to find they were ordinary middle-aged businessmen, putting on good faces but a little bored. Their wives were well-tended Portlanders, with healthy natural good looks and unfussy clothing. One wore a beautiful white scarf and gave Lavender a big armful of white roses. "You said no gifts," the woman said, "but I couldn't bear to come empty-handed."

"They're beautiful," Lavender said, and kissed her cheek. She held the roses in front of her tutu and said, "Now, don't I look like a ballerina?"

Ginny, never without her camera, shot the moment and dozens of others, feeling slightly antsy as the time crept closer to seven and there was no sign of Jack.

At seven, they gathered around the tables and held up champagne glasses filled with Bellinis, Lavender's favorite. Ruby stood, holding a nonalcoholic version, and said, "I only hope to live half so well and shine a

435

quarter as brightly as you do, Lavender. Thanks for inviting all of us!"

Lavender, looking fit and elegant in the silvery dress, held up her own glass. "This is one of the best nights of my life, and I thank you all for coming. Right now let's sit down and eat!"

Ginny glanced over her shoulder one more time, but still no Jack. She shook it off and sat down next to Ruby. The Foodie Four sat on one side of the table, opposite Lavender's nephews and their wives. Ginny saw Hannah snare a seat farther down the table, next to Noah, and smiled to herself as the girl sent a cat-with-the-canary glance over to Ruby, who lifted her glass in a toast to Hannah.

The evening was still and warm. Ginny sipped her Bellini and picked at the watermelon salad, nibbled a little roll, but she was deflated. It would be unkind to show it, so she made a point of laughing at the jokes. When Lavender told one of her stories about the glory days of the airlines, she tuned in, intrigued as ever by the spirit of those bygone times.

Ginny found herself chewing on her thumbnail. Maybe she should get her phone. He might have been delayed for some perfectly legitimate reason.

But if she got the phone, she'd have to listen to the message from Kansas, likely Matthew calling from some secondary phone to leave messages. Or her mother, telling her how she was ruining her life.

Hadn't she just resolved to face her life the way it was instead of ducking things she didn't want to see or deal with? She sighed. Where was the difference between facing things and setting boundaries? She didn't really know.

Unable to sit there one more moment, she jumped up. "I'll be back in a few minutes," she whispered to Ruby.

Ruby slapped a hand over hers. "Wait. Do you know that truck pulling in to the lot?"

Ginny heard it then, the enormous horsepower of a gigantic engine, and she turned to see Jack's rig making the turn into the lot. It was designed to handle big trucks, though maybe not one as big as this, and he navigated into place, parked, and leapt down gracefully.

Willow barked a welcome and ran toward the man. Ginny followed behind more demurely, forgetting her flip-flops so that she was walking barefoot through damp grass, her eyes fixed on his lean, loose-limbed form. He'd dressed up a little, with a tie and a blue-striped shirt she liked very much and his usual jeans. He carried a black cowboy hat with a turquoise-studded band.

The first thing he said was, "Sorry. I borrowed a car and it had a flat and there wasn't time to get it fixed, so I had to drive the rig. Kinda foolish, but I didn't want to miss —"

Ginny rushed the last few feet and flew up on her tiptoes to kiss him. "I am so glad you're here," she said, and took his hand. "Come meet my friends."

They'd already rearranged things at the head table, making room for him. Ruby had slid around to sit next to Noah, making Hannah glower a bit and Noah sit straighter. Still holding tight to Jack's hand, Ginny said, "Everybody, this is Jack Gains, my friend from Colorado."

He raised a hand. "How're you all doing?" He pulled Ginny around the table with him as he greeted her friends individually, starting with Lavender. "Happy birthday, young lady," he said, and offered the perfect white daisy he held in his hand. "I'm glad to meet you."

Lavender tilted her head appraisingly, and the jewels in her crown sparkled. "You, too, son. We sure appreciated your care of Ginny when she was sick."

"I was glad to be there."

He paused before Ruby and bowed. "You have to be Ruby of 'The Flavor of a Blue Moon.' You look exactly like I pictured you."

"You've read my blog?"

"Some of it. I liked your cherries post." With a wicked glance at her pregnant belly, he added, "Looks like you swallowed a few of them."

Laughing, Ruby put her hands on her tummy. "Maybe so."

As they took their seats at the table, Ginny was aware of her bare feet against the grass, and Jack's tight grip on her fingers, and the fragrance of him, which was enhanced by some kind of shaving lotion or cologne that she liked, slighty musky and oriental. She was aware, too, that her ears were hot with the speculation of the others, with the stark wickedness of her actions, and with the secret thrill she got from that.

But mostly what she felt as she sat next to him was starvation, a hunger for him, for his company and the sound of his voice as he talked to Ruby on one side and to the nephews who had seen his truck and asked about it. She ate watermelon that suddenly tasted a hundred times sweeter than it had five minutes ago, and she memorized the angle of his nose and the shape of his jaw. She noticed his fingernails and his hands.

He didn't eat very much. He kept taking her hand below the table, touching her thigh, crinkling the tulle beneath his fingers. With his other hand, he fed Willow tidbits of chicken. The dog loyally sat behind his chair, guarding him from all comers. Or something.

As the meal wound down, Lavender stood up, her glass in hand. Her color was high from the alcohol, her cheeks bright red, making her eyes beneath the white hair especially bright. "Hey, everybody, in a minute we'll start dancing. There's plenty more to eat, so don't be shy, and we have plenty of sodas and microbrews and wine, and you're free to sleep in the pasture with the chickens if you need to."

A smattering of laughter danced from table to table.

"Now, I'm eighty-five today and I reckon I've earned the right to ramble a little bit, so bear with me."

"We love listening!" Ruby cried, raising her empty glass.

"Thanks, sweetheart. All of you should meet Ruby Zarlingo, who writes an earthy blog called 'The Flavor of a Blue Moon.' She's a vegan, but we forgive her because her writing is so terrific and because she's a pretty spectacular cook."

Ruby shone, standing to do a little bow, like the ballerina on a jewelry box.

"That brings me to the fact that this is a rare and magical day," Lavender said, more seriously. "It's the blue moon, a time when you can have second chances, and new hopes, and new starts."

Ginny looked up at Jack at the very instant he looked at her. They shared a long moment, hands touching palm to palm beneath the table. Blue sparks shone between their hands, slipping out like tiny fireflies.

"Think about that, friends. What would you do, if you could do anything? Where would you go? What life would you live?" Like a goddess, Lavender shimmered in her silver dress, the rhinestones on her birthday crown sparkling. "That's really something to think about, isn't it?"

A wife looked at a husband. A mother glanced at her son. Hannah leaned forward intently. Next to Hannah, Valerie listened without betraying what she felt.

"I've had a lot of lives in eighty-five years. Some of you have lived a lifetime in one or two years, I know. Noah, my manager, is one of them. He served in the Army for four tours, and that'll mark you. You see how the land has given him new life."

Ginny looked at Noah, wondering if he

minded, but he only nodded.

"Valerie and Hannah there: They have a chance to strike out and become whoever they want, and they're traveling across the country to a new life away from the tragedy they survived."

Valerie reached for her daughter's hand.

"I've been a stewardess, an adventuress and a secretary, an accountant and an organic farmer and a perfumer. There are just times you know that a new life is calling. If you don't listen, that's when you get in trouble. If you're brave and listen to that siren call" — she smiled at Ginny — "you might find something brand new."

Ginny was glad that was all Lavender said. The words brought back some of her conflict over the situation. Jack's hand landed on her shoulder, his fingers brushing along her neck, and she shivered ever so slightly.

"This farm called to me at a time in my life when most people would have been thinking about retiring, and although it was a tragedy that brought me back here, I'm forever grateful to" — she choked up momentarily and bent her head; one of the nephews wiped his eyes — "Glen, my dear, dear nephew, who also had big dreams for the place and made it prosperous for the first time in thirty years.

"Turns out my true work was right here. I brought everything with me, the secretary and the accountant and the stewardess who knew how to talk, all right back here to this farm. I made something beautiful, and I am very proud, and I do not want to see it pass into the hands of a mega-farm corporation that will not run it the right way." She looked at her nephews without blinking. "I'm hoping to see it carried on when I leave, by people who love it."

The nephews exchanged mild glances. Ginny noticed Ruby, however, glaring at them. Were they going to sell the land?

"And that's that. I've got little presents for everybody, in a basket by the porch, to help you remember to do your own work and find a good life, so don't forget to take one on the way home. Now, let's get down to some dancing!"

Lavender sat. The band began to play. The nephews excused themselves, their wives with them.

Ruby ran after them, her skirt swishing bright in the gathering twilight.

"Do you want to dance?" Jack asked.

"I'm not very good," Ginny replied, "but I'll try."

"Nothing to it. C'mon."

443

CHAPTER 35

Ruby ran awkwardly, off balance thanks to the baby. "Gentlemen!" she cried. "Wait a minute, will you?"

They turned, the little army of four. Ruby stuck out her hand. "We met, you might remember, in McMinnville earlier this week?" She was out of breath and panted, touching her chest. The men looked, which had not been Ruby's intention, but she straightened, unashamed, and met the eyes of one of them. "I have no doubt that Lavender is going to outlive all of us, but she is very worried about the farm."

"That was uncalled for, making us look like fools. We're here at her party, and she acts like that?"

"You don't want the farm, though, do you?"

"We're city people," the other one said, shaking his head apologetically. "We don't know anything about this place. We'd lose it in no time."

"I get that. Why sell to that guy, though, the one she really really doesn't want to have it? Why not find a better buyer, somebody who'll respect what Lavender has built here?"

"Like you?" one of the wives said, dismissing Ruby with a head-to-toe glance. "What are you? Twenty-two?"

"Twenty-six," Ruby corrected. "But, yes, me. I don't know if I can get the loan I'd need, but I'd like to try. I want to tell Lavender that I'm trying. She invited us here, the Foodie Four, because she wants an heir, and this has felt like my true place since I got here."

"You're bamboozling my aunt, aren't you?" said the first nephew.

"I don't need to bamboozle anybody. That's not who I am." She shook her head, stepping back. "Just think about what she said, okay? Like exactly what would you need? Think about that."

The first nephew's wife took his arm and turned him away. They walked up the hill without speaking — stopping by the basket, though, to get their presents. Ruby grinned.

The second nephew said, "He's offering a lot, Wade Markum is."

Ruby's heart plummeted. "Well, think

about it, anyway. I'm going to stay here and work with Lavender, learn the business. There's time."

To Ruby's surprise, the nephew stuck out his hand. "Thanks, Ruby. I can tell you love her."

"I do."

She watched them leave, then stood where she was, looking back over the scene, at the sparkling lights, the people dancing, including Ginny and the guy, who looked at Ginny in a way that made Ruby's throat hurt. Also dancing was Lavender, with a man from town. As Ruby watched, Lavender waved a hand in front of her face and excused herself, going to the table to have a long drink of water. She sat down, hands on her knees, and smiled at the scene.

"Hi, Ruby."

She spun around at the familiar voice, and for a long moment she simply gaped at the also-familiar face. He looked gaunt, too thin, but maybe that was because she'd been looking at the robust Noah. "Liam!" she cried. "What are you doing here?"

"I couldn't stop thinking about what you said, about the baby." He moved closer. Ruby took a step back. "I told Minna I had to talk to you in person. I flew out this morning. Jesus, that's a long flight!"

"How did you know where I was? Oh, the blog."

He nodded. Hands in his pockets, he looked over her shoulder to the dancing and the tables so prettily scattered over the grass. "It's your friend's birthday, huh?"

"Yeah." Ruby spied Noah standing off to one side, Hannah swaying beside him, and she suddenly didn't want to talk to Liam. "You know, this is not a good time for me. We'll have to talk tomorrow."

"I only have tonight. And I've come a long way to talk to you, Ruby."

How had she never noticed how peevish he could sound, how small? "You can't just fall into my life and fall back out. It doesn't work that way." She made a smoothing gesture over the baby, over her skirts, and started to turn away.

"Don't do it, Ruby!" He grabbed her arm. "I've been flying for ten hours today, two stops, since I couldn't get on any damned direct flight."

"Take your hand off me right now."

He froze and dropped her arm, backing up two steps with his hands in the air. "Come on. It's my baby, too. You owe me that much."

"No. I don't think I *owe* you anything." She turned away, then said over her shoulder, "If you want to come back tomorrow morning, we can talk then."

She walked away, feeling the pull of him on the back of her neck, but she kept going, away and away and away, giddier with every step.

By the time she reached the table where Lavender sat, however, she was shaking all over. "Liam," she managed to say, "is here."

"Where?"

Ruby looked back up the hill, and there he stood, brooding, with his hands in his pockets, those baggy big chinos she always thought looked affected. From this distance, he was very ordinary and small. "There," she said.

"Huh," Lavender said. "What does he want?"

"To talk to me. But I don't want to talk to him."

Lavender gave her a long look. "You might as well get it over with."

"No," Ruby said, quite sure. "He doesn't set this schedule. I do." She jumped up and went through the milling people to find someone to dance with. When she looked later, he was gone.

They had their photo taken, the Foodie Four and Hannah, all in a row in their dresses, with their feet bare and the lights strung behind them. Noah took a bunch of shots, making sure there would be a lot for each of them to choose from, and Ginny kept breaking out of the lineup to see how they looked. From the sidelines, her man gobbled her up with his eyes, and Ginny was a floating star, the peach dress with its tiny crystal beads catching the light in winks and blinks, very subtle beneath the netting. Her dark hair had been piled up to start the night, but as it went on, tendrils fell down on her freckled shoulders. She looked sexy and at ease, and Ruby thought with wonder, *How did that happen in a week?*

But look at her own self! Instead of throwing up and crying, she was happy and getting more pregnant by the day, and she *was* going to stay on the farm and learn everything she could. At least that way she could be ready to help buy it if that came to pass. If not, maybe she could find other farmwork.

After Noah took the pictures, he came over to her. "It's my turn to dance with you."

"Okay. I've been dying for you to ask. You look like Antonio Banderas, only taller and younger."

"And better looking."

"Well, that goes without saying."

They danced easily together, a two-step he led with expertise. Ruby yawned and let herself lean into him. She found herself falling into the music, into the starry night, into the dance. "I think my baby likes you," she said dreamily. "She kicks me when she hears your voice."

"I'm glad." He swayed with her for a while, humming along with the music, his voice in her hair. "Ruby, can I ask you what you saw? When we kissed?"

"It's not seeing, exactly." She put her head on his shoulder, feeling very tired. "I just feel things about people sometimes, like things around them, energy or memories or ghosts, maybe."

"Hmm." His voice rumbled up through his chest. After a long moment he asked, "So what did you see or sense about me? Something bad?"

"No," she said, trying to hang on to the thought. "More like . . . sad . . . I guess." She yawned again. "You have to get something off your chest."

They had slowed, were barely moving, but Ruby didn't notice. Like a baby, like a safe and drowsy child, she'd fallen asleep on his shoulder. She was somewhat aware of him picking her up and carrying her off the platform, aware that she wanted to tell him something, but sleep was so overpowering that she fell with it to the other side. Far away, far away and safe.

CHAPTER 36

When the partygoers began to drift off one by one, Jack said to Ginny, "I suppose I'd better be going."

She knew what she should say. *Let me walk you to your truck. Thank you for coming.* She liked it that he didn't presume any intimacy, despite the way they'd been dancing, heating up their skin, rolling against each other. They generated so much power that they could have lit the night by themselves.

"Okay," she said. She picked up her sandals by the table, kissed Lavender good night, and, holding hands with Jack, walked up the hill to the parking lot.

"What a great night," he said. "Thank you for inviting me."

"You're welcome. When do you head back?"

"Tomorrow, bright and early. I've got to pick up a load and be on the road by nine."

A pinch of loss squeezed her chest. "So soon!"

"I know. It's the way my life goes, unfortunately. But I need to see you again, Ginny. I can't — This is . . . something." He squeezed her hand. "Something."

"It is," she said. Smiling, she tugged him away from the path to his truck and toward her trailer, enjoying the slow build of heat that kindled between them, the anticipation of what they had been hoping for, thinking about, all evening. "Can you stay, at least for a while?"

"Until dawn."

She led him up the steps to her home, the only home she'd made for herself alone, a space that belonged utterly to her. It was small inside, but not so small that they couldn't figure out how to peel away the layers of clothing between them and make their way to the bed, where Jack laid her gently down on her back. When she wanted to reach for him, he said, "Wait," and he kissed her everywhere, shoulders and thighs, belly and the lower curve of her breasts, her inner elbows, the springy triangle of hair between her legs. Then he touched her, and kissed her mouth, and she said, "Please, please, please, come inside!" and he did, filling her — oh, sweet heaven! — all the way up, living hot flesh, and she grabbed his behind, holding him still, holding him inside her, not moving, so that she could really feel it for a long, long moment. Him, filling her, holding her, sucking on her neck, suckling her lips, his belly sweating against hers, his legs slightly awkward in the small space.

"Now," he whispered, and she said, *"Yes, now, yes, move, yes,"* and she exploded all around him, all over her body, in each place his lips had touched, in her lips and her tongue, which sucked at him, in her fingertips, which dug into him. He whispered, too, *"Yes,"* and *"Yes,"* and *"Ginny, Ginny, Ginny."*

And when they were done and sweating and breathing hard, she laughed, wrapping her legs tightly around him, and kissed his face, his shoulders, his arms. "Thank you."

"We're in trouble, sister," he said, and bent toward her again. "I'm an old man and I'm already wanting you again."

"Good," she whispered. "Good."

It was, Ginny thought, one of the best nights of her life. They dozed and drank bottles of cold water and raided the fridge at three A.M., taking out cheese and crackers, which made a mess in the bed.

The best hour was at four, when he said

he would have to go in one hour. They opened the curtains to see the sky and curled up on a pile of pillows, with quilts flung over them, and talked.

And talked, and talked. Not about anything, really, but about everything. Ginny told him that she wasn't going home but she would miss her roses. He told her that he'd been thinking of giving up the driving but wasn't sure what was next, especially for a man over fifty. She asked if she could shoot photos of him, and he agreed, letting her take pictures of his bare feet and his chin and his eyes, staring at her through the lens.

Their bodies were tired, sated. "I'll feel this tomorrow," she said.

He chuckled, tracing her thumbnail with the pad of his index finger. His cheek was against her hair. "Yeah, me, too."

"I'm worried that you haven't slept and have to drive. That's dangerous."

"I'll have a good hour or two before I pick up my load, then break every couple of hours for a half hour. I'm sometimes a bad sleeper, especially on the road. I've learned to deal with it."

She nodded.

"If you're not going home, what are you going to do?"

"I have no idea, Jack. None." She tipped her head back to look at his face. "It's exhilarating."

"Sounds like heaven to me." Soberly, he traced a line down her neck, over her breasts, connecting dots. "Will I see you again?"

"Yes," she whispered. "We'll figure something out." She paused. "But I need to be sure you understand that I'm still looking for myself, that it would be bad for me to get too serious about you."

"I get it." He touched her lips. "I'm patient. I also believe things work out the way they should. We shouldn't have met even one time, much less over and over." He smiled. "I've got fate on my side."

A prickle of tears touched the back of her throat, and she pressed her face into his softly furred chest, breathing in the smell of him. "I am going to miss you."

"Me, too. You have no idea." He stroked her hair. "We'll take it one day at a time. You have things to work out. So do I."

Ginny nodded silently, willing time to stop so that she could stay here in this moment with Jack for a couple of thousand years.

But all too soon he had to step around Willow and find his clothes. Ginny watched him dress — underwear, then jeans, shirt, and socks. He sat down on the banquette to put on his shoes, the tie strung around his neck, and she wondered sharply, fiercely, if she would ever see him again. "Whatever happens, Jack, I want you to know that this mattered to me, okay? A lot."

He finished putting on his second boot and walked over to her. "Whatever happens," he said, bending down to kiss her, "I love you, Ginny Smith. You woke up my world."

She smiled. "Be careful."

"I will."

She forced herself to stay where she was, calling Willow to keep her company in the cold and empty bed. Every cell in her body buzzed with satiety, as if he'd poured some honeyed elixir into her body. She laughed at the thought, covering her mouth and pressing a hand between her legs. She supposed he had.

She supposed he had.

Exhausted, she fell asleep like a child in an enchanted forest, the last thing in her ears the fading sound of his big truck driving away down the road.

CHAPTER 37

Somewhere just before dawn, Lavender awakened suddenly and completely. She'd fallen asleep fully clothed, too tired to even slip out of her shoes.

Now she got up, feeling strangely alert and bright, and peered out the window to see that there were still people in the garden, talking and laughing beneath the big willow. From here she couldn't make out who they were, but there was music playing, one of her old favorites, "Wang-Wang Blues." She and Ginger had learned to swing dance at some point and loved every chance they got to show off their skills.

Intrigued and feeling so refreshed, she padded down the hall and through the kitchen. Things were piled helter-skelter, the food put away but dishes still waiting for morning. She'd insisted. Plenty of time for all that tomorrow.

The music drew her, and she wandered

outside. A pack of dogs chased one another around the perimeter, dashing away from people who tried to catch them. One of them raced toward her and she said with glee, "Rome!" but he raced too fast to be sure he really was the dog of her heart.

A little dizzy, she paused, feeling disoriented. Was she dreaming? A woman approached her, a woman with long red hair and smiling eyes. "Come sit down," Ginger said. "You look pale."

"I'm fine," Lavender insisted. "Better than I've been in days."

"Still," Ginger said. "Let's sit."

And now that she'd agreed, Lavender realized how out of breath she was, how very uncomfortable she felt, that wretched indigestion returning to ruin what was such a very nice dream.

The dog came padding back, just as Rome always had, bringing her a slobbery ball. "It *is* you," she said, and gasped as a roaring train pushed upward through her chest.

"It will only last a moment," Ginger said, holding her hand.

And it was a moment, a long moment, while Lavender traveled through the length and breadth of her life, seeing herself at four and at nine and twenty-two. She saw her strong, middle-aged self striding through the world, saw her heartsick self when her nephew died and she came back to the farm. She saw it all, outlined with love, every precious minute of it, and then the pain left her.

"There now," said Ginger. "We've been waiting."

Jubilant dogs were suddenly flipping and leaping, and Rome licked her fingers. Lavender scrubbed his side and let him kiss her face, and she walked forward, with Ginger and her dogs. She spied her mother, and her friend Reine, picking flowers, and, finally, there was her nephew Glen, who'd died too young, too soon, and broken all of their hearts. He looked well, hale and hearty.

"Well done," he said, and hugged her.

CHAPTER 38

Ginny awakened to the sound of her phone buzzing angrily in a circle. She'd been asleep for only an hour or so, and she wondered who was calling so early. Naked, and remembering happily why, she padded over to grab it off the table where she'd left it last night. The number was a Kansas one she didn't recognize, but she decided she ought to take it anyway. Bracing herself for an irritable Matthew, she punched the button. "Hello?"

"Thank God," said her mother. "Do you ever answer your phone?"

"We were celebrating my friend's birthday last night, Mom." She rubbed her face. "I don't carry my phone all the time. What's up?"

"Take a deep breath, honey, because I have bad news."

A pang stabbed her right through the heart. "What?"

"Well, he's alive, but your husband was in a car accident. He's in the hospital."

"What?" Grabbing the blanket off the bed against the chill, she wrapped herself up. "When? What happened? How badly is he hurt?"

"Last night," Ula said. "He wrapped his car around a telephone pole and broke his legs. He has a concussion, too, but they say it isn't serious. The legs will take a while to heal. You need to get home right away."

A sense of resistance — actually a sort of terror — enveloped her. If she went back, would she be snared? "I don't — I drove here, Mom. It will take days."

"You're his *wife*, Ginny Smith. You have an *obligation*. Use some of that cash of yours to buy a plane ticket and get yourself back here today."

"What about Willow?" The panic, the resistance, swelled until she thought she would choke. "My Jeep and my trailer? I can't just leave them."

"Your friends will look after things for you, won't they? You can fly back in a month or two if you have to, or hire somebody to drive it back."

No, no, no, no, no. "Mom, we're getting divorced. I can't do this."

"Ginny May Smith, if you don't come

back here, I swear by all that is holy that I will come out there and drag you home by your hair. You have a responsibility."

And for no reason she could name, Ginny knew she would have to go, that somehow this was her punishment for cheating. Her lungs squashed down until she nearly fainted from lack of oxygen. "Fine. I'll call you with the details."

Willow had awakened and now came over to sit in front of her, focusing kindly eyes on Ginny. She hung up, with tears streaming down her face, and opened her laptop.

She had never flown in her life, but she had often arranged for Christie to come home from college. She discovered that she could fly to Wichita at two o'clock. With a sinking heart, she paid for the ticket and packed up some of her things.

Then Ginny got down on her hands and knees with her dog and hugged her tight, crying as if she were going to jail for years and years.

She showered and dressed, then headed over to the cottage to make a pot of coffee and get some breakfast going for everyone. Willow trotted along beside her, blissfully unaware that she was about to be left behind. Fresh tears ran down Ginny's cheeks at the thought.

So close, she thought. She'd been so close!

In the kitchen, she measured coffee and poured water into the coffeemaker, eyes still leaking tears. Her body reminded her of the way she'd spent the night, and she sat down at the kitchen table to write a note to everyone. She needed to make sure someone could look after Willow until she got back. She would drive the Jeep to Portland, she supposed, and leave it in the airport parking lot.

She felt exhausted, the one hour of sleep not nearly enough.

She called Matthew's phone, but there was no answer, as she had supposed would be the case. If he'd been in an accident, the phone was probably still in the car. He always plugged it into the cigarette lighter, worried about running out of power. She hung up and called her daughter.

Christie answered on the second ring. "Mom! I've been worried that you didn't pick up! Did you get my messages?"

Ginny shook her head. "I haven't checked them yet, but I got the news about your dad. Are you going home?"

"I can't, Mom, but please keep me posted. Grandma made it sound pretty bad last night. He was in the car for two hours before anyone found him."

"I didn't hear that part. Where the heck was he?"

"Out on County Line Road."

"I'm flying back this afternoon," Ginny said, to reassure her daughter that her father would be all right. Her voice came out airless, weary. "I'll let you know."

"You sound depressed."

"It's complicated," she said, unwilling to burden her daughter. "I'll call you, okay?"

"Okay. Love you. Safe travels."

As the coffee brewed, Ginny walked to Ruby's camper and knocked but got no answer. Next she went to Valerie's trailer and knocked there. Val answered with crazy hair and wearing a bathrobe. "What's up, Ginny?"

"I have to go. My husband was in an accident, and I have to fly home. I'm leaving my trailer and Willow, but I need to find Ruby before I leave."

"Oh, sweetie." Val came down the steps and hugged Ginny tightly. "I wish you didn't have to go. Damn it."

Ginny hugged her hard, trying to keep her tears contained. "I'll call you, okay?"

"You're coming back, right?"

"I'm leaving my dog. I have to come back."

"Good move," Val whispered. "Don't let

them get to you. Just be you."

"I will. Take care."

"Yeah." Val stepped back and wiped tears off her own cheeks with long dark fingers. "Sorry, but I'm going to miss you."

Ginny kept her eyes wide. "Don't get me going again."

"Check Noah's cottage for Ruby. She was very chummy with him last night."

At this, Ginny grinned. "Well, good for them. Both of them."

"And you," Val said, squeezing her hand.

Ginny shook her head. "I can't talk about that right now."

"All right. Go, do what you need to do, and get back here."

But when Ginny got back to the kitchen, Ruby was there, eating peanut butter toast. "Did you spend the night with Noah?" Ginny whispered. "I went to your place and —"

"Yes," Ruby said, "but not like that. I fell asleep when we were dancing and he carried me down to the cottage. Sweet, right?" She ate her toast. "Did you also see that *Liam* was here last night? He flew from New York to talk about the baby!"

"No way!" Ginny poured the coffee she was desperate for and stirred in two heaping spoonfuls of sugar. "What did you say?"

"I told him to come back today. He said he couldn't, so I guess that's that." She eyed her toast. "But I think I might be over him."

Ginny sipped her coffee — super hot, super strong, super sweet — and a fleeting memory of Jack ran over her eyelids, down her neck. She swallowed the memory away. "Really."

"I kept hoping something would bring us back together, you know, but when I saw him last night, I felt nothing. Like, *nothing.*" Ruby shook her head. "It was weird."

"That's good, though, right?"

"It's great!" She smiled. "And what about you and Jack! I saw you take him back to your Airstream, you wicked woman."

"I can't talk about that right now," Ginny said for the second time in ten minutes, and hot tears streamed down her face, copious and unbidden. "I have to go home."

Ruby leapt up. "Oh, no! Was he mean to you? Did you not get along? What happened?" She put an arm around Ginny. "Tell me."

Ginny dropped her face into her free hand, overcome. "It's not Jack," she said. "It's Matthew. He got in an accident and I have to go home. He's in the hospital with broken legs." Grief, as enormous as the ocean, poured salt through her. "I hate it."

"You don't have to go, Ginny. You can stay. Make a stand."

She shook her head, still crying, the tears dripping through her fingers to the floor. "I have to." She wiped a sleeve over her face. "Will you take care of Willow for me? I'll try to get back in a couple of days."

"Of course. Take as much time as you need. Maybe I can sleep in your trailer, too. Mine's kinda cramped, actually. Would you mind if Ninja Girl comes, too?"

"Not at all."

"All right, so what can we do to get you ready? Want me to drive you to the airport?"

"Would you?"

"Absolutely. Let me grab Noah, too. He knows where things are. And then you don't have to pay all that parking for the Jeep."

CHAPTER 39

Ruby was the one who finally found Lavender, sitting beneath the willow tree in the grass. When they'd returned from dropping Ginny at the airport and Lavender still hadn't come out for breakfast, Ruby went to check on her. The bed was empty.

"She's not there," Ruby said, coming back to the kitchen. "Maybe she's walking the perimeter."

"I've been in the kitchen since you guys left," Valerie said, shaking her head. "She would have had to fly."

"Where are the dogs?" Noah asked. "They're usually wherever she is."

"I haven't seen anybody but Willow this morning."

Noah looked pale. "Let's go look around."

He headed for the meadery and the lavender fields, while Ruby checked the shop and the vegetable garden, and it was only as she was wandering the back way up the hill that she spied Lavender, still dressed in her silvery dress from last night, leaning against the willow tree, looking toward the valley. The dogs were in a half circle to her left side, some sleeping. One leaned on her leg.

Ruby said, "Oh, thank goodness. We were so —"

And then she realized that Lavender was unmoving, too still to be sleeping. She knelt beside the old woman and touched her cheek. It was cold. "Oh, Lavender, I'll miss you."

But it was a good death. The best.

She went to find Noah, so they could decide what to do.

CHAPTER 40

Ginny was afraid she would be nervous, flying, but she fell asleep within five minutes of takeoff on the first plane and slept until they touched down in Dallas. But changing planes freaked her out, especially when she discovered that the airport was gigantic and filled with so many people. She'd never been anywhere with such crowds in her life, and there were so many different *kinds* of people, in so many different kinds of clothes, speaking more languages than she could begin to name.

Sitting at her gate, eating a pretzel, she watched them stream by and wondered where she would go if her next plane was her choice. Would she fly to Madrid? Hong Kong? New York City?

On the second plane, she tried to sleep, but despite the lowered lights and the sleepiness of the passengers around her, she couldn't slip away from the depression that crept closer and closer with every mile they flew east. It had taken her nearly a week to drive to Oregon, and all of it was gone in a day. Erased.

As they taxied to the gate in Wichita, Ginny listened to her voice messages, three of them. The first was from Christie, who wanted to know if she was there yet. The second was from Ruby, who said, "Hi, Ginny. I have some news. Please call me when you have a chance. It's important."

The third was from Jack. "I reckon I shouldn't call you, but I just wanted to tell you that I've been thinking about last night all day. I can't stop thinking about you, and I hope the feeling is mutual. I'm turning in for the night, but call tomorrow if you want. I'd love to hear your voice."

She played it three times, her face turned toward the window so that she could hide the tears. She couldn't stop crying! It was as if she was crying three tears for every one she'd never shed over the years, as if something in her was melting.

The regional airport was small. It smelled like Kansas the minute she stepped off the plane — humid air and sweat and the promise of a thunderstorm later on and the dusty fragrance of wheat growing.

Her mother was waiting under the fluo-rescents, and at the sight of her, Ginny wanted to turn around and run away. Her mother's face was hard, her too-long gray-ing hair pulled back into a ponytail. "Hey, Mom," she said. "Thanks for picking me up."

Ula gave her a surprisingly heartfelt hug. "I'm so glad you're here, sweetie. I've been worrying about you every day."

"I've been fine. I've had a great time, honestly." She shifted her backpack a little and walked with her mother toward the doors. "How's Matthew?"

"Not good, Ginny. Really upset about ev-erything."

"I don't mean about the divorce."

"Well, why do you think he wrecked his car?"

Ginny took a breath. "I don't know. Maybe it was an accident."

"It was because he was distraught! He loves you! He's always been a wonderful provider and a good, kind man to you. You're outta your mind if you leave him."

"Stop," Ginny said, and halted right in the middle of the hallway. "I'm here to see if I can be of use, and I'm trying to be a decent person, but I don't want you all over me."

Ula shrugged. "Fine."

They drove to the hospital in silence. Wind blew in through the open windows of the car, bringing the smell of cow dung and pond water. Ginny tried not to think of the high thin air in Colorado or the soft purple glory of the Columbia River Valley. Tears rose in her eyes again, and she blinked them away.

Over.

The adventure was over. She was back home, back in Kansas, and somehow, she didn't know how, they would trap her here.

"You go on in, honey," Ula said in the corridor outside Matthew's room.

Ginny hesitated. The television was turned on, and the light fell in a blue wash over the body in the bed. For a moment she felt as if she couldn't breathe, that if she walked through the doorway, she'd be squashed flat.

But she made herself step into the room. "Hi, Matthew," she said quietly. "How are you doing?"

His neck was in a brace, and his face was battered. One arm was in a purple cast, but his legs were beneath the covers, only his feet sticking out, and they were encased in some contraption. "Ginny?" he croaked. "That you?" The words were slurred through fat lips.

"Yeah, it's me." She stepped up to the side of the bed and took his free hand.

"Baby, thank you for coming back. I was such a fool. Such a fool." Tears streamed out of the corners of his eyes, a wrenching sight, and it nearly made her cry again, too. "I have a concussion, did they tell you?"

Ginny's throat tightened. She wanted to say, *I'm not back, not like you think,* but it seemed unnecessarily unkind. In a day or two she could tell him the truth. "Yeah. Broken arm, too, huh?"

"Yeah." He gripped her hand. "Now that you're back, though, things will work out okay, won't they? We'll just talk things out. We've been married a long time. We gotta keep trying."

The room was too warm, too humid. She felt herself shrinking, fading, growing thinner, and it made her dizzy.

But she found she did not have enough cruelty in her to dash his hopes while he lay broken in a bed, hungry for love and reassurance. The mother in her put a hand on his head. "Sleep. We don't have to talk about anything right now."

Her mother drove her home to Dead Gulch, a twenty-minute drive, and it was only as Ula pulled in to the driveway that Ginny realized she was stranded. Her Jeep was back at the farm, and Matthew had totaled his car. "Can somebody lend me a car?"

"I'll come get you in the morning, hon," her mom said. "Eight o'clock too early?"

"No. But you don't have to drive me around. I'll rent a car if nobody has one to lend me. I'd rather do that, honestly."

"Don't be silly. No point in spending all that money when you've got family to do things for you."

Exhausted, Ginny didn't argue. "All right, I'll see you in the morning, then."

"We can get you to the grocery store, too, at some point. You know men — they never shop. He's probably been living on pizza and Chinese since you left."

"I don't need to go to the store," she said, getting out, and before her mother could insist, she slammed the door, waving as she strode to the garage and punched in the lock code on the door. It clicked into motion, and Ginny ducked under, not waiting for it to rise all the way.

The house smelled of old food and a stagnant drain, and when Ginny flipped on the lights, she saw that Matthew had probably not done the dishes since she'd left nine days ago. They were piled in the sink and stacked without care along the counter.

Her mother was right: She spied pizza boxes, some with dried-up pizza still inside, and the white boxes from the local Chinese. He'd at least rinsed those but hadn't thrown them away.

Woodenly, she dropped her backpack on the floor and fetched a black trash bag from the cupboard. It took six minutes to throw away the boxes and load up the dishwasher and even wipe down the counter, another thirty seconds to take the trash out to the container beside the house. Maybe a full seven minutes, but Matthew had preferred to live with the mess. Feeling sorry for himself.

When she finished that, she scrambled a pair of eggs — thinking with longing of the fresh, fresh eggs at the farm — with a slice of American cheese, washed up, and headed for bed, trying to stave off the monster of depression stalking her. She was exhausted from so little sleep the night before. She missed her dog and her friendly little Airstream. She missed Ruby and Lavender and Valerie and even sulky Hannah.

She didn't bother to go to their bedroom. The bed would not be made, and their bathroom would be a mess of discarded clothes and towels. Instead, she went to the guest room, stripped off her clothes, and crawled under the covers in the overly air-conditioned, deadly silent house. As she drifted off, she remembered that Ruby had called, but by then she was too far into her sleep to make the call. She would do it in the morning.

THE FLAVOR OF A BLUE MOON
a blog about great food . . .

Recipes   Appetizers
Main dishes   Sides   Sweets
Sort by Name   Sort by Category
About Ruby

Lavender's Birthday

Here are some photos from the big Blue Moon Festival at Lavender Honey Farms. This is the Foodie Four, plus Valerie's daughter Hannah, in the red dress. That's me in the blue, and, yes, friends, you would be right if you guessed I am pregnant. Woo-hoo! How's that for a beautiful surprise? The baby is due in October.

The beverage of choice was Bellinis, which is an Italian favorite made with prosecco and peaches. Because of my condition, I did not drink the alcoholic kind, of course, and the drink I came up with was delightfully refreshing and festive. You might want to try it.

THE TRADITIONAL BELLINI

2 cups prosecco
2 cups pureed white peaches
Few drops of grenadine

Blend and serve in champagne glasses.

479

Ruby's Nonalcoholic Bellini

2 cups sharp nonalcoholic cold-pressed apple
    cider
2 cups fresh peaches
1 liter Pellegrino or other Italian sparkling wa-
    ter

Blend and serve cold.

CHAPTER 41

Noah had carried Lavender into the house and laid her gently on the couch, then called the right people. Lavender — ever sensible — had given him all the information ages ago. He had the numbers of the funeral home she preferred, her lawyer, the relatives who would need to be notified. Ruby was cleaning the kitchen when she spied Hannah sliding in through the back door and into the living room.

Ruby turned silently, alert for signs of breakdown or overwhelming grief or hysteria.

But today Hannah wore her curly hair loose on her shoulders, and she was dressed in a pair of ordinary jeans and a T-shirt. She simply stood beside Lavender, head cocked, for long moments, then she looked over her shoulder. "Is it okay to touch her?"

Ruby nodded, wiping her hands on a dish towel. She eased closer, pretending to gather things into piles on the table. There, but not.

Hannah knelt and put her hand on Lavender's face, just as Ruby had done, stroking the lined cheek. She picked up her hand. "Why isn't she stiff? I thought people got stiff?"

"It probably hasn't been very long."

"She's cold, though." Hannah peered at something on Lavender's neck. "And all the blood has drained away from her face."

Ruby blinked back tears, wishing Lavender could be here, listening to Hannah's clinical assessment. Lavender would find it amusing, no doubt. "What are you looking for, Hannah?" she asked gently.

Hannah frowned, perplexed. "I don't know. It's just — where does the life part go? I don't get that. Something is living and breathing and then it stops. What is the part that is alive?" She turned to look at Ruby, and tears were streaming down her face. She didn't even seem to notice. "All those kids you knew who died — did you ever think of that?"

Ruby nodded, unable to speak. "I don't know."

Hannah took Lavender's hand. "My sisters disappeared. Like, there was nothing left of them. The plane went straight down into the ground, and they just disintegrated." She wiped tears off her cheeks impatiently. "I hate thinking of that. How scared they must have been when it was going down. I don't know why I wasn't there. I don't know what keeps me alive. I just don't know."

Ruby grabbed the girl and brought her close as Hannah dissolved into sobs, her shoulders shaking violently. She clung to Ruby so fiercely that Ruby almost could not catch her breath. Her shoulder grew soaked, and Hannah poured out a thousand days of tears she'd held back. "I miss them so much," she wailed.

"I know," Ruby whispered, smoothing the girl's hair over and over and over. She thought of her mother, who had wandered away and never come back. "I know."

An ambulance came and took Lavender's body away, and they spent the day cleaning up from the party, getting things in order, getting ready for a wake. Noah said he'd leave the platform and lights up, and they would have a raucous second party, and Ruby agreed that was just right.

By evening, Ruby sat in the kitchen with Valerie and Hannah, drinking leftover Bellinis and eating cake.

"She wouldn't want us to be sad," Ruby

said. "But I am, anyway."

"Me, too," Valerie said. She covered her daughter's hand. "How are you, honey?"

Hannah's face showed the ravages of her earlier crying jag. "I'm cool. Just tired." She stood up and put her plate in the sink. "I'm gonna go read." She squatted to rub Willow's head. "Can she come with me? Sleep in my bed tonight?"

"I'm sure she'd like that. I have my kitten."

"Thanks." Hannah whistled like a pro. "Come on, Willow."

Dog and girl headed out. Ruby poked at the cake on her plate. "I wish Ginny would call back. I hate it that she doesn't know."

"I hate it that she had to go back there to those people. They really, really do not appreciate her."

"Are you worried that she'll stay?" The possibility had not crossed Ruby's mind. "She's changed so much!"

"I know. But getting out of there took a lot of grit. Doing it a second time might be hard."

"We have her dog. And her Airstream. She'll be back."

"I hope so."

Hannah came back in, Willow trailing. "Um, Ruby? This guy is outside and wants

484

to talk to you."

"Guy?" She frowned. "I'm coming."

"It's me, Ruby," Liam said, coming into the kitchen. "Can we talk now?"

"I thought you went home to New York."

He stood just inside the door, looking wildly uncomfortable. "I thought we should talk. I came all this way — it seems important." His hair was combed over his forehead in a deep side part, and he'd donned hipster black-framed glasses. His jeans were low on his hips.

She didn't see the Liam she knew anywhere in this outfit, but she took pity on him. "Come inside and sit down." She gestured toward the living room. He took the couch and she took the chair. *Lavender's rocking chair,* Ruby thought, rubbing the arms with her palms. "What do you want to talk about?"

"Well." He laced his fingers together. "The baby, I guess. Like, how do you want to do things? Split up custody or whatever. Do you want to come live in New York again?"

"No, I don't. I'm going to live here." If she could, anyway. If not, she'd figure out the next step. "You'll have to come here. I'll be nursing for the first year or better, and pumping breast milk all that time would be unhealthy for both the baby and me."

"I'm not leaving New York. My work is there. My life is there."

"Your wife is there, too. Or wife-to-be."

"Yeah. She's freaking out. She's sure we're getting back together. You make her feel really insecure."

Ruby narrowed her eyes. "Maybe she shouldn't cheat with somebody else's boyfriend. Kinda leads to expecting he'll do the same thing again." As she said it, she realized that she felt the truth of it, deep in her belly. He would do this again — fall instantly, madly in love with another woman. "No offense, but she's not my problem."

"I know, you're right." He took off his glasses, rubbed his face. "I feel conflicted over this. It seems a gift, but I am not sure what the meaning of it is, showing up so late, after we broke up."

Ruby rolled her eyes. "There is no meaning, Liam. Honestly, that's an exhausting way to live. Sometimes things just are. There's no message from the great beyond or God or whoever. Life evolves."

"Why did you tell me about the baby?"

She took a breath. "Because it was the right thing to do. Because Lavender told me I should." She rubbed a palm on her thigh. "Probably because I was hoping it would

486

wake you up to what we had, too, but now I'm seeing how little I want that back."

"You're just mad at me, Ruby." He leaned forward earnestly. "Maybe we should give it a try. Maybe we should get back together, for the sake of the baby if nothing else."

Two months ago — heck, one *week* ago — Ruby would have burst into tears, thrown herself at him, let him hug her and assure her that all would be well, even if she knew in her heart that it would not. "No," she said now. "I don't want that."

"Is there someone else?"

Noah's face fluttered over her imagination, but he wasn't the reason things had changed. "Yes," she said. "There is a baby who deserves to have a fully present mother and a fully present father, and you're never going to be that guy. She's my priority."

His jaw hardened. "You want to play hardball, then?"

"No, I don't. I want us to play fair, with each other and with our child. That means my needs matter as much as yours."

"I want to be part of her life."

"Good. Let's find a way to make that work. Maybe for the time I'm nursing, you can come visit on a regular basis, until she's old enough to visit you by herself."

"That's not enough, Ruby. Would that be

enough for you?"

She smiled. "No." She rubbed her hands over her belly, then rocked forward and held out her hand, palm up. For the space of long moments, he held himself apart.

Finally he capitulated, placing his hand in hers and holding on.

"We made a baby, Liam, and whatever happened at the end, it was born in love from my side."

"Mine, too," he whispered.

"There's time for us to figure out the details of how we'll do this, but if we both try to be kind, it should work out okay."

He nodded. "We can try."

Hours later, when all the phone calls had been made, when all the relatives had been notified, when Liam had been sent on his way, and when Ruby had fed her kitten and made sure that Willow was comfortable with Valerie and Hannah, she flung a sweater over her shoulders and walked down to Noah's cottage.

It was a small place, only four rooms in a square, with a front porch looking down to the pastures and the mountains beyond. Noah was sitting on the steps, a sturdy white cat stretched out on his legs, covering him from knee to waist, his tail dripping down the side of Noah's thigh. "Hey," Noah said as she came up. "You work things out with your baby daddy?"

"Did you see him come back?"

He nodded.

She half-grinned. "I guess that's what he is, huh?" She laughed. "Yeah, we're good for now. I suspect it will get testy in a little while, but tonight I sent him on his way and we're good."

"Good."

She twisted her arms out in front of her, clasping her hands and stretching. It eased the muscles in her shoulders and back of her neck. "How are you doing?"

He bent his head, and Ruby saw that he was fighting tears. "Okay."

"Oh, honey." She scooted closer and put her arms around his shoulders. "Go ahead and let it out. I'm here. I don't mind."

"I'm going to miss her like an arm," he said in a raw voice. "It was her time, and it was a good death, but she made me whole again. Just being here, being accepted." Tears dripped on the cat, and his tail flicked. "I don't think I realized how much better I felt until today."

"She was very special, that's for sure." Ruby rubbed a circle on his back, and he rubbed the cat on his lap. "Tell me about when you first came here."

"I was so tired of death and destruction and blood and noise," he said. "I wanted to grow things."

He talked about his conversations with Lavender. He told Ruby about their first meeting, when she'd looked him over with despair. He talked until he was hoarse, one story after another, and Ruby listened. When he wound down, she told him about Lavender tracking her down on the Internet and laughing when she found out Ruby was only twenty-one. It was impossible, she said, but they became good friends and founded the email loop that sustained the Foodie Four. She told him about when Valerie's husband and daughters had died, how Lavender had raised nearly $10,000 in relief funds so that Valerie could have time and space to figure everything out.

Talked out, they sat in silence on the steps. Crickets sang in the grass, and far away a cow mooed. Stars shone, and the moon was still bright and white. "I'm over him," Ruby said.

"Are you?"

"Definitely." She leaned on his shoulder, her arm touching his side. No ghosts crowded in today. It was only the two of them and the baby dancing inside her and the crickets and the cat.

Noah took her hand. "Good," he said, content. There were things that were coming — what to do with the farm and how to keep it, and all the details of living — but Ruby felt a quiet, clear certainty that it would somehow all work out.

CAKE OF DREAMS

I'm in Dead Gulch, friends. Nothing to worry about, a family emergency. I'll tell you everything later.

CHAPTER 42

Ginny awakened with the dawn shining through the window, a hot bright dawn, unlike the ones she'd met recently, and she stared at her feet for a long moment, trying to place herself in time and space. It was her grandmother's old Singer sewing machine that oriented her. A stone dropped in her gut.

Home. Back in Dead Gulch.

She got up and showered quickly, washing the travel day out of her hair, scrubbing the last of Jack away. She didn't cry this morning. There were no tears left, only a hard little kernel of loss.

As the coffee brewed — the pot had stood empty the entire time she was gone — she dialed Ruby's number. It went straight through to voice mail, and Ginny left a message. "Hey, Ruby. I'm sorry. I just realized it's practically the middle of the night there. Give me a call when you get up. I'm so depressed I feel like I'm walking around in concrete shoes."

She carried her coffee out to the deck, an elaborate thing Matthew had built a couple of years ago, complete with high-tech grill and seating for twenty, even though they never had parties or even much family over. He didn't grill, either, but thought maybe he'd figure it out.

Someday.

She sat on one of the deck chairs, looking over the view of fields planted with corn and soybeans and, in the distance, a silo. The water tower squatted like a flying saucer in a bad movie, the letters fading so badly that only E DG CH was visible. As teenagers, the local kids dared one another to climb it, but Ginny never had. She was afraid of heights, afraid of getting in trouble, afraid of —

Afraid. Afraid to drive, in case she ran into a drunk driver and died a terrible, bloody death. Afraid to climb the water tower in case she fell off. Afraid to apply to anything but Kansas colleges in case she failed or there wasn't enough money. Afraid to look stupid. Afraid to break up with her boyfriend, who bored her, because maybe nobody else would ever like her. Afraid of getting pregnant. Afraid of —

Afraid, afraid, afraid.

Afraid to stand up to her mother. Afraid to live somewhere else.

The same feeling swamped her now: fear that somehow she would get trapped here, losing letters, fading away until there was nothing left of her.

The only antidote was action. Rather than sit here and stew in the juice of fear, she would take her camera downtown and shoot whatever she saw. It would be a good blog, anyway.

She was only a few blocks from downtown Dead Gulch — what little there was of it — and even so early there were plenty of vehicles already parked in front of the Morning Glory Café. She stood across the street and shot the scene: The big pickup trucks that ranchers and farmers used to haul water and hay and whatever else they needed. The Morning Glory's cheerful window, painted with vines and blue and pink and white flowers. Trees lined the street, giving deep shade during the hot summers, and they were fully leafed and glossy at this moment. A blue heeler, apparently free for the day, trotted with purpose down the sidewalk. Two men in cowboy hats and jeans stood talking in front of the drugstore. Looking through her viewfinder, she saw it objectively. A country village street, peaceful, productive, even beautiful.

How had she never been able to see that before?

Leaving the lens cap in her pocket, she crossed the street and shot a long view of the sidewalk — sideways, with the shops on one side, the street on the other — then headed into the Morning Glory for some breakfast.

She sat at the counter, swiveling on the stool, camera in hand. "Hey there, Ginny," Bill Miles said from three stools down. "Heard that husband of yours had a doozy of an accident. How's he doing?"

"I think he'll be all right," she said. "My mom and I are driving back up to Wichita in a little while."

"He's been through a bad patch, with the company closing and all, I guess."

Ginny blinked. She rubbed a finger over the rough surface on the barrel of the lens, letting the information sink in. She nodded, giving him space to talk.

"Well, look what the cat drug in," the waitress drawled. Hattie had been working at the Morning Glory since high school, which was probably about the time Ginny had started grade school. A tiny, busy, hipless figure on stick legs, she wore swoops of

496

black eyeliner on her bright blue eyes. Her hair was dyed black and hung down her back in a coy curl. "Want some coffee, hon?"

"Yes, please."

Ginny shot the coffee cup as Hattie poured, the swoop of light along the counter, the light coming in from outside. People glanced at her curiously but didn't seem to mind. "Can I have pancakes and bacon, please? And some tomato juice with lemon."

"Coming right up. How's that husband of yours? He's been eating here sometimes twice a day while you were off traveling."

"We were just talking about that," Ginny said mildly, stirring cream and sugar into her cup. "He's banged up, but I think he'll be okay."

"Shame about the company, but he's a smart guy. He'll land on his feet."

"Not so easy," Bill said, shaking his head, "when a man's pushing fifty. And what's left around here, anyway, I wonder? He'll have to go to Wichita. Kansas City, even."

Another block of cement grew around her ankles. Matthew had lost his job. Wrecked his car.

Did that mean she had to stay? What did you owe another person? What were the bounds of decency?

The questions dogged her as she choked down pancakes and bacon that was too salty. Behind her, the murmur of breakfast voices, the clank of silverware, the ordinary, pleasant sound of morning in a café, took her back to breakfast on the road, and she wished that she could turn around and see the Rockies through the window, or some of her fellow RV'ers. She wished Jack was sitting here next to her, talking about peach trees or *The Twilight Zone* or the book he was listening to on tape.

What was her obligation?

She paid for her breakfast and carried her camera outside, her feet so heavy she felt she might drown. Her shoulder blades itched again.

In her pocket, her phone rang. It was her mother, who said, "Where the hell are you, Ginny? I've been waiting for you for ten minutes, honking and ringing the doorbell."

"I came downtown for breakfast at the Morning Glory," she said.

"By yourself?"

"Yeah." Ginny looked over her shoulder and realized that she had done exactly that, eaten alone in public in her hometown. It hadn't been strange at all. "I was hungry."

"Well, stay there and I'll run by and pick you up."

"I need a cake shot, so I'll be in front of the bakery."

"Can't believe you're thinking of your blog when your husband is in the hospital."

"It's my job. I can't just let it go."

"Whatever. I'll be there in a second, so take your pictures fast."

And it was the tone that made her linger, made her walk slowly down the block, shooting whatever interested her, as she'd done across the West — a trio of planters filled with geraniums, a pair of forgotten garden gloves beside them, the jewelry-shop window reflecting her face, and then the bakery. She went inside. "Hey, Renee," she called. "Mind if I take some pictures of your lemon cake here? That's so pretty."

"For your blog? You go right ahead. I'm honored, honey. I've got the recipe, too, my own special one, if you want to run it."

Ginny lowered the camera. "Really? I've wanted to make this cake for a dozen years, at least."

"All you had to do was ask. I don't mind some publicity for my little shop."

Out of the corner of her eye, Ginny spied her mother's blue sedan creeping down the street. "I gotta go, but can I email you?"

"Call me and I'll give it to you."

Waving, Ginny dashed out into the street

and flagged her mother down, feeling lighter. Lemon cake could do that to you.

"Mama," she said, slamming the door, "when did Matthew lose his job?"

"Where'd you hear that?"

She clicked backward on her photos, trashing a couple that said nothing, pleased with a couple of others. "In the diner."

"He didn't want you to know. It was a few weeks ago that he found out. They're closing the local office, and he's got to go to Kansas City or be out of a job. He wanted you to have your trip before he told you."

"Huh." Ginny stared out the window. Digesting.

"He's one hell of a good man, Ginny. Better than you deserve, with all your gallivanting."

"I told you last night that I wouldn't listen to this, and I mean it."

"You just don't appreciate —"

"Mom."

"You can't tell me to stop speaking my mind."

From her pocket, Ginny pulled out a pair of white earphones. "Then you won't mind if I listen to music." She stuck the buds into her ears.

Her mother kept talking, and Ginny could make out some of the words, but mostly she didn't. She hummed along with the music to help block the sound. Quite adolescent, she supposed.

Also not bad boundary-setting. She checked it in the plus column.

A phone call rang in, and Ginny pulled out her earbuds and answered without bothering to see who it was. It didn't matter if it helped her block her mother out. "Hello?"

"Ginny, it's Ruby. How are things going?"

"Um. Okay. How are you?"

"I . . ." She cleared her throat. "I have some news."

Something cold moved over the sun. "Not the baby?"

"No. But it's bad." Ruby took a breath. "Lavender had a heart attack and died. We found her under the willow tree, just sitting there in her dress."

"Oh, my God. She *died*?" Ginny's mind raced through the weekend hours, the trip to the emergency room . . . "It wasn't her gall bladder. It was her heart."

"Yes."

Ginny made a noise of pain, pressing her fingers to her mouth. A burning started in the middle of her throat and behind her eyes. Hot liquid tears spilled over her lower lids. "I'm so sad. I can't believe it took me so long to get there and now I'll never see her again."

"I know. But we're all saying the same thing — that it was the kind of death you want. She went fast. She must have gone out in the early morning, still wearing the tutu, and sat beneath the tree. Her dogs were with her."

Blinking, unmindful of the tears, Ginny peered out the window, thinking of the beautiful party. "And at the end of a perfect day. I'm glad she ate a lot of cake." Her composure broke, and a sob escaped from her lips. "When is the funeral?"

"She didn't want a funeral, just a memorial. She's being cremated, and of course she wants her ashes scattered around the farm. We can wait to do the memorial for a few days. As long as you need. We all agreed, even the nephews."

Ginny nodded, tears streaming down her face. "I'll call you later, okay? I'm in the car with my mom right now."

"Do you need me to come and be with you?"

"Oh, honey. No. Thank you, but I'll be fine." She steadied her voice. "Thank you for offering. Take care of yourself and the baby. And my dog."

Ruby laughed softly. "Yeah, I think Hannah might fight you for her when you get back. She's really in love with her."

"That's good. A dog can heal a lot of wounds."

"So can cats!"

Ginny was surprised to find she was smiling through her tears. "Of course."

"Call me."

"I will." She hung up and held the phone in her hand. There was no need to put her earphones back in; her mother was quiet.

"Bad news?" she asked, signaling to change lanes.

Ginny nodded. "Lavender died. It was her birthday we celebrated. She was eighty-five, and had" — Ginny's tears welled up again — "an amazing life."

"I'm sorry, hon." Ula patted her hand, then dug in her purse and pulled out a packet of tissues. "Here you go."

"Thank you." Ginny wiped her face, but the tears kept spilling out. All the way up the road, she stared out at the fields beneath a hot blue sky and thought about Lavender laughing. She thought about the Rockies, and the ocean, moving and moving and moving.

"She really meant a lot to me," Ginny said to her mother. "She used to work as a stewardess in the sixties, and then, when she was almost sixty, she took over this farm and planted it with lavender."

"That's brave, at sixty."

"Yeah," Ginny said, and the tears choked her again. "I can't believe I'm never going to see her again."

Lavender.

Lavender and her life, her courage, her power, her absolute zero tolerance for bullshit. What would Lavender say right now? What would Lavender do?

She wouldn't be whiny and weepy, that's for sure. Taking a breath, Ginny dried her tears and sat up straight in her seat. She didn't speak until they got out of the car. She flung her purse and her camera case over her shoulder. Her mother closed and locked the doors and headed for the entrance.

"Mom, wait, before you go in."

Ula turned warily. Her feet were bad from decades of hard work, her hair thin and too long for the texture. She had put on lipstick, but Ginny could not remember the last time she'd worn anything but that. No makeup, the same loose button-up shirts and baggy jeans and tennis shoes she'd worn every weekday of Ginny's life.

But what Ginny could also see now were the chains around her ankles, the chains of circumstance and time and missed chances. "I love you," she said. "I know that you mean well in all of this. But I am not staying here. I am not going back to Dead Gulch today. I'm going to the airport and I'm leaving."

"You can't leave a man who's injured and out of a job! That's not decent."

Ginny raised a hand, maybe blocking the blow of the words. "I have been trying to be a good daughter and a good wife and a good mother my whole life." She took a breath. "It didn't get me anything, because it's never been quite good enough. I had to find out what it was like to be loved for myself before I had the courage to stop being a good girl and just be me."

"Oh, who do you think you are? Ever since you started writing that blog, taking all your pictures, you think you're better than us."

"I only wanted to — feel something else," Ginny said. "See what *I* thought about the world, what *I* saw when I looked through the lens of a camera or talked to somebody who wasn't always tearing me down." A fresh spill of tears ran over her face. "I do love you, Mom. I hope you know that."

She turned and started walking, a strong rope of Lavenderness burning up her spine. She took a breath and blew it out.

"Ginny! You can't just —"

But she didn't listen. She went into the hospital and found her husband's room.

Marnie was there, and when she spied Ginny, she hopped up. "Hey!" she cried. "How're you doing, girl?"

Matthew's best friend, Grange, was there, too, an overweight man with a little goatee that framed his full lips. He looked gray with worry, and circles under his eyes attested to the lack of sleep. "Hey, Gin," he said in a raw voice. "He's been hoping you'd come in this morning."

Ginny eyed Grange and heard Ruby's voice: *Is he gay, maybe?*

But honestly, no, she didn't think so. She thought Matthew simply didn't like sex. Maybe it was low testosterone; maybe it was lack of interest in his wife; maybe he worked too hard; maybe his back gave him trouble. She didn't know, and, really, she didn't care anymore.

"You guys want to give me a minute here?" she said.

"Ginny," Matthew said, "it was harmless. It didn't mean anything."

Marnie smacked his leg. "Shut up."

Ginny held up a hand. "I don't want to know."

"Ginny, it's —"

"Don't talk!"

Ula came puffing into the room, face red and sweaty as she made a grab for Ginny's arm. "My daughter has lost her mind."

"Stop talking!" Ginny roared. "Listen!"

They were all so shocked to hear her shout that they did exactly what she said. They turned their faces to her and closed their mouths.

And Ginny said, "I am leaving you, Matthew. I'm sorry you're hurt, and I'm sorry you lost your job, but you'll be fine. I just can't be your wife anymore. I can't be in Kansas anymore. I can't be the person you all want me to be. I tried, and you got so mad at me for not being able to do that that I lost everybody. I lost my family and my husband and all my best friends, not because I did anything wrong, but because you couldn't see *ME*."

Marnie rolled her eyes.

Rolled her eyes.

For one long minute, Ginny saw herself smacking that supercilious expression right off Marnie's face. Rage as clear and clean as grain alcohol poured through her, burning everything unnecessary away. She swallowed the murderous impulse and stepped over to her husband. She kissed his forehead. "I don't hate you. I hope we can be

507

nice to each other. And I am sorry."

There were tears in his eyes, but he only nodded, grabbing her hand. "I didn't really break my legs. That was a lie. Your mama thought you wouldn't come back unless the accident was worse."

Ginny looked at her mother. "Really?"

"Honey, I'm just —"

"I'm done." Ginny squeezed Matthew's hand. "I'm glad your legs aren't broken." Laughing, she wheeled around and headed out the door, not looking back. She strode through the Wichita hospital halls, seeing open blue skies ahead, all hers for the asking. As she stepped out into the humid, hot Kansas day, she called a cab over.

"Airport, please."

On her shoulder blades, wings sprouted, muscular and powerful, ready to carry her into the next stage of her life. She thought of the ocean, and the promise of redwood trees, and flying.

And freedom. And friends. And people who loved her.

Faintly, she thought she heard a voice, raspy and no-nonsense:

Atta-girl.

CHAPTER 43

October

The morning was damp and drizzly as Ginny puttered around her tiny kitchen. The rental, a place only about double the size of her trailer, sat right on the Oregon beach, overlooking waves that were, this morning, crashing in drama and noise on the rocky coast. She hummed under her breath, stirring blueberries into pancake batter, cracking eggs from a carton marked LAVENDER HONEY FARMS. She picked them up every couple of weeks when she drove in to check on Ruby, who was due any day.

"Mmm." Jack ambled into the room, bare-chested, his hair tousled with sleep. He bent in and kissed her neck. "That smells great."

"You can make the coffee if you like."

Ginny's phone rang and she snatched it up. Ruby's number showed on the screen. "Is it time?"

"Come now, Ginny. She's coming fast! We'll meet you at the hospital."

"I'm on my way. Love you! Can't wait to meet her!"

Ruby made a noise. "Oh. Oh. Gotta go."

Jack was already putting on his shirt. "We'll get coffee on the way, huh?"

"I'm so excited!"

They drove in her Jeep, since Jack's rig was way too big. He usually parked his truck at a Walmart in town when he came through, about every three or four weeks. He reached for her hand as they waited for coffee at a drive-up booth. "I'm so glad you've settled in one spot for a bit," he said, kissing her hand.

After Lavender's memorial service, Ginny had traveled down Highway 1, along the coast of California, then back up, stopping in different spots. She chronicled the special pastries in each place she went, a fresh offering for her blog. She'd met more of the backbloggers, too, and had even conducted an in-person photo workshop in San Clemente. She met with Jack when she could, but it was not as much as either of them would have liked. The relationship had grown enough that she was willing to let him step a little closer. She'd rented the cottage outside Astoria, and Jack would be moving his center of operations to Portland next month. He'd live in Astoria, too, in his own apartment, but they could spend a lot more time together.

"Me, too." She kissed his hand in return. "I knew she'd go into labor the minute you were able to stay for a day or two. It just works out that way, right?"

"I'm glad. I want to see the baby." He handed over a cup of coffee. "And we'll have our Thanksgiving adventure."

They were going to Tofino, in British Columbia, to see the crashing waves. Both of them had had to apply for passports and were as excited as twelve-year-olds when they arrived. "It's only Canada," Ginny said. "But it's cool."

"It is cool," Jack said, and had tumbled her backward, kissing her mouth and her face and her throat. "You're cool."

"You're cool."

Now, in the cradle of the Jeep, with the windshield wipers slashing the water away, Ginny admired his profile, craggy and not perfectly handsome but astonishing to her nonetheless every time she looked at it. "I'm so glad I met you," she said.

He smiled, reaching his hand over to grab hers again. "It was going to happen, one way or the other. Even if you hadn't left

Dead Gulch, I would have stopped on my way through, and you would have been standing there, and our worlds would have turned upside down."

"That way would have been much harder for me."

"Yep. But you would still have loved me."

They all gathered in the waiting room. Ginny and Jack perched on hard plastic chairs. Valerie sat next to Ginny. Ruby's father, a tall, lean man with a balding pate and a very serious face that seemed exactly the opposite of Ruby's cheery one, paced. "Do you think she's all right?" Paul asked anxiously. "It's been a long time."

"I'm sure she's fine," Val said. "Do you want to get a cup of coffee or something? Sometimes first babies can take a pretty long time."

"It's already been three hours," he said.

Valerie smiled. "Yes."

Paul went back to his pacing. Jack leaned over. "I think I'll take the poor guy to get some coffee."

"Good idea."

As the two men made their way down the hallway, Ginny said, "How's it going in San Diego?" Valerie had flown back to Portland a week ago, to be on hand to help with the baby.

"Better than I anticipated, honestly. My parents have needed the help for a while, I think, and I was too immersed in my own troubles to see it. They have a big house in La Jolla and plenty of room, and we all enjoy the company but can escape one another when we need to."

"That's great. And Hannah?"

"She's like a new person. I don't know if it was just time or she's blooming with her grandparents or the trip, but she's doing well. I made her see a counselor for the first few months, but even the counselor said she's fine for now."

"It seemed like meeting Ruby really helped her."

"Funny how things turn."

The men came back in from the hallway, carrying paper cups of vending-machine coffee. Paul peered into the coffee with a sad face.

"That bad?" Val asked.

He looked up and gave her a crooked smile. "Worse. But it'll do."

"Any coffee in a storm."

His expression lightened, and he took a sip, wincing with exaggeration. "First World problems, right?"

Val laughed, the sound as rich as a cello. Paul frowned, then seemed to actually focus on her. "Are you the wine blogger?"

"Yes. Or I was."

"I loved the blog you wrote about the old vines. The Norton, right?"

"That was a long time ago."

"Ruby turned me on to the blog," he said, moving a step closer, "but I kept reading because you were so entertaining and didn't take it all so seriously."

Val smiled, and Ginny noticed the little sheen about her mouth, an ever so slight straightening of her spine. "Are you a wine enthusiast?"

"I don't know that I'm all that knowledge-able." He tucked his hands into the pockets of his well-cut but loose-fitting wool trousers. "The science is interesting. The product is creative. That intrigues me."

Val patted the seat beside her. "I agree with you. It's like perfume — so many possibilities."

Paul sat and tilted his body toward Val, leaning closer to listen.

Ginny smiled. Jack nudged her and raised an eyebrow in their direction.

Perfect.

Labor was, Ruby thought, about five thousand times more work than she had expected. Her body felt as if it were being turned inside out, one agonizing inch at a time. "This HURTS!" she cried at the top of her lungs.

"You can do it, sweetie," a nurse said. "Don't yell. Save that energy for pushing."

"I can't push anymore," Ruby said, sweating. "My eyes will pop out."

Noah laughed. He had begged and cajoled and pleaded to be allowed to be her coach. Ruby had resisted for three months, all through the new sweetness of their blooming love affair, all through the time she grew more and more huge and marveled that he could find her attractive at all, all through the struggle to secure the farm — which they had finally done with a combination of loans from the VA, the sale of the food truck (on which she had made a fine profit), and a low-interest loan from Ruby's father, who had proved to be agreeable once he saw the farm.

In the final month of Ruby's pregnancy, when she had begun to waddle and her face was like a moon of fat, Noah knelt down and asked her to marry him, for real, so that he could be the baby's father, and Ruby had burst into tears.

"Your eyes are fine," he said now, and the

laughter in his voice enraged her.

"I am *exhausted*," she cried. "How long can a person push?" But the waves of energy built up again in her body, wilder and wilder and wilder. She gripped Noah's hand and held her breath.

"Wait, wait, wait," cried the midwife. "I need you to hold on for as long as you can, Ruby, then give it all you've got."

She closed her eyes. *Come on, daughter,* she thought, reaching for the tiny soul she could feel anxiously trying to get free. *Let's work together.*

Ruby gathered all that she was and took strength from the beings she could sense around her, whispering and urging and touching her with encouragement. She became something else, some being of light and power and fierceness, and spied her daughter wearing a funny little medieval gown. She gathered her up and they dove into the world.

A cry rang out, and then they were putting her baby in her arms. Her daughter, who settled immediately, looked up at her mother with big blue eyes, and stopped crying.

"Welcome," Ruby said. "You are so loved and wanted. I am so glad you came to be my daughter. Thank you."

Everyone said newborns couldn't smile, couldn't even see, but Ruby saw the rosebud lips do exactly that as the baby's eyes rested on her mother's face. "Welcome, Lavender. I've been waiting for you."

And, in the distance, Ruby heard the kind laughter of the other Lavender, off having adventures in the other land. "Thanks to you, too," Ruby said, and fell back on the pillows. Noah bent and kissed her forehead, then kissed the baby, too.

Late that night, Ginny cleaned up the kitchen after their dinner. Jack had already headed over to her Airstream, parked beneath the tall tree she loved. Paul and Val had stopped to have dinner at a celebrated restaurant in McMinnville and would come back later.

Ginny hoped they hit it off. Neither one of them had had a lover or a partner in a long, long time. As she put sheets on the foldout bed in the living room, she thought of what Valerie said at the hospital: *Funny how things turn.*

She plumped pillows in the quiet, and puffs of lavender came out of the feathers. She closed her eyes and inhaled, missing Lavender very much, all at once. If only she'd been able to be here for the baby's birth!

But that was the turn of the wheel, wasn't it? Ginny placed the pillows carefully against the top of the bed, smoothed the blanket, and looked around one last time to make sure it all seemed welcoming for Paul or Val, whichever one chose the couch.

A photograph caught her eye, one of a cluster that covered most of one wall. During the day the photos were in shadow, but now, at night, the lamp illuminated the march of Lavender's life.

The one that caught Ginny's eye showed Lavender in her Pan Am uniform, at thirty-four or thirty-five. She was stunningly beautiful and elegantly coiffed, her hair rolled back smoothly from her face, her body as lean and lanky then as it had been in her eighties. The woman with her was a redhead, laughing, a braid falling over her shoulder.

Ginger.

Riveted, breath coming in shallow bits, Ginny looked carefully at the other photos for confirmation of what seemed utterly obvious, and there she found it. Lavender and Ginger, camping, both dressed in pedal pushers and sneakers and plaid shirts, their long hair hanging in braids. This photo was black-and-white, but Ginny still recognized her, the woman who had shown up along the road, in bathrooms and restaurants. Ginger. It was Ginger who had been her companion.

She smiled and touched the faces. "Thank you," she said, then grabbed an umbrella and ran up the hill to the trailer spilling out yellow lamplight into the darkness, to a man who took her in his arms and rumbled, "There you are," before he put his hands on her, and made her laugh, and then made love to her the way she deserved.

ACKNOWLEDGMENTS

Every now and then the universe bestows a sudden, unexpected, and quite fortuitous gift in your life. For me, one of those events was the arrival back in my life of my cousin Sharon Jensen Schlicht. With brains, creativity, and a thoroughly astonishing organizational ability, she has brought more blessings into my work life than I can possibly enumerate here.

Farmwork, whether it is food or lavender or any other agricultural product, is not a minor undertaking, and I needed to understand that life. On a research trip to Yamhill County (along with Sharon), I met two extraordinary women who gave me the bones of this book.

The first was Chrissie Zaerpoor at Kookoolan Farms (visit them at www.kookoolan farms.com), who responded to my tentative request for insight with a generous, rich depth of material that is still reverberating

521

with me. Without that serendipitous afternoon and a multitude of emails, much of this book would never have developed. I was charmed by the chickens and the kittens, by the meadery and the lambs, and by the very no-nonsense, hardworking, brilliant Chrissie herself. Thank you, Chrissie, for your thoughtfulness, your grim truths, your emotional honesty, and your wit.

Any mistakes are entirely my own. I hope I got it mostly right.

The second person I must thank effusively is Debbie Gorham, at Willakenzie Lavender (and Alpaca) Farm, also in Yamhill County (www.willakenzielavender.com).

It was Debbie who provided the background for the growing of lavender, the various forms of oil and products, the challenges and joys of growing lavender. Not only did she generously offer all this detail with humor and deep passion, she did it on an afternoon when she was preparing for the massively popular Yamhill Lavender Festival, which was only two weeks away. Thank you, Debbie! Again, all mistakes are my own.

I also want to tip my hat to the magazine *Artful Blogging,* which provides me with many hours of reading pleasure, and from which the seeds of this novel began. Over and over women in those lovely pages say, "Starting this blog changed my life. . . ."

Finally, I'm grateful as ever to my publishing team, especially Shauna Summers and Meg Ruley, who encourage me and push me and (gently) roll their eyes when I get off track. I am a far, far better writer because of you both.

ABOUT THE AUTHOR

Barbara O'Neal fell in love with food and restaurants at the age of fifteen, when she landed a job in a Greek café and served baklava for the first time. She sold her first novel in her twenties, and has since won a plethora of awards, including two Colorado Book Awards and six prestigious RITAs, including one for *The Lost Recipe for Happiness*. Her novels have been widely published in Europe and Australia, and she travels all over the world presenting workshops, hiking hundreds of miles, and, of course, eating. She lives with her partner, a British endurance athlete, and their collection of cats and dogs, in Colorado Springs.

The employees of Thorndike Press hope you have enjoyed this Large Print book. All our Thorndike, Wheeler, and Kennebec Large Print titles are designed for easy reading, and all our books are made to last. Other Thorndike Press Large Print books are available at your library, through selected bookstores, or directly from us.

For information about titles, please call:
    (800) 223-1244

or visit our Web site at:
    http://gale.cengage.com/thorndike

To share your comments, please write:
    Publisher
    Thorndike Press
    10 Water St., Suite 310
    Waterville, ME 04901